AMERICAN GOLIATH

Also by Harvey Jacobs

AMERICAN GOLIATH

Inspired by the True, Incredible Events
Surrounding the Mysterious Marvel
Known to an Astonished World as
The Cardiff Giant

HARVEY JACOBS

ST. MARTIN'S PRESS
NEW YORK

This fiction is based on fact, inspired by what is called "America's Greatest Hoax." The story is real. As for the details, since history leaves many questions unanswered, best consider *American Goliath* a work of the imagination. Enough to say that *something* happened, once upon a time and place.

Several illustrious ghosts play parts in this story. None has complained of his or her role, nor confirmed or denied what is written here. If any has been badly served, the author expresses regret. No malice was intended nor harm to preserved reputation. Quite the contrary.

Black and white illustration of the Cardiff Giant on title page reprinted by kind permission of The New York Historical Society. From pamphlet #F127.06C2C3, Collection of The New York Historical Society.

Design by Nancy Resnick
Edited by Gordon Van Gelder

Library of Congress Cataloging-in-Publication Data

Jacobs, Harvey.
    American Goliath / Harvey Jacobs. — 1st ed.
       p.   cm.
    ISBN 0-312-16771-7
    1. Forgery of antiquities—New York (State)—History—19th century—Fiction. 2. Cardiff giant—Fiction. I. Title.
    PS3560.A25A8   1997
    813' .54—dc21   97-15344
                                                 CIP

First Edition: October 1997

10   9   8   7   6   5   4   3   2   1

There were giants in the earth in those days.

—GENESIS

For Kermit Rose and Tex Weinper.
Young soldiers. Old wars.

1868

FORT DODGE, IOWA, MARCH 21, 1868

My life is perfect. I know my place. I connect to the planet. No demands are made on me. From time to time I am cradle-rocked. Jolted. Thus reminded of Source, which is comforting if disquieting. Time is no concern. Rumblings above of no consequence. Mysteries below irrelevant. I am entirely defended. Safe beyond sensation. Congealed eternity. I think I will sleep now. Or am I asleep?

BINGHAMTON, NEW YORK, APRIL 10, 1868

George Hull drifted through a dream, smoking himself. He'd turned into a cigar, a Partagas El Cid Corona: thick, mellow, and slow-burning. George enjoyed the transition to dead ashes. His marvelous aroma wafted shimmering rings through the streets of Binghamton, New York, then fractured to color and gave the town a rainbow.

His flesh rang the alarm that spoiled the metamorphosis. He woke shivering, naked in his bed, with no cover for protection. George looked over at his skimpy wife, Angelica. The blanket thief. She'd managed to wrap herself in their brown comforter and looked more like a cigar than he had in his dream.

George, who had entered her the night before and filled her with a hive's worth of honey, thought, "Maybe somewhere inside something provident is happening." He owed her a baby.

Angelica breathed in shallow little gasps. George imagined she must have lungs the size of snow peas to suck such tiny gusts of air. Sometimes she slept so silently he would shake her to see if she was alive. No matter what the hour, when he woke her, Angelica jumped to attention, alert, cordial, ready to serve him. Then he would snap at her, accusing her of sleeping too quietly, of feigning death. A smiling Angelica would make some effort to apologize through her puzzlement. She confused his rage with concern.

For all Angelica's vulnerable grace, she was the one who had rolled herself in the blanket and left her husband rubbing his body to get the blood flowing. He stood naked doing knee bends, stretching his arms, trying to connect with the icy first light.

George heard noises from the factory downstairs. His father, Simon Hull, and younger brother, Ben, were already breakfasted and at work. Industrious men of vision and conviction, they began their labors while owls still blinked at dawn.

George put his ear against the wall of his brother's room. The chilled ear flamed with sounds from a boiling sea. George was suddenly alive. He went out to the hall, quietly as a man of generous proportions could go, his large feet making old boards groan. Angelica was sealed in sleep, a jar of preserves protected by glass and wax.

When he came to the door of the room where his sister-in-law slept, he caressed its milky-white knob as if it were a breast. That door was a friend. It opened silent as a curtain.

It amazed George that two women could be so unlike. Hushed, skimpy Angelica with her miserly breathing and plush Loretta who gave out the sounds of a bellows. Angelica smelled like a candle. Loretta steamed vaporous rose-water fog, enough to confound the seasoned captain of a clipper ship.

Loretta Hull chewed on a moan, her jaws moving slowly from side to side as if she munched music. Her mouth opened like a salty wet shell. Her wide face smiled, the face of a cherub with a halo of red-gold hair. Awake, that hair was disciplined into a tight bun. Asleep, it wandered like wild vines, trickled like spilled wine.

Loretta awake was different too, a staunch, ample woman often grave as a tombstone. But in bed, ah, well, a marvelous island. And even though her bed was half empty, she rationed the blanket into equal shares. Ben would never rouse from his sleep with a rattling blue behind and balls shrunk to pits.

George dared to move closer. He lifted Loretta's woolen cover from the bottom. There were her feet, toes curled, ten startled witnesses to an unfolding crime. She trembled and shifted like an earthquake, rolling onto her stomach. Her nightgown pulled up to her waist and George confronted her glorious rump. He raised the blanket higher to examine her powerful legs and thighs. A few wisps of auburn hair blossomed between her legs. God's garden. George mapped her landscape with the eyes of an ancient troll.

His sister-in-law sighed and turned on her back. A shaft of young sunlight made her sex glow. He reached out and slipped her gown off her shoulders. Breasts with nipples like pussywillow destroyed all restraint. George kissed those flowers. Then he spread her legs and mounted her. Her hand guided him into Binghamton's warmest nook. When he came he bit his tongue to keep from screaming.

While George deflated, Loretta opened her eyes and whispered, "Nothing happened, did it?"

"Nothing happened."

"Go back to your room, George. Don't you have any respect for me or for yourself?"

"I'm lower than a beast. A moth flying to flame."

"This is the third time this month that you've come sneaking in here. Take no for an answer. Go downstairs. Roll your cigars and be grateful for your wife, your work, and a place to live. Leave well enough alone."

"Well enough? I am the unhappiest man in America."

"There must be a more miserable man."

"You'd be hard put to find him. Loretta, let me kiss your fruit basket. The peck of a starving sparrow."

"We have an order for twenty dozen Ulysses Supremos to get out by Tuesday. Go downstairs. And before you go do me one favor. The chamber pot. You're positive nothing happened? I was in such a deep sleep."

"An innocent sleep. No, you woke in time to save your honor and my conscience. I thank God for that and ask, if not for passion, then for compassion. I promise never to bother you again. I am a changed man. Only allow me to watch you relieve yourself." George loved to watch her squat.

"Why, George?" Loretta said, settling onto the ironstone throne. "You've been to Niagara Falls. You went there on your honeymoon. Remember?"

"Not a nice thing for Venus to say."

Back in his room, George watched Angelica's flat face while he dressed. She was moon pale. The little mouth had stopped gulping air like a goldfish. It was sealed shut, tight as a pod. Her blanket didn't move up and down to confirm her existence. He resisted the urge to shake her.

Loretta's rotten remark about Niagara Falls reminded George that a year before, almost to the day, he'd come within a shriek of committing murder. He was standing with Angelica, looking out at the silver torrent, watching time spill to frenzied water. The endless hemorrhage frightened him. Why was Niagara considered a haven for lovers? Ah, the endless gush of passion. Ah, the majesty of nature. Ah, the reminder that fragile creatures must huddle together, cleave together for survival.

Maybe with a woman like Loretta beside him, a more substantial lady, sweet fury and moans to match the turbulence outside, he would have felt differently. As it was, the newly married George Hull stood on a cliff growling back at the falls while the silent bride beside him gazed into their future like a mirror reflecting nothing. George almost pushed her over the edge.

He had done the decent thing and honored his agreement with Hamish Flonk. The widow Flonk was now Mrs. Hull, and better off than before. But did she know it? Angelica was so yielding, so giving, so permanently gracious, it was impossible to read her heart.

When the contract had been drawn with her former husband, George focused on the sum involved. Three hundred gold dollars, an honest and respectable agreement by any standard. The provision that George would replace him in the nuptial bed "should the Lord in His infinite wisdom choose to strike down the said Mr. Flonk in the course of battle" seemed a meaningless conceit.

Hamish Flonk agreed to serve as George Hull's surrogate in a war that couldn't possibly last for more than a year. Would America allow herself to be torn apart? Besides, being a lumpish sort of man and not the brightest, this Flonk might suffer some wound or even capture, but Flonk was the Salt of the Earth, a fellow blessed with a long if lugubrious destiny, an honest New York farm boy surrounded by his own band of turgid angels. He would never volunteer to lift a fallen flag or challenge Confederate cannon.

Hamish Flonk had no fervor, no patriotism or politics or cause he cared about. He worried about weather, the planting, the harvest. Here was the perfect substitute, eternally protected, dependable as turnips, certain to live out his days, father his crops, eat, sleep, shit, procreate, wither, die, decay, fertilize the land with his old corpse. Not meant for a hero of the Grand Army of the Republic. Not meant to writhe with his skull split by an Alabama bayonet.

Something had gone terribly wrong.

George remembered his first and last meeting with the late Hamish Flonk. Angelica had come with her doomed mercenary. She waited outside during their negotiations, dainty as a daisy. After the signing and the transfer of funds, they had all gone to celebrate over lunch. George remembered tempting thoughts about that gentle girl left alone while her husband trampled alien corn. George put those thoughts aside as easily as he dropped his napkin.

When word came of Mr. Flonk's abrupt demise, there was much talk about the contract. The Simon Hull & Sons Tobacco Company had prospered, what with its dependable supply of contraband Southern leaf. Angelica Flonk was offered a generous settlement. But she refused to accept another penny for her husband's life. The woman was intractable.

George Hull reasoned with her for days, offering excellent alternatives to himself as a substitute husband. She could have money enough to run, even expand, Hamish's dismal farm. Or a shop of her own in the city. A thousand men, ten thousand, would gladly take a woman of property to have and to hold.

Angelica refused any sensible compromise. She didn't get a lawyer or sulk over her fate. She stopped eating. A wisp to begin with, it was clear to everyone she wouldn't last to the Spring.

"Marry me as you promised Hamish and give me a child. Or do nothing. I won't blame you, George. I won't hound you. I won't haunt you. I'll turn to dew drops and be done with it." That was the note she wrote him a month before their wedding.

On his wedding night, after George disconnected from his bride's slender body, he fell asleep to the sound of Niagara's mocking thunder. Hamish Flonk waited for him. The young soldier used both hands to hold the hemispheres of his skull in place. He apologized for his bloody jacket and a few missing buttons, then congratulated George Hull and praised him as a man of honor. George offered him a Ulysses Supremo and they sat on a rock smoking together. Hamish oozed blood that absorbed into stone. "Earth has an infinite capacity to accommodate the dead," Hamish said. "Praise the Lord."

"I'm perfumed by your widow's juice," George said. "The Lord works in mysterious ways, Private Flonk."

"Yes, sir!" Hamish said. Then he tried a salute to some flag or other and his broken head shattered like an egg.

George went downstairs to the kitchen. Two loaves of bread lay side by side on the counter. Angelica's was shaped like its maker, sourdough with burnt crust. Loretta's bread was Loretta, a luscious gold kitten. He ripped off a piece of Loretta, savored it on his tongue, and washed it down with a mug of Ben's bull-wash coffee.

In the factory, George nodded to his father and brother. They nodded back. He was always late. His habits were past apology or Simon Hull's disapproval. George was George. He sat at his bench, lifted his knife, and cut Honduran binder into half-moon shapes. The crop, still warm from the sweat room, had a nice spongy feel, a sweet, organic aroma.

If George Hull hated the factory, he liked its tobacco air, armpit air, gorilla air. The mix of leaves smelled like mummy skin, slightly rotted, fermented, dried, moistened, perspired, entombed in the dark, liberated, stemmed, ribbed, piled into vegetable pages thicker than Bibles.

Simon Hull, who had invented the Ulysses Supremo (thick as a Corona, tapered Perfecto for the mouth, blunt on the tuck like a Londres for easy lighting, and designed to produce an ash as long as a finger), cut strips of Havana filler and rolled it into perfect diagonals. Ben Hull wrapped the final product, orchestrating Colorado browns, dark *maduros*, reddish *claros, oscuros* black as charcoal. He banded each finished cigar with a picture of General Grant in a gold oval, then arranged the Supremos like ammunition into wooden boxes. The same portrait of Grant was burned into the lid of each box along with the legend SIMON HULL & SONS TOBACCO COMPANY, BINGHAMTON, NEW YORK, UNITED STATES OF AMERICA. It was George who had named their premium product and designed its formidable container. He had a talent for catching a customer's eye.

Simon Hull and his offspring worked efficiently as oarsmen taking pleasure in the family rhythm. Ben sang the "Battle Hymn." Simon hummed along in his cracked falsetto. George joined loudly for the *glory hallelujahs*, crunching the words. His father and brother knew how much George hated God. He might as well have served in the war and returned without arms and legs, deaf and blind from a shell burst.

FORT DODGE, IOWA, MAY 2, 1868

————◆◆◆◆————

I am anchored in place. Immune to disaster. Why this growing sense of threat? Felt presence of terror. Centuries ago, eons ago, grumbles and groans. Fountains of fire. Memories so remote I could hardly bear witness. Lately I play with those distant visions. Liquid dreams of something before.

ACKLEY, IOWA, MAY 11, 1868

————◆◆◆◆————

The Reverend Mr. Henry Turk looked at goblin eyes looking back through a darkness he could never fathom. The little savages were cut and combed, nicely groomed, dressed to resemble children. Surely a tribute to those like Mrs. Samantha Bale who shepherded that flock. He winced to think that he participated in a futile exercise. That these pretend children were far past redemption. It was entirely possible that they lacked human souls.

It could very well be that the remote hollow in which familiar souls dwelt was, in their special case, filled with some primal mist. Perhaps blessed with a trace of spirituality more common to the animus of birds and beasts. Possibly plants and trees. But with no hope of Heaven.

Reverend Turk kept his thoughts to himself. Accurate or not, they were inconvenient. The prevailing conceit was that even Red Indians enjoyed a remote possibility of salvation.

The acknowledged achievements of the Ackley Academy made it clear that Indians, caught early enough, could absorb and retain a degree of useful information. Some, Mrs. Bale said, could actually read and cope with numbers. If the pretend children could be taught to pretend civilization, then why not pretend Jesus Christ was ready to embrace them?

Certainly innocent Samantha Bale believed in her mission. That simple woman couldn't see the snakes wriggling behind those placid eyes or the devils beating drums in those violent young hearts. Mrs. Bale had prepared her class for his visit, read the story of the Creation, led them through Eden like a cherub guiding felons, determined to harvest Christians from Satanic seeds.

"Good afternoon, children," said Reverend Turk.

"Good afternoon, Reverend," slurred voices replied. He felt a chill and began to hiccup. There was no laughter. They watched his small spasms without expression but he knew they rejoiced in his misery.

Reverend Turk refused to sip the water Mrs. Bale provided. "I understand this class has had the excellent advantage of a fine and dedicated teacher to encourage your education through the holiest of books. You have heard how the all-powerful God created the heavens, the firmament, the flora and fauna, and, yes, man and woman. You know now that, despite urgent warning, Adam tasted forbidden fruit from the Tree of Knowledge at Eve's misguided behest. Startled and confounded by the evil serpent, seduced by slime, Eve chose to barter paradise and immortality for earthly wisdom and banishment to a world of pain and death. Adam must share some blame for that sad decision. He should have known better than to confuse Eve's beauty with God's truth.

"Yes, the Bible begins with a frightening tale of betrayal and arrogance. But take heart, for this story has the happiest of endings. Though banished from Eden, we are given the chance to visit a place more sublime, there to gaze upon a countenance more radiant than a thousand suns. To be cleansed and made whole in the glow of our Father's smile. Say amen."

"Amen."

"And again."

"Amen."

"What you have learned here at Ackley Academy must have stirred many questions," Reverend Turk said. "We welcome your questions. Our beliefs do not fear challenge. Quite the contrary. Many with white skins who call themselves Born Again face moments of doubt. If any among you feel the need to speak out, I am here to listen and reply. Be not afraid, for the Lord is compassionate and understanding and instructs us to suffer the children. Especially those who, like yourselves, have been raised in ignorance and encouraged to worship false pagan gods."

"If you have a question, please raise your hand and sit quietly in place until the Reverend Turk calls upon you," Mrs. Bale said. The room went quiet. It did not surprise Turk that none in that displaced herd would risk voicing distrust, even to a sympathetic ear like his own. Mrs. Bale had warned him to expect no sign from them, not of comprehension, acceptance, or rejection. Their way was to remain self-contained as cocoons. He was about to continue his lecture when a small copper hand rose in the air like a flower with a clenched fist for its bud.

"You have a question, Herbert?" Mrs. Bale said. "Very well. Stand and state your name for the Reverend Turk, then tell him what bothers your mind."

"I am called Herbert Black Paw. I ask of the beast with the twisted back."

"What is he saying, Mrs. Bale?"

"I'm sure I don't know. Explain yourself, Herbert."

"He who drinketh no water."

Samantha Bale let out a sudden giggle and covered her mouth. "You mean the camel, Herbert? Is that what you mean?"

"Yes. That one. You have shown him to us in the morning."

"Reverend Turk, Herbert, who is a bright and responsive boy, has a question he wishes to ask you about a camel. He seemed very much taken with the illustrations we studied before you came. Excellent depictions of life in the Holy Land. We are not here to talk about camels, Herbert. Sit down."

"Let him ask, then," the Reverend Turk said warmly. "If I can answer, I will, though I am no expert on the ways of the dromedary."

"That beast is not of my place," Herbert said flatly. "That beast is of another place. I have never seen a beast with a more foul face or hurt body. Is your god so shaped as the camel? Does your god carry hairy hills when he goes?"

"Are you asking if Lord Jesus Christ is a camel?"

"Your god has nothing in my land. Why does he come here?"

"The God I speak of is a universal God, young man, the one God. All gods tremble before Him. He rolleth up the sea and maketh the mountains to kneel. And I think He would willingly take responsibility for creating the camel. For your information, child, there are those who believe, on scientific evidence of bones and such, that this land was indeed home to the species in centuries past. That American camels were commonplace."

"Your god gives no thunder to me or rain I think, sir. And I do not in my heart believe that any such creature as the camel was known to my fathers or their fathers or their fathers before them. The idea makes me laugh. *Ha ha ha.* And the buffalo laugh with me. *Ha ha ha.* And every deer, rabbit, and horse. *Ha ha.*"

"Herbert Black Paw, you are out of order," Mrs. Bale said. "Now apologize to Reverend Turk immediately. Reverend, you must understand how difficult it must be for these orphans——"

"Not orphan. My family lives still now."

"You are all orphans," Mrs. Bale said. "When you came here to this school because of the kindness of our government you renounced the old ways and old ties. We have talked about this many times. Now, Herbert, tell the Reverend how deeply sorry you are for your disgusting outburst. The whole class is mortified by your behavior."

"Because a hungry man is given fruit by his woman is no bad thing. To seek wisdom from such a magic fruit is no bad thing. Then why does your hairy god of the dry mouth and lumpish back spurn such a man? This god is for another place and time. I am not sorry, Mrs. Bale. And I am no orphan. I am the first son of Singing Fox, a chief among the Dakota. My mother is dead but yet a weeping ghost who rides on wind. How should I be sad to this Reverend whose god is a camel and should shit where he lives?"

The Reverend Mr. Henry Turk grabbed the boy's arm and dragged Herbert Black Paw to the front of the room. The boy was told to bend over and drop his pants. Mrs. Bale left the room while Reverend Turk pummeled him with a wooden switch shaped like a baton. The switch left thin bloody streaks that looked like war paint. The blood stripes gleamed. "My God is everywhere," the Reverend said softly, even as he slashed flesh. "He knows no nations, no borders. He covers the Earth like a luminous sky. For Him, these United States of America are the new Jerusalem. He has blessed this nation as no other. He has given us victory in war and reconciliation in peace. Praised be His wondrous name. Say amen."

"Amen."

"My God loves this land, its rivers, its oceans, the grass, the trees, the hills and valleys. He is a cool spring in the desert, snow on the mountaintops, rain on the rose. He createth all things and dispenseth forgiveness to all who accept his dominion. He is the resurrection and the life. Be purged, my child, of Lucifer's pus and bile. Know that Jesus walks the earth like a giant. He hath just and righteous title here. We are made in his image and revel in His grace."

Riding home, Reverend Turk smiled at the sunset. Calm now, he saw humor in Herbert Black Paw's confusion. *God is a camel.* He wondered at the workings of the primitive mind. And the thought that the Lord of Hosts was alien to the very nation He had so carefully chosen as the place for His modern miracles.

Of course Mrs. Bale was correct in her comments, over tea and cakes, that it was difficult for those lads to dismiss the idea of Christ as invader. What vision of Heaven could they share? The damned are the last to appreciate rescue.

Still, the Indians did have some inkling of immortality. They spoke of a Divine Spirit, Wakonda, whatever. Probably every insect, slug and worm had that intimation, ancient memory of the sublime Creation. For Mrs. Bale that was a glimmer of hope, the tiny chance that even a bee might suspect salvation. For Reverend Turk, her notion was a bit farfetched. His Heaven required at least minimal credentials.

Tranquil on the back of his loping horse, he remembered a time from his own childhood when the robed and bearded patriarchs of The Book seemed foreign, remote as a Sahara sandstorm. Those austere Disciples had little to do with St. Louis, Missouri, where he was born and raised. It took time and patience to learn that Bethlehem was Everyman's cradle. No question, it would have been easier to embrace a Jesus who walked through Boston, Philadelphia, Chicago, or even New York.

Reverend Turk thought perhaps he had been too hard on Herbert Black Paw. No. Lessons etched in pain endureth longest.

FORT DODGE, IOWA, JUNE 3, 1868

Thumps and echoes? Why ponder variables? To help me pass the ongoing? Should I be bored with so much nothing to do? I can never catch up at this rate. Wasting hours in speculation. I am all there is. A clunk? A violent thwack? So? Shame on me. Unworthy of majesty.

BINGHAMTON, NEW YORK, JUNE 10, 1868

As they walked through the streets of Binghamton, George Hull looked at his father's crumbled face. Simon Hull had lived for nearly eight decades. His skull popped through its cover. His hair was dead leaves. His lips were purple rivers bracketing a swampy valley defended by broken walls. Only Simon's eyes showed life. Deadly blue, they stared up at the Dipper, thirsty for renewal. George thought to himself, "This is me if I am lucky enough to endure. What a system."

"I'm worried about you, George," Simon said. "This business with your brother's wife."

"Loretta? Why? What lie did she tell you? It's Ben you should be worried about. That bitch is out for trouble."

"Loretta told me nothing. I am an old man living in an old house, George. Every board speaks to me. I hear things I don't want to hear. If a mouse moves it sounds to me like an army."

"What are you saying?"

"Loretta is Ben's temple."

"Are you suggesting that I would ever entertain thoughts of compromising my own brother?"

"I am suggesting that George keep his chickens in their coop. I am suggesting that your sword be sheathed in its proper scabbard. I am suggesting that you accept Angelica as your woman and behave with some semblance of dignity."

"I am thirty-eight years old. I am not an idiot."

"I wasn't questioning your wisdom or lack of it. I am not unaware of the magnetism of an incandescent woman resting naked only inches away. I live in the same house."

"You? Is this my own father with hardly the energy to draw smoke from a stogie telling me that he lusts to pet Loretta's prize poodle? Or am I hearing words spoken by the wind? I must be insane. Yes, that's it."

"Don't dare mock me, George Hull. I was simply trying to tell you that I won't condemn your repulsive desires. But I warn you to keep your stallion in its stall. Leave the stuff of tragedy to Shakespeare and the Greeks. We enjoy a balanced life, a fine business, a hopeful future. Before I die, I would like to see our home blessed with a happy brood of bustling grandchildren, the only medals your mother and I ever wished for. What I lust for, George, is family harmony, health, and a measure of prosperity."

"From your mouth to God's ear. You think I want anything more?"

"I do think that, yes. I suspect you are a restless and impatient spirit. A disruptive sort. Transcend the clutch of despair, those tentacles of rapacious greed that yearn for every drop of honey in every hive. Make your motto *control, accept, be grateful.*"

"Thank you, father. I will try to remember."

"You have a snide mouth, son. And amazing arrogance. I have decided to put both to good use. I think it's the right time to expand our enterprise, widen our horizons, seek new markets, create new products. I am already at work developing a cigar with appeal to the newly liberated Negroes, an affordable *breva* Colorado *medura* to be called Pickaninny. The label will feature a happy ebony toddler swaddled in white bunny fur."

"Bunny fur. Yes, that might work."

"My intention, George, is to give you the task of bringing the concept to fulfillment. It will require substantial effort and dedication, but the potential reward is enormous."

"I don't know what to say."

"I want your plate clear of debris, your mind in fresh focus before you embark on this venture. I want you to enjoy a deserved vacation. I am sending you to visit your sister Samantha."

"In Iowa?"

"You leave in one week. When you pack your bags, fill them with more than clothing. Load them with your rage, your unbridled appetites, your obscene impatience and misdirected ambition which must rival that of Alexander, Attila, and Genghis Khan. Pack those things along with any other demons that plague you. Take the bundle West and leave it there to bleach clean as the abandoned animal carcasses we see depicted in the press. Amuse yourself with new experience, arouse yourself with fresh vistas, broaden your outlook through new acquaintances, shape yourself to a finer person. You have potential, George. Your dear mother and I knew you could go farther than good, honest Ben. Now you have your chance. Go and refresh your spirit. Take time to discover your wife."

"You want me to take Angelica?"

"Can rain in the west nourish fields in the east? Certainly take Angelica. Who can say which of my daughters will give me a grandson to flaunt before angels?"

FORT DODGE, IOWA, JUNE 12, 1868

Questions of origin are certainly a sin. The world is rock. All else is rock. A sweet continuance of stone. Darkness surrounds our continuity. Then, Source, with such a shield who is my enemy? If I am everything, can I be diminished? Are you amused by these rantings? I am. Where is my mind?

GETTYSBURG, PENNSYLVANIA, JUNE 16, 1868

Barnaby Rack looked out at a field of tombstones. They seemed to belong where they were, a natural foliage neatly arranged. The endless rows in perfect symmetry gave a comforting sense of order.

He wrote: *A garden of silence. Blanketing coffins filled with splintered bones, outraged flesh, decapitated limbs, skulls holding echoes of martial music. The detritus of patriotic pride carefully hidden, covered with grass. Broken soldiers in eternal formation, flat on their backs, with their monuments rising like futile erections probing a dispassionate sky.* Good.

"Rest in peace. You are peace or close as we come," Barnaby said to the air, then wrote that down in the notebook. He went back to copying names off the markers. *These names belong to nobody now. They are ownerless, free to use again and again by other armies in other wars. Here is a kind of miracle. There will always be names enough and never a shortage to worry about. An infinite arsenal of names to match Mother Earth's infinite capacity to house the battalions of dead. What a marvelous resource for the nation!*

Barnaby browsed the battlefield on assignment for the *New York Clarion*. His managing editor, John Zipmeister, told him to trundle his ass to Gettysburg before the bodies buried there cooled to oblivion. "I don't want a war story," Zipmeister had said. "I want a postwar story. And not the usual crap about reconciliation under death's umbrella. Go up to Cemetery Ridge and pick out a few of the poor bastards. A Union man, a Reb, at least one salt-of-the-earth, New York–bred stiff. The idea here is to track down their families because we want to know who they were, what they were about, where they worked, who they stuffed, did they like apples, and how are they mourned. What did that bomb or bullet take away, and how do the living cope with their loss? Do they light candles in church or curse God and Lincoln? Where do they see their lives going and the country heading? Do they dream of vengeance or have they come to terms? You know what we're after here, Rack. Human drama, emotions, consequences. You're always pissing and moaning about how you don't get the chance to use your talent. Be my guest. Bring back something I can use, like three thousand words to make my pimples explode."

Between taking names, Barnaby made notes on the look and feel of the place. A gliding bird, a clump of wildflowers, a little torn flag plugged into the ground, trees to bear witness, a breeze to soothe any ghost, a mud-spattered doll, splayed bellydown, left to comfort one fallen warrior.

Barnaby went around, jotting names at random. Final selections could come later. It was no small thing for a man to be resurrected in the pages of the *Clarion*. To have handfuls of dust, shards of flesh, chips of yellowed teeth flung in the face of the relatives. Barnaby had the odd thought he should ask for volunteers.

That idea made him laugh out loud. His laugh magnified and echoed off statues of angels and eagles and abandoned cannons left to guard the sanctuary. Then his legs were pushed out from under him and he found himself spread like the doll, embracing a mound of wet dirt.

Barnaby lifted his head to see what cut him down. An imp danced around him, arms poised and fists clenched like a prizefighter. The imp wore a black suit, white shirt and tie, patent leather shoes, and a derby hat. Its mouth sprouted a cucumber-size cigar curling smoke like the stack of a puffer belly locomotive.

"Is this a place for shallow laughter?" the imp said. "Where so many gallant fellows from both North and South ask only for our respect? Realize, sir, that but for chance you too might rest in this sodden bed, forever deprived of all things meaningful, including the pain of pleasure."

"I wasn't making a mockery of the fallen," Barnaby said. "My laughter was ironic. If I laughed at anything it was capricious fate." "Ah," the imp said, lowering its arms. "I understand now and I owe a profound apology."

Barnaby stood and brushed himself off, then bent to retrieve his notebook and pencil. The imp approached him with its face tilted toward Barnaby's groin and an outstretched hand. "Charles Sherwood Stratton," the imp said, tipping its derby. "Pleased to make your acquaintance."

"The General?" Barnaby said. "It is you."

"One and the same. But you have me at an advantage."

"Rack. Barnaby Rack. We met once before."

"Then I must know you, so we are old friends. Shake my hand. Go on. I won't snap."

"General Tom Thumb. Yes, I was there when Mr. Barnum presented you to Mrs. Lincoln. I remember Mr. Barnum's very words. What has two hands, four feet, and an iron-clad contract?"

"Ah, yes, poor sullen Mary Todd. She thought I was a bug. I expected her to swat me like a fly. Impulsive woman. Very troubled, as I recall. Not what I expected, but who is? Of course, the First Lady might have been offended when I asked her late lamented husband, 'How's the little woman?' It was an honest attempt at humor and no malice intended. And you? Are you a diplomat, then?"

"A reporter. *New York Clarion.*"

"A gentleman of the press. Impressive. I dabble in writing myself. I have always thought my short life worth a long book."

"May I ask why Tom Thumb is in Gettysburg?"

"To pay tribute. As a General to his troops. Though this battle was none of my making and I'm glad of that. The carnage, the carnage. Why must the future be built on blood? And you?"

"My job is to choose a few from these anonymous thousands and tell their stories."

"Excellent. Have you learned to interview the dead, Mr. Rack?"

"Not yet. My interviews will be with family and friends."

"I see, yes, very interesting. You should interview me someday. I am a repository of fascinating tales and experiences to charm any reader."

"I will suggest that to my editor."

"My card, Mr. Rack." The General's card was the size of a postage stamp.

"And mine in return."

"Now, if it won't distract you, I intend to perform for the boys. It's what I do and all I can do."

Barnaby watched the tiny man dance and do cartwheels while he sang "Dixie" in a high falsetto. Then General Thumb ran along the rows of graves and vanished down a hill.

Barnaby tucked the minuscule calling card in his shirt pocket and took notes on their meeting. Another gift, another bonus, another toy for Zipmeister. Then he heard thunder and saw the sky go black. Lightning streaked through the clouds.

Barnaby followed a shaft of light to one stone and read its inscription:

PVT. HAMISH FLONK, FIRST NEW YORK INFANTRY, BORN 1841, DIED 1864. FOREVER A STAR IN THIS NATION'S PROUD BANNER. MAY HE STAND EXULTANT ON THE DAY OF JUDGMENT AND PROCLAIM, "I DID MY DUTY FOR THE UNION!"

Silver fire streamed in the direction taken by General Thumb. Barnaby was certain so small a rod was an unlikely target for a lightning bolt. Since the odds against mayhem were so enormous, he didn't bother to investigate Thumb's fate. If Barnum's midget had been hit, only a crisp the size of a moth would remain and there would be news worth printing. But knowing so much good luck was too much for any reporter to expect, Barnaby ran for cover.

He stood under an oak tree while the drizzle turned to a torrent. *Leaves and grass release a delicious green smell. The field is transformed as nature conspires to camouflage evidence of the horror that once frightened birds with screams and shrieks and unanswered prayers. Those complaints lasted only for a moment. That moment rushes backward to memory, washed by the storm that makes the tombstones shine even as this shower of pelting hail erases their legends.* Nice.

Barnaby saw General Thumb rise over the horizon, spinning like a fragile pinwheel, dodging fire, still singing anthems to his audience of skeletons.

FORT DODGE, IOWA, JULY 1, 1868

Impossible. Huge clatter and crash. Ripped and lifted. Dropped upside down. Severed. Separate. Up to your old tricks, Source? Rearranging the furniture, are you? Well, I don't accept it. Not for a minute. I demand attachment and my full share of gravity. I have tenure by right of service. This is no grain of sand. This is me. Displaced. Disoriented. Detached. Compromised. Irritated. Your whim. My indignity. Not the last of this.

ON THE UNION PACIFIC, JULY 5, 1868

Each time he thrust at his patient wife, George Hull's rump rapped the ceiling of the new Pullman Coach. His body, moving up and down while the train moved east to west, refused to allow him release.

George pumped Angelica's well for what must have been fifty

miles and through two tunnels. She moaned like the train's mournful whistle but with considerably less conviction. From his own experience in such matters, George knew that Angelica was more accommodating than appreciative of his marathon effort. That was no surprise since their couplings had never been odes to passion. He didn't even feel anger anymore as he had in the early days. She did the best she could. He functioned like a dependable machine. The process of procreation didn't demand earthquakes.

Finally, matching the *click-clack* of the wheels, George found a rhythm that transcended indifference and exploded in her lap. Angelica did smile and lock her legs around him, which he took as a measure of gratitude. It gave George some satisfaction to think that theirs might be the first infant conceived in a Pullman Coach.

As she reached for a towel, he kissed Angelica on the lips, wished her sweet dreams, exited the upper berth through a heavy curtain, and climbed into his cubby below. Lying on his bunk, made mellow by climax, George let the *click-clack* lull his restless spirit. He had not been alone in bed since his wedding day and welcomed the privacy.

George appreciated the mobile miracle provided by the Pullman Company, a splendid example of technology in the service of affluence. It certainly boded well for the nation's future. Civil war left the country dazed, licking bloody entrails, hearts leaden with guilt. Things were changing. A great surge of fresh energy had begun to flow like gore from the wounded.

A statesman summed it up nicely: "New railroads, new factories and foundries . . . are linked with the grand march of humanity." What the pundits predicted, A Great American Barbecue, was already under way. Sullen spirits would be purged on the grill.

That the grand march trampled and murdered, gutted and burned, was unfortunate but inevitable. Progress was a bloodthirsty benefactor nourished by human sacrifice. Sad that the future feeds on the past. Let music from the grand march burst sensitive eardrums, that was the way of things. The art, George knew, was to keep in step.

There were those, like Angelica, who clenched against the new momentum, their noses still clogged by the smell of death. But others strained to go forward, cross horizons that spread like Loretta's legs. The factories and foundries oozed steel like spiders ooze web. Webs of steel would soon cover the American continent. As George Hull rested, his pinched wife floating above him, coolies sweated track across the Sierras. Irish roustabouts raced to meet them. Rails and telegraph wires were splitting the skulls of savages and spilling out their red brains for fertilizer. Chunky cities transformed the wilderness. Even mourning lovers must yearn to join the frantic dance.

George felt hot between his legs. He wanted to wake Angelica again, feel his ass banging like a mallet on the Pullman's metal roof. But there wasn't much point. Mrs. Hull was always compliant, but it would be like dipping into a tub of wet nails. So, instead of climbing to a higher perch, George put on a wool robe and slippers, then left his capsule for a walk down the train's narrow aisle.

He went thinking about Andrew Carnegie proclaiming his gospel of wealth while he forged empires. And about George Hull's fetid shroud of tobacco leaves.

"Are you all right, sir?"

"Fine. Never better."

"Can I get you something? A cool drink?"

George looked into the round black face of an attendant keeping the night watch. The man was hardly in his thirties, a squat-bodied sentinel wearing a white coat and Pullman cap.

"Nothing, thank you."

"My name is Elwood though all Pullman porters answer to George. After George Pullman. Call me what you want. Something you need, please let me know."

"Since I am another George, Elwood will do. I suppose there are people sleeping behind all those curtains?" George said for no particular reason.

"Every one filled. These new coaches are quite a success with the public."

"It's like being in a moving mausoleum."

"Wouldn't have said that. But I see your meaning, what with the stacking. You can tell they ain't dead by the snores and such. Most of our passengers sleep like babies. I expect it's the rocking."

"Well, there's not an ounce of sleep in me," George said.

"You want a periodical? To occupy the mind?"

"My mind is fully occupied. That's the problem, Elwood. So tell me, what do you think now that His Accidency is on the way out of the White House? You think you'll get your forty acres and a mule as they promise?"

"I never talk politics with the guests. My folks was in service to the governor of Virginia. House Negroes, not field hands. I like being with the railroad and wouldn't trade for no acres or mules."

"Do you smoke cigars?" George said, remembering his father's vision. If four million darkies got the habit, it could add up. The old man was on to something.

"Never tried one."

"Would you like to? Cigars are my business, you see. We're very interested in developing a following among Coloreds. We have a new product, Pickaninnies, a blend of the finest leaf, crafted to produce a continuance of pleasure and an aroma like perfume."

"You don't say. Never took to cigars."

"Ah, but you never smoked one of ours. Suppose I find a few samples back in my berth and we allow ourselves to indulge."

"I can't do that, sir. I'm not permitted to socialize beyond polite conversation."

"We'll keep the conversation polite, then, Elwood."

"Besides, I'm on duty here."

"And on duty you remain. Some of the best minds in our most important offices function at maximum while they smoke. You must know that."

"If the conductor should come checking . . ."

"He's probably deep asleep. This will be our secret, Elwood. And I would most value your opinion of this proud new creation of ours."

"May I ask, sir, how much do your Pickaninnies cost?"

"Free of charge during this limited test period. No cost, no obligation. Are you game for a sample?"

"We'd have to stand out between the cars."

George fumbled in his berth until he found a leather case of Pickaninnies in his jacket pocket. He could hear a restless Angelica flap like a fish in her flying bed. It was her first trip West, her first trip of magnitude. Certainly exciting for that innocent. Could she have ever imagined herself propelled across the dark miles riding like a princess in a Pullman Coach? Had Hamish Flonk returned of a piece, such a journey would have remained in the realm of a fairy tale. If the trip did nothing more it might teach Angelica to appreciate her legacy. That Fate shouldn't be judged too harshly, too soon.

The train rushed through an endless forest, its pine army splashed in moonlight. "Well? Say something, Elwood." George pulled his robe around him, fending off the night wind. "Your opinion is of interest."

"Very nice, I think," Elwood said, a smoke trail snaking from his mouth. "Mellow with a tad of a bite."

"Exactly. A tad of a bite. You people appreciate a tangy taste. What we suspected."

"I should go back in now. Make my rounds."

"You've hardly had two puffs. Go on, Elwood. Take a deep draught. Like so. *Savor the flavor. Mild as a child.* That's our new motto, for which I take some credit."

"I guess I savor the flavor, all right."

"Elwood, how can I know if you're telling me the truth? Or are you saying what I want to hear?"

"You can't know."

"Smoke it to the hilt. Down to the stub."

"I'll save the rest for later."

"No. Don't worry. You've earned a box for your trouble. This should be a fair test. The taste changes as it burns closer to the root."

Elwood took another mouthful, a gray cloud rising around his head. "It does. That's a fact."

"I'm counting on you to tell your friends about these Pickaninnies," George said. "Word of mouth is the best advertising."

"I'll do that, sir," Elwood said. "Count on it. But if I could speak my piece without upsetting you?"

"Say what you want. You won't upset me. That's what research is for."

"The name. Pickaninny."

"What about the name?"

"And the thing about mild as a child. I know it ain't your intention to give out the message that a cigar is any particular child. But others, less educated, might feel some resentment."

"Mild as a child is the whole idea behind the name," George said. "Can't you understand that? The association between mild and child? Everybody likes children. Don't you like children?"

"Some yes, some no," Elwood said. "But face it, there are such Negroes as dislike the word pickaninny. If I was you people, I'd come up with another name that don't give cause for offense. Say, Uncle Tom. Nobody would be offended by that."

"Uncle Tom? That says zero. It doesn't create any kind of emotion. None whatsoever. Pickaninny is a name with substance. You can't forget it. It sticks with you. If there happen to be five or six misguided niggers out there who might object for some stupid reason, well, that gives me no incentive to squander a name as powerful as that. I don't recall asking you what you thought of the name, Elwood. Only the cigar."

"That's exactly right, sir. If I overstepped, I offer my apology. Black folk will welcome those Pickaninnies into their homes, men, women, and even the children. *Savor the flavor. Mild as a child.* Yes, sir."

"We didn't anticipate women and children among our customers. Should we? Frankly, the preferences of your people are largely unknown to us."

"Oh, I think the ladies and the little ones are fair game."

"That's good news," George said.

"Now I do have to get about my chores."

"One puff for the road."

"For the road."

George and the attendant took a final drag, then tossed the spent Pickaninnies onto the tracks. "I am a little tired now," George said. "Time to grab a few winks."

"Yes, good night to you, sir."

"Aren't you coming?"

"In just a moment. I think I'll stay out here in the air and savor the flavor."

"Savor the flavor." George laughed, shook his head, and went back to his berth. He stripped off his robe, lay on his bunk, closed his eyes, and drifted with the train's steel lullaby.

Above him, Angelica had her legs pulled up so her toes touched the Pullman's roof. She tried to think of herself as a lake drinking in streams of fresh water. Water from rain, water from melting snowcaps and dripping icicles. She knew it wasn't working. She could feel her body defend against George Hull's seminal burst. No baby would get its start that night on the Pullman Coach. Hamish would have to wait for his surrogate immortality.

Between the cars, the attendant, Elwood, emptied his guts onto the track bed contemplating the price of freedom.

FORT DODGE, IOWA, JULY 6, 1868

Is this my final spasm? A return to the swirl? Will I be rendered again to frivolous atoms tweaking infinity? Which is better: the confusion of fission or illusion of fusion? To be a Prince of Chaos or a clod in this lumpish continuum? Is terminal germinal or germinal terminal? I deserve explanations. Not take it or leave it. Beginning or end, I need time to make ready.

ACKLEY, IOWA, JULY 8, 1868

The Reverend Mr. Henry Turk sat surrounded by his most trusted books, tracts, and broadsides preparing the sermon he would deliver ten days hence. He paused in his reflections, closed his eyes, and projected himself to the stage of a gigantic tent where a thousand lost sheep would gather for their annual ritual of renewal.

This year he had designed the setting himself. There would be no decoration or distraction in that theater of purification. Only a raised black pulpit on a bare stage, stark as Judgment, and a large cross of oak daubed with splashes of red paint in those places where the Lord shed His blood. On both sides of the stage, behind the speaker's rostrum, a choir of children from the Indian school would waft hymns of praise.

The Reverend saw himself speaking to the eager crowd. He watched his words fly like sparrows to nest in eager ears. His problem was, those sparrow words were not flowing easily from pen to paper. No wonder, since this sermon must produce nothing less than astonishment. This was no time for platitudes. Each spoken phrase must be a young flame. Nothing less would cauterize the mind-rotting plague of complacency.

Turk stood up from his desk and stretched. Did his own lethargy have its roots in self-doubt? Had he bitten off more than he could chew? Was he a prophet or merely a sounding board? The challenge was to break through every obstacle, to enter into a room of shimmering revelation.

Being a humble man, the Reverend Turk allowed for the vague possibility of failure. That was only a courtesy to his modesty. With the Savior's help and a better attitude, he knew he would find his way. Confident or not, he had to get on with his writing.

Some immediate stimulation was needed. Turk opened the lowest drawer of the cabinet where he kept letters, diaries, an assortment of trivia, and a bottle of sour mash whiskey. The consumption of alcohol was an evil thing, except to muffle pain. The agony of elusive language was the worst pain of all. Reverend Turk uncorked the bottle, prayed to transform its content to ink, then tasted the fruit of his alchemy.

Next he consulted a book left behind by a fallen dove who called herself Bottomless Patricia and once sold her favors at the Blue Eye Saloon. After a dream, that dedicated whore renounced her ways and went East to join celibate Shakers. The Reverend Mr. Turk had reluctantly blessed her journey.

Her gift to him was the whiskey, along with a suspect manual of Shaker customs. There were detailed instructions concerning the vile dances those Shakers employed to generate spiritual ecstasy. Blatant illustrations confirmed their shame.

He had studied the manual out of curiosity and allowed himself to experiment with the movements and patterns, tappings, trippings, and turnings that seemed designed more to pacify Pan than encourage true bliss. During those experiments, Reverend Turk noticed a kind of elation that left a pleasant lilt, especially when he allowed a bit of whiskey to lubricate his arthritic knees. He was forced to admit the demanding cavorting did leave some residue of what could be taken for grace.

The room suddenly seemed very warm. Reverend Turk stripped off his shirt and trousers. Using his hands to clap and his shoes to stomp, Turk let himself test Shaker gamboling, most complex, he thought, for a sect that heralded simple gifts.

Following instructions, he began by trotting in slow circles, then whirled himself around until he felt himself near fainting. He circled and whirled, whirled and circled, while perspiration spilled down his face. His most private part throbbed and stiffened.

The Reverend Mr. Henry Turk patted at the bulge in his union suit, grasped his own handle, and used it to pull himself around and around. Owlish hoots escaped from his mouth. No question, he felt a welcome rush of creative impulse. When he saw Samantha Bale standing at the door, the Reverend tried to halt his momentum and dropped like a top then curled to a fetus.

"I brought cookies and bread," Samantha said, staring at the ceiling while she held out a cloth bag embroidered with swans. Her face was the color of sunset.

"How good of you to come, Mrs. Bale," Reverend Turk said, reaching for his pants, then his shirt. "What must my behavior seem to you? No, I have not gone mad. Here is a manual of rituals performed by a radical cult called Shakers which designate themselves Christians and have managed to draw converts to their bastion. They promise epiphany through scandalous dance accompanied by self-generated percussions. You see why I felt myself obliged to investigate this heresy?"

"I should go now."

"No. Stay. Can I offer you some refreshment?"

"There is something I would like to talk about if I am not interrupting your work."

"By all means. The work can wait. I trust the Shakers will keep shaking for a time, *heh heh,* until they shake themselves out of existence. They are celibates, you see, entirely dependent on new recruits. But enough of the Shakers. Please say what you came to say."

"It's my brother George," Samantha said. "He's on his way with his wife for a visit."

"How nice for you, Mrs. Bale."

"I hope so, Reverend Turk. I have received a most disturbing note from our father."

"Disturbing in what way, may I ask?"

"George is a turbulent soul. A good man but momentarily conflicted and confused. I was hoping to bring him to your meeting next week and that you might spare a moment to speak with him. He most desperately needs guidance and direction, and I know he will be inspired by your message."

"Of course I will see your brother, Mrs. Bale. And pray for his safe arrival."

"Thank you. Yes, it will be good to see George. He was last in Ackley when my Dr. Bale passed on some six years ago."

"May he rest in peace. Tell me, is our choir of young seraphim ready to be heard? Has the one called Herbert Black Paw learned something of humility?"

"The choir is marvelous," Samantha said. "They've come so far and from such beginnings. Herbert, alas, remains a special case. He has refused to join in song with the other children. I can't know what to expect from him."

"Let me ask a favor of you. Bring the boy to my meeting. I want him to hear what I say. Him especially."

"What if he proves disruptive?"

"I'll return him to the void. But give him this chance to sing."

"What a compassionate man you are, Reverend."

The Reverend Mr. Henry Turk patted Samantha Bale's hand. "And now I must return to my labors," he said. "Thank you again for your thoughtful offering. I do look forward to meeting brother George. Allow me to walk you to the gate, Mrs. Bale. And let me apologize for any embarrassment I may have caused you."

"It is I who should apologize. When there was no answer to my knocking, I might have realized that you were indisposed. But I did want you to have the bakery warm and fresh from the oven and when your door swung open . . ."

Back in his study, the Reverend Turk saw that the bottle of sour mash sat naked on his desk. Had she noticed it? There was no label. It could have been liniment. Or even cologne. Besides, that woman was discreet as she was forgiving and far too caught up in concern for her brother to speculate on reasons why her spiritual leader would twirl like a dervish with a corn cob stuck in his underwear. The innocent accept. That is their innocence.

CARDIFF, NEW YORK, JULY 10, 1868

William C. Newell, Stubby to everyone who knew him, surveyed his miserable plot of land. The Newell farm, with its sulfur-smelling lake, seed-rejecting soil, miserly trees that produced such acid fruit even insects refused to leave larvae on the apples, peaches, and grubby cherries, collapsing barn, caving house, sullen cows, angry goats, bald chickens, bloated cat, toothless dog, frumpy wife, and logy son, lay like a blight on creation.

That sterile farm was surrounded by verdant fields, gentle hills, blue lakes where plump ducks floated and trout leapt, forests filled with deer, rabbits, pheasants. Pious farmers worked prosperous acres covered with ripening wheat, perfect corn, pungent alfalfa, orchards erupting with plenty, gardens bursting with melons, and squash in huge abundance. Men blessed with God-fearing wives who dropped obedient children from welcoming wombs, happy beasts, and sturdy homes, had good reason to thank Heaven for their bounty.

Even the weather that hung over Stubby Newell's place was hostile to life, sweltering in summer, frigid in winter, fog-damp in autumn, last to green in the spring. How Stubby's farm got misplaced in beautiful Onondaga was a mystery.

The local Minister once explained that, had the Deity worked even another hour past the end of the Sixth Day before resting, only on the morning of the Seventh, Stubby's life would have been easier to endure. As it was, Stubby Newell did the best he could.

His farm came cheap, made cheaper by nervous whispers. The previous owner dug up a string of bones, what looked like a human spine, along with a rusty razor, then stupidly rushed into Cardiff to announce his grisly find. He'd heard that rare artifacts and burial mounds unearthed across the valley, everything from Indian beads to Jesuit ribs, were bringing high prices from the state's new museum.

What the farmer forgot was that a citizen of Cardiff had vanished the year before leaving only a blood-soaked hat behind. When the man from the museum rejected the bones as not very old and the rusty razor of recent vintage, a rumor grew that the vanished man had been murdered on what was to become Stubby's property.

The farm, always considered a cursed plot, was then said to be haunted by vengeful demons. That suspicion gained strength when the bone-finder hanged himself and his hound after rot took what was left of his planting.

Stubby sat on a rock and lit the last of the cigars Uncle Simon Hull sent him for Christmas. At his wife, Bertha's, urging, Stubby tried many times to compose a letter to his uncle asking for a job down in Binghamton at the Simon Hull & Sons cigar factory. It was hard for Stubby to write anything, much less plead for help. And for all its horror, the farm was still home.

He felt himself a gladiator, wrestling invisible monsters that lived on his land. There was something exhilarating in the contest. Stubby was defined by misery, more frightened of sedentary comfort than he was of malevolent forces that made his lettuce turn to pulp and his wasps take detours to sting with no provocation. Tilling soil mixed with the virulent remains of a murdered man had certain rewards. His struggle was legendary, even if nobody but himself knew its epic dimension. Someday minstrels would sing songs about Stubby Newell, but only if he stayed where he belonged.

FORT DODGE, IOWA, JULY 12, 1868

No frame of reference for any of this. I am in crisis. Not myself. Unknown now. There is just so much loyalty. Source, don't take me for granted. Why abuse and antagonize your best creation? We nourish each other. Give me my mountain!

FORT DODGE, IOWA, JULY 15, 1868

Angelica Brewster Flonk Hull accepted God as a cluster of stars in a moonless sky where heavy clouds drifted. A comforting umbrella, certainly awesome, signaling with erratic old light. Tantalizing. Pretty. Remote. Preoccupied with splendor, indifferent to much else.

Her life moved through good times, bad times, slow times, days and nights strung together like beads in a necklace that once belonged to someone and would someday be passed along.

When she prayed she talked to herself. It always surprised her to hear others petition Jesus as if He were standing beside them or hovering like a dragonfly. To ask gifts and miracles, the keys to Heaven, seemed imposing and in bad taste. But Angelica respected different beliefs.

"The Reverend Turk is a marvelous speaker," Samantha Bale said. "Watch. You'll both thank me for the experience."

"He draws a crowd," George Hull said, looking around at the congestion of farmers and tradesmen, the young and the old, the strong and the crippled, come together to partake of invisible energy.

Unlike his young wife, George believed strongly in a God who paid close attention, making absolutely sure that each of His children turned slowly on a spit until their fat dripped and sizzled while they sang His praises. The Jews said God was filled with wrath and vengeance, a jealous God who condemned vanity even as He insisted on constant reminder of His marvelous power. Their God demanded gratitude for dispensing a brand of mercy that was only a postponement of disaster. George suspected the Jews had it right, though even Jews cherished a slim chance at paradise. Heaven in exchange for giving up pork chops.

George could easily see why the likes of Carnegie or Vanderbilt would be devout, they of the foundries and railroads, mansions and millions, good health and good news. But why these sodbusters with dead eyes, tired women, and multitudes of feverish children?

"Are you comfortable?" Samantha asked. "These benches are a caution."

"Comfortable enough," Angelica said. "And you, George?"

"Oh, yes. Comfortable."

"Isn't the choir a marvel?"

"Beautiful," Angelica said. "What voices. And you say they are savages, newly brought to the Lord?"

"Divine transformation," Samantha said, beaming. Even Herbert Black Paw looked like a figure emerged from the stained glass of the Ackley Academy's chapel window.

"I wish your Reverend would begin before my ass ruptures," George said. "Would it be wrong to smoke here?"

"Please, no," Samantha said.

"He knows," Angelica said. "George just says things."

"George just says things," her husband mocked. "George says things."

The choir went silent as the Reverend Mr. Henry Turk made his appearance to a gasp from the assemblage. He wore a black suit, black shoes, a white shirt with black tie. On his head was a headdress of radiant red and blue feathers held together by a white band of birch.

"My dear friends, my sisters and my brothers, may the Lord bless thee and keep thee. We are gathered together in this tiny corner of the universe united by love and mutual belief in Jesus Christ as healer, protector, and shepherd on the road to life eternal. As you know, it is God's way to convey His wisdom to mankind through avatars, ambassadors chosen to carry His message of righteousness. Those messengers stand tall as telegraph poles, arms outstretched to grasp His wondrous wires. Across those wires flow currents of revelation and enlightenment.

"Tonight I say to you that I, Henry Turk, have been asked, nay, *commanded,* to serve as such a pole, and I accept with humility and pride. For each and every one of you, I have a telegram from Jesus bringing glorious news.

"Ah, but there will be a price to pay for all this. Don't reach into your pocket, reach into your heart. That price is your entire attention and a willingness to allow the Lord's electric voice entrance to your soul.

"The telegram you are about to receive is a birthday greeting. Happy birthday! If you came here burdened and broken, you will leave reborn with a new vision of yourself and of a nation also reborn.

"The Reverend Henry Turk does not address a crowd. He speaks to one person, you. Forget that your heads bob like flotsam in this sea of shining faces."

The Reverend Turk left his podium and crossed to where the boys' choir stood. He reached out both hands to grasp Herbert Black Paw by the shoulders and pulled the lad to him. Herbert kept his posture and his poise though Samantha could see him quiver like a tuning fork.

For days that renegade child had been isolated, ostracized,

soundly thrashed, fed on oatmeal, forced to sit like a statue until he agreed to sing with the others. Samantha felt his decision was no more than submission.

Actually, Herbert Black Paw was caught between fury and acceptance. In Herbert's mind, Wakonda, the Great Spirit, danced and whooped while their Christ watched, dangling from His cross. It seemed as if Jesus' magic eyes drained power from gods who ruled over a defeated people.

While Wakonda raged, Herbert Black Paw considered deserting the temple of the sky. Trees and mountains, rivers and lakes, birds, fox, deer, wolf, bear, buffalo, the wind itself fought to keep him. Through Samantha Bale's passion Herbert felt the sting and seduction of Jesus' wounds.

Reverend Turk led the silenced singer to the pulpit, took Herbert Black Paw's chin in hand, and turned his alien face toward the audience. "I speak to one, I speak to all," the Reverend shouted. "I deliver Thy telegram, Lord, and if Thy holy pronouncement penetrates the red darkness that fills this pitiful child, no Christian soul could dare reject Thy call." Reverend Turk lifted the war bonnet from his own skull and dropped the dazzling crown onto Herbert Black Paw's twitching head. It came down over his eyes and the crowd let out a laugh.

"Friends, restrain your mirth. This boy needs no eyes to see the vision I bring. And know one and all, that this Indian spawn was, if not the source, then the inspiration for that which has been revealed to me. And through me to be trumpeted from this modest place to every golden city, yea unto Jerusalem itself.

"It was this boy, this pagan whelp, who challenged the Reverend Mr. Henry Turk with a question that rocked me to my boots. *Suffer the children,* sayeth the Lord. When I was invited to speak to him and his kind at Ackley Academy, I told them of the miracles of the Holy Land, of its endless deserts, and burning sands, of its lush fields and barren plains, of the tribes who wandered there, of their flocks and herds and beasts of burden, and of the false gods they worshipped and the sinful lives they led.

"My subject was Genesis. 'There were Giants in the earth in those days . . . when the sons of God came in unto the daughters of men, and they bare children to them, the same became mighty men which were of old, men of renown.' Giants in the earth who somehow yielded to temptation even as Adam and Eve gave ear to the serpent's wretched hiss. 'And God saw that the wickedness of man was great in the earth, and that every imagination of the thoughts of his heart was only evil continually . . . And it regretted the Lord that He had made man on the earth, and it grieved Him at His heart. . . . And the Lord said, I will destroy man whom I have created from the face of the earth; both man and beast and the creeping thing and the fowls of the air; for it repenteth me that I have made them.'

"I told those startled students how the Lord found mercy enough to spare the righteous Noah and allow our race of men another chance at life, and even life eternal through the sacrifice of His only begotten son, the Christ we cherish.

"And what was my reward? They smirked at me. And that took a brand of courage, make no mistake. They defied me, but I had to find the strength to understand and suffer their defiance. They told me these Giants that were in the earth were not of *their* earth, those holy places I described were not *their* holy places, the God I bow to could not be *their* God. And those words cut hard.

"I went home to fast. I scourged body and mind. I prayed for means and method to share Christian glory with these foreign beings. And, truly, I myself was racked with doubt. As some among you can attest, I was driven to the edge of madness. Could it be that Reverend Turk had given himself to a God from some antique land with little relevance to the American continent? Could it be? Were the stories I so prized of the elders and apostles, of Jesus Himself and His wanderings, nothing but tales for strangers?

"And then, friends, then, praise to the Almighty, my telegram came and I knew it came from the highest pinnacle. It was revealed to the Reverend Mr. Henry Turk that the Holy Bible is *not* someone else's, that the Living Christ is *not* someone else's, that the geography of wonders is *not* someone else's. It was shown to me clear as the dawn that my God worked the marvels of Genesis right here, in these United States! That this is where those mighty Giants walked! That America is where Jesus was born and slain to rise again! In America!

"And how could that be? Why then does the Bible say otherwise? It does not! It does not! Blame not the book but its flawed translators. Blame them for stealing our righteous heritage, then conspiring to conceal this truth for more than two thousand years! Blame them, and forgive them for they knew not what they did.

"Eden is here. You and I are God's first children, and that explains our splendor and our greatness. What was the test of Civil War but another scourging flood to cleanse us and show us a new path to glory? We live in Jerusalem! That is my news!

"Now let this *American* choir sing 'Amazing Grace' in the *American* tongue and let us sing along in perfect harmony!"

Herbert Black Paw felt light-headed as his mind watched bearded disciples in tattered robes roam his hunting grounds. The hills and valleys filled with those dauntless invaders. Their eyes burned with a sense of mission, their voices drowned every bird song, their grotesque flocks gnawed on buffalo and deer and the bodies of his people. The parade of giants was endless, unstoppable. They sucked up the rain and farted thunder.

It was too much for Herbert Black Paw to fathom so he turned himself off. He toppled and lay prone on the stage, the feathers from his war bonnet spread in every direction.

The Reverend Turk bent over and kissed the boy's cheek as the choir's hymn escaped the tent and soared over the land. "I have brought this boy to Jesus," the Reverend said softly. "He listened and *heard*. He *knows* and is transported." Reverend Turk held out his arms as God's telegraph pole should, drinking in the tonic of gratitude and sweat that burst from his flock.

Samantha Bale left her seat and dashed to the pulpit. She

kneeled to revive Henry Black Paw, but when she examined him she saw that effort was wasted. "He's dead," Samantha said. "This child is dead. We have a dead Indian here."

The Reverend Turk heard her the first time. "Let's keep that to ourselves for the moment," he said. "Whatever the cause, worldly or divine, we know at least that the boy has gone to a much better place."

"Your sister seems distressed," Angelica Hull said to her husband, who swatted a mosquito against his arm. The insect splattered a tiny circle of his own gorged blood.

"She should be distressed." George said. "Giants in the earth. This is Fort Dodge, Iowa, not Bethlehem. Her Turk is demented. He should be burned at the stake with chestnuts roasted in his embers."

"I don't know, George," Angelica said. "It could be possible. So much is hidden from us. Don't you agree?"

A week after Herbert Black Paw was buried in the sanctified ground of the churchyard, George Hull had his private meeting with the Reverend Mr. Henry Turk. The two men argued while Samantha Bale sat listening, quietly mortified by her brother's blasphemous and vulgar behavior.

"Giants up my bunghole," George said. "Tell me this. How big were those American giants of yours?"

"By measure ten to twelve feet tall and quite substantial in girth," Reverend Turk said with such immediacy and assurance that George Hull could only throw up his hands and stomp out of the room.

Samantha was forced to smile. She had never seen her brother in full retreat.

BINGHAMTON, NEW YORK, AUGUST 3, 1868

On a sweltering August afternoon Loretta Hull sat waving a Japanese fan while she sipped a refreshing glass of lemonade. The Simon Hull & Sons, Fine Cigars, retail store, newly appended to the factory, was hardly famous yet. If three customers came in a day there was jubilation.

Ben and his father were off to Poughkeepsie, gone to examine a site for what Simon envisioned as a flourishing chain. This despite her husband's objection. Business was good as things were, selling only to wholesalers. Ben had no taste for the retail trade or for what he called "spreading ourselves too thin." But lately Simon Hull was consumed by ambition.

Loretta guessed it was because her father-in-law felt himself in a race with death. The old man whistled and wheezed while he spoke of expansion. Still, he sent George west and went east with Ben while Loretta was left to stoke the home fires. Loretta enjoyed her privacy as much as she disliked being alone in the large house. It was a nice change to have the men away and be free of Angelica's syrup.

If she missed any of them, it was George and his strange morning visits. Ben was an automatic man, in, out, and asleep. George browsed like a bee before he stung. Straining to keep his ardor in harness but always betrayed by the protest of bedsprings.

Still, that game had to stop. If Ben was deaf as a post, his father had ears like a predator. Loretta knew Simon never liked her. Not from the day Ben first brought her home. But he hid those feelings for his son's sake. Now Simon's runny eyes betrayed wrath the way George was betrayed by the groaning springs. As for Angelica, if that one knew or suspected her husband's philandering, there was no sign of it. And what if she did? The worst tribulation wouldn't ruffle her prissy composure. Angelica was a pleasant stranger in the house, a grateful cat who wandered in and stayed. She did her chores and sewed clothes for a baby who cooed in the shadows of her mind.

Simon Hull must know Loretta would give him his future long before Angelica gave him more than a scrambled egg. That was why Simon ignored the tattletale floorboards and a bed that played morning music. Simon was desperate to see the face that would roll his cigars into the next century. Whoever its father, that face would manage to resemble his own.

Loretta put down her lemonade and browsed the book Angelica sent from Iowa. THE TRUE GEOGRAPHY OF GENESIS, *by the Reverend Mr. Henry Turk,* inscribed by its author and dedicated to a saintly Indian boy. She flapped her skirt to cool her thighs.

The bell over the door tinkled like a wind chime. Loretta smoothed her dress and positioned herself behind a cedarwood display case where refulgent cigars of all types and sizes awaited inspection.

A tall, gangly man entered the shop, sniffing the seasoned odor of mellow tobacco. Loretta knew he was not a local from his city suit and tie. He was dressed like a lawyer, carrying a leather case in one hand, a straw hat in the other. The thing that struck her was his cranberry bush of red hair, red eyebrows, red moustache, and blue button eyes. He looked like his face was drawn with crayons.

"Good afternoon, sir. May I help you? Please feel free to browse the merchandise at your leisure. We have something for every taste. We call our products Fingers of Pleasure, all handmade in our own factory and of fine quality. As you see, every cigar is freshly kept in a cool humidor. The case is designed to preserve and enhance natural flavor. We sell singly or by the box. Prices vary depending on your choice. More costly items are on the upper shelves, the more modest arranged on the lower. Any questions are welcome."

"Thank you for that comprehensive introduction. Do I happen to be addressing Mrs. Hull?"

"Yes, as a matter of fact."

"Mrs. Hull, my name is Barnaby Rack of the *New York Clarion*, a major daily newspaper with which you might be familiar."

"I'm afraid not," Loretta said.

"It doesn't matter. The thing is, I know I should have written in advance of this visit, but I was on an assignment in Albany and chose to stop here in Binghamton on the chance you might find some time for me."

"Time for what?"

"Time to talk. You see, Mrs. Hull, I was recently wandering the field at Gettysburg gathering the names of certain fallen soldiers. I know this is a painful subject, but among the names I copied from their tombstones was that of Hamish Flonk, your former husband, may he rest in that special place kept for heroes. My object is to write a series of articles so our readers may be reminded of the ultimate sacrifice so many made to preserve our Union."

"Those poor boys," Loretta said.

"Indeed. I want our readers to know who they were in life and the memories they left behind among those they cherished. In my research, I learned that you and the late Private Flonk were once man and wife. And though the flow of years has carried you to new shores, I hope it won't distress you to share your feelings with thousands of strangers who are, in truth, your invisible friends."

"Journalism. What a fascinating vocation. You must visit everywhere and meet everyone of consequence."

"Sometimes rewarding, sometimes exciting, mostly a job like every other. There are many days when I envy people like you, Mrs. Hull, whose effort produces something useful and tangible. Like a good stogie as opposed to transient prose. It does smell good in here, better than my office. Well, what do you say?"

"About what?"

"An interview. My schedule requires that I return to New York City by tomorrow morning. I only have a few spare hours so I must press for your willing cooperation."

Loretta was about to tell Barnaby Rack that the woman he

sought was Angelica Hull, Mrs. George, not Mrs. Ben. But she'd had long talks with Angelica about Hamish Flonk and knew exactly what Angelica would say to the reporter. If the interview was refused, an article would be written with no mention of Hamish, and that would deny him a last chance at fame. Loretta thought about George moving inside her like a steam engine trying hard to muffle its noise. In a way she was as close to George Hull as his wife. Maybe closer. And besides, the day moved slow as a slug.

"I would be delighted to participate," Loretta said. "I was just about to draw the shades and close shop anyway. There's very little trade abroad. Men don't think much about a smoke when the world is smoking."

"Nicely put," Barnaby said. "I see you have your own flair for words."

"I admit to small praise from certain parties for verse I once composed," Loretta said.

Barnaby watched Loretta move like a drifting balloon, lowering shades, dusting the counter with a feather brush, wiping the stoical face of a wooden Iroquois.

Barnaby loved the women of Manhattan, a splendid assortment of every kind, from vestal virgins peddling velocipedes along the Battery to sedate sophisticates riding Concord Coaches through Central Park, from melon-rumped slum queens peddling fresh fish on Fulton Street to factory girls taking lunch on tenement fire escapes. If there was one thing New York City made well it was women. But even in the smallest of hamlets, the most remote regions, other blossoms bloomed with an appeal all their own. These were the priestesses of corn-from-the-fields, apples-off-the-tree. Less wise than their city sisters but no less delicious. Barnaby knew his appeal to those rural nymphs whose corseted lives had such strangled horizons.

"Now follow me into the house," Loretta said, "where it's cooler and where we can sit and converse. You were correct to assume that speaking of Hamish will never be easy for me. I have found new happiness with a generous husband, but Hamish Flonk was my first love and I still feel his kiss."

Barnaby readied pad and pencil. He knew he'd found a treasure.

"We shall have a quiet moment together, Mr. Rack, since both my husband and father are away and even my brother and sister-in-law are off to Iowa to visit a dear relation. We will sit in the parlor and sip some wine made from local fruits and berries."

"Fruits and berries," Barnaby said. "That sounds like a treat."

While the New York reporter with the crayon face took notes, Loretta told the story of meeting Hamish Flonk at a church supper, of love's quick flowering, of her parents' firm opposition to any alliance, of furtive nocturnal elopement, of first consummation in a stable since there wasn't a room to be had in the town where they'd fled. "It didn't escape us that ours weren't the only troubled hearts to find solace on straw."

None of that was true, but it might have been. Actually, Angelica was bartered away by her father for a pond that went dry a month after her nuptials.

The more she talked the more Loretta sensed she was saying too much, but the words kept coming and Barnaby kept writing. When she told about how, when she was swelling with child, Hamish rented himself as a mercenary to pay for their keep, she wept like the ill-fated infant, destined to die of a pox the same day its father was slain. "It was as if little Horace was summoned to go with him," Loretta said, weeping.

"Are you telling me you married the same man who sent your spouse to war?"

"Yes," Loretta said. That part was valid, though she sensed she'd released a family skeleton. "I admit to some qualms but George was very insistent. I was frightened of his advances since the man is a bit coarse. Did I have an alternative but to submit? Hamish Flonk's parents offered me no support. My own dear folks left me orphaned the year before. I wanted my baby back, and still do. When

George and I are blessed with a child it will also belong to Hamish in some way. My new husband is fully aware of my feelings and full partner to that hope."

"You have found this new marriage agreeable?"

"More endurable than agreeable. Now that George has learned to curb his fits of jealous rage, my fears are less frequent. He even buys me new items for my collection of miniatures. I have shelves of little houses and animals and furniture cute enough for elves to sit on. When George drinks, well, life is not roses, but is it for any of us? At least I mend fast and was taught that to heal is to forget."

"Are you saying your husband is guilty of physical abuse? A surly drunk who beats you?"

"George Hull is a short-tempered man. If I fail to please him, though I try, I do try in every way, he cannot be faulted." Loretta's eyes squirted fountains. Exhausted by her monologue, she swooned and fell to the floor.

Barnaby Rack, who hadn't shed a tear since his teething, felt his own eyes turn to puddles. He dropped his pad, left the chair where Simon Hull usually sat, then bent to embrace Loretta, possessed by a fierce urge to protect her from further misfortune. They clung to one another, tasting the salt of all sorrow. Barnaby found himself soothing a breast popped free of its bodice.

Minutes later, Loretta said, "Nothing happened, did it?" while Barnaby Rack buttoned his pants.

"Nothing wrong," he whispered with great warmth. This was no transient seduction, no infamous lechery, no tumble in a haystack. This was a matter of necessary respite and reparation. "Let me assure you, Angelica, that I speak for myself and my readers when I say that you are a remarkable person and a credit to your sex and our nation."

After the reporter left, rushing to catch up with his schedule, Loretta fixed herself a light supper and sat down to read Reverend Turk's revelations. That biblical patriarchs might have walked streets just outside was a most curious prospect. She wondered why Jesus or Adam would stroll through Binghamton. If either chose to visit Simon Hull & Sons to buy a Ulysses Supremo, they wouldn't pay a penny, not even tax. But what if they asked for a box?

Before she went upstairs, Loretta checked to see if the smudge on the scatter rug had dried where she'd scrubbed it. There was no mark, no evidence. Because nothing had happened. If it had Simon Hull might find himself squinting at a grandson with a head haloed russet. She imagined Ben's father trying hard to conjure more colorful ancestors than he easily remembered. Fuzzy from Angelica's medicinal wine, Loretta dampened the lamps, lit a candle, and watched her shadow dance on the wall.

FORT DODGE, IOWA, AUGUST 7, 1868

Now I am hot. Then cold. There seems to be less of me. Shaped sounds from unexpected directions. What sounds? Source, could it be your intention to give me company? Thanks for the gesture. But please understand our former arrangement was best. Why crowd the world?

ACKLEY, IOWA, AUGUST 13, 1868

July 31, 1868

Dear George,

I trust this finds you and yours in good health and enjoying your visit with our sister Samantha. We have returned to Binghamton from Poughkeepsie, then Kingston, where Father and I have leased certain properties in keeping with our planned expansion.

Father is most pleased with this enterprise. Our retail store here at the factory has aroused growing interest from the community. We are encouraged that customers arrive, in increasing numbers, even during this sweltering season.

Father is anxious that you visit Chicago in the very near future. He has read of a large migration of Negroes to that metropolis and is convinced they will prove a source of important revenue. Who would have thought it possible!

We were both astonished by your comments concerning the name Pickaninny, but if that name is a detriment and offensive to certain of the darkies, then by all means let us consider your suggestion. Uncle Tom seems an acceptable substitute, and we congratulate you on the choice.

Enclosed you will find new bands and boxes which should, of course, be substituted for the old. The picture showing lovable Niggers circled around that happy elder evokes a warm feeling as you predicted it would— One can almost hear their squeals of delight at his gentle avuncular epithets.

All of us send our regards and best wishes to Angelica. We hope her journey home will be tranquil. We understand your concern about her brittle health and the negative effects of further travel.

Please convey our affection to Samantha with the sincere hope that she will soon venture east. News of her growing interest in the Reverend Mr. Henry Turk comes as a welcome surprise. Her Reverend has grown quite famous here since publication of his remarkable tract, which is widely circulated and often debated.

Father asks me to tell you that he is considering purchase of stock in the Pullman Company of which you wrote with high praise. You see, George, he does take your words to heart and has every faith in your success. We wish you Godspeed and an easy mind.

Your Brother,
Benjamin Hull

George Hull left the letter on a table and lifted Angelica's hand mirror. Its border of gilded sea nymphs framed a face that showed other than an "easy mind." His glossed eyes were a frightening shade of crimson, blood vessels streaked eggy white. For all Iowa's fresh air and Samantha's good food, George looked peaked, putrid, and pale.

He'd had no restful sleep for weeks. Not since his encounter with the same Reverend Turk who now courted his sister. Since then they had met many times. Samantha gave the comrade of giants nothing but encouragement. Turk was a welcome guest at her table, already a family member.

The Reverend being a celebrated author, George was forced to listen to glowing reports from his publisher. There were public readings of his sermons. A ton of mail from around the nation reported sightings of giants who hid in forests or skittered naked over fields, thus confirming the Reverend's intuitions while stirring massive new visions.

Reverend Turk was rich, his star on the rise, destined for greatness. George Hull was destined to prowl Chicago, hawking Uncle Toms to ebony faces. This time God went too far.

George Hull's swollen brain uncurled a worm. George allowed it to suckle the venomous breast of revenge. The imp gorged poison. Giants they wanted? Giants they needed? Should such a gigantic appetite be ignored?

"I must tell you, Samantha, you were right about your Reverend," George told his sister one morning. "He has somehow managed to shake me awake from a long sleep. If, as you say, I have not looked well, it's because I've consorted too long with demons. But I am cured now and on the golden trail."

"I rejoice for you, brother," Samantha said. "And I will tell Reverend Turk what you said."

"Tell him. Thank him. I am too shy a man to express myself with proper emotion. You know that."

"Yes, George, I know," Samantha said. "I know. But if you can't acknowledge gratitude, at least treat Henry with obvious respect. He actually feels you resent him."

"Oh, I will show respect," George said. "More than that. I will become his proudest convert."

Then, beginning his *grand march,* George ran upstairs to the bedroom where Angelica still rested. He stripped off his pants, turned her, and rammed from the rear. When he was done and gone, Angelica Hull crossed herself, said prayers for her husband, for herself, for both their families, for strangers, for Hamish Flonk and other soldier angels.

LAFAYETTE, NEW YORK, AUGUST 21, 1868

Aaron Bupkin picked up his harmonica and played the old song, singing between blowing.

> *I gave my love a cherry*
> *That had no stone.*
> *I gave my love a chicken*
> *That had no bone.*
> *I told my love a story*
> *That had no end.*
> *I gave my love a baby*
> *With no crying.*

"Why did God inflict this musical Jew on my house? This is your last month, Bupkin. It's over and done with. I have a long list of Christians who'll gladly pay twice what you pay me and no complaints," his landlady, Agatha Elm, yelled from her bedroom next door.

"Sure, sure, Mrs. Elm," Bupkin yelled back. "The line is two miles long. My congratulations and don't worry about me."

> *How can there be a cherry*
> *Without a stone?*
> *How can there be a chicken*
> *Without a bone?*
> *How can there be a story*
> *Without an end?*
> *How can there be a baby*
> *With no crying?*

"I hate that song. Stones, bones, dead babies."

> *A cherry when it's blooming*
> *It has no stone.*
> *A chicken when it's pippin'*
> *It has no bone.*
> *The story of I love you*
> *It has no end.*
> *A baby when it's sleeping*
> *There's no crying.*

"The baby is *sleeping,* not sick. That never occurred to you, Mrs. Elm, did it? The baby is a fat, healthy, happy baby."

"My ears hurt from you. I get shooting pains."

Aaron wrote the words under a line of notes that looked like fawn prints in snow. It was his habit to preserve the songs of Onondaga Valley. He heard "The Riddle Song" from a street drunk in Cardiff. It amazed him that such a sour and sullen collection of human beings had such tender and beautiful ballads boxed inside beveled brains.

"It's a love song, Mrs. Elm. A love song."

"For Jews," Mrs. Elm said. "A love song for Jews."

Aaron Bupkin had lived in Mrs. Elm's house for two years, since he discovered his latent talent. When he came to Onondaga County, peddling fabrics and thread, he didn't know the word *dowser*.

It seemed to Aaron his whole life was based on a series of accidents. In Poland, his parents were killed in a pogrom after taking a wrong road by accident. When Aaron was three, he came to Boston with his grandfather, Isaac Bupkin, sponsored by Isaac's brother, who was crushed by a milk wagon a week before they got there. Fifteen years later, while Aaron showed his goods to a farmer's wife on a farm near Ithaca, the lady stuck a forked willow branch in his hand and asked him to find water under her land. She knew Jews were capable of all kinds of magic.

Aaron humored her to clinch the sale of five yards of calico. He wandered around a meadow waving the forked stick, pretending to doven in Hebrew. His intention was to stop after a respectable tour, rattle the stick, and say, "Here is water. Don't thank me. No extra charge." Instead, the rod showed a mind of its own and began shaking of its own accord. It nearly jumped out of his grasp, then pointed down at a crocus.

When Aaron Bupkin returned to the territory six months later with a new load of merchandise, he found himself famous. The purest water bubbled from a hole dug where his stick pointed. After that triumph, along with selling cloth on commission, he could sell himself as a water witch. He didn't know if his gift was a blessing or curse.

Aaron's service was in heavy demand as word spread. The dowser delivered, more amazed than his clients when a new well gurgled up from earth's belly. He took a room at Mrs. Elm's in Lafayette, had his goods shipped from Boston, dowsed on the side, and made himself a living. Aaron Bupkin shrugged off abuse from his landlady and assorted local anti-Semites. She needed his rent; they needed water. He liked life in the country.

Aaron quit his singing when the ugly blue cuckoo in Mrs. Elm's Black Forest clock came flying out like a hound's hard-on. Aaron listened to twelve raucous squawks, took up his willow wand, and headed downstairs. His new customer, a sweaty scarecrow, was already waiting hunched on the seat of his wagon.

"You the water witch?"

"So they tell me," Aaron said, climbing aboard. "What's your story? The old well quit on you? It happens." While they rode out of Lafayette Aaron pulled out his harmonica and played a few bars of "Old Zip Coon." He stopped playing and said to the driver, or the trees or the sky, "Suppose you heard a song about a man who teases his lady with a riddle. He offers her pitless cherries, boneless chicken, an endless story, and a baby who never wails. When she asks him where he was going to find such impossible things, he tells her, in a tender poetical fashion, the answers to his riddle. Would you know you were listening to a love song? You would know. How could you not know?"

"Why would a love song talk about chickens?" the waterless farmer said. "Is the baby dead? Is that it?"

"Why not?" Aaron said.

"Never had trouble with the old well," the man said. "Never knew a year so dry. It don't remember how to rain."

The water witch nodded in sympathy. But the farmer knew Bupkin made his money from drought. Nobody fooled anybody.

NEW YORK, NEW YORK, SEPTEMBER 1, 1868

In lower Manhattan's Printing House Square, Barnaby Rack sat nose to nose with John Zipmeister in the conference room of the *New York Clarion*. The text of Barnaby's article, "Squadron of

Dust," was spread on a table carved with a generation of initials obsolete as the names on Gettysburg tombstones.

"The Hamish Flonk section goes. It's out of step. Can't you see that?" his managing editor said.

"The Flonk is the heart and soul of the piece. Can't you see that?"

"Rack, do not agonize. The other profiles are fine. I read them and feel good about myself. But the Flonk is deadly. What did you give me? A soldier who didn't believe in the war. A loser who sold himself for a handful of cow shit."

"To save his farm and feed a pregnant young wife is a handful of cow shit?"

"So after he's dead she quits the farm, loses the baby, then serves up her coochiecoo to the draft dodger who paid three hundred greenbacks for her husband's balls. That's inspiring."

"She promised Flonk a baby. He wrote in the contract—"

"Screw the contract. I hate the contract. I hate the whole idea. What's the purpose of this piece? To stir up positive feelings about warm, loving human beings facing up to the tragic loss of their loved ones. In every case but the Flonk you have struggling widows, orphans with big, sad eyes, parents who light candles in windows that face brick walls. Nobody complaining because their men fought for a cause, not a few bucks and a bag of cucumber seeds. Is it our job to make our readers vomit guilt out the window?"

"It's not about guilt. It's about nobility. It's about real mourning. It's about womanhood. It's about ultimate sacrifice."

"I know: 'BEREAVED WIFE USES UTERUS TO HONOR SACRED PLEDGE.' Hooray, hurrah. I'm not saying I don't admire the lady. I never said that. But I'm damned if I'm going to nourish America on subtlety, ambiguity, or abstraction. They need hope out there. Hard hits of hope.

"Sorrow, yes. Tribute, yes. Regret, no. You read the papers? The war is over. What's over is over. The whole point is to get up and get moving, North, South, whites, niggers, chinks, even injuns. New horizons, new vistas. *Rum-ta-tum.* I don't want to feel sorry for the survivors. I want to feel proud of their guts and fortitude. Speaking of which, your title is a lead weight. 'Squadron of Dust.' I hear 'Bold Bugles.' "

"Give me the Flonk, I'll give you bold bugles."

"You'll give me bugles and stuff the Flonk."

"So what do I tell that woman? That the *New York Clarion* rejects truth?"

"Tell her the *Clarion* don't want to get sued. Did you see any contract? Did you talk to the husband? Where's corroboration? Even if I was creaming to run that story I couldn't get it past a blind lawyer. Say it is true. You think what's-his-name will sit still while the whole country reads about how a slacker beats on a war widow in between pokes? He'd come here with a shotgun, and who'd blame him? The subject is closed."

"This is very bad," Barnaby said. "I sold out a trusting woman who dared open her heart."

"So buy yourself an ulcer. And next time, Rack, please use the machine for your copy. We're supposed to be learning how to typewrite. Play the 'Literary Piano,' remember?"

"I hate that thing. I can't write on that thing."

"Christopher Sholes happens to be our beloved publisher's favorite nephew. When he comes in here I don't want to tell him Mr. Barnaby Rack don't like his toy. I want to show him pretty pages. I want to tell him how we can't wait to throw away our little pencils and dump our ink in the sewer. You might have some talent, Rack. You're not just a sprinter. You could go the distance. But there's fat on your eyeballs and you're stuck in the past. Like the former Mrs. Flonk, may she rest in peace."

"Her name is Angelica. And she's far from dead."

"Angelica? Oh, Christ, don't tell me. You didn't. You couldn't have. I thought you told me she opened her heart. What else did she open on company time? Off the record, Sir Galahad, how was it?"

FORT DODGE, IOWA, SEPTEMBER 4, 1868

George Hull washed down the last of his sirloin and potatoes with a long drink of ale in the dining room of the St. Charles Hotel in Fort Dodge. Samantha's delicate cooking, more refined since her dyspeptic Reverend began pleading his belly, didn't stick to thick ribs. And the bilious Turk convinced her to purge the house of all potable alcohol.

Samantha served boiled chicken, stewed lamb, baskets of leaves, fruit punch, buttermilk, and chamomile tea. Those measly meals hardly sustained George's riotous hunger, magnified of late by devilish intentions. He needed red meat and a brew he could feel sting his throat.

His energy was severely depleted.

In the days before Angelica left for Binghamton, George prowled her like a lion in heat. Angelica's response to his husbandly chores was as bland as Samantha's cooking. Angelica didn't seem to mind being frequently entered but showed friendly patience more than passion or even noticeable enthusiasm.

George worked hard to make her shake under him. He looked for a shudder but got hardly a tremble. They coupled twice a day and three times every night. When Angelica headed home George's penis dangled like a defeated flag. His scrotum sagged like a goiter. Sore genitals was a small price to pay if his efforts bore tangible fruit. George suspected Angelica's body was like Cousin Stubby Newell's farm up in Cardiff: adamant soil that rejected seed and blunted the planter's passion. A fertile Angelica was as likely as a bountiful harvest for Stubby.

George ordered more ale.

That morning he'd written his cousin an incendiary letter on deckled hotel stationery. George outlined his maniac plan on posh paper. He wrote in simple detail, saying just enough to kindle fire in Stubby's cold hearth. Including a promise of money. If his dense cousin couldn't grasp every facet of so outrageous a scheme, let greed substitute for insight. Courage was possible without conviction.

The letter mentioned nothing of pitfalls or punishments. To give a man like Stubby Newell too many worries was needlessly cruel. Sins of omission were the merciful course. Besides, George knew an agreeable Stubby was essential. This was a family matter with no room for strangers.

Could Stubby be trusted with more than a hoe? George depended on his cousin's stupidity to keep him discreet. Stubby wouldn't let a cat out of the bag if he didn't recognize it for a cat. Even Stubby would be smart enough to keep his mouth shut after George made it clear that all chance for profit was linked to their mutual silence.

George Hull swallowed his ale and heard himself chuckle. He patted his satisfied mouth with a linen napkin, poked his teeth with an ivory toothpick, lit up a Ulysses Supremo. He paid in gold for his lunch, mailed his letter to Cardiff, belched in God's face, then went about business. For the first time in his life George felt at peace with his madness.

FORT DODGE, IOWA, SEPTEMBER 7, 1868

I admit I am set in my ways. Logic tells me there is but one Source, and possibly a Source for the Source and quite possibly a Source for the Source of the Source and so forth. A comfortable cosmology. Then how to explain this edgy suspicion that I'm under new management?

FORT DODGE, IOWA, SEPTEMBER 9, 1868

George Hull climbed a wood ladder down into a pit hacked out of rock. The quarry reminded him of drawings he had seen of Pompeii's desolation. Dusty air had the gray taste of murder.

Five bare-chested men sat on granite blocks. Two whites, three blacks, segregated by color, gnawed at food from their lunch pails. Their drink came from a keg of warm beer. George was ignored. They could have been a herd of grazing steers.

"Good afternoon, gentlemen," he said. "Tell me, who is your foreman?" One of the whites, biting into a wedge of cheese, held up a massive arm decorated with a tattooed dragon. The dragon's body snaked up the arm, curled its coils around the man's hairy trunk, trailed its green tail down inside his pants. The dragon's head was the hand attached to the waving arm. Its fingernail teeth clutched a wad of brown bread.

"Me. Mike Foley."

"I don't mean to interrupt your meal," George said. "But time is a factor, Mr. Foley."

"Then say what you want to say."

"My name is Hole, employed by the United States Government as a geologist. I have been sent to gather samples of stone from around the nation, each indigenous to a specific state or territory. I come as a representative of the President."

"My prick in his ear," Foley said.

"The stone will become part of the monument to Abraham Lincoln even now in design," George said.

"Well, if you want rocks, you've come just in the nick of time, for we're down to our last chips here. All we got left to mine is the whole bloody mountain range. How much do you need for your statue? Iowa gypsum should be represented in some prominent way, such as for carving Honest Abe's beard or a cheek of his sanctified ass."

"You didn't admire Mr. Lincoln?"

"The man in some measure. Not his war to make the monkeys rich and us white men poor. Is that true or false, boys? You jigs know your worth now, eh?"

One of the black miners went to the beer keg with his cup. He only got a few drops and kicked at the barrel.

"See, there you go," the foreman said. "You saw the ape help himself to the last of the lot and no word of contrition. It's Mr. Lincoln we've got to thank for that."

"Getting back to my purpose," George said. "I require a slab of your gypsum in the following dimensions: twelve feet in height, four feet in width, two feet in depth, the piece then wrapped in burlap. Can you satisfy me?"

"It so happens. But now we must talk price. Since we're dealing with the government here, and all of us voters, I think we must show our patriotism, boys."

"Even the government keeps to a budget," George said.

"What should we ask for a choice bit of royal anatomy?" Mike Foley asked his dragon hand. Then he lifted the hand to his ear and listened as it whispered the answer. "Would a fresh keg of lager be excessive?"

"You want to be paid in beer?"

"Within the hour before we all turn to sand. Beer in a full tub of ice. And a hundred dollars for charity."

"How long will it take to find the right piece of stone?"

"By a curious twist, we fractured out a slab only this morning. There it lies, ready to be cut into chunks. It was our next project. The measurements, I think, are within inches of those you gave me. The Lord works in mysterious ways to quench the thirst of His laborers. Slab number twelve, laying there on the ground waiting for you to take it. It's as fine a piece as you'll find for a thousand miles. We'll trim it and wrap it, then what?"

"I'll find a wagon to carry it."

"It will have to be a very strong wagon to hold that thing in one piece. How far must you go?"

"Forty miles to the railroad."

"Over muddy dirt roads with such a load? We're talking five tons. Let me slice the block into three equal pieces. That service is free if the ice is still ice when it gets here."

"Uncut. Intact. As it is."

"Whatever you say. But don't ask a receipt for these dealings. This transaction is private, between citizens and the White House. Our small contribution to the common good. Are we agreed, Mr. Hole?"

"Agreed, Mr. Foley."

"Jason, lift your emancipated butt and go with the diplomat. Show him the quick way to the brewery. By the time you're back with our holy water, Your Grace, we'll have the President's chunk of Fort Dodge packed tidy. With a minute to spare to toast the Republic."

NEW YORK, NEW YORK, SEPTEMBER 19, 1868

To my surprise and amazement, a tiny fellow appeared, not from under a mushroom as in familiar fantasy, but from behind an austere marker. He was garbed as immaculately as a mannequin, down to his spats, his minuscule head crowned with a black derby hat.

Was this an apparition? Some sprightly spirit come to entertain those fallen comrades? In a direct sense, yes! For the little man proved to be none other than General Tom

Thumb, P. T. Barnum's marvelous mainstay, come to pay his respects and cheer the troops.

There, in that somber theater, under a petulant sky, the General offered what solace he could. Did his mute audience laugh at his antics? Who can know? But this writer must confess that, during this energetic and masterful performance, he felt a tear spill from his astonished eye.

In a private room of the Blossom Club on Fifth Avenue, Tom Thumb crinkled the *Clarion* into a ball and threw it toward the table where Phineas Barnum was being massaged by a barebreasted woman who called herself Miss Moon.

Thumb's own back was being kneaded by her assistant, Kite, a young Oriental whose own breasts, not nearly so spectacular, bounced with the optimism of the recently bloomed. Miss Moon had bulk but Kite had sincerity. Her fingers were dancers. The General didn't feel envious or deprived. The former impresario, now a member of the Connecticut State Legislature, deserved the Moon with big tits.

"You should have told me you were going to Gettysburg. There would have been fifty writers weeping," Barnum said.

" 'Mr. Barnum's marvelous mainstay, an energetic and masterful performance.' You can't argue with a review like that, P.T. I went on a whim. Not for the publicity. I went for myself."

"Whims are a luxury neither of us can afford, Tom. The article is sympathetic enough but still, a wasted opportunity. You should have realized every potential well in advance."

"Each move, waking and sleeping, must be calculated? Is that your philosophy?"

"And Miss Moon's. More of that, dear. Yes, yes."

Tom Thumb flipped over and watched Kite's digital ballet on his abdomen. "And everything spontaneous is for your suckers?"

Kite moistened her lips and leaned down.

"Not yet, you dunce," Miss Moon said. "Excuse her, please, General. She don't have the language."

"No offense given, none taken," Tom Thumb said.

"We live in the limelight," Barnum said, breathing harder. "We create our own reflections. We're a breed apart and must meet our public more than halfway. Our curse is that we can leave nothing to chance. Alas, Tom, we must anticipate, manipulate, and control what we can. Our currency is delusion."

"Not illusion?"

"Show me the difference since both are wedded. There's *us* and there's *them*. We must make them believe what we tell them. Which is what they want to believe in the first place. And even when we allow a sucker to glimpse the truth behind a humbug, it's only to leave him more credulous. When a sucker learns he's been suckered, and sees other suckers in the long line behind him waiting the same fate, then he feels the smirk of superiority. He's in the club, as it were. And now we have our sucker tight by the balls and snap the next trap."

"It must bother Barnum that his mainstay, Tom Thumb, is what he seems. I am your only honest creation, P.T."

"The world's smallest man? The General? A marvel? Would you admit to some slight exaggeration? In other circumstances, I doubt your splendid wedding to Miss Mercy Bumpus would have brought out society in droves or caused much commotion. That man from the *Clarion* would have written of his outrage had he observed some a dime-a-dozen midget desecrate hallowed ground. You're as much an illusion as real, Thumb."

"I doubt I could be replaced for a dime or even a dollar."

"A figure of speech. Don't get me wrong, Tom. You know how much I respect you and your talent. But the both of us would be put out with the garbage if we forget who we are and what makes us able to afford afternoon dalliance with affable Miss Moon and delectable Miss Kite. Our mission is to startle and amuse, to make our audience pay too much for too little and forget to hang us from the nearest lamppost. Remember to let Barnum orchestrate your encounters with the press. Do we understand one another?"

"We do. There's another article in the *Clarion* concerning a sermon by a Reverend Mr. Henry Turk from someplace out West. He claims the giants described in the Book of Genesis were American made, that Jesus himself was a Yankee Doodle. The paper reports Turk's view is gaining considerable popularity. Which gave me an idea I think excellent. Mount a musical extravaganza leading to a huge climax of anticipation. At which point, in a blaze, a mythic colossus is expected. But instead of a giant from Genesis, they see me, in a garden with Mercy. Adam and Eve, surrounded by a flock of bleating sheep. Do you like it?"

"My honest reaction? Worse than suicide. Never tamper with freckles or religious conviction. The audience would eat you alive. Thank providence you have me for a mentor. Otherwise, Tom, you'd be kept on display in a cage. A rule for Thumb: In this business, never let your guard down, never let your God down. And don't trade a cow that lays eggs for a chicken that gives milk. What you save in size you lose in prestige."

"You are forever a font of wisdom, P.T."

"Enough rhetoric. Now, Miss Moon, Miss Kite, descend from your house of stars. Shower blessings upon this humble public servant and his abridged associate."

"Miss Moon, please explain that commandment to your acolyte," said General Thumb, "lest she miss my friend's poetical nuance."

"Kite," Miss Moon said. "Find his thimble."

ON THE ILLINOIS BORDER, OCTOBER 14, 1868

Abbreviated. Abandoned. Assaulted. Mistreated. Disoriented. Demeaned. Disgusted. Dishonored. Bounced. Buffeted. Pushed. Pulled. When I think it is done, more punishment. Lifted then dropped in a flood of vibrations. I wake to the sounds of damp snorting. Cracking. Yanking. Noises urging. My optimism is strained. It's hard to keep cheerful.

CARDIFF, NEW YORK, OCTOBER 19, 1868

Stubby Newell could almost hear his mother saying "What's got ears, can't hear, but ain't deaf?" He'd scratch his head trying to remember the answer from the last time because she said it about a thousand times. Then it would come to him and he'd yell, "Corn, Mama." Now Stubby wasn't so sure the answer was right. His corn seemed to listen to his curses with droopy green ears and send back sorrowful sighs.

Stubby spent hours stuffing the stalks upright after a stiff night wind uprooted half his crop. The soil he owned didn't put up much of a fight to guard its bounty. If a bird farted in the next county a stalk would go down.

Stubby took Cousin George's letter from his back pocket and read it again. For all George's curlicue penmanship, the message was far from clear. This much came across: that *something* would be buried on Stubby's property and left there to ripen. That the spot chosen for the burial should be a good place for a well. That the well would gush gold.

What would be hidden, or *why*, George never defined except by vague hints that made no easy sense. Stubby concluded George Hull was involved in some hanky-panky and needed help to make it work. The letter said all would become crystal clear when George came to visit before the first snow.

Spelled out was the prospect of a windfall if things fell together. Maybe George, in his travels, had come on some new tobacco leaf to replace Stubby's scabrous corn. No, the tone of the letter suggested something more ominous. Stubby hoped George's scheme stopped short of murder. The idea of burying some new evil, a strange corpse to further corrupt his miserly ground, gave Stubby pause.

All the Hulls were shrewd apples; George the shrewdest. They knew the way to a dollar. But Stubby had no wish to hang for a profit. Still, George was right when he wrote "reward twins with risk." If the plan proved too repulsive, there was time to back off.

George seemed to be acting alone, independent of his father or Ben. He said: "Stubby, this is between you, me, and the doorpost." All the Hulls might well be in league. Was it coincidence that, the same day George's letter arrived, Stubby got another note from Simon Hull that spoke of expansion and held out hope for a future as part of their firm?

He examined George's letter again. There was a list of instructions arranged one to ten like the Commandments. The last commandment repeated the need for caution and told Stubby to "burn this letter and scatter its ashes." Stubby saw that was a stupid idea. Without George's list of the other commandments, how could he follow them? For all his smartass education, even Cousin George had his lapses.

Stubby watched a crow circle, then leave. His scarecrow was demolished in Winter and never replaced. That cornfield didn't need a straw man. Winged scavengers were frightened enough by the prospect of eating dinner there.

CHICAGO, ILLINOIS, OCTOBER 21, 1868

George Hull followed his beefy host along a corridor of stone statues and blank-faced grave markers that led to a ramshackle shell of what looked like an icehouse. "Good to meet you in person, Hiram

Hole," Gerhardt Burquhart said. Burquhart & Salle is glad to do business."

"You come highly recommended," George said. "I want only the best. Mediocrity is my enemy."

"I could tell from your letters that you are a man of taste. But how did you get the slab here from Fort Dodge?"

"It took six weeks," George Hull said. "The trip was no picnic. Three wagons split like matches. Once the damn thing tumbled into a gully and we had to find a ditching machine to get it back on the road. When we reached the railhead in Montana, it looked like the promised land."

"What did you tell the teamsters who brought it to us?" said Gerhardt Burquhart, a top-shaped man with a turtle face.

"They never asked for explanations."

"Chicago don't care about nothing. Well, you are here now and Herr Salle has made us a good place to work. We won't be bothered. This barn has been empty for years. We do our work in the open."

"This Salle, you never mentioned much about him."

"No worry about Edward. We have worked together since Germany. A brilliant stonecutter. Pay him his wages, give him his bottle, and that one is content."

"He knows what we're about?"

"He knows what he needs to know. I said to him you are a crazy from the East with money in all your pockets. I never said even your name."

George explored the rotting barn. What had been a window was covered with a sheet. Leaks in the roof were plugged with canvas. Burquhart had stripped the gypsum slab of its burlap. It lay on a butcher-block table held up by cement blocks and surrounded by kerosene lamps hanging by chains from a scaffold. A smaller table held an assortment of hammers, chisels, and drills.

"A hospital from Hell," George said.

"A nursery," Burquhart said, unrolling a charcoal sketch. "You like your baby?"

George looked at the drawing. A tall, robed, barefoot figure, its chubby face surrounded by curls, stood with outstretched arms. One hand held a nest filled with robins.

"I hate it," George said. "This belongs in an Italian cemetery. I don't want a memorial to St. Spaghetti. I thought I made all that clear."

"People love our creations, Mr. Hole. We don't get complaints."

"Which is why I came to you, Herr Burquhart. But we are not here to manufacture a churchyard fountain. We are dealing with a higher art. What I want is a petrified giant who died hard, in gross agony. His body is twisted, his legs contorted, his feet arched in spasm. His right arm rests across his stomach, his left arm is locked behind his back. Only his face contradicts his suffering. It is a strong, calm face, a gentle, knowing face, it could be the face of a long-suffering Jesus."

"Yes, you wrote all that, Mr. Hole. Instinct led me in another direction. Look closely at this sketch. See how he cradles birds in his hand? You can hear them chirping. Listen to me. We know what pleases the family. In the long run, it is best to stay on familiar ground."

"Familiar ground is the last place I want to be. Give me a creature of such mass and terror as to inspire awe and wonder. I know what my man looks like because he comes to me night after night. He haunts me, Herr Burquhart. He is my obsession. My giant hides in that stone, and I depend upon you to release him."

"Frankly, Mr. Hole, we are more used to heavenly creations. Myself and Herr Salle have no equal for angels, seraphim, garden nymphs. Even our gargoyles are more friendly than fierce."

"I don't want you to father a devil. Give me a man, true and tortured, who saw eternity's landscape in his final anguish. A huge and powerful mortal, brought down in his prime without knowing why, who accepted his doom as God's judgment. Reach into yourself, Herr Burquhart." George slapped at five tons of rock on the table. "Find him!"

"If he's there, we will search him out."

"Oh, he's there. He's there. Rest assured."

"First more sketches. Then a plaster model. This might take more time than we bargained for. It could involve a further negotiation."

"Moving this lump cost me a fortune and the month of June. My giant must be finished and on his way by October. Meet those conditions and I'll meet your cost."

"On his way where?"

"North, south, east, or west. His destination is secret."

"Ah, well. Four months for what should take a year. In agony, you say. But his face resigned. His muscles in knots, his toes locked together, one arm grabbing in front, one clutching in back to rip out the rot that kills him. On his chest, I see a raven."

"No raven," George said. "No vulture. Not a pigeon."

"Ah. He has a massive beard?"

"We are confronting a victim of petrification, Herr Burquhart. An ancient fossil. He has no hair on his body."

"A bald giant? You hear that, Edward?"

"So?" said a thin voice from above them. Herr Salle peered down from a roof beam, a slender old man propped on all fours. "A hairless giant? It don't make no sense."

"Don't pay attention to him," Herr Burquhart said. "He's drunk. Always drunk. Edward, you look like a schnauzer. Come down."

"A bald giant is impossible," said Herr Salle. "I refuse to accept this commission, Gerhardt. Send him away."

"I was his apprentice in Dusseldorf. Edward has da Vinci's hands and Michelangelo's eyes. One good eye, to be truthful, but it's enough. With God's help I can hold him together a whole Summer. We'll get your job done."

My ordeal is done. I am in the next place. I look forward to unbothered centuries. My fluster forgotten. Peace and repose. Forgive me, Source, for my petulance. So it goes.

"Take a sample, Edward. Just enough to know the grain."

"This is gypsum. For masons. House builders. Why not marble?" Salle's stringy gray head jerked like a weather vane in shifting wind.

"The man is shaking. He's out of control," George said.

"When he takes up his tools, a sea change comes over him, Mr. Hole. Edward, the large mallet I think," Burquhart said.

"The small chisel," Salle said.

George watched Salle make the first cut. His body steadied. His left arm went rigid at his side. His right hand froze around the mallet's shaft. He struck like Thor.

oww! Vain calcification! Stupid stalagmite! To think myself spared! Fracture! Fragmentation! Affront!

BINGHAMTON, NEW YORK, OCTOBER 28, 1868

Angelica dusted the curio cabinet that held souvenirs of Hull generations. There were silver teething rings, baby cups, porcelain figurines, sad-faced dolls, a pipe in the shape of a fish, pewter mugs, a flintlock pistol, the Bible that came from England with the first Hull expatriate in 1713. The last treasures to be housed there were a wooden fork and spoon that fed George Hull his first solid food.

Loretta sat playing "The Blue Danube Waltz" while her sister-in-law primed and polished. The package addressed to Angelica lay unopened on the parlor table. It had been delivered an hour earlier with some fanfare from the postman impressed by the tony return address. "Stewart's Department Store in Manhattan, *ding dong,*" he'd said when Angelica signed for her parcel.

Angelica had no idea what the package contained or who sent it. George was still somewhere in the Middle West writing orders for

the company. She had never been to New York City and knew nobody there. Puzzling over its content gave Angelica a surge of good
anticipation; she was in no hurry to give up that heady suspense.

"You are one of a kind," Loretta said. "I would have torn off the
paper the minute I got it."

"Where does this grime come from?" Angelica said. "Ben's baby
cup is all tarnished black."

"Let the trolls have Ben's baby cup," Loretta said, slamming the
ivory keys. "I can't stand not knowing."

"Then you open it, darling," Angelica said.

"You want me to open your package? I will, then."

Loretta ripped the brown wrapper and found a fancy box waiting inside. The box itself was a prize, flecked with gold and printed
with a pastoral scene. Loretta undid its blue ribbon and lifted off
the cover.

"Dear Lord," Loretta said, holding up a dress for a goddess.
"This would please any bride. But who sent it?"

Angelica stopped her dusting and came to finger the satin. "How
would I know? Is there a card enclosed? Here, let me see for myself."

Angelica fumbled through layers of tissue. She found a blank
envelope holding a note: *For lovely Angelica Hull who was so generous to this sorry scribe. —B.R. Clarion.* Angelica had never been generous to a scribe and knew no B.R. Clarion. "The whole thing is
impossible," she said. "It must be returned to the store."

Loretta looked down at a slight discoloration on the rug while
her mind identified the sender. She reeled from a rush of heat.

Angelica held the dress against her body. "This is closer to your
size than mine," she said.

"I don't think so," Loretta said.

"But look for yourself. I could swim in it."

"Never mind. It was sent to you, dear, not to me. Some simple
alteration would give you a fit."

"No matter since it's going back."

"Send back a gift? That would be both foolish and insulting. Besides, how would they find the customer?"

"Perhaps they know this Clarion."

"There must be dozens in and out of Stewart's every day," Loretta said. "New York isn't Binghamton. If I were you, I would keep both the dress and the mystery of its origin. Leave well enough alone."

"And what would I tell George?"

"That you saved your pennies and bought it to look marvelous on his birthday."

"It *is* beautiful," Angelica said, touching the fabric to her face. "What a curious turn of events."

"You might consider getting rid of that note," Loretta said. "However innocent, it might require excess explanation. I would like the box, though, unless you intend to keep it."

"The box is yours," Angelica said. "And the dress to wear should a party spirit move you."

"How proper that your reward came for some generosity, because you surely are generous. But Ben keeps me well covered and my wardrobe is quite complete." Loretta went back to her playing: *Ta-de-da-ta-tum-ta-tum-ta-tim-Ta-de-da-ta-tim-ta-ta-tim . . .*

"You play that so well," Angelica said. "I can almost feel those blue waves splash at the shore."

Loretta had a vision of her sister-in-law floating down the Danube in her B.R. Clarion dress, belly-up, bloated as a blowfish.

CHICAGO, ILLINOIS, NOVEMBER 3, 1868

By November, George Hull finished his business for Simon Hull & Sons with mixed success. While he had interested several new merchants in carrying the firm's expanded line, his efforts with the Uncle Tom brand produced less than spectacular results.

It wasn't that the Negroes weren't pleased by the smoke; it was the ten-cent retail price that caused problems. He had written several letters to Simon and Ben suggesting they find ways to cut the cost of producing the Uncle Toms. "Use horse shit and hay if you have to," George told them. "but get the price down to a nickel or under."

What he didn't tell them was that Chicago's darkies had discovered what they called *cigarettes*, little worms of tobacco wrapped in plain paper. They gave minimum pleasure and lasted only minutes, but they were cheap and came packaged in colorful cardboard boxes convenient to carry. George couldn't believe those paltry mutants were anything but a passing fad. Cigarettes didn't produce juice enough to hit a spittoon. Only their novelty made them attractive. What gave him pause was seeing a white woman smoke one, and though she was only a whore in a bar, George felt himself shiver. He was bound to clue his father and brother to the dangerous possibility of new competition. In time. There was certainly no imminent menace in the behavior of a few coons and whores.

It would be wrong to dilute the excitement he sensed in the messages from home. That positive mood made Simon Hull generous with George's expense account. George needed every cent he could get. Any news that would temper the family's euphoria could only be counterproductive.

The stonecutters Burquhart and Salle had gone through six detailed clay models. All expensive. All tepid visions. Their giants were more qualified to stand guard over a children's graveyard than spin the eyes of believers or traumatize orthodox atheists.

Before he'd gone off on his last selling trip, George sat both sculptors on a hard bench and read selections from the Old Testament. He led them to realms of fire, brimstone, and virulent vengeance. He showed them a jealous, wrathful Jehovah ready to vaporize rebels, cities, earth itself in tantrums of cosmic frustration. George used his voice like Reverend Turk, milking the last drop of boiling blood from every citizen of Sodom. Then, in a panting whisper, he took Burquhart and Salle through the pulsing tumescence and honeyed dilation of The Song of Songs.

He tried his damndest to show them what his giant took for granted in the course of a usual day. "If a sparkling ball of archangel turd flew down from the sky to spatter his dearest and closest friend, my man would hardly notice," George said. "If his lover turned leprous and her nipples came off on his tongue, all in a day's work. Understand what we are dealing with here. My man saw Jesus crucified and felt the scorpion sting of each Roman spike resonate in his own mortified flesh. He was *there,* gentlemen. He was *there.* It shows on his face. It shows in his body. Any autopsy of his parts would yield traces of Heaven and Hell. His prick dipped in lava. His feet walked on coals. His brain knew apocalypse. His eyes were seared by comets. I asked for a *giant* and you give me the Mayor of Dusseldorf. There's no more time for models. Take your tools to the stone. Let the brute who lives there propel inspiration."

Edward Salle drained a pint through the lecture and dozed but Gerhardt Burquhart was moved. He let out a scream. That sudden comprehension gave George some faint hope.

Leaving those hacks unsupervised was a terrible risk but George Hull had no choice. His funds were at bottom, his father wanted him home to fill Angelica's oven. Whatever the stonecutters gave him would have to do, or the project would be abandoned forever.

A week later George headed back to Clark Street. Gerhardt Burquhart answered his knock. "Ah, Mr. Hole, good to see you again."

"Is it done?"

"Did you bring our final payment? And enough for the cooper who built a magnificent cradle to carry your infant?"

"I have your money. Do you have my giant?"

George waited for his eyes to adjust to the sickly yellow light in the barn. His first sight was of Salle, asleep inside a great box of heavy pine lined with copper sheeting.

"I think your man will be comfortable," Burquhart said. "The coffin will be stuffed with sawdust and banded with iron."

"The container is not the content," George said. "A box is the least of my problems."

"Well, if our work doesn't please you, you can take Edward instead. He likes sleeping in there. Tell them your giant shrunk up from mildew."

"Spare me your humor," George said. On the worktable he saw a mound covered with a sheet.

"Let me wake Edward before the unveiling. He wants to watch your face."

George waited while Salle was prodded to consciousness. "More lamps and candles," Salle said, yawning. "Did you tell him my feelings?"

"Not yet, Edward."

"He is our masterwork. I will not sell him for any price. We have created life here. You shall have full recompense for your block of granite and the cost of bringing it. But never the giant."

"Shut up, Edward," Burquhart said, lighting a lamp. "He don't mean it, Mr. Hole. He gets attached."

"I mean it," Salle said. "I wouldn't let you see him if it wasn't for Gerhardt's pleading. So now have your look and go away."

"Ten feet two and one-half inches in height," Burquhart chanted while he pulled off the shroud. "From his chin to the crown of his head, twenty-one inches. Six inches of nose. Three and one-quarter-inch nostrils. Eight inches of lips. Shoulders three feet apart. Seven-inch palms, eight-inch fingers, five-inch wrists. Three feet from his hips to his kneecaps. Thighs a foot wide. Calves nine and one-half inches front to back. Feet seventeen and one-half inches long. A phallus like a Maypole. His weight is near three thousand pounds. Look at the expression, the detail of the jaw, the tension of tendons and muscles. Not the Mayor of Düsseldorf this time."

"Schönes. Schönes Kind." Salle patted the giant's gray cheek. "So what do you think and who cares what you think? Now we settle accounts and you go on your way."

George Hull stood with his throat in a knot.

Undark? Moving noises? What's left of me? Who are those shadows? My servants then? I say cover me quickly. Hide me away. This light is affliction. These sounds unendurable.

"It makes me sad to see his misery," Burquhart said. "With a few chips Edward could make a smile."

"What you've done so far is perfection," George said.

"*So far?*" Salle said. "You heard the Philistine?"

"We still have work," George said. "The fellow's unblemished."

"Of course there's no blemish. We rubbed and we rubbed."

"I didn't ask for polish. He must show his age."

"Time and the weather will age him fast enough." Burquhart said.

"Too long for my purpose. We make our own clock."

"Tell this man to go home before I kill him," Salle said.

"The customer is always right," Burquhart said.

"I hate when you tell me that," Salle said.

The next day George Hull bought a gallon of English ink and bathed his giant cerulean blue. "He looks like an eggplant," Salle said from the cage Burquhart built where Edward could dry out and recover his senses.

"Does he have to be kept in here?" George said.

"He contributes," Burquhart said. "You never know when Edward will say something useful. That is the way with a genius."

"Damn you both," Salle yelled, rattling the bars.

George worked all night to make a mold from layers of paper pierced with needles. In the morning he melted lead in a cauldron and cast a spiked hammer he called Iron Maiden. When the hammer cooled, George slammed it into the giant's blue body.

"Why?" Salle wailed.

"Scars and pores," Burquhart said.

Next the gypsum was scoured with metal brushes. The hammering and scrubbing made up a few centuries but the bluish hue clung.

"Still an eggplant, *ha ha*," Salle said.

Through the following days, Gerhardt Burquhart kept a time sheet listing each extra hour of labor. At night he totaled George Hull's mounting debt. The money was good but not good enough. Between Edward raving and Hull who was crazier, Burquhart began to doubt his own sanity. Sometimes he thought he heard complaints from the giant in a language without any words.

"Mr. Hole," he said, "we all need some rest. You've been carrying on for four days straight without stopping even to eat or drink. If you don't quit, that box will carry you home to your family."

"We must get him right," George said.

The next morning, before dawn, George Hull collapsed. Burquhart was pounding more pores with the Iron Maiden when his client gave out. He let George lay where he fell and went to make coffee, then carried a cup to Edward Salle.

"No more shakes," Salle said. "Let me out for some exercise. Everything hurts from the cramping."

Burquhart unlocked the makeshift cage, happy to see his friend returned to some semblance of stability. The two stonecutters sat drinking coffee, watching George suck for breath.

"I wish I never saw him," Salle said. "He makes me discontent."

"Don't grieve. We're done with him," Burquhart said. "I throw him out tomorrow with his pockmarked Satan."

Salle circled the giant, humming "Tannenbaum" while he surveyed his ruined work. Burquhart let his eyes droop, remembering with relief that their next commission was a generic St. Peter.

Burquhart opened his eyes when he heard Salle cackle. He saw his partner pouring fluid on the stone man. Burquhart's nose burned.

"What?" he yelled loud enough to wake George from his faint.

"Acid," Salle said. "Sulfuric acid. It will eat him up. He will go back to the house of smoke."

When Salle was put back in his cage, Hull and Burquhart poured buckets of water on the giant but the damage was done. Blue skin gave way to a vomitus mixture of grays and browns. Veins in the stone turned nearly black. The thing stank of wet ashes.

George Hull flopped to his knees and cursed God. Burquhart considered offering him a discount. When his cursing was done, George kissed Gerhardt Burquhart and paid full in gold.

CHICAGO, ILLINOIS, NOVEMBER 5, 1868

Pecked. Pocked. Painted. Caressed. Corroded. Was this last violation voiding? Or am I improved? I have never condoned vanity. But if I am my shell I would like to know if mordant immersion made me more or less handsome. Wounded. Now wafted. Risen and swung to another bed. This one softer. Tugged and taken. From? Toward?

CARDIFF, NEW YORK, NOVEMBER 14, 1868

Riding his horse, Pegasus, from Lafayette to Cardiff, Aaron Bupkin felt Autumn's first chill. The Onondaga Valley exploded color. Each tree a poem. Every leaf a celebration. This red, gold, and orange world would soon be a sorrow of iced, empty arms. All life snow-smothered. A blank kingdom of silence. But what a way to meet death. Vain as a sunset.

Aaron blew disconnected notes on his harmonica looking for a tune. His thoughts were unformed as his music. What set him off was the preposterous book he carried in a saddlebag. Mrs. Elm shoved it into his hand the night before when they passed on the stairs. She grunted twice, a remarkable endorsement from that critic.

The book made the case for America as the Holy Land where biblical giants once frolicked like rabbits. Its author, a Christian evangelist named Turk, presented a premise entirely absurd but surely intriguing.

Riding to Cardiff, Aaron speculated that if there were giants in Onondaga County, a few of them must have been Yids. He imagined an enormous Jew breaking through the trees, blocking the trail, waving a staff, proclaiming in thunder: "Shema Yisrael Adonai eloheinu Adonai ehad!" Hear, oh Israel, the Lord is God, the Lord is One. So tell me, is this the best road to Syracuse?

"What's your opinion, Peggy No Wings?" he said to his plodding mare. "Is this a land of giants? Don't be such a cynical horse. Did you know that only months ago a man in France, a Monsieur Lartot, dug up a Cro-Magnon in his own backyard. In the southern part of France where they dance without their pants. You know that song? If they find Frog Cro-Magnons, why not Yankee giants? The schlubs around here act like they descended from hippos. All things are possible."

When Aaron found the Newell farm he reined in the horse. "Look at this place. The leaves are already dead. Even the pine trees are brown. The soil is sand. What grows here? Look at that house and the barn. Like rotten teeth. See the cow? It don't have an udder."

Stubby Newell came out to meet the famous Jew water witch. Aaron Bupkin's fee, ten dollars, was a sin and a shame. It was George Hull's money, easy come, easy go. In Stubby's opinion, the whole exercise was stupid. The one good thing about the Newell spread was a surfeit of water. Stubby's silo was empty but his well was always full. A creek gurgled behind his barn. He needed more water like he needed more beetles.

"Good afternoon, Mr. Newell. Aaron Bumpkin is my name. Mrs. Elm gave me your note."

"I hear you got the touch," Stubby said, while Aaron dismounted. "I guess we'll see about that. My property runs from the tree line here, to that hill there, and the fence back behind the house."

"Beautiful spot," Aaron said. "Wonderful view."

"I'll take the horse so you can get to your work."

"She's called Pegasus."

"My druthers is to dig near the barn," Stubby said. "Maybe you can find me a spot."

"It's late to start digging," Aaron said.

"Don't I know that? I aim to finish the digging next Spring. But there's time to get started now which I can't if I don't know where to start."

"That's true," Aaron said. "I hope I can help you."

"For ten dollars you better help me," Stubby said.

"Ten dollars is a dollar a year for ten years of water," Aaron said. "And the next fifty years free. Is that your old well there?"

"I boarded her up. Went sour, then to dust. I take from the creek when it runs clear but most of the year it's a swamp."

Aaron got his dowsing rod out of its fancy wrap. "I like to say a little prayer before I go to work. It's in the Hebrew language, but don't fret about that. I ask God to guide my hand."

"What I don't hear can't hurt me," Stubby said, crossing himself. "I'll take the horse to my barn. The wife would have fixed you a lunch but they say your people don't eat same as we."

"I'd take an apple," Aaron said.

While Stubby and Pegasus crossed a field of dry weeds, Aaron closed his eyes, swayed back and forth, and said the bracha for wine. It was odd that a desert tribe had no special blessing for plain water, but Aaron assumed wine would cover enough liquid territory. He felt something should be said to acknowledge his fantastical gift, knowing how many ladies would have to buy how many needles and spools of thread, patterns, notions, and yards of cloth to earn him ten dollars.

Finding underground streams usually took sweaty hours. This

time his prayer paid quick dividends. The minute Aaron grasped the forked stick it jumped like a grasshopper. He could hardly hold it. Wherever he pointed the willow rod twanged. Aaron knew he was standing on top of a bathtub, that the whole Newell farm was practically floating.

In such circumstances it was really peculiar that Newell's first well went dry. You could find a lake walking blindfold and shoving a finger through that crust of earth. So why wasn't this farm the Garden of Eden? Aaron knew the story of the man murdered there; he must be a vindictive, malevolent soul.

"So close to the barn?" Stubby said as Aaron marked out the place for his well. "Better than I asked."

"You saw my stick. To tell you the truth, I'm tempted to cut my fee by two dollars. Are you sure the old well can't be saved?"

"Don't tell me my business," Stubby said. He had boarded up the well just in case the dowser got curious. This Bupkin was one dangerous, suspicious, powerful Jew. "You'll be paid what we agreed. Here's your apple."

"For my horse," Aaron said. "Peggy thanks you. If my work proves successful, please don't be shy about telling friends and neighbors. I live by recommendations. When it's warmer, I'll come by with my fine line of yard goods and accessories. Perhaps Mrs. Newell . . ."

On the path home, Aaron leaned forward to swat at a horsefly that browsed near Pegasus's ears. "This whole valley is filled with phantoms," he said. "More phantoms than bushes. I suppose they don't bother animals but they make people edgy. Some for no reason, others for good reason. Take William Newell. That man is oppressed. You know what they call him? Stubby. Ask me why. Because that man is half turnip who can never stand tall. You saw his vegetables? Like cramps on the vine. You saw his pig? If it was *kosher* I wouldn't eat it. You saw his chickens with yellow feathers? How much milk comes from a cow with no udder? Did his ghost of a horse tell you anything? I'm throwing his apple away. A voice tells me you're better off without it. Who knows what worm lives in that fruit? Who knows what the roots of the tree that produced it sucked up for nourishment? You noticed I didn't ask Mr. Newell if he knew any songs? You thought I forgot? I didn't forget. I was frightened to hear them."

ALONG A DEVIOUS ROUTE, NOVEMBER 19, 1868

Peter Wilson, a Chicago drayman, delivered a monster box to the Great Western Railroad. It took a crane to load the package— 3,730 pounds of deadweight—onto a freight car. The man who hired Wilson, one Herman Hooper, said it contained finished marble to be used for the lobby of a millionaire's mansion. But Hooper, complaining and carping, behaved as if the box held his dead mother. Wilson, an easygoing fellow, was glad to see frantic Hooper leave on the same train.

On November 22, that same box was transferred to the Delaware and Lackawanna. There, at the Great Suspension Bridge where the rail lines intersected, the transfer was supervised by a Martin Moriches, who told the conductor he acted on behalf of Cyrus Field, who wanted a perfect stone monument made to honor the men who laid his Atlantic cable.

The box was taken on board the New York Central bound for Syracuse, watched over by Rufus Troom, who introduced himself as agent for the sculptor, John Rogers, who needed bronze for his newest creation, a tribute to Thoroughbred Ruthless, who won the first Belmont Stakes.

Next, the Syracuse and Binghamton line took the box, and a certain Pritchard Dobbs, its high-strung guardian, to the Erie Railroad terminal, where Barton Berlman paid sixty-seven dollars for the ride to Union, New York.

The well-traveled container lay unclaimed at the railyard in Union until the twenty-eighth of November. Then it was fetched by Mr. Gibberson Olds, who presented a proper receipt. Olds waited while the box was placed, with prolonged difficulty, on a rented wagon. The rental included a sturdy team and a seasoned driver, for which Mr. Olds paid the sum of seventy-seven dollars and fifty-two cents.

At dusk in a drizzle, Olds and the wagon left on the five-day journey to Cardiff. His driver, Loomis Zane, was informed that their ponderous load was a tobacco press of superior and hitherto unknown design and that details of the journey must therefore be kept quiet.

Harassed by bad weather, fallen tree limbs, ruts and welts, with one of his beasts showing bad temperament, the taciturn Zane kept his eyes full on the road. He didn't notice when the pelting rain dissolved all residue of Hiram Hole, Gibberson Olds, Herman Hooper, Martin Moriches, Rufus Troom, Pritchard Dobbs, and Barton Berman, leaving a smug George Hull in their place.

Before sneaking off to Union, George spent a long week in Binghamton, reunited with his family. When Simon and Ben were caught up on George's reports of sales and rejections, and he with their recent accomplishments, George convinced his father and brother that his next trip should be a quick visit South to make firsthand contact with tobacco growers and carry the word of Uncle Tom cigars to Virginia, both Carolinas, Georgia, Alabama, and Mississippi where the ebony forests bloomed thickest.

Simon hesitated out of concern for Angelica. When George told him Angelica seemed abstracted, off her feed, not primed for the process that might lead to ripening, his father agreed to the journey. George left for Dixie with their hopes and blessings, taking a devious detour that led to the drenched Cardiff road.

On that road, licking rain, he realized how much he enjoyed

this delicious duplicity. George understood why captured spies smirk when they're tied to a post. While the firing squad aims, rifles crack, bullets fly from barrel to heart, they must hear incredible music.

"Noxious, stinking, putrid, puke weather," Loomis Zane said.

"Press on," George said. "Press on, sir."

BRIDGEPORT, CONNECTICUT, NOVEMBER 29, 1868

"I visited the ruins of Iraniston," Barnaby Rack said. "It must have been a glorious showplace."

"It was modeled after King George's home in Brighton where I guested many times," said P.T. Barnum, spinning in his leather chair. "I miss the humble palace, as does my dear wife, Charity."

"Fire has been your constant nemesis. First Iraniston, twice the American Museum."

"The first time my museum burned, when the Johnny Rebs torched her out of misdirected malice, cost me twenty-three years of my life," Barnum said. "But the blaze last March was worse. To rebuild and then watch destruction repeated might shatter a weaker man."

"You must have been devastated."

"I remembered the words of a paraplegic friend: 'I take my paralysis in stride.' The irony is, both times there were rumors that Barnum was the Prometheus who lit the match to advance his own cause. There were cartoons showing me followed by a fireman holding a bucket of sand. Expensive publicity, I'd say, Mr. Rack."

"Do you have plans to build again? The word in New York is that you'll soon be back among us weaving new spells. General Thumb tells the *Clarion*—"

"General Thumb will say anything to keep his name prominent in the press. No, I think not. My present life of public service satisfies me. Barnum's modest plan is to run for Congress, then be ready to run for President. When we finish with the next team of humbugs. I voted the Grant-Colfax ticket myself. First, because Grant is the bigger fool. Second, because better Ulysses Grant and Schuyler Colfax than Horatio Seymour and Francis Blair. Horatio and Francis can't come close to Ulysses and Schuyler. Such names ring out like bells. Come Ulysses, here Schuyler! Yes, those are the men to lead us closer to perdition. In any case, the majority will always vote for the biggest impudence, and that's Grant. And Barnum likes to be with the winner."

"So I should tell my readers that P.T. Barnum is devoted to pursuing his political career? Not the Drummond beams or calcium light of theater but the limelight of office?"

"Tell them that. Use those words."

"Sir, do you believe that the electorate would rally to the man responsible for exhibiting the Freejee Mermaid, which proved to be an amalgam of glued fish and animal parts? Or the bearded lady, whom many say was no lady. And George Washington's wet nurse, Joice Heth, whose real age fell eighty years shy of the hundred and sixty years you announced?"

"Proved? What was proved? I stand by the mermaid, the lady, and Joice Heth who held Washington to her breast and had milk-stained documents to prove it."

"But you yourself admitted to perpetrating those frauds."

"My confession was the fraud. Am I wrong, Mr. Rack, to remind you that you are addressing a member of the Connecticut State Legislature? A favorite son of this not inconsequential city of Bridgeport? Of course my public will respond to me. They must know that, in Congress or as President, Barnum would outhumbug the world. Our nation would thrive under my leadership."

"Your history bothers me," Barnaby said. "And also your philosophy. Where's the line between humbug and lie?"

"A humbug's a good thing. A purge for the body politic. The best antidote for sanctimonious pomp and bulbous aggrandizement. I admit that a humbug may in part be a lie, but a lie that does harm cannot be labeled humbug. Never call Barnum a liar to his face. I am your best patriot, America's friend and defender. Say that to the *Clarion*'s constituency."

"Your fortune was made on fleecing the gullible yet you claim your motives are altruistic?"

"If the people lose the ability to laugh at themselves, then you'll see fires much hotter than those that took my home and my business."

"I visited your New American Museum many times. What a collection of fakes, freaks, and fossils. Ancient artifacts made in your basement. One couldn't tell the real from the false. The children especially were left dizzy, more hoodwinked than educated by your displays."

"What is real? What is false? The triumph of the place was reminder of that very confusion. And you're wrong about the kiddies. They were best at detecting the difference. A child knows a humbug before its mother."

"But when a humbug succeeds and yields profit, there's every temptation to delay its exposure. A humbug become dogma can be worse than fire."

"Nothing is worse than fire. Or better than fire. Fire feeds like a glutton and is never satisfied. Fire is as ruthless as time. Both time and fire level the playing field, alchemists that transmute yesterday's horror to next year's nostalgia. Time and fire give us the future. They make tomorrow the place to bank our penny's worth of optimism. Barnum has been victimized by both and holds no grudges.

"Mr. Rack, I just said something worth writing down and also worth at least a guffaw. You failed to take notes and forgot to laugh. Young man, I suspect your problem is youth. Youth is always too serious."

"If I seem too serious it's because I sit here talking to Barnum the candidate, not Barnum the clown. As showman, Barnum has my admiration. Barnum as politician gives me pause."

"Some of my best friends have paws, Mr. Rack, and wet noses to the bargain. Another witticism ignored by your pen. When you define the difference between candidate and clown, let me know quickly. In the meanwhile, I find your manner unacceptably brash and I will so inform your superiors. On your way out, my secretary will hand you an engraved portrait of myself quite suitable for reproduction. Along with your coat. This interview is ended."

CARDIFF, NEW YORK, NOVEMBER 30, 1868

Bertha Newell sat watching the storm. She kept her nose to the window glass whenever she could, somehow in league with foul weather.

Alexander Newell whittled at a piece of birch, carving the shape of a heron. Stubby Newell watched his son, a boy who seemed old at fifteen. Alexander's head was shaped like a gourd. He had his father's body but the head was definitely his mother's heritage. Everyone in Bertha Newell's clan resembled some kind of squash, as if they'd come down from a race of pumpkins.

Stubby's attention turned to the fireplace, his favorite theater. Each flame seemed to be playing some part in a drama where the actors crackled and spit sparks. He never wondered what their play was about but enjoyed each performance.

The Newells never talked much to one another, but each felt the weight of family and the bond of linked flesh. They would have all

winter to sit together, night after night, sharing a silence that somehow gave strength.

If Simon Hull came through with a job in Binghamton and the
Newells were lifted from their treacherous farm to a city of
promise, Bertha might rejoice and Alexander do a dance, but
Stubby knew he would miss the heavy comfort he found on his five
forlorn acres. That knowledge of his discontented contentment
made Stubby angrier and more ashamed the longer he stayed on
that sorrowful patch.

In years past he could lessen his burden by thrashing his son, but
Alexander had grown too big and too strong. Once he slapped
Bertha for some release, but she slammed him with a kettle while
he slept. His last dog, Tinker, willingly accepted his boot, but Tinker died. The new mongrel, Sherman, snarled at insult and had
teeth to mince iron. In that fallow season there was nothing for
Stubby to do but wait out the clock.

"Somebody outside," Bertha said.

"This time of night? I don't think so," Stubby said.

"Didn't hear nothing from Sherman," Alexander said.

"Sometimes Sherman won't bark," Bertha said. "Somebody out
there. Near the barn. What I see is too fat for a firefly and too
small for the moon so it must be a lantern kind of hanging on air."

"You see a light? Why didn't you say that?"

"I said it."

"Not what you said, not what I heard."

Stubby lit his own lantern and went to investigate. He wiped
rain from his face and slogged through muck toward the bouncing
blob of light and the sound of men's voices.

"Who's there?" Stubby yelled. "What do you want here?" Sherman came at him, snapping. "It's me, you shitbag hound. Them by
the barn are the trespassers."

"Stubby?"

"Who's calling?"

"George. George Hull."

"Cousin George? That you?"

The cousins bear-hugged and back-slapped while Sherman turned his attention to a third man who stood nearly invisible.

"Damn. I gave up on you, George. You said October."

"I said October but I guess I meant November. Better late than never. Are you ready for me?"

"I'm ready, all right. But I don't know what I'm ready for. I mean, I did what you wrote me to do but I didn't fully get why you asked me to do it."

"Get this mutt off me," said the wagon driver. "It's spooking my animals."

"Who's he?"

"Drove us down from Union."

"From Union? *Us* being you and who else?"

"Us being me and my Pandora's box," George said. "The new to-bacco press."

"Tobacco press? I guessed it was some such thing."

"Just let's get the damn thing down off the wagon," George said. "You got somebody can help?"

"Can't we wait for daylight?"

"No," George said. "Now. Show me the place where you dug the hole but don't mention the digging. The less that driver hears and the less he sees the better I like it. I want that man out of here soon as possible. Then we can talk as much as you want."

"You wrote me to hire a water witch to find a likely place for a new well. This Jew came up here for ten dollars and pointed over there behind my barn."

"Then that's where we unload. Which ain't going to be easy. What about the ropes and the pulleys?

"Like you said. Stashed in the barn. Another nine dollars. Nineteen dollars between the dowser, ropes, and pulleys."

Two hours later, when the rain turned to fog, the driver inched his wagon back toward the Cardiff road with Alexander leading blind horses.

"Bad trip to go through this soup," Stubby said.

"Don't fret about him, Cousin. The man was well paid for his work."

Stubby kicked George's box, half sunk in mud. "A tobacco press. I get it now. You want me to grow tobacco up here. It must be some new kind of seed because you know I tried that years ago and the leaves I got tasted like hog hair."

"Get an ax and a saw," George said. "We got to get that thing opened."

"In the dark? It won't sink no deeper, it's packed tight as young pussy, no rust going to seep in there if it ain't already. Come inside and have a hot drink. My back's acting fierce."

"Bear with me, Stubby. Let George have his way. What's got to get done should get done before morning and forgot by the afternoon. Get the ax and the blade. We'll go slow and careful. What's in there is precious cargo."

"That's good news," Stubby said. "Whatever you say. Tell me, George, am I breaking some law here? Because if I am, I think I should know it."

"No law I heard about," George said. "We're legal as candy. That's the beauty part, Cousin. Nobody gets hurt."

"I'm relieved. Your letter left blanks in my mind. Made me think you don't trust me."

"If I didn't trust you, would I put my life in your hands? I told you, all will come clear following the funeral."

"Now that's what I mean, George. You say we're breaking no law but we got to work at night in the fog and you talk about a funeral. I don't know any funerals where the box gets opened before the burial and I don't want to know. Why are we burying a tobacco press? Explain your intentions and don't skip details. I'm entitled. Otherwise call back your wagon and find someplace else for your planting."

"I like your spirit," George said. "I've got the right man in my corner. You'll have your answers. Get the tools. We can talk while we cut. First about Alexander. Can you assure me what that boy sees and hears will be kept to himself?"

"Alexander don't have friends and says maybe ten words in a year."

"Ten words could kill us. You'll keep the boy straight?"

"Leave my son to me," Stubby said. "What kind of tobacco press needs time underground?"

The constant in all this is the one called George Hull. He allows me escape. Then I'm dropped in a pit and the same George who freed me shovels muck with the rest. Let me lay here and mold. Moss. Fungi. Spores. Green rot clogs my crevices. Things wriggle and crawl. I measure infliction by the trickle of water tingling the truncheon between my legs. This damnable itching! I saw something in the boy's rolling eyes. They fear me! I'll wait for you, George.

NEW YORK, NEW YORK, DECEMBER 16, 1868

"I don't confuse you with Stanley or myself with Livingstone," Barnaby Rack said. "But I think by now you might have discovered that I might be ready for something more than dribble about a spent windbag like Barnum or vital news alerting mankind to the creation of the game of Badminton by some demented British duke. I noticed that we elected a new President, nearly lost San Francisco to a quake, that General Lee is on trial for treason. Does John Zipmeister send Barnaby Rack to cover those insignificant stories? No. He decides to send Rack the Hack to Hell's Kitchen to kiss a gangster's behind and then to report on an elevator. An *elevator*, for God sakes."

"Get it through your head that you're a feature writer, not a war correspondent. Those are both solid stories worth the telling. People read the *Times* and *Tribune* frontward. They read the *Clarion* backward. For us, its sports, comics, features, then maybe the news. I happen to like backward papers that value daily obsession higher than crass reality. I call that a proper sense of priorities. But if you feel differently, tell me. I want to be first to know. Because you might want to try your luck on one of the other sheets. See what they'd give you to do and how much you'd get paid to do it. And by the way, Rack, your Badminton story was twice too long. You saw the sign over my desk? GOD CREATED HEAVEN AND EARTH IN TWO PARAGRAPHS."

"I noticed the sign, yes. But the story of the Duke of Beaufort, the cretin of Badminton Hall, so intrigued me, the brilliance of his shuttlecock so involved me, I wanted every New Yorker to share my excitement. Excuse me if I got carried away, Mr. Zipmeister. As for your other suggestion, the minute prosperity replaces depression, I just might sniff opportunity across the street."

"Meanwhile sniff where I tell you to sniff or you'll be more depressed than you are."

"And your instinct for news tells you a carol to a lowlife thug is what our readers want the week before Christmas? Not to mention the biography of an elevator? You're serious about assigning an adult human being to write that shit?"

"Rack, I had all to do to smooth over Barnum's bitching about your callous attitude. He was right, you know. You weren't sent to Connecticut to antagonize a national treasure. Or to compare him with Thomas Jefferson. Don't push me too far. Just get off your high horse and back on the ground."

"I didn't mind that you deballed my Barnum. But it hurt when you slashed at the Badminton."

"Your line about 'a whirlwind of feathers spinning like a tipsy sparrow through a chasm of space'? Did I cut that? And lose my chance at Heaven?"

"Forget Barnum. Forget Badminton. I'll even ride your damned elevator. But why would the *Clarion* whitewash Brian?"

"Whatever he is, he's close to the power. And word came down from upstairs. So swing your brush."

Barnaby Rack went to meet Grinder Brian at Knuckle's Silver Mine on Tenth Avenue. Silver dollars paved the floor and decorated the walls and ceiling. The waiters and bartenders wore silver-dollar jackets and derbies. That palace of opulence, with its fragrance of tobacco and beer piss, was Grinder Brian's favorite property and the seat of his throne. The reporter and his subject shared a circular table covered with more silver dollars.

Touted as leader of the Fish Head Mob, nicknamed the Pickle Czar, Brian was credited with extortion, shylocking, theft, and mass murder. Barnaby expected to confront a fuming rhinoceros. The man who collected ransom for every marinated cucumber sold from the Bronx to Manhattan, the same man who owned whore-houses and clubs where perverts danced naked, the scythe for Boss Tweed of Tammany Hall, was a pencil-bodied fellow with a crescent-moon face. He dressed like a bank clerk in a black suit, white shirt, and bow tie. His voice was so low Barnaby leaned into his breath to hear him.

"My business is business, no more, no less," Brian said. "The charges against me are trumped up and false."

"And why do they call you Grinder?" Barnaby asked, knowing the name came from Brian's habit of grinding inconvenient corpses down to their shoelaces in an abattoir somewhere in New Jersey. "It's a provocative moniker, I'd say."

"Because gents like you need fiends and villains," Brian said. "My real name is Sean Shamus Brian. There's a scoop for the *Clarion*. Of course, I'll deny it."

"You're known as a private man, a shy turtle adverse to publicity. Then why did you ask for this meeting?"

"Good question. I'm a family man. I live a quiet, plodding life. More a snail than a turtle. Still they shout *Grinder Brian!* whenever a foul deed is done or a citizen drops to the pavement. Those head-lines hurt my wife, bother my kiddies, and don't make me happy. I grew up in these streets, worked hard on the docks to improve my-self and earn my position. I want to set the record straight once and for all. Brian is guilty of nothing but success."

"You want to be loved, then?"

"I won't ask for love. Respect is enough."

"Those men standing there at the door seem to respect you."

"Don't let those thugs bother you. They're my friends and associates, all bought and paid for. You know why I asked the *Clarion* to send you, Barney?"

"I didn't know you asked for me and my name is Barnaby, not Barney."

"It was because of what you wrote about Gettysburg. 'Bugles of Hope.' It touched my heart. The war was very good to me. I admit it. And I know that but for the grace of God I might be asleep in some field. Your article reminded me of my own mortality. How fragile we are. And myself the object of such malice and vituperation. Is early death the price of fame in this cold city?"

"Can we talk about pickles?"

"No."

"Then may I inquire about a certain meat processing plant across the Hudson in Jersey?"

"No."

"Can we talk about anything, Sean Shamus?"

"My mother, rest her soul. We can talk about her."

"We're both busy men," Barnaby said. "Suppose I go back to my office and write off the top of my head. Say I fill in the gaps and make Grinder Brian seem human, even larger than life. If I were to do that, would there be any need to stay past one beer?"

"If you were to do that, you and your rag would have my full gratitude. But be gentle with me. It's my first time so close with the press."

"Gentle as a tyke with a kitten, allowing some flavor of mayhem for spice. Just a sprinkle, of course."

"That would be most acceptable, Barney. Do you like to get laid? What is it you like under your tree?"

Barnaby left Knuckles Silver Mine with a handful of souvenir dollars. He walked briskly toward his next assignment, the new Equitable Insurance Tower where the first elevator ever installed in a commercial building awaited his talents. He already wrote his lead: *Rising and falling with the human tide, a modern marvel of elevation and descent. Only an elevator? Nay! More than that! Lusty harbinger of a city of splendor whose structures scrape the sky. In years to come, grand cathedrals of commerce . . .*

Barnaby stopped to look at a store window where a bent old man placed hats on wooden heads with no faces. He realized with a shudder that, elevator or butcher, he could write most of his *Clarion* prose without ever leaving home. *Grinder Brian—Is he an enemy of the people or maligned innocent? A tarnished diamond trapped in a nether world whose violent code forces compliance . . .*

What would it be like to write the truth? *Your reporter sensed that this black-suited, gore-dripping, mick bastard knows he's doomed to die by the sword. That his profits from pickles and pussy will soon jam the pockets of other silk pants. Yet Sean Shamus Brian, scion of the Fish Head Mob, has my sincerest respect and envy! For he lives on the brink. Each tick of his gold pocket watch is a drop of his own hot blood. My own watch ticks slower but swallows less time. Grinder Brian's days are shorter and sweeter than mine, his nights longer . . .*

At the Equitable Building, Barnaby was met by a good-looking lady named Elizabeth representing the company. "We're very proud of our lift," she said. "It works wonderfully well."

"But don't the employees feel queasy riding so high, so fast?" Barnaby had his own problem with elevators.

"Some, in the beginning, did complain. Now they are united in their enthusiasm. Take the ride yourself, Mr. Rack. Be a bird without wings."

"A bird without wings. I like that, I'll use that. As for the ride, let me take your word."

"Oh, go ahead, be brave," Elizabeth said. "We're an *insurance* company. Do you think we'd take risks in our own home? How can you write about our astounding elevator if you refuse to experience its actual flight?"

Barnaby, intimidated by gender, took a deep breath and entered the cage. Elizabeth signaled the operator to take him to the top floor. As the door slid closed, a rotund passenger rushed inside gasping.

"Sorry," the stranger said. "Got to get back to the mill."

When the elevator lurched past the fourth floor, Barnaby burped, felt dizzy, and grabbed for a handrail. The operator saw his discomfort and reacted by stopping midfloor. Barnaby had a picture of himself held dangling over the world's end by a strand of steel hair.

"Please don't get sick in here," the operator said.

"We'll get off at five. My floor," the round man said.

"I was told to take him to six."

"Look at his face."

The pudgy samaritan led Barnaby off the elevator on five, then down a long corridor. He unlocked a frosted-glass door with the name Oliver Elversham stenciled near the knob. Inside Elversham's windowless cubicle, Barnaby was placed in a leather chair while his host poured a tumbler of water.

"I feel quite idiotic about all this," Barnaby said. "I've always reacted badly to heights."

"At least there's no window to bother you," Elversham said. "I'm new to the Equitable. Here one aspires to a window as one might gaze at a distant horizon."

"What do you do here?" Barnaby asked to be polite.

"I sell life insurance. The universal product. Being a novice, my only clients thus far are my own family members. But I have confidence."

"Life insurance has always fascinated me," Barnaby said, swallowing bile. "Your company wagers I'll live to dodder. I bet I'll die young and pay for the privilege."

"Well, there's more to it than that. And if one does manage to beat the actuarial tables, one expires on a high note leaving at least one secure mourner whose grief is all the more genuine. Tell me, do you carry a policy?"

"Me? No. Who would be beneficiary?"

"I gather you're unmarried. A young bachelor might well ask

himself why he requires ample coverage. The reason is simple. Probability. I mean, the probability that you will marry and become a loving husband and father. If you contract young, your premiums are much lower. Take my word for it, someday you will need my services, Mr. . . . ."

While Elversham spoke of inevitables, Barnaby sipped Equitable water and thought unexpectedly of Angelica Hull. He'd entertained the idea of sending that woman another anonymous gift in the spirit of the Christmas season. Now there she was with him at the Equitable, along with the memory of their instant together in Binghamton. Insurance for Christmas?

"Sean Shamus Brian is my name. Glad we met, Mr. Elversham."

"Likewise, Mr. Brian. As I was saying, at your time of life and considering what I assume to be your obvious good health, the cost of a generous policy would be minimal. To plan ahead makes excellent sense and, if you allow me, I could sketch out the terms and conditions. As for beneficiaries, whoever you might select in the interim, that name or names can be easily changed to accommodate life's alterations. There must be a parent, a brother or sister, an uncle, aunt, or cousin, a friend, a charity, whose name would serve nicely for the time being. If you keep your policy a private affair, they'd never have reason to lament future exclusion. And if you should pass away, God forbid, think of the gift you would leave."

"You're a good salesman," Barnaby said. "You have my attention. But tell me first, is there a staircase down?"

"I think Equitable Life will win any bets we make with you, Mr. Brian. I see you're both sensible and cautious. Yes, there is a staircase. But should you become my client and decide to take the elevator instead of the steps, you'll ride with serenity. I can guarantee that."

To give a bet on the life of a Pickle Czar seemed a highly original toy for anyone's stocking.

"Is there a medical examination required? Or the need for complex documentation?"

"I saw you speaking with our Miss Elizabeth downstairs. As a friend of the Equitable family, you'd get our best rate. We could waive the formality of an exam. Your word and signature would be sufficient."

"Our dealings must be confidential. For certain delicate reasons, I wouldn't want even dear Elizabeth to know that . . ."

"I understand. No problem. I don't mean to pressure you or influence your decision, Mr. Brian, but let me say that you could be fully protected five minutes from now. I must ask for your age at your nearest birthday . . ."

While Oliver Elversham tallied numbers, Barnaby Rack did some calculating of his own. To commit the crime of forgery and risk good money against the odds Grinder Brian would last for a year was clearly the act of an inspired madman. To do it in exchange for a roll on a rug was an act worthy of Lord Byron. Such anonymous gallantry enforced Barnaby's image of himself as the last true romantic. In some curious way, Barnaby felt buying insurance for a faraway lady gave some center to his transient existence. And there was always the chance that, down the line, it would make a hell of a story to tell Zipmeister.

"I came in feeling wretched," Barnaby said. "Now I feel good about myself."

"That's the way with insurance and why I'm honored to be part of the profession," Elversham said.

"As you should. As you should," Barnaby said.

CHRISTMAS EVE, 1868

Winter camouflaged its own despair and did it so cleverly thoughts of Spring were rare as birdsong. Snow covered the Onondaga Valley. Under that vast quilt, thawed by wool and friendly flame, made tranquil by food and drink, with souls lulled and languid, the more fortunate citizens of Cardiff ignored icicle daggers that hung from their eaves, looked away from goblin faces hiding in the frost on their windowpanes. Bertha Newell was one of the few who recognized the gray horde that clouded her view of the impacted land. The goblins watched her, she watched them. Even Bertha felt content, wreathed in Christmas peace.

Stubby Newell stoked up the fire after he fed his pagan stock extra rations. Even Sherman, who gave back nothing but grief, got a bone from the leg of the lamb that gave the Newells their holiday dinner. Such bounty came unexpected. Stubby's last crop already bore fruit. Cousin George sent fifty dollars tucked inside a card with a picture of the Wise Men.

Alexander Newell whittled at the hull of the clipper ship, *Cutty Sark,* nursing dreams of the sea. Since the night he'd helped shovel dirt over the twisted stone man, then spread clover seed on its grave, the sea filled his mind with temptation. He took salty excursions to faraway shores and returned from his reveries with bags full of savage mementos.

In Binghamton, Simon Hull, in his favorite chair, smoked a Corona Corona. He watched its plume drift over his sons and their wives.

Loretta played "Little Lord Jesus" on the piano while Ben and Angelica sang the words. Ben had Loretta's gift in his pocket: glass candlesticks no bigger than toothpicks. He knew how Loretta would coo when she saw them and maybe smoke his best cigar out of gratitude.

Even George seemed to feel the holiday. He sat with his eyes shut, a cat smile on his face. George, in fact, was in an odd place, a frozen manger where dark heralds hovered over a new holy hatch.

The Hulls, ringed and contained by Simon's sweet smoke, made a peaceful canvas.

In Ackley, Iowa, Samantha Bale and the Reverend Mr. Henry Turk laid dried flowers on the grave of Herbert Black Paw. They prayed the Indian boy enjoyed Christmas Eve in Heaven. That celebration had to rank high among eternity's diversions.

At the *New York Clarion,* Barnaby Rack clinked glasses with John Zipmeister. They toasted the Savior, the New Year, the American nation. After work, Barnaby went back to his rooms on Greenwich Street, where he found a present waiting: a Yuletide tree of a lady, naturally decorated, with a gold star in her hair and a note dangling from her wrist on red ribbon: *Compliments of the Season from Sean Shamus Brian. Her name's Mary Purple.*

General Tom Thumb handed out gifts to the drunks on the Bowery: socks, gloves, scarfs, booze, and good wishes. A few blocks away, his surrogate father, the Honorable Phineas T. Barnum, hosted a party at the Clarendon Hotel, where an English guest spoke of a notable behemoth named Jumbo at the Zoological Garden, twelve tons of pachyderm with a seven-foot trunk the wags called Victoria's Best Consolation.

In the Dorchester section of Boston, Aaron Bupkin sat with his grandfather, Isaac, arguing the meaning of *Nephilim,* which the New Testament translated as *giants.* "Not giants who live on a beanstalk," Isaac said, questioning claims by the Reverend Henry Turk, *"Nephilim.* More *machas, mavins.* What the Hasids mean when they talk about spiritual Jews who *look down at the sky."*

"Maybe yes, maybe no," Aaron said. "There is something to be said for giants who are giants, not philosophical concepts. To tell you the truth, I like the idea of literal giants clomping around."

"You worry me, Aaron," Isaac said. "You sing their songs, now you like their giants. What did I do wrong?"

In Chicago, Edward Salle forgot making a giant. Gerhardt Burquhart remembered the creature with paternal pride. In his Winter sleep, the thing came home wearing tight lederhosen with a bride who called Burquhart Papa.

Grinder Brian stood by while a rival who'd kept seven whores in Chinatown was reduced to a mulch then washed down the drain of a Hoboken warehouse. Grinder heard a loud gurgle, crossed himself, and bawled while his men turned away. He had nothing personal against the pulp in the septic tank. One whore or two, but *seven* make a statement. Any echo of treason can tumble a king.

In Binghamton, after church, Angelica Hull followed her husband upstairs. She considered telling him first about the unexplainable dress from Stewart's Department Store and, next, about a peculiar letter she got from the Equitable Life. But George was inside her before she could say "Merry Christmas." Angelica watched snowflakes tumble and thought about Hamish, safe and away.

Earth tight around. All heat withdrawn. The bugs hibernate. Time turned to ice. A mountain to fill a sump hole? Nothing makes sense. Between a scream and a yawn. At least wake the ants.

1869

SYRACUSE, NEW YORK, OCTOBER 16, 1869

Stubby Newell, pinched in the suit he last wore to his wedding, sat waiting for an officer of the Collendale Bank and Trust. He'd been to this bank twice before pledging flesh and farm in exchange for a loan. Flabby bankers rejected his pleas, assessing his total collateral as less than a dead leaf in the wind. While Stubby shared their opinion and admired their wisdom, he hated their imperious manner. They had a way of making him feel invisible, disappeared from the family album.

But on this crisp October morning, Stubby was eager for his interview. He expected quick rejection and was prepared to make the most of it. Cousin George wrote how important it was that his feeble petition be a matter of record and remembered.

Following George Hull's detailed map, Stubby had spent Spring and Summer wandering through Cardiff, as far as Lafayette, singing a ballad of misery: His cursed farm was more cursed. Some malefic sponge sucked water from his land. His creek was down to dregs. His well turned to bile. He'd seen it coming for a year, when he spent his last money to hire Jew dowser Bupkin who showed him where water waited. Fresh water. Clear water. But what good was Jew water with no way to tap it? No money to dig. Turned down by the bank. A season of drought. More weevils than corn.

Stubby's neighbors commiserated but claimed empty pockets. More than one thought a merciful God was finally acting to end the prolonged agony that kept the Newells in perpetual pain. Sell the farm. Hitch the team. Go someplace else.

Stubby enjoyed what sympathy he got and the prayers said for his family in Cardiff's Congregational Church. The Newells became famous as a tribe of black shadows. Their awful presence reminded other sufferers to count blessings. Alexander and Bertha were embarrassed by the attention and puzzled at its origin, but Stubby forbade them to ask any questions. "It will come clear," he said, quoting George. "Our luck is changing." By August even Stubby believed that was true.

In Onondaga Hollow, not fifty miles away, a farmer came up with a bundle of bones. Scientists from Cornell University in Ithaca declared the bones fossils of unknown origin and paid plenty to own them. When the newspapers printed the story of the find, every dog in the valley was sent snorting for ossified gold. Cousin George was one lucky man. If anybody would ever believe in his giant, the time was at hand. Stubby sent those newspaper clippings to Binghamton urging George to make the next move. His cousin answered quickly: "No hurry. We'll wait for October. Credibility's worst foe is coincidence."

"William Newell?"

"Ready and waiting," Stubby said, and went through a low wooden door where Mr. Collendale Bank & Trust beckoned.

"Don't I know you?"

"I've been here before. I asked for a loan."

"And did you get the money?"

"Not exactly. Things are different now." Stubby said, handing the inquisitor his papers.

The last time his pastor helped fill out the bank forms. Every word was proper, the penmanship grand, and to no avail. This time, Stubby did the application himself. He used question marks for answers and let his pen drip blots the size of squashed moths. All George's idea.

Stubby watched his inquisitor wince at the document. "The thing is," Stubby said sincerely, "I need a new well dug and I need it dug fast. In fact, just yesterday I said to myself, Stubby, when they hear your good news that bank won't refuse you again. So I picked myself up and hired Gideon Emmons and Henry Nichols to dig my well for me. On the very spot picked by the best water witch in the county.

"While we sit here talking, that well is being dug. Because without it I'm ruined. Hell, my wife gives more milk than my old well gives water. But with the new well, excuse me for whispering but I can't know who's listening, *alfalfa.*"

"Alfalfa?"

"That's where the money is. *Alfalfa.* So if we can just get on with the necessaries, I can start right away to make myself rich. The amount I wrote down pays for seed, fertilizer, and the damn digging. When we strike water, we'll join hands and drink the first glass to your health and long life."

The officer shuffled through a desk drawer and came up with a file. "William Newell, yes. We sent our assessor down to your farm the last time."

"You did. Not the best Christian I ever met."

"His report was not encouraging."

"I know it," Stubby said. "But that was before alfalfa. Or pure water. So forget his report. Put it behind you. By this time next year we'll be sitting here laughing at that report, *ha ha ha. Hee hee hee.*"

"Maybe you were too hasty to hire your diggers, Mr. Newell. These matters must take their course. Sometimes weeks and months . . ."

"But I can't wait, you see. Gideon and Henry asked for money in advance, but when I said I was seeing you today to get some they agreed to put down that well. And not only them. Smith Woodmansee to stone it up and John Parker to draw the stones."

"I'm sorry to hear it, Mr. Newell, because I'm afraid this institution can't be so quick to grant your request. Money is tight these days. Your farm is not exactly in prime condition. We would like to help, but let's just suppose that dowser was wrong and there is no water for your alfalfa. Or that the demand for alfalfa should prove transient."

"That dowser is never wrong. He could find a river in a rock. Alfalfa they say is the new sure cure for constipation and who do you know that don't constipate?"

"We're bankers, not gamblers, Mr. Newell."

"But Gideon and Henry are digging today. I owe those men. You hear what I'm saying? Do you hear me? Or is wax got you plugged?"

"Calm yourself, please."

"Calm myself?" Stubby yelled. "Calm myself? There's good water down there, maybe twenty, thirty feet under my soil. With an honest flow I can care for my own. Without it, Stubby Newell's a dead man. Calm myself? Give over that money and give it now." Stubby grabbed the officer by his shoulders and shook off his spectacles. Then he stomped the tortoise-frame glasses to sparkling dust.

"You got me excited," Stubby said, falling back in his chair. He dropped a gold eagle on the officer's desk. "Excuse my tantrum. As you see, I am not entirely destitute. Twenty dollars should cover my damage and then some. If you don't mind, I think I'll take myself over to the First Fidelity where I might find a hand worth shaking."

"We won't forget this behavior," the officer said.

"Don't suppose," Stubby said.

CARDIFF, NEW YORK, OCTOBER 16, 1869

———◆◆◆◆———

Gideon Emmons and Henry Nichols slammed their shovels into the soft clover patch behind Stubby Newell's barn. The earth was butter soft and came up in clumps.

"Shoulda had us out here back in May," Henry said.

"Couldn't pay in May," Gideon said.

"Wouldn't put my well here," Henry said. "Got a feeling we're going down a mile 'fore we see wet."

"Maybe yes, maybe no," Gideon said.

"He put down cash, didn't he?"

"Enough for today. How he got up the money is a mystery to me. Maybe somebody died."

"What about tomorrow?"

"Stubby headed up to Syracuse to drop in on the bank."

"They wouldn't lend him measles. You see his house? You see his barn? You see his old lady? That melonhead boy? Even the dog ain't worth its own shit or anything else around here."

"The man was in good spirits when I talked to him," Gideon said. "He was a different man this morning when he left. Full of vinegar. Maybe he went crazy."

"Wouldn't blame him," Henry said. "What he been through."

"It has been a trial."

"I'm hitting rock," Henry said. "I knew it. Just like a Jew to take Stubby's money and keep quiet about there's ten foot of stone to get through."

"Maybe that Jew didn't pick up the stone."

"He knew, don't worry about that."

"Maybe it ain't ten foot of stone. Maybe it's just a thin sliver," Gideon said.

"You watch," Henry said. "I'd bet a dollar we got a assbreaker on our hands."

"Hear that? Now I'm scraping rock," Gideon said.

"Newell luck," Henry said. "Let's see what we're dealing with."

While Henry probed with his shovel, Gideon knelt in the pit to brush away a clot of loam.

"Solid granite," Gideon said.

"What did I tell you?" Henry said. "We should quit now. It don't make sense to keep going since Stubby's coming home empty-handed. I don't want to be here listening to him say how we got to finish for the sake of religion."

Gideon brushed away a mound of reddish clay. "Small wonder nothing but a fungus could grow here. A few inches of topsoil and the rest . . ." Gideon Emmons let out a howl. A gray face looked up from the circle he cleared.

"What's the matter with you?" Henry said. "Some kind of snake in there?"

"No snake," Gideon said. "Something down there but no snake. I might settle for a snake. I swear it's a face like no face I ever saw."

"What face where?"

"Right here lookin' up at me," Gideon said.

"Jerusalem," Henry said. "It's some kind of dead injun."

"Don't look like no dead injun," Gideon said. "Looks like a white man."

"See if there's more to him than his face."

"Drop the shovel and get down with me, Henry."

"I don't know about that."

"Look at the size of his head. It's like three heads in one. If this was a injun we'd all be living in wigwams."

Henry and Gideon scooped up handfuls of earth.

"I found a foot," Henry said. "Got toes on it bigger than bull-frogs. There's a whole leg laying here."

"We need us a witness," Gideon said. "To see what we found."

"We're each a witness," Henry said. "One for the other."

"I'm going for somebody else just in case. I don't like this."

"Nobody home at the house. Mrs. Newell and the boy went into town."

"Wagon on the road," Gideon said. "Hail him over."

"Hold up," Henry said. "Maybe a witness is the last thing we need. Maybe we should just haul this thing out of here and tuck him away somewhere safe. Stubby Newell don't need to know what we found."

"It's on Stubby's property," Gideon said.

"Even so. We found it."

"Look at this neck. I can't even reach down to where the back is. He must weigh a thousand pounds naked so how would we move him without help if we had the notion to do it? Which we don't."

"You heard about what happened in Onondaga Hollow. This stone man could be worth a dollar a pound to them scientists."

"Two dollars a pound, he's Stubby's to keep," Gideon said. "It's only right. Gideon Emmons ain't a body snatcher nor ever will be."

"That's John Hagens in the wagon," Henry said. "Let him go on his way. We got to talk this over."

"A arm," Gideon said. "I found a bent arm."

"I don't like the look on that man's face," Henry said. "Maybe he's the feller got murdered."

"More reason Stubby deserves him," Gideon said. "Get John Hagens to come over here."

"If he has a mind to. That's a stubborn man."

"You tell John Hagens what we found and try to keep him away. There's never been nothing like this in Onondaga County. Look at that belly with its muscles pulled in. However he died, I wouldn't like to know it. I don't envy this man for all his size."

"Come to think on it, if he died and got buried how come he ain't bones?" Henry said.

"You never heard about petrification?" Gideon said. "Don't you read? It happened a lot in the old days. Skin turned to stone. Body to crystal. They even found petrified cabbages. It was a most natural thing."

"John, John Hagens!" Henry yelled to the passing wagon. "Hold up! We got something to show to you worth seeing!"

"Henry, Gideon, good day to you both," the driver yelled back. "I'd like to see what you've got there but I'm on my way into Cardiff with my last load of watermelons."

"You don't want to miss this," Henry said. "We got serious petrification."

"A giant dead man," Gideon yelled. "Stuck in Stubby Newell's new well."

"New well?" John Hagens said. "Where did Stubby Newell get the money for a new well?"

ON THE ROAD TO CARDIFF, OCTOBER 16, 1869

———◆◈◆———

A pair of bats rose from the forest, circled, and dove back to cover. Stubby Newell clucked to his horse. He wanted to get home before dark. He was losing that race. A red sun slid over the edge of the planet while a new moon rolled through plum-colored clouds.

Stubby pulled over his rig to light a lantern that dangled from a hook at its base. He touched the same match to a fat cigar he'd bought in Syracuse. The flare of the match startled a turtle crossing the road. Stubby blew a mouthful of fifty-cent smoke at its mottled shell then picked up the turtle and tossed it into a patch of reeds.

He got back up on his wagon and jiggled the reins. Jerked to motion, Stubby watched the sun die, the moon born. Carrying fire between his teeth, Stubby enjoyed the death of the day.

He didn't know what to expect on his homecoming. Gideon and Henry would have dug up George Hull's friend around noon and probably crapped in their pants when they met him. When they told their story, Stubby would *show agitation but don't seem excited or even much interested. The opposite. All you care about is your well and the water. Tell them you want that thing out of there fast. Go with them to Cardiff to ask the minister for advice. Get the word out then sit back and wait.*

After his performance at the Collendale Bank & Trust, Stubby was sure he could do what George wrote him to do. The hard thing would be to keep a straight face and act like he didn't comprehend the commotion. If there was a commotion.

Stubby didn't expect too much. The people in Cardiff were slow to enthuse and hard to excite. He wrote back to George, *Don't expect July 4th* and George wrote he'd settle for July 5th or 6th. *Got to work up momentum before a stampede.*

"Maybe yes, maybe no," Stubby said, shoving his cigar at a firefly's flash. Nothing ventured, nothing gained. If the whole thing fell flat he could prop up that giant in his cornfield and give his neighbors more reason to genuflect when they passed Newell land.

Stubby followed the road around Daniel Archer's dairy farm. Three of his own cows could fit into one of Archer's with room to spare. The Archer barn, with a tin bull for its weather vane, was sound as a castle. In the dusk Stubby saw stacks and bales of cattle feed ready and waiting for Winter. Archer's house had a new roof, new shutters on the windows, and a gate carved like stalks of wheat. And Archer was lazy. He worked less in a week than Stubby did in a day. "So how come?" Stubby asked Venus, low on the horizon. "Where did I go wrong?"

Stubby took a long drag on his cigar and forgot not to inhale. His lungs went to spasm. He coughed and cried, spitting brown juice at Archer's lush island. When he recovered, Stubby realized his wagon had stopped. He reached for his switch, took a swipe at his horse, then saw that a shape held the horse by its bridle.

"Pa?"

"Alexander? That you? What are you doing out here on the road in the dark?"

"I got scared of the candles."

"Son, what are you telling me?"

"There be least a hundred all holding candles singing 'Great Is Thy Faithfulness,' 'Rock of Ages,' 'Onward Christian Soldiers,' and such. Some saying to string up the dowser."

"Let the horse go, come sit up here with your pa, and say it all slower. Who's holding candles and singing? And why do they want to hang my Jew?"

"I can't answer all of that. Most everyone in town is up at the farm. I don't know why they're singing or what they got against the water witch. It's something to do with the stone man Cousin

George hid back of the barn. The well diggers found him like you said they would and got John Hagens for their witness. He and Henry Nichols tailed for town and there's watermelons all over the road now."

"Alexander, if I told you once I told you a thousand times to forget Cousin George had anything to do with any stone man. And I don't understand what John Hagens or watermelons have to do with this."

"I surely don't neither, Pa. But people say it's about the murder of some saint or apostle. When they heard who first found the grave Ben Hawkins fell down on his knees and began the singing. Somebody else said find the dowser and string him before it's too late."

"Too late for what, son?"

"Don't ask me. Too late is all. And I never said nothing about Cousin George nor did Mama."

"Well, that's good news. What's Mama doing?"

"Last I saw she was selling them water a penny a cup. Gideon Emmons asked her where she got water since the old well was poisoned and dry and Mama said it got unpoisoned and filled to the brim like a miracle. She said it had to be the work of the Lord."

"She said all that? Good for her. George Hull didn't send directions for this kind of turn. And I don't want them hanging no Jew just on general principles. All he did was his job and what he got paid for. If there is water under the spot where he pointed. Which we can't know and won't need to. We'd best get home and see what's what."

"I got to go back there?"

"It's where you live, ain't it?"

The wagon climbed Papoose Hill then dipped down to Carson's Crossing. From there, Stubby heard "The Old Rugged Cross" and saw enough candles flicker to call every moth. "What did I tell you?" Alexander said.

"Mama's getting a penny a cup?" Stubby said. "Who's keeping

account?" He tried to remember if his deal with George touched cups of water. Knowing George, it probably did. But to give away nine cents out of ten seemed a sin and a shame what with George down in Binghamton having no cups to wash.

NEW YORK, NEW YORK, OCTOBER 17, 1869

General Thumb, livid, left the Hippotheatron Theater followed by his bodyguard. He walked across Madison Park in a rage. That night he'd played to what Barnum called the mouth without teeth, a theater two-thirds empty of life.

It was the reviewers who'd gutted him, lashing out with raw venom. The production Thumb staged, *In Camelot's Court,* deserved raves, not rebuke. The play was a tribute to his namesake, Thomas Thumb, a gallant knight a few inches high who fought for King Arthur, rode around on a mouse, and died valiantly doing battle with a spider. The show had every element for dramatic success: humor, pathos, romance, and regret.

Thumb saw his role as the problem. Rejected by stately Guinevere, betrayed by Mordred, sent to his death by a jealous Arthur, his heroic character was beyond critics who wouldn't allow any midget to stretch his talents. The audiences laughed when they should have cried. They wanted only happy endings from the General they knew from theatrical farce.

Thumb sat on a bench while his bodyguard watched for stray dogs or assassins. He thought about sending the man on his way. Being torn apart by a rabid hound or hit on the head by a felon could bring relief. A final assault would have left him in a better place. The General had an expensive turkey on his hands and hor-rendous decisions to make.

Thumb took deep breaths to clear his head of rancor. When the scurvy notices came out, Barnum suggested he abandon *Camelot,* cut his losses, lie fallow for the rest of the season. But what was the master really saying? That Thumb's novelty was gone? His career in twilight?

Thumb put his face in his hands. He needed Barnum in harness again. And the atrophied old goat needed Tom. After one run for Congress, now back in the State Legislature, P.T. rocked on the porch of his mansion, Lindencroft, praying for burglars. Barnum's pride was the alarm he'd designed to shoot rockets from the roof if prowlers came calling. But Barnum required rockets with his morning coffee. He'd turn to leather up there in Connecticut. Maybe it was too late for the two of them. Moments pass. Only fools and salmon try to swim up waterfalls. But if something woke Barnum from his enchanted sleep, they both could strut up Broad-way like peacocks.

"A man must make his own luck," General Thumb said to the bodyguard, then jumped down from the bench. The bodyguard, who had not the good fortune to be born a talented midget, con-sidered the General's proclamation.

BINGHAMTON, NEW YORK, OCTOBER 17, 1869

———

"Albany, Kingston, Plattsburg, Binghamton," Simon Hull said, banding samples of the new Hull De Luxe Signature Reserve. "Four stores in a year and all of them thriving. The Uncle Tom brand is our only discouragement."

"That disaster can be laid at my feet," George said.

"No, son. You can't blame yourself if Negroes are taking to cigarettes, God forgive them. Infants eat mush but soon outgrow it. Let's look ahead, George. I've been thinking it's time Simon Hull & Sons had a presence in New York City."

"New York City? Where there's a tobacconist on every corner?"

"But only a few *humidors* with fully stocked keeps where a gentleman can go with his friends for an evening. Brandy, wine, conversation, and a Simon Hull smoke."

"Hold up," George said. "I've been to places down there with walnut walls and appointments from Europe. Men of means already have their clubs to rely on. Does New York need us?"

"There's a new class emerging who'll learn to appreciate luxury. They may not have the power of a name but they do have power of the purse. And they need us."

"First class for the second class? First aspiring Negroes, now the nouveau riche? Simon Hull & Sons. Oasis to the almost?"

"Energy flows from faith, faith from vision," Simon said.

"I seem to be lacking all three," George said.

"You and too many of your generation. Malaise is the legacy of civil war. But we're an optimistic people with a great destiny. Yesterday's pain is tomorrow's pride. I wish your outlook could be brighter."

"I was born with the colic."

"When you have children your feelings will change."

"You might be right, Father. Though I can't understand why a barnyard of babies would make a sour grape sweet."

"It might help the grape sweeten to hear me out. Your brother has shown a fine ability to supervise our expansion. My plan is to send Ben to Manhattan to live for a while and survey possible opportunity."

"You send me west and south and save Manhattan for Ben? There's a vote of confidence."

"George, I am trying to help you find your niche in the scheme of things, and I don't think it's organization or sales. I'm not chastising you in any way, only facing what's true and trying to do what's best for us all. My inclination is to take a trip to Cuba and South America to explore new sources of supply."

"Ben in New York, Simon exploring, and where is George Hull?"

"Here in Binghamton in charge of the factory and fulfillment of orders from our branches. Binghamton is the hub and heart of our enterprise. Does that show lack of trust?"

"And what about Loretta?" The prospect of mornings without his dip into Loretta's Blue Grotto was grisly.

"You mean Angelica?"

"Of course, Angelica."

"She'd manage the store."

Simon's strategy for the Hulls grand march hardly interested George since his future was elsewhere. He waited to hear of developments in Cardiff. Stubby was clearly instructed to send a wire with the news, but no wire came.

"So what are your feelings?" Simon asked. "Tell me you see some glimmer of hope for our success. Give your father that much."

George felt like his giant, twisted and writhing, denied even decay. A fraud preserved to prove a fiction. "These are my feelings. The name Simon Hull & Sons will be revered by men of goodwill for as long as there's history. For a woman is just a woman, but a good cigar is a smoke."

"From your mouth to God's ear," Simon said.

Next morning Ben Hull rose even earlier than usual and went down to check a fresh batch of Connecticut leaves. George tracked Ben's sounds then went on pilgrimage to the Shrine of Loretta. Tucked between Loretta's legs he found a yellow envelope.

"It came late yesterday," Loretta said from her faraway place. "I forgot to give it to you."

George opened the telegram and read the message he'd composed for Stubby Newell in advance: *He is risen.*

"Is it important?" Loretta asked from the far place.

"Not important," George said, lifting her shift and tonguing true treasure. George lapped like a puppy.

"Stop that, bad boy," Loretta said softly. "Nothing will come of it."

"I know, dear," George said, lifting his nightshirt. "Now go back to sleep."

CARDIFF, NEW YORK, OCTOBER 18, 1869

On Saturday morning Bertha Newell sold mugs of black coffee to a shivering crowd at three cents a cup. Stubby and Alexander went into town for provisions. Stubby bought the biggest roll of canvas Boljer's General Store stocked.

By early afternoon, with the help of Gideon Emmons, Henry Nichols, John Hagens, and some neighbors, the canvas transformed to a humongous tent that protected the giant's vulnerable grave.

While Alexander directed a clog of traffic, Stubby dragged a table out of the house and positioned it near the tent's narrow flap. A gifted artist, Jane Kloster, who ran Cardiff's Elementary School, lettered a sign that said: 50 CENTS PER TEN MINUTE LOOK/CLERGY 25. The discount price for clergymen was agreed to after strenuous negotiation with Stubby's own Congregational minister, Hethrow Locke, and three of his colleagues from the town of Lafayette: Presbyterian, Dutch Reformed, and Methodist. Those four men of the cloth were exempted from waiting on the long line that snaked to where a cluster of wagons jammed together in the cornfield. They were left alone with the giant for as long as they wanted at no additional fee. Stubby hoped they'd hurry their browsing. Every minute they dawdled was costing him money.

The waiting crowd had opposite feelings. Novelty had been reason enough to bring out the curious. But seeing that holy quartet vanish into the cavernous tent hushed the strange congregation. There were murmurs, gasps, and sudden hallellujahs. Viewing an oddity was one thing; visiting a miracle different.

Stubby flexed in the quiet. He realized those churchmen could make him or break him. If, God forbid, they emerged belly-laughing, slapping their thighs, he'd be left with a rock and a hat-ful of shame. If they exited with humbled faces his stone man would be certified, deserving respect. The stakes were higher than Stubby had realized.

The more time the ministers took, the more he tensed. Gone silent, the festive mob that invaded his land reeked more of men-ace than merriment. A voice told Stubby to confess on the spot before Christians turned lions ate him alive. If he told how he'd been pressured, forced into sin, there was a slim chance for mercy. The whole sinister scheme could be blamed on the Jew, who would likely get lynched anyhow. Stubby saw Bertha's blank face at her window and guessed she was having the same second thoughts.

The tent flap parted while Stubby gulped vinegar. The four min-isters came out in a rigid line. They formed themselves into a half circle, joined arms, and sang "Nearer My God to Thee." Hethrow Locke, being the most vocal, spoke for them all. "Friends," he said in his stained-glass voice, "today in this modest place, this tiny cor-ner of Onondaga, the truth of the Bible is affirmed. From antiq-uity's bowels a fossil hath appeared, a fallen giant who, even in demise, hath strength enough to smite any cynic who dwelleth among us. Welcome, creature of stone revealed in the pages of Genesis. O Lord, forgive us for disturbing Thy servant's long rest. His exhumation was a happy accident, the result of honest effort undertaken with no intent to defile. Our brother, William Newell, who instigated this dig, sought a well to gush water. Instead, Lord, Thou hast given to William and to all a taste of the precious water of life eternal. Lord, in our hearts we know had Thou wished to conceal this astonishment of petrified bones, this Giant of Cardiff

121

would stay undisturbed. We believe his discovery was no accident but Divine Will enacted. Your giant is come down to us through miraculous days. Let all who gaze upon his stilled might and majesty contemplate our own brief, perilous journey through the days of our years. And let each of Thy children recall Thy most blessed directives. Welcome, Giant of Cardiff!"

"What about the Jew dowser?" a voice said from the crowd. "Do we hang him or not?"

Stubby knelt with his peers, closed his eyes like the rest, and lifted a handful of powdery earth from his suddenly sanctified land. He told Jane Kloster to change the sign to FIVE MINUTES/ONE DOLLAR/PLEASE NO EXCEPTIONS.

The verticals stare but what do they see? First their eyes are twin terrors then puddles of love. They throw flowers and wait for some message. I have nothing for them. Enough to remember a time without color. Am I of two worlds, Source, and neither? Where is the George to explain?

Reverend Locke called Stubby Newell aside. He patted Stubby's head. "Your face shows me that all this attention has numbed your senses, William."

"I should bury the thing again. He belongs in his crypt."

"Perhaps at some future date. But your giant deserves to be experienced by the public. There's divinity in this."

"I opened a can of worms for myself and my family."

"The opposite. This creature is our victory over worms. Through his excellent preservation he reminds us of the glory day of resurrection. But there is one conundrum."

"What's that, Reverend?"

"How shall I say it? The giant is proportionate. By which I mean all his parts are consistent. It was thus inevitable and understandable that his privates would be of substantial dimension."

"You mean his prick and balls?"

"His penis and testicles, yes. Excessive."

"Oh, absolutely," Stubby said. "Imagine carrying that bump in your pants every day. But I guess in those times they had women who expected no less."

"William, you must arrange some modest covering before any viewing continues."

"Strike me dead," Stubby said. "I should have known that much. What is the matter with me?"

"Don't fault yourself. But take action today. The shock of such confrontation can only distress men, women, and the children. For some, like the elderly, it could be fatal."

"I can see that. Thank you for saying it. I'm going inside right now and talk to Bertha. She knits like a beaver in heat and already started on a sweater for her sister in Manlius. It's a pretty good size and might do the job of concealment."

"That sounds more than adequate."

"Later she can make something special, maybe in black, measured to the purpose. A neat bag and a pouch maybe to save us from shame."

"There is no shame in the stone man, William. But to mitigate religious emotion with any suggestion of prurience is wrong and could leave you open to a charge of exploitation."

"Exploitation? I don't want nobody exploited," Stubby said. "Only to pay what's fair. If God gave me the giant that must mean He wanted Stubby Newell to have some benefit to make up for the years of denial."

"I don't doubt it. Or that you will remember the church when considering dispensation of your bounty. Charity is the soul's best nourishment."

"Don't I know it?" Stubby said. He would talk to George Hull on the subject of charity. Charity should come from George's ninety percent of the gross, not from Stubby Newell's ten. And the cost of a mat for that pole and those globes should come out of George's share by any honest arithmetic.

"Be strong, custodian," Reverend Locke said. "God's watchman at the gate."

"His will be done," Stubby said.

NEW YORK, NEW YORK, OCTOBER 20, 1869

"From the *Syracuse Daily Journal,*" John Zipmeister said. "Listen up, Rack." Zipmeister read in a low, rolling growl:

> There were strange stories circulated throughout the city, to the effect that a wonderful discovery had been made—that a human being, a petrified human body had been exhumed, and was there to be seen on the farm of a Mr. Newell. The story passed from mouth to mouth, growing as such stories do, until it was believed by many, pooh-poohed by others, and received with allowance by the more credulous. It was ascertained, however, in a short time that an object had really been found.
>
> Our observer can give no description that will convey to the mind of the reader anything like a correct idea of the object as it appears to the beholder. The trench in which it lies is about four feet deep, and is cut down a couple of feet on either side, making it some fifteen feet in extent. The earth is removed to the clay upon which the body rests. Above this clay is a deposit of four or five inches of gravel and sand, in which the body was half embedded. The exhumed object is the complete semblance of a giant. It rests in a very natural reclining posture, and appears as though it was a person who had fallen there and died. The right

hand rests upon the lower abdomen, and the left hand is pressed against the back directly opposite. The left foot is thrown partially over the right one, the leg resting partly upon its fellow, but not crossing it. The muscles of the lower limbs are fully developed and seem greatly contracted. The whole body reclines slightly to the right, and the left side is consequently somewhat raised above the other. The head is likewise inclined to the right. The position of the hands and feet, the contraction of the muscles and the attitude of the body indicated, to our view, the agony of intense physical pain. But the face is perfectly calm. The head and face are remarkable developments, and impress the beholder with a feeling of admiration akin to awe.

The reader can form some idea of the colossal proportions of this curious object. Its like has never been found upon this continent. The proverb tells us that "there were giants in the earth in those days" and though we are not able to tell the exact date and origin of the human and beastly monsters which are, now and then, brought to notice by accidental means, yet the fact of their occasional exhumation tends to verify the asseveration that there *were* giants in those days. Of course, the question at once arose, Is this object a petrification or is it a colossal statue?"

"Where again?" Barnaby asked, looking up from his typing machine.

"Outside Syracuse," Zipmeister said.

"Why in Syracuse?"

"Is that a question, Rack? How the hell do I know why in Syracuse? Anyhow, they go on to give the measurements. Enormous son of a bitch. Creepy story."

"You're not going to reprint that bullshit," Barnaby said. "It's an obvious Halloween prank."

"I thought I was a cynical man," Zipmeister said. "But I have a way to go to catch up with you. Why is it bullshit? How can you say to me sitting here at the *Clarion* that they didn't find a giant laying in a ditch in some dumb farmer's backyard? And it's too early for Halloween."

"You're right. They found a giant in Syracuse. I'd better pack my sling because it must be Goliath. Could be I'll find David and a Philistine down the road munching cow pies."

"I don't know what you'll find down the road and neither do you. What you should know is that this kind of story is meat and potatoes."

"Did the *Times* or *Herald* pick up on it yet?"

"No. It's just off the wire."

"I see. Well why not the *Clarion?* What's wrong with our printing fiction?"

"The *Syracuse Journal* said they sent an observer."

"No, they said 'our observer' observed. Their observer was probably some field mouse. I wouldn't rush into this unless you want to wake up with scrambled eggs on your face."

"I'm not rushing into anything. You are, Rack. I want you on the night train. They found *something* in that hole, bet your ass."

"But you promised me the Republicans. You said—"

"I got a hunch about this one."

"Then why not go up yourself? I bet you've never once been up to Syracuse. You don't know what you're missing. And I'd hate for you to be deprived of the Second Coming if you missed the first one."

"Hear this.

> As we draw near and see the groups of men standing about the house, talking in low voices, as though it would be a sacrilege to raise the tone above a whisper, the impression at first is that the services are being conducted with all their awful sublimity. But reaching the ticket office, the reality bursts forth then, and the tent, surrounded by hundreds of anxious sight-seers, brings us face-to-face with the fact that we have gone to a show, wonderful, how-

ever, in its character. One man, who has come a long way, anxious to believe the remains to be a fossil man was heard to say:—Now then, look here; I ain't going to believe that that's a putrefied man unless you show a feller some of the coffin. Is he dead?—then expectorates tobacco juice toward the prostrate form. Thus rudely are our dreams and cogitations disturbed.

"Ticket office? Fossil man? Tobacco spit? Mr. Zipmeister, I'm the one going to die up there."

"Be on that train, Rack. And print me a picture of what's laying in that pit enough to stir dreams and cogitations."

"Syracuse dreams," Barnaby said. "Upstate cogitations."

CARDIFF, NEW YORK, OCTOBER 21, 1869

Stubby Newell, chin in hand, sat at his kitchen table drinking brandy with Professors Othneil Marsh and Benjamin Sillman of Yale University, Professor James Drator of the New York State Archaeological Museum, and Dr. Andrew White, the president of Cornell University in Ithaca. Stubby was impressed by his guests, each one with a college diploma. While the scholars debated, Stubby looked out toward the tent.

Alexander supervised a huge crowd of visitors, allowing five at a time to see what they came to see. Just laying there, the Cardiff Giant was earning sixty dollars an hour, which meant six dollars clear for the Newells; hour after hour, day after day, sunup to sunset, maybe forever. Subtracting the cost of the guards Stubby hired to protect the stone treasure, a seven-day week, twelve hours a day, allowing for a noon start on Sunday, meant four hundred seventy-two dollars and sixty cents for Stubby, nine times that amount for George Hull. Stubby didn't need professors to tell him who held the short end of that stick.

That morning Daniel Archer had come to offer Stubby a swap of their farms if Stubby's threw in the stone man. Archer had his deed in hand, waving it like a wand. The Archer Dairy Farm with all its land, barns, and stock, one of the richest spreads this side of Bear Mountain, in exchange for a granite slab.

An hour before Archer, three lawyers and a dentist from Albany showed Stubby ten thousand gold dollars in a trunk for his prize. Ten thousand dollars on that same kitchen table. Both times Stubby choked not to say *done deal*. What stopped him was a mind picture of George Hull goosing the air with his thumb. Stubby told his suitors, "Got to think about that, things being what they are."

George's plan was to show up in Cardiff a few days after the find when the trip was more natural-seeming. Stubby thought his cousin better hurry before good intentions gave out. Even family blood is only so thick. He could taste the cream from Archer udders and remembered how that gold trembled light.

Professor Marsh held up a magnifying glass to examine a chip from the giant's thigh. That chip alone cost those professors a hundred in cash. Stubby figured George would have stopped any chipping before it got started so the hundred would be his little secret. As it was, he'd put up a fight. "What if you crack him?" Stubby said. "What if a whole hunk splits off? Then what?" But those men had silk tongues and amazing credentials. Stubby capitulated and sold them their fragment. They were right, nothing split, cracked, or crumbled.

"Possible fossil, Mr. Newell," Professor Marsh said. "Still . . ."

"You all heard the hollow wump when I thumped him," Professor Sillman said. "There could be organs inside, no question. Though I cannot vouch for their condition without a full autopsy."

"Hold on," Stubby said. "That chip is as far as I'll go, and I shouldn't have gone that far. We got a sacred man on our hands. Please don't talk autopsies in this house."

"Nothing can be done without your consent," Professor Marsh said. "We are aware of that fact, Mr. Newell."

Mr. Newell poured another round of drinks.

"I am of the opinion that we have a statue outside," Professor Drator said. "Albeit a statue of great antiquity and possibly the most valuable object brought to light in this century."

"You say a statue?" Marsh snapped. "Then answer me this. Why would any classical artist make a statue to celebrate a man so horribly contorted? And where is its base?"

"A base will be found."

"One would think a base would be found where it belongs, either under the statue or nearby. Which convinces me, Drator, that your theory is baseless."

"I think it's too soon to judge," said Cornell's president, wiping steam from his glasses. His inclination was to call the giant not ancient but adolescent, a bad example of amateur sculpture. Dr. White was too prudent to announce that suspicion while Marsh and Sillman wavered. Cornell was not Yale. "Tell us again, Mr. Newell, how the giant was discovered."

"Gideon Emmons and Henry Nichols were digging me a well. That's the long and the short of it."

"And you chose the location for the well?"

"No, sir," Stubby said. "The Jew water witch did all that a year ago. You should have seen his dowser rod jump when he came to the spot. Like he found a new ocean."

"A year ago, Mr. Newell? Then why the delay in digging?"

"I didn't have the money to dig last year. Fact is, I didn't have the money in hand when I went out and hired Henry and Gideon this year. But I was pretty sure the bank would lend it. I guess I was wrong. If they'd found ordinary water down there instead of Goliath I'd have two angry men up my ass. Halellujah is all I can say. Halellujah again and again."

"This needs investigation," Dr. White said.

"I respect your caution," Professor Marsh said. "Too soon to declare the thing human. Such a conclusion would surely have incredible ramifications, echoing back-and-forth across endless centuries."

"A glorious statue to honor some ancient hero who kept his composure even in defeat. Mythic, gentlemen, but not human flesh. Some kind of gypsum, though not of a type quarried in this immediate region," Drator said, pounding the table.

"Then why, when you rub at the chip, do you not feel ordinary grit in your fingers but a powdery substance? Is it because we are dealing not with gypsum but the petrified remnant of human skin?" Sillman asked.

"And if it was a statue of such mass and proportion, why is it here and how was it transported?" asked Marsh.

"You won't sway me," Professor Drator said. "I repeat, though, fossil or statue, the thing is remarkable."

"Oh, yes, it is remarkable," Dr. White said. "Quote me on that. Though I still think it too soon for public proclamation."

"So Cornell is conservative and carefully shy?"

"Cornell is careful," said Dr. White. "Shy and skeptical."

"Skeptical? In the face of what we've all sampled and seen, considering the conditions of exhumation, how can you possibly harbor suspicion of fraud? Admit, at least, that . . ."

Stubby stood up and stretched. "Can't sit too long anymore," he said. "My own petrified bones won't let me. If you'll pardon me, gentlemen, I'm going to check on my son, Alexander. That boy never had more than fifty cents in his hand at any one time and the Devil's always looking for converts."

"I use the word skeptical in its broadest sense," Dr. White said. "Can one presume Mount Blanc from a single pebble?"

"Delay is a sister to science," Professor Marsh said. "But too much delay is the kin of self-doubt. We are here to share our expertise and best intuitions. Dr. Drator says icon, Professor Sillman and myself are stymied, and you sniff at fakery. No wonder the masses pillory academia, always eager to crucify her ambassadors. And why, Dr. White, do you bring Mount Blanc into this when we have our own noble mountains to draw on for metaphor? The majestic Rockies or even our neighboring Adirondacks or Catskills? If this giant is American and bespeaks a new reading of Genesis, how long should we hold back that news? Should someone else sound the trumpet?"

"Sound away," Stubby said from the door. "Blow the horn. Look at the crowd out there. Some highly educated folks among them. Would they grab up their kiddies and drive all those miles, sing hymns and psalms, then trample on each other for a chance to pay their dollars to see any statue? Fossil's the word here."

"Mr. Newell has a good point," Dr. White said. "Perhaps their faith will be confirmed. After full autopsy."

"Forget it," Stubby said. "I already told you my feelings on that. And what about Lot's wife? Didn't she go to a pillar of salt, which ain't too far removed from what we got here? Was there talk of any autopsy on that poor woman? God is always turning people to something else from what they began. How much school does it take to see my giant has been through enough to turn Jesus to stone? Don't we call Him Rock of Ages? Am I right or wrong?"

Stubby punctuated his argument with the sign of the cross then went out the door and caught himself a deep breath of October's apple cider air.

ACKLEY, IOWA, OCTOBER 23, 1869

Samantha Bale sat in her rocker worried about Halloween. It was not an easy holiday to explain to her pupils at the Ackley Academy. Samantha's attempts to convince the Indians that All Hollows Eve was a time for pleasantries, games, and jolly songs—*for the glory of the Jack is in the lantern and the glory of the pumpkin is the pie*—left the children befuddled.

They knew very well that the holiday sanctioned their white counterparts to carry on like fiends, slamming heads with flour sacks, smearing nasty epithets on doors and windows, tipping gravestones, loosening wheels on wagons, running and screaming like banshees, lighting fires in litter heaps, breaking fences, stealing pets, prying open barn doors and pigpens, terrorizing travelers, wearing demoniacal costumes, disguising their faces with hideous masks, and dribbling red paint like trails of blood. The privileged children of Ackley did not set a good example for their less fortunate brothers and sisters.

The Indian school was a favorite target for ill-conceived pranks by roving bands of ghosts and goblins from respectable homes. The year before, six Indians from the elementary class had been kidnapped, tarred and feathered, then left tied to trees on the Common Ground. Such excessive celebration gave the Indians reason for doubting their teacher's insistence that bobbing for apples was more fun than torturing kittens. Samantha Bale's enthusiastic plans for carving up pumpkins, a party where cookies and candy corn would be served, a performance by the choir and a memorial ser-

vice for the dead, didn't seem sufficient to capture the limited imagination of her charges.

The hardest thing to explain was the custom of trick or treat.
"The idea," she'd told an assembly, "is actually good-hearted. One
taps on the door of a house. When the knock is answered by one
of the inhabitants, the Halloween reveler, sometimes garbed in a
charming costume representing some famous person or even a gentle animal, asks the question, 'Trick or treat?' At which point it is
traditional for the inhabitant of the home to offer some gift. A
fruit, a sweet, even a penny. The gift is accepted, the reveler says a
polite 'thank you' and withdraws. I admit, once upon a time, if no
treat was offered then a trick was the result, and admittedly those
tricks could be annoying, destructive or worse. Before the Enlightenment, the phrase 'trick or treat' implied a kind of blackmail
and signified implicit threat. But today, children, it is all a wonderful charade. Those solicited feign apprehension and fear while
the revelers pretend to be fearsome. In truth, both are willing participants in a reenactment of ancient ritual. In most, but not all,
cases, some treat is proffered, gratefully accepted, and acknowledged. But when there is no treat, there's no retribution. One passes
on to the next house and repeats the process.

"Now, let us rehearse a proper Halloween encounter. Joseph
Snake Tooth, come forward."

"Yes, Miss Bale."

"Knock on my door and say 'Trick or treat.' "

"Knock. Trick or treat."

"Oh, who can it be tap-tapping at my door? Is it a phantom?
Woe is me! Please spare this house! And here is some fudge for
your trouble. Happy Halloween."

"Thank you, Miss Bale."

"Very good, Joseph. Now, Andrew Buffalo Horn, your turn."

"Knock. Trick or treat."

"Sorry, Andrew. I have no treat for you. And what will you do?"

"Slice off your skin for a saddle. Feed your guts to my dog. Hang
your ears from your nipples. Thank you."

"You are not welcome, Andrew, not at all."

Samantha, rocking, considered Reverend Turk's advice to ban all mention of the ambiguous celebration despite its religious purpose. "Remember Pandora? Better keep the box closed," he said. "It seems a shame to deprive the Indians of Halloween joy, but the safest solution might be to lock the doors against confusion. For those savage children, good and bad spirits are no seasonal visitors but constant companions. To mock their ghosts with glowing pumpkin faces might be considered a sacrilege. More danger than diversion. Perhaps your pupils are too close to their origins to distinguish a frivolous trick from barbaric vengeance. Halloween, as we know it, is an acquired taste."

As the Reverend often told her when Samantha's strength wavered, "Education is not a stroll down the lane or simply a matter of numbers and letters. The hardest lessons to deal with concern subtleties of discipline, ethics, and values. But when the spark of truth leaps over the chasm from teacher to child, ah, what reward!"

Samantha was startled by an insistent tap-tapping at her own door. She found the Reverend Henry Turk standing breathless on her threshold, spreading newspaper in her face.

"I was just thinking of you," Samantha said. "Come in. You seem agitated, Henry. Is there trouble?"

"Trouble? No, my dear, not trouble. Vindication! Vindication! I must remain humble. I must not crow. Samantha, I am given the sign I have prayed for these many days and nights."

"Sit, Henry. Relax. What sign do you mean?"

"Here in the *Tribune* from Chicago. On page nine near the bottom:

> Reliable reports have been received of an astonishing discovery, the accidental exhumation of a petrified man of gigantic proportions and unquestioned antique origin. The find came on the farm of one William Newell of Cardiff, New York, in the County of Onondaga, while workers set about the task of digging a well. According to Mr. Newell,

eminent scholars among the first to examine the stone man quickly concluded that this fossilized colossus, amazingly preserved, descended from a race of giants.

"Do you understand what this means, Samantha? My assumptions are validated. The scoffers are routed. I knew it would happen, but not so soon!"

"Henry, that is marvelous news. Tell me the name of the farmer in Cardiff."

"The farmer? William Newell. But what difference? Farmer or carpenter, New York or Nebraska, the find is the thing."

"I feel faint," Samantha said.

"No wonder," said the Reverend Turk. "So do I. A colossus, Samantha. An ancient behemoth!"

Samantha Bale experienced a depressing flash of memory. Little Samantha Hull, before she knew right from wrong or could weigh the relative worth of the trade, alone in her attic with pubescent Stubby Newell lifting her dress, dropping her drawers, and gazing too long at unmentionable parts. In exchange for a ratty straw doll he found in a field. *Trick or treat?*

LAFAYETTE, NEW YORK, OCTOBER 24, 1869

———◦•◦•◦———

"So you're here to see the Bogey Man?" the bartender at the Blue Lion Inn said to Barnaby Rack. "They're running coaches every hour to Newell's plantation. I think they get a quarter each way, but it's a nice enough ride through the hollow and past the Onondaga Indian reservation. Where you coming from? I'd say a distance."

"And you'd be correct. New York City."

"Well, I hope the trip is worthwhile. I ain't seen the giant myself and don't plan to. The whole thing gives me jitters. A man dies, let him lay. Don't dig him up and put him on exhibition."

"What do you boys think about your petrified neighbor?"

"No fossil laying there," said the bearded customer to Barnaby's left. "He's naught but a monument, and I know who made him though nobody takes me serious."

"You know who made him? Tell me, I'll take you serious. It's worth the price of a beer."

"Save your money," the bartender said. "Jabez Cloog is crazy as a bat in a box. What comes to his head comes from the moon."

"Crazy? I don't think so," Jabez said. "You remember that man we called Mr. Croaker? Because he looked the spitting image of a bullfrog? Croaker came here from nowhere. Bought what was left of the Dickerson cabin near Tully. You'd see him come and go but sometimes not for months at a time. That man told me personal that he was a sculptor. The new Michael Angelo. His words, not mine."

"And why do you think Michelangelo made a giant?" Barnaby asked.

"Just to make something big," Jabez said. "Can't think up any other reason. Why does anybody make anything?"

"I mean, what makes you think Croaker fashioned the stone man?"

"Because of what I saw when I went with Sheriff Platz and found Croaker dead. We had us a bitch of a winter three years back. Couldn't move from your home for the snow. Along about March it occurred to somebody that nobody seen Mr. Croaker since November. So we went out to check on him and found him froze to a cube. And there was cute little statues all over the place and the tools to make more. Does that tell you something?"

"Not much," Barnaby said. "Why would you conclude it was Croaker who made a giant and buried him on somebody's farm?"

"I told you the statues we found were little. Croaker said to me, and I swear to it, he was making a master piece. Big enough to see from ten miles. We didn't find no master piece, now did we?"

"Jabez's been living on that story all week," the bartender said. "Him and Tyler Spoon over there got it all figured out."

"What's Tyler got figured?"

"Ask Tyler. But expect it to stand you another pint. Hey, Tyler, come over here. Tell this man what you know about the doings up at Stubby's."

Tyler Spoon, with a bean body and a face that curved out ahead of his shoes, reminded Barnaby of half a parentheses. He got up from his table and took the stool to Barnaby's right.

"Tyler don't know nothing," Jabez said.

"I know this," Tyler said. "About a year ago on a miserable night this heretic came in here with a teamster for company. They sat right over there near the fire. That man raved and raved against all religions. I said to myself, Tyler, if you're ever going to do some favor for God do it now. So when they left here I followed them out with intention to punch his heathen face. But the rain came down so hard and the wind so furious I told myself he's punished enough just to be on the road. Which brings me to their wagon. It carried the biggest box these eyes ever saw. And where were they pointed if not toward Cardiff?"

"That's no story," Jabez said. "None whatsoever. And nobody re-members that man but you."

"You wasn't here to have what to remember," Tyler said.

"Where was I?" the bartender asked.

"It was the time you went up to Cazenovia to look at a patch of land. I don't recall who took your place that night. Same night the creek flooded over."

"So the giant was made by a froze sculptor and carried to his grave by the anti-Christ?" Barnaby said, chewing on bacon rind. "That explains everything. Thank you both, gentlemen, but I think I'll go take a look at the marvel myself before he gets up and heads out of town. You never know with giants. They're an erratic race."

"That's twenty cents you owe me," the bartender said. Barnaby paid and noted the expense under "Local Color."

"My regards to Goliath," the bartender said.

"I'll tell him you said so," Barnaby said.

"They was in with the Jew, you ask me," Tyler said, while Barnaby buttoned his coat and pulled down the flaps on his cap.

"In with what Jew?"

"Bupkin the water witch. Lives at Mrs. Elm's though I don't know why she lets him. Won't do her no good."

"I miss the connection."

"Jew dowsed the spot where the stone man was laying," Jabez said. "Darn good dowser. Almost hung for his trouble, though."

"Knows more than he's telling," Tyler said.

Even John Zipmeister would spark to reports of a Hebrew who'd dowsed up a mammoth. Hell, President Barnum might cotton to a whopper like that. Barnaby Rack was beginning to enjoy this assignment. It firmed his conviction that everybody west, south, and north of Manhattan were kinfolk to vegetables.

CARDIFF, NEW YORK, OCTOBER 25, 1869

Alexander Newell divided the waiting line so that two tributaries fed into the Cardiff Giant's tent. One line was made up of the ordinary curious. The second was a sorry collection of the sick and the maimed. The former were there for amusement, the latter for succor.

Out of natural compassion, Alexander let one foursome of normals enter the giant's sanctum sanctorum for every two groups of the stricken. Alexander couldn't grasp why anyone believed the stone man had healing powers, but his mother explained how the desperately afflicted needed a shrine.

Alexander felt queasy about the sham and deception. Cousin George said the whole scheme was a joke, but where was the laugh scratching dollars from gaspers and groaners? Still, his guilt diluted when the Newells tallied profits. "At the rate things are going," Stubby said, "you'll have your own ship with silk sails."

"Get on in, hurry up," Alexander told the next quartet of life's victims. "You got ten minutes." A blind man was led into the tent by a deaf girl. They were strangers who joined forces to save the blind man a separate charge for the sister who brought him. "You look out for that one," Alexander said to the deaf girl. "We don't want him falling all over the place. If anything gets broke in there, it's on your head, lady."

The second pair in the set was a uniformed soldier in a home-made wheelchair and a bent-over hunchback so old Alexander couldn't tell its sex. "Move along. Plenty are waiting for a look at the petrified marvel and we don't want none disappointed. You know how the sun drops down early these days, so don't waste any time. Your ten minutes start when you pass through the flap."

"What do you see?" the blind man whispered to the deaf girl.

"She don't know what you asked her," the hunchback said. "And don't talk all the time we're inside here. I want it quiet enough to feel feelings."

"That giant is something to behold," the soldier said. "There's a pit dug and shored up by boards where he lays. You can see he was ravished and tormented to the end. His hands are grabbing his ass and his belly with both legs pulled up like a newborn. There's no hair on him, not a whisker. His face is the face of an angel except for it's pocked and splotched black and brown. There's some redness near his nose and eyes which could be from dried blood."

"You ain't here for a speech," the hunchback said. "Just be quiet. We're all on our own."

The blind man lost his sight at age five when he saw his pet dog cut in symmetrical halves by a plow.

The deaf girl survived smallpox at three. To ease the tot's supposed final hours, her parents moved her bed to their room. The last thing she heard through feverish ears was the grunting and moaning of what she thought was the beast come to kill her.

The crippled soldier, kept far from battle, came through the war whole and unscathed. His legs gave out suddenly while his father read him newspaper tales of the feats of dead heroes.

The hunchback was twisted by time. In the quiet of the tent, staring down at the stone man, he remembered halcyon days and sweet nights lost forever.

Endless the parade. Now one with white eyes. One with stuffed ears. One with round legs. One ossified dreamer. Firefly bellies empty of candles. Come to steal my light. Then take what you want and to Hell with you all!

In less than his fair share of time, the blind man ran out of the tent kissing flowers, screaming that he could see.

He was followed by the deaf girl who could hear his hoots and wild shouts.

The young soldier stumbled after them pushing his empty chair.

Only the bent one was left the same, but none in the crowd heeded his sorry condition.

Alexander automatically gestured the next party forward, but nobody moved. It took him a minute to grasp what he saw. When the blind man kissed him, panic hit. He dropped his roll of tickets, grabbed up the money box, and dashed for the house.

Bertha Newell watched from her window. "William," she said to her husband who added up numbers, "we got our hands full. Send for George now."

When Barnaby Rack arrived at the Newell farm, the public was dancing with angels. He found out the reason and sought interviews with the saved.

"What about me? I'm worse than I was," the hunched old man yelled to Barnaby. "My whole trip was a waste. Write that down."

"Sir," Barnaby told him, "I heard a tale of two dismal men who visited St. Bernadette's spring. One was carried on a litter, paralyzed by chronic arthritis. He was a total believer, buoyed by faith. The second man was a desperate atheist, a victim of rheumatism, wheeled to the shrine by orthodox friends. Both were lifted and dipped into blessed water. The reluctant atheist came out of his bath entirely restored. The believer came out still paralyzed and complained bitterly to a priest about God's inequity. 'Rejoice,' the priest said, 'for your litter has been blessed with new handles!" The bent man swung his cane at Barnaby, who managed to dodge hard contact.

It was near five o'clock by the time Barnaby Rack had his audience with the giant. The Autumn sun was weakening fast. Stubby Newell lit a circle of candles to add light inside the tent. Barnaby shared his time with a middle-aged couple from Schenectady and a lusty lady from Buffalo. The couple held hands and kept silent. The Buffalo lady reached over the guard ropes to rub the stone man for luck. "Ain't he just like a cuddly dawg," she said. "Or a bear who et too much honey? You never know what's laying in yer backyard these days."

Barnaby examined the stone miracle worker as if he observed a corpse at a crime scene, distancing himself from emotion. He compared what he saw to a sketch he'd bought from an artist who worked the crowd outside. The likeness was adequate and true in detail but nothing like the actual object. A shifting tide of shadows made the giant seem like a restless sleeper. The pain in his body, the peace in his face, clashed like angry surf against a tranquil beach.

The couple embraced and danced a waltz without music. The lady said, "Isn't that sweet?" Barnaby felt the corpse reach out to grab him and pull him closer, insisting that Barnaby touch its cold skin. "Dance me around," said the Buffalo lady, "if you don't mind." Barnaby complied, glad for her heat.

His ten minutes used, Barnaby left the tent and watched the crowd. There were no more miracles that afternoon but, since the moment of grace, many who were sick claimed improvement. The rejected blamed only themselves.

Is there more to me than I know?

NEW YORK, NEW YORK, OCTOBER 26, 1869

Exclusive to the *New York Clarion:* Cardiff, New York, 25th *instant.* While awaiting transport to this tiny hamlet in the fair County of Onondaga, your reporter used the delay to visit the Unitarian Church in the proud city of Syracuse. News of the discovery of a petrified giant which has excited each citizen prompted a sermon by Reverend S.R. Calthrop who debunked the opinion that the object was a fossilized man, much less of biblical origin.

The good Reverend supported his argument by citing evident marks of stratification in the stone corpse indicating a series of artful cuts as those done by a skilled sculptor, and never by Nature herself. He went on to point out that no limbs are detached, not even a finger, and that a slash near the wrist seems the result of a slip by an artist's hand.

Said Dr. Calthorp, "In the ancient world only the Greek School of Art was capable of such a perfect reproduction of the human form. I have seen no Egyptian or Assyrian sculpture which approached this in anatomical accuracy. Was the artist, then, from some highly civilized society now utterly extinct from this continent, or was he someone from that French colony which occupied Salina and Pompey Hill and Lafayette? The only other hypothesis remaining is that of a gross fraud. One need only say with regard to this that it would require a sculptor of supreme genius wedded to impossible audacity.

"But what did the artist, sighing over lost civilizations, intend his creation to represent? Had he known of the discovery of America by the Northmen, he might have had in his thoughts some gigantic Eric or Harold, shot through with an Indian's poisoned arrow; his body is dying but the strong soul still rules the face which smiles grandly in death. If you had objected that there was too much mind shining through the features, the sculptor might have answered that the closed eyes saw in prophetic vision that men of his race would one day rule where he had lain down to die."

Is the Reverend Calthorp correct that a statue has been unearthed, or is it, as many scientific observers say, a genuine fossil? I can tell you this much: Today your reporter was privileged to observe not one, not two, but three marvels of instant healing which defy explanation and seem far beyond the power of any statue of stone or even the finest Carrara marble.

Glorious sight was returned to a blind man. A deaf woman could suddenly hear. A crippled warrior left his wheelchair behind him. The splendors of vision, the raptures of song, the gifts of mobility, all were restored in the presence of a man turned to stone!

In Cardiff town, an extraordinary hush prevails, as befits the aftermath of wonderment. Tonight, the church is filled with worshippers who forgo thoughts of sleep. They pray and they sing, they wave Old Glory as if in trance, and their mood is infectious. Who could fail to be moved by such events and their broad implications? This reporter, for one, who is not made of stone, joins with the mass in devout appreciation! *Land where our fathers died, Of Thee I sing!*

"This came from Rack?" John Zipmeister said to a copy boy. "Swear it came off the wire, you little bastard, or I'll fry your liver in a skillet."

LAFAYETTE, NEW YORK, OCTOBER 28, 1869

Mrs. Elm opened her door and felt her heart skip. A large man looked down at her through burning black eyes. The coal eyes were set deep in a face hidden behind a bush of white beard. He wore a wide-brimmed black hat and a long black silk coat. Gray curls hung down from his ears. He carried a carpetbag ornamented with olive trees and a paper bag smelling of fish. Mrs. Elm thought Death came to claim her, disguised as a snowman dressed like a scarecrow.

"Good morning, lady," he said in a dangerous accent. "Is this the residence of Aaron Bupkin?"

"Bupkin has a room here," Mrs. Elm said. "So what?"

"Please, I would like to see him. My name is Isaac Bupkin. His grandfather. He wasn't expecting me so when you tell him I'm here, tell him slowly. It will come as a shock."

"Bupkin," Mrs. Elm yelled upstairs. "Another one here to see you. This ain't no hotel."

In Aaron's room, Isaac Bupkin sat on the bed, drinking cold tea from his own bottle. "What did she mean, another one here to see you?"

"I'm not sure," Aaron said. "She could have meant another Jew or she could have meant another visitor. Some New York reporter came earlier asking all kind of questions. This business with the giant stirred up a hornet's nest."

"Your letter frightened me, Aaron. I want you back in Boston. It's better for us in the city. We shouldn't be spread out one by one."

"If I was going to leave I would have left. I'm staying here. I wrote you, I saw twenty acres near Ithaca."

"If you had money to buy land they wouldn't sell to you."

"The farm is abandoned, falling apart, owned by a widow who moved to Vermont. She'll sell to anybody."

"I have a fool for a grandson."

"Grandpa Isaac, when I came here I knew this was my place to be. Like I know my name. I can't explain the feeling."

"Your place? You wrote they almost hung you. Some nice place. You get a good night's sleep around here, Aaron?"

"Besides, I have a business here. Between the dowsing and peddling, I make a living. Did you get my goods? When will they ship?"

"Everything ordered. They should ship any day."

"This thing with the giant has got them all boiling. Everybody and his uncle making flags. I can sell anything red, white, or blue."

"You saw the shlimazel?"

"I'm dying to see him but I'll wait a few weeks."

"It, not *him.* Thank God you didn't see *it,"* Isaac said.

"What does that mean?"

"You want something to eat? At least what I brought is glatt kosher."

"I'm not hungry."

"Since when?"

"Grandpa, tell me, why did you say thank God I didn't see it?"

"You know Rebbe Lowe?"

"From Dorchester?"

"From Prague in the Middle Ages. He made the golem. You know the golem?"

"The fairy tale? About a creature made from dirt and clay who protected the ghetto?" Aaron said.

"Some fairy tale. The golem was strong like a house. Rebbe Lowe found out he could bring it alive by putting a scroll with God's name under its tongue."

"It had a tongue?"

"Why shouldn't it have a tongue? The rebbe needed a place to put the scroll so he added a tongue. In the beginning, the golem was the Rebbe's best friend. It went out and gave knocks to bad goyim. The Jews never had it so good. But the golem was made. from what the Bible calls 'unformed substance.' There was life in it but no trace of God. So the golem blew around like a storm. It wouldn't listen even to Rebbe Lowe any more. All that golem could do was kill, burn, destroy. Even pious Jews and nice goys. Whatever got in the way. So the Rebbe had to crack it apart with clubs and hammers, whatever they had in those days. He was sad about it but what else could he do? I would have done the same thing myself."

"What was he sad about?"

"Rebbe Lowe created life. There was affection. The golem was like a member of the family. The Rebbe's own son. Lowe was a great Rebbe with good intentions yet he committed the worst sin. He played God. Not bad to have a golem around when you need one, but what comes from 'unformed substance' goes out of control."

"What did the Prague paper say? 'SCHMUCK RUNS AMOK'?"

"It's no joke. We shouldn't get too close to certain secrets. Maybe someday, not yet."

"I feel for Rebbe Lowe and the golem. But why bring it up? Is it my fault I dowsed a giant? I was looking for water, not golems. I don't know if the Cardiff Giant has a tongue but, believe me, I don't carry around God's name on scroll and, if I did, I wouldn't put it under my own tongue. So why come all the way from Boston, Massachusetts, to Lafayette, New York, to warn about golems?"

"Tell me something. Suppose what they found is a golem from some other Rebbe with good intentions?"

"It's definitely no golem. They say it might be a Viking."

"A Viking down here? That makes no sense."

"More sense a Viking than a spare golem."

"Is it circumcised, Aaron?" Isaac whispered.

"How should I know if it's circumcised? Somebody told me it has a long schlong. I know they covered its parts for the sake of the women and children. I never heard the word circumcised."

"Would they tell you?"

"They probably would have hung me if it was circumcised."

"Maybe it's the real reason they covered the parts. To keep quiet that it's circumcised."

"I'll go take a look in a few days, Grandpa Isaac. Then I'll send you a telegram."

"I always thought to myself maybe if Rebbe Lowe circumcised his golem, he could have saved himself trouble. A circumcised golem would behave better."

"That's a theory you'll never prove. But take credit for an original idea. Write a letter to the *Globe.*"

"That thing you found might have a tongue and something under the tongue. It could be of 'unformed substance.' "

"I didn't find it. They found it. And it's more Goliath than David. I don't think their stone man is a special friend of the Jews."

"We can't take the chance."

"What chance can't we take?"

"To let loose such a monster. Because you know who'll get blamed."

"Their giant is laying there. It's not bothering anybody."

"It heals the sick. What the golem did to make its reputation. But later, vay is mir."

"You must be tired, Grandpa Isaac. I'll find you a blanket. Take a nap."

"It's got to be circumcised."

"You want some schnapps? Apple brandy?"

"Promise me, Aaron."

"Promise you what? Am I a mohel? I live here. I don't go around circumcising strangers."

"We all have a purpose in life. We are here for a purpose."

"I believe that. But that's not my purpose."

"Listen to the peddler, the dowser. Aaron Bupkin, do something your grandfather can talk about in the synagogue."

"You'll stay here tonight. Tomorrow you'll go home to Boston.

The giant has nothing to do with me or you or the twelve tribes of Israel."

"What must be done will be done," Isaac said. "Alevi."

CARDIFF, NEW YORK, OCTOBER 29, 1869

Alexander Newell raked earth on the floor of the tent. Finished combing, he patted down ruts with the back of a shovel. Then he took his mother's duster, jumped the rope that kept gawkers away from the giant, and slapped its face with turkey feathers. Powdery dust flaked off the stone.

Alexander didn't like being alone with the creature. He knew it was only a statue Cousin George put there and no cause for conniption. But even the white puffs of grit gave him goose bumps. They floated like clouds on the moon.

He dusted under the loincloth without looking down. That giant was hung like his pa. When Stubby went around naked, Alexander stared up at the ceiling and wished his old man was more modest about exposing his parts. It was Alexander's feeling that a father should not put organs on display for his son to compare. In gross violation of natural law, Stubby flaunted his equipment and joked how he had to take care not to trip on his balls.

Alexander thought about the toils of the day. At least a thousand people showed up at the farm, a few hundred stayed long after dark. He had all he could do to clear them out before midnight. A few families still hid in the cornfield, afraid to light fires no matter the chill; men, women, and their children with no place to go, wanting to be there in case of a miracle. It bothered him to know how dumb people could get.

It burned Alexander that his own parents, like Cousin George, distrusted him keeping their secret. Stubby had a fit when he saw the man from the *Clarion* write down what Alexander told him, and all he told was common knowledge. "Nothing to nobody, how many times I got to say it?" Stubby yelled, then gave Alexander a whack on the cheek.

Alexander slapped the stone face with his duster and saw more smoke rise. If anybody had reason not to trust, it was Alexander Newell himself. He was there when a cripple, a blind man, and a girl with no hearing were cured of their blight. He heard the Reverend Locke say the statue was petrified flesh. He saw people on their knees, even his pa on the ground, to give thanks. Hell, the newspapers wrote it all up. So where was the truth and who to believe? Alexander put his ear to the stone man's chest, listening for a heartbeat.

These are my hours with no eyes pleading. I am back to the time of formation. Swirl of stars. Dance of comets. I frolic with my Source. Ride meteors. Splash through molten pools. Whee. Hooray. Hurrah. Take your hands off me, Pimple Face. Go away.

Cousin Angelica once gave Alexander a conch shell. When he held it to his ear, he could hear every sea in the world and the moaning of mermaids. Now, from the giant's barn of a chest, Alexander detected similar sounds. Was it water running deep in the earth that sent up those echoes? Alexander closed his eyes. He saw porpoises, dolphins, whales, great serpents. Squid trailed tentacles through a shower of pearls. Fish with wings leapt at a rainbow. He saw the ship he knew for his own rise and dive through purple waves. Alexander pulled his ear away from that euphony, opened his eyes to close out those visions.

"I'm cold as a bone and sweating like a pig," he said to the giant. "You miserable sonabitch, whatever you're up to, I'm done around here."

BRIDGEPORT, CONNECTICUT, OCTOBER 30, 1869

General Thumb was announced, bowed, dashed into the room, jumped onto Barnum's wide lap, and let his body go limp. Barnum waved Thumb's arms then twisted his head side to side, up and down.

"Hello, Thumbkin," Barnum said, while Tom flapped his gums.

"Hello, you gross fraud," Thumb said in a falsetto voice. "They saw your lips move."

"My lips did not move," Barnum said, tipping Thumb's head toward the floor. "I am the greatest ventriloquist and you the worst dummy God ever made. Why did I rescue you from the garbage heap?"

"The one who tossed me away threw with more accuracy than you throw your voice."

"You ask for a sound thrashing, Halfman."

"You're not half the man to do it," Thumb said while Barnum made his arms flail.

"Be cautious, Thumbkin. My patience is thin."

"It's the only thing thin about you."

"Do you dare call Barnum obese, you twit?"

"Haven't you heard? Barnum's become an obese obtuse recluse."

"Recluse? I'm a prominent figure. Who don't know my name?"

"That your figure is prominent I do not dispute, sir. But names and fames are quickly erased. They may know you in the suburbs, but memory fades fast in New York."

"If I spend my declining years declining, does it mean I'm forgotten?"

"No, they'll remember you as a colossal fossil, P.T. But not the fossil you might have been. And speaking of fossils . . ."

"Don't tell me, Thumbkin," Barnum said, yanking Tom's thinning hair. "I can still read your mind though the type is so small. Does the fossil you're ready to speak of reside up in Cardiff?"

"So Barnum keeps up with the news instead of making news himself?"

"I'm familiar with current events," Barnum said.

"And when you read of the petrified giant, did that odd event stir some current in your copious gut?"

"I must admit, Thumbkin, I experienced a twitch."

"Well, well," said the General. "I'd say you should have felt a twitch, twang, and tingle."

"You're the dummy, sir. You say what I want you to say."

"This dummy says Barnum's a gas bag tied too hard to the past and beyond levitation."

"Do you?" Barnum bounced Tom on his thighs. "And what would you say if I told you I've already dispatched my ambassador to visit that very stone man in person?"

"If Barnum said that, I might kiss him."

"Then he won't say it."

"Can it be true, sir, that your resurrection is imminent?"

"And possibly Tom Thumb's. If his terms are agreeable." Barnum made the General's hands clap.

"I hear the General's dance card's full," Thumb said. "The offers pour in."

"A pity, but so what? There are scores of tiny men ready to waltz with Goliath."

"But none more graceful."

"Alas, that's the truth," Barnum said. "Though it hurts me to say so. Now, Thumbkin, will you join us for dinner?"

"I'm famished from my journey. I could eat a flea."

"For you there's a flea on the menu," Barnum said, lifting his guest in the air. "God, it's good to see you in the pink, Tom, and looking so fit."

"And a treat to see you posture in your pasture, P.T. You haven't changed a bit since last month."

"Some refreshment to whet your appetite, General? Would a drop of port be in order?"

"Any port in a storm, Mr. Barnum."

Barnum poured the wine into Waterford crystal. "To the giant from Genesis and his diminutive nemesis."

"That's the long and the short of it," Thumb said, lifting his glass.

CARDIFF, NEW YORK, OCTOBER 31, 1869

George Hull sat in Stubby Newell's kitchen, going over Stubby's ledger of income and expenses. The numbers were sweeter than George had imagined. He tried hard not to demonstrate too much satisfaction. "Impressive," George said.

"The money keeps flowing," Stubby said. "I can't believe what's going on here."

"Just the beginning," George said. "Tip of the iceberg."

"The only sour note here is Alexander. No sign, no trace. It was all too much for the boy. It's hardest on Bertha. She's sure Alexander headed to Gloucester for the life of a sailor."

"There are worse lives than a life on the sea."

"He was never an easy boy. I wish you'd got here sooner, George. You might have talked him out of it. He'd have listened to you. Bertha says he'll get himself drowned."

"It's Alexander's time to wander. I'm sure he's well and thriving. You'll see I'm right. He'll walk in here one day with a stuffed whale on his back."

"Amen to that. And your kin? How are they?"

"Father's fine. Full of plans. Ben and Loretta are in New York building a fancy new Hull's Humidor for Manhattan."

"None of them know what we're up to? Not even Angelica?"

"No, not even Angelica. I hope Bertha won't let anything slip."

"Bertha won't say two words on the giant. She's a strange woman. Part of her here and part elsewhere. She knows and she don't know. I mean, she knows but I can't tell what she thinks about knowing. Bertha's hard to pin down."

"Well, so far so good."

"Better than good. Yesterday I went up to Syracuse and popped six thousand dollars in my account. Six thousand dollars. When do you want your cut of the pie?"

"Not yet, Stubby."

"You're a trusting man."

"When you do the accounting of what's yours and what's mine, take another five percent for yourself. I think you deserve it."

"George, I am glad to hear you say that. Fifteen percent is fairer than ten considering the work I put in."

"Just keep in mind I have others to pay. I won't name names, but don't think George Hull too greedy."

"Did I ever think that? All this is your doing and thank God for it. Since the miracle was told in the papers they're coming so fast I can't count them. We set up three more feeding stands and sell out what we got. Oysters to oats, cider to milk."

"I had a hunch we'd hit big, but not so hard or so fast. Nor that the vultures would be so quick to circle."

"Who don't want to buy in? The last offer I got was thirty-seven thousand five hundred for three-quarters ownership. That's more money than I knew was in the world. Maybe it is time to consider doling out shares."

"The whole of America is panting to see the petrified man."

"They can't all come to my farm, George."

"But we can go to them. Before the heavy snows, we'll ship Goliath to Syracuse. You find us a hall up there. In the Spring, to New York. Then maybe Boston. After that . . ."

"I don't know, George. I don't know. You got me following a stone man for the rest of my life."

George closed the ledger and shook it at Stubby. "Any time you want off the train, you tell me."

"Don't get me wrong. It's not like Stubby Newell ain't enjoying himself. Christ, have we got them by the short hairs or not? Though sometimes it anguishes me to see men of such reputation arguing man or statue when the answer is neither. Makes me wonder what reputation is and what it's worth. Are we all rattling around in an empty washtub? Is the whole world full of beans?"

"I'd say so, give or take."

"I don't relish the feeling of protecting a lie."

"No lie to protect, cousin. Did you say what you found? Did you ask for opinions? All you did was turn up dirt on a rock some call a giant."

"The praying and moaning got to Alexander."

"They moan, they pray. What's that got to do with you or me?"

"Not a damn thing, George. But I'm glad you're here to remind me and I wish you could stay."

"Only a few days. My excuse for coming was to try out Simon & Sons' Goliath brand."

"It's a good smoke. They might catch on. Ten cents is steep though for folks around here. You should put a flag on your wrappers, George. To go with the flag I draped over Goliath's plunger. Since I switched Old Glory for Bertha's sweater, I get plenty compliments. People hanging flags from every pole they can find."

"Good idea, Stubby. 'Land of the pilgrim's pride.' "

Upstairs, in Alexander's abandoned room, Bertha Newell tried to plump a depleted down pillow. She gave up on the pillow and laid out a patchwork quilt made by her mother for a wedding gift. That quilt kept its color and cheered the small space.

While she straightened the bed, Bertha watched Angelica Hull unpack a fancy suitcase and unfold a dress fit for any queen. It was good having another woman in the house. Bertha liked what little she knew of George's wife and sensed she might be a soulmate. They were both private ladies who hardly stirred air when they moved. Angelica was younger, pampered by Hull money, but Bertha could forgive those advantages. She knew Angelica's trail of tears. It was hard to envy the girl's good looks or begrudge her a few luxuries.

"This is a nice room," Angelica said. "Very airy."

"We added it on for my mother but she passed on before moving in. Just as well. How would she have got up and down the stairs?"

"I'm sorry," Angelica said.

"Ten years already. Rest in peace. That was her bed, though. I made Stubby get it to bring here. I like those carvings all over the posts. All kind of birds. When I was a girl I made believe I could hear them singing. I could. Alexander slept there before he run off."

"A beautiful bed," Angelica said, careful to skirt talk of the newly departed Alexander or his older sister, who'd died of the cholera. George warned how a wrong word could snap Bertha shut like a scallop. She'd stay silent for months at a time.

Bertha also had a few subjects to keep off Angelica's table, especially anything to do with the stone man. Angelica hadn't mentioned those goings on but she would sooner or later. "Could you show me that dress, or is it a gown?" Bertha asked.

Angelica lifted the mystery dress from her trunk and spread it over the quilt. She was startled to see it in Cardiff. Her sister-in-law must have packed it without asking. For some reason it bothered Loretta that the dress hadn't been worn yet, especially after Angelica took so much time to alter it. The Newell farm in Cardiff was certainly no place for its debut.

Loretta should never have taken such a liberty. It was probably because Angelica wouldn't let her borrow the dress for New York. When Loretta asked, Angelica said no in such a strong voice she turned herself pink. Something about that dress irked Loretta as much as it intrigued Angelica. It would serve Loretta right if she gave it to Bertha, who surely needed something to raise her low spirits.

"Do you like it?"

"That's a dress for a dream," Bertha said.

"Please don't get the notion that your cousins in Binghamton go around wrapped in satin," Angelica said. "I just didn't know what to pack for this visit or what exactly to expect up here with all the excitement. You've got to tell me the whole story and leave nothing out."

"You mean about the fossil?"

"Of course I do."

"What's to tell? We found a big doll. He's laying out there in the tent and that's all there is to it. Bunch of fools make a fuss over nothing. He cost me a son and I don't want to dwell on him."

"I understand," Angelica said. Embracing her, Angelica discovered Bertha Newell wore her bones close to her skin. "I'm sorry I brought it up."

"Don't matter. Why don't you go see Old Stony? That's my name for him and it fits."

"No hurry," Angelica said. "I was never much for giants, gnomes, trolls, elves, or the like. Not since a girl and never will be. It's not in my nature."

"I guess he'll wait for you," Bertha said.

Stubby stopped the sale of tickets and led George into the tent. "There he is, cousin, right as rain."

"The year underground did Goliath a favor," George said. "He never looked better. So damn real."

"He does look like he belongs there," Stubby said.

"The setup is perfect. You did good, cousin."

"Just followed your instructions and added my touch here and there," Stubby said. "The hard part was getting the seepings drained from the trench and the sides shored up. If I dowsed the spot instead of the Jew I'd have picked us a drier place."

"If you'd dowsed the spot alarms would go off in some curious heads. Got to keep a step ahead at all times. Think things through. That's the art."

"You're the man knows the art, George."

"Yes, I'll admit it. It's a gift, I suppose, and I've got it."

"With Alexander gone, I hired Smith Woodmansee to sell tickets and John Hagens to keep count. Those two hate each other like Cain and Abel, so taken together I trust them."

"Well, let's let them sell tickets."

"I'll go check the cigar table. Should be up and working by now. Got John Parker selling your Goliaths. Deal we made, John keeps three cents on the dollar, fifteen cents on a box. And there's some man from New York waiting for me in the house. Always something to do."

"I'll just wander around for a while," George said. "Maybe take Angelica for a trot up the mountain. She likes watching the leaves change."

"Sure, take my rig," Stubby said. "If there's any fresh miracles I'll holler."

"If Goliath's in a mood for miracles, let him get my bowels moving. Whenever I travel what I eat turns to brick. Least he can do's let George Hull take a well-deserved dump."

The George returns to mock me. Too late for that. This ground altered more than my surface. THEE and THY is my name now. Goliath has his own flag. I bequeath. I bestow. I am to the verticals as my Source is to me. Here come others. More need and more noise. I can't go so I'll stay. Let them come. What are bowels which won't move? When I know they will quake, George. My mood is good today.

From the heights of Bear Mountain, George Hull saw caravans of coaches and wagons head for Stubby Newell's farm. Watching from his catbird seat, George felt such a surge of elation he whooped like an Apache. Angelica, who never heard her husband make such a sound, jumped like a startled fawn. She nearly lost balance and fell off the wagon. George reached out to catch her arm. It was their first human contact in months.

For almost a year her husband kept himself sealed in an unlabeled wrapper. George went on his sales trips and functioned well enough at home, but Angelica knew he lived outside his body. In sleep, he had long debates with invisible adversaries. Awake, he watched weather like a desperate farmer.

For peculiar amusement, George buried a curious assortment of objects—broken crockery, glass, iron, a crèche complete with plaster figures of Mary, Joseph, the Magi, a sheep, goat, horse, cow, and of course Baby Jesus—out in the garden. Days later, he dug them up only to plant them again.

When he wasn't talking to Simon or Ben, George talked to himself. He read biographies of heroes, ancient and modern, or absorbed himself in archaeological texts. He browsed catalogues from expensive stores as if he were studying the classics. He sent for travel folders and pamphlets on finance and investment. He clipped articles from magazines and newspapers reporting on theatrical spectacles from as far away as London and Paris.

Between his work in the factory and those odd recreations, George used himself so thoroughly each day that at night there was no energy left for other activity. He would flop into bed, pull into a ball, and blow out like a candle.

At first, Angelica enjoyed the relief from their automatic couplings. After months of avoidance, she felt deprived. Not of the exercise but of its consequence. Without George's slamming and gushing, no tenant would fill the cradle waiting empty in a corner of their bedroom.

She saw George grow thinner, his face turn pale, his manner go skittish, and wondered if she was to blame for her husband's decline. Angelica didn't want to be widowed again, a dry eggshell rolling through indifferent rooms. She cooked his favorite dishes, bought new nightgowns and perfumes, tried to interest herself in his latest obsessions. Nothing helped. George kept to himself, pristine and preoccupied, as if he waited some sign or signal to return him to life.

His sudden whoop in the wagon, and the grin on his face when he saved her toppling, came as a shock. When he laughed loud and long at Angelica's fluster, her amazement increased.

"Why the outburst, George?"

"Natural exuberance, my dear. Look around you. Taste the air. Appreciate so much beauty. Soon the last leaf will be gone and forgotten. Do you think those leaves know they're doomed and enjoy one final celebration? What color! What a fabulous bounty for us to enjoy."

"The country seems to agree with you."

"Oh, it does. I'm a country boy at heart, and nothing like nature to nurture body and soul. From up here all things seem possible. This wagon of ours is like a toy boat on an ocean of orange and gold. I could envy Alexander Newell, wherever he is, bouncing on waves. Do you feel the majesty of the mountain?"

"But you must know the answer. I'm a child of the woods."

"Of course, so you are. Look down there. That colorless patch is Stubby's farm. See, there's the tent where his stone man holds court. And those dots are people. Hundreds of people and more on the way. I feel good for the Newells, up from the dead. I feel good for myself and young as a sunrise."

"And for us, George? Do you feel good for us?"

"It goes without saying."

"I've been worried about you. You seemed so distant of late."

"Never worry about George Hull or his powers of recuperation. If I've been floundering, now I'm solid in place and ready for conquest."

George let out another war whoop and gave the horse a hard swat. They headed higher, toward more splendor. Angelica wondered why she felt so alone in that radiant bath.

When night fell in Cardiff, Stubby went back to his ledger. "Our best day yet," he said, adding columns. "I think we've earned a short snort."

Bertha poured white lightning from a jug. George stood to offer a toast. "To you, cousins," he said, "and to Uncle Fossil. 'There were giants in the earth in those days,' but none richer or more generous."

"First thing I'll do with my share is buy a new dog," Stubby said. "Maybe the one up the road who killed Sherman. Mean bastard, but hell, he's got spunk and did me a favor. George, you don't mind if I filch a few simoleons from the box, now do you?"

"Go ahead, but don't make a habit of it."

"You heard him, Bertha. A real gentleman. That calls for another libation. And this time, don't skimp on the juice."

"Douse the light," Angelica yelled from the porch. "Here I come, ready or not."

"Let's watch our talk," George said, holding two fingers over his mouth. "Come on in," he yelled to his wife.

Bertha snuffed out the table lamp. They heard the door creak and Angelica's footsteps. A pumpkin face with slit eyes, pyramid nose, and fanged mouth floated toward them sizzling. Yellow candle flame seared its wet pulp.

"Happy Halloween," Angelica said, holding out the pumpkin to George, who recoiled. Something about that thing gave him the willies, a hissing reminder of death.

"You got a real talent," Bertha said.

"Scooped enough of his brains for two pies," Angelica said.

"Light the lamp," George said. "I don't care much for sitting in the dark."

"That's some face you carved out," Stubby said. "I think you earned yourself a drink."

"She don't drink," George said.

"Maybe one for the holiday," Angelica said.

"There you go," Bertha said, pouring. "Elixir of life."

"To loved ones here and gone," Angelica said. The drink slashed her throat like a sword. She felt it snake gullet to gut trailing fire. Angelica's vision jiggled. Her pumpkin's face flattened and spread in a puddle then snapped back to itself.

"Home brew," Bertha said. "Don't ask what's in it."

"Stimulating," Angelica said.

"Put hair on your chest," Bertha said, pouring more.

"That's a disgusting expression to use on a woman," George said.

"No harm done," Stubby said. "Don't think Angelica should run up and shave."

"No need for vulgar conversation," George said.

"We're country," Stubby said. "Me and Bertha don't know better. Maybe now with the stone man we'll both go to Yale. I got friends there these days."

"Do you have a guard at the gate tonight?" George said.

"Hear, Bertha? You turned him serious. No, George, no guard. I tried to hire Gideon but he's occupied with family. Wouldn't worry. Halloween or not, kids don't bother us this far out. But with the giant for attraction, I suppose I should check around. Want to walk with me? Get some air?"

"Why not?" George said. "Do us both good."

"Those two," Bertha said when the men were gone. "Do they like each other or hate each other? I can't tell about men."

Angelica was focused on her pumpkin head, expanding, shrinking, twirling its eyes, gnashing ugly teeth. "I'm sure George is very fond of William," she said while the pumpkin popped its cheeks and let its head whirl like the planet.

"If you say so," Bertha said, tilting the jug toward Angelica's glass.

"No more for me." The candle sputtered inside the orange skull. Angelica saw pumpkin eyes blink to black. "Well, maybe a smidgen for the ghoulies and ghosties."

Later, in bed, Angelica listened to George Hull's violent snores. They spun out of him like spiderwebs filling the bedroom. The webs were turned silver by the Halloween moon. After his whoops on Bear Mountain and his talk of conquest, she'd expected a bit more attention. But Bertha's brew sang a powerful lullaby. George had to be helped upstairs.

Angelica remembered that Bertha's own mother died in that

bed. If legends were true and ghosts swam through moonlight, the old lady might be with them under the patchwork. Just as well George stayed asleep.

Angelica got up and crossed to the curtained closet. She pulled off her nightgown and found her mystery dress. The satin felt delicious against her bare flesh. She decided the dress would be Bertha's, but wearing it once seemed only proper. She saw herself split down the middle in Bertha's cracked mirror. All in white, Angelica looked like her own wraith.

The room suddenly swirled. Angelica knew she was drunk as a sot but what of it? In George's jacket, hung over a chair, she found a Goliath, stripped it, bit off the tip, and lit it with a sulfur match. Then she dodged George's snores, sneaking lithely between them, and edged out the door blowing smoke.

She heard Stubby cough and a wheezing from Bertha, intimate sounds owned by the house. Angelica headed for the porch where strangers belong. A cold wind sneaked under her skirt.

She wanted a moment alone and invisible but the wide night wouldn't hide her. Every star kindled her mystery dress. Every bat and owl watched while she ran for the tent.

Even inside, light clung to her dress. She saw the light came from a lantern turned low. Stubby must have let it burn for protection. Angelica surveyed the house of the giant. High time she paid him a visit, and properly dressed for the moment. There he was, sleeping stone.

Angelica took a puff on George's cigar and curtseyed her greeting. To see better she moved toward the rope defining his space. Even that vantage was too dim for good vision. Angelica crawled under the rope to see better.

In an instant she knew him. Contorted body, arms in grotesque self-embrace, legs locked together, face past rage. She saw it was Hamish. Ashen, bloodless, betrayed. Angelica screamed and fell on the body, kissing his thighs, hands, and mouth. She pulled off the flag that covered his sex and licked the stone wet. She lifted her dress and straddled his hips, shoving at him while she pounded his chest. Giant arms grabbed her. Her legs pulled apart. Stone lips pressed her mouth. She was entered, filled, dissolved to frenzy, burst like a pod.

When Angelica opened her eyes she saw George Hull's face looming over her, calm as the giant's. Without saying a word he lifted her up off the ground and carried her outside.

"Wait," George said.

He went back into the tent and found Alexander's rake propped in a corner. He slammed its iron head against the giant's grand phallus, again and again until the stone fractured. George used the flag to wipe his wife's blood from stone thighs then threw it back over Goliath's wounded prick.

"Come," he said to Angelica, who sat on the ground watching the dawn. He led her gently to the house and up to their room, undressed her and put her to bed. He climbed in beside her, pulled the quilt over them, and held her close.

"Sleep," George said.

Angelica lay with her eyes shut sorting through dreams. Hamish was dead, done with, final. She reached to wipe tears from her cheeks and felt her hands burn.

"You'll feel better tomorrow," George said.

"I have something to tell you," Angelica said. "I have my child. You can go now."

George lay awake thinking. The power of the giant was gigantic. The stone man would crown him emperor, make him sultan, lift him from cigars to sainthood. Give him more choices than trees in the forest. Anything, anywhere, his for the taking.

George Hull had been chosen to cross the horizon but with no map or compass and no turning back. He looked at the dawn as frightened of freedom as he had been of bondage.

George listened to Angelica's breath. Who was that woman? Whose child did she carry? Whose wife was she now?

Patience, please. If this is a bother, forgive in advance. Here is what happened. I lay enjoying my rest. Mindless. Lulled by the night. Then, Source,

I became aware of an alien presence. First, a lambent glow examined my form. I thought it Your messenger. It moved closer until I determined a she thing, one of them. Only another with starving eyes. But then I feel her. Do I make any sense? She washes through me hotter than acid. Astonishment at such blatant invasion. Nothing like it to compare. More, Source. I smell her. What fragrance. She holds me. I know her hands. Next her mouth. Again I say, This must be Your courier come from first fire. Then she mounts me, beats me, pushes my third leg with such urgent passion I thunder amazement. I am possessed by the urge to consume her. Be contained by her. Vanish into her. I feel juncture. Nothing makes sense. I verge on motion. I swear it. I know it. Wait! The George appears. Dares rip her away. I rage. I fume. Next tilts her backward and puts himself in where I was and belong. I am left rumbling, retching, reaching. Then he carries her away but, hear me carefully, Source, returns alone to smash at me like a madman. Unlike the hour of my shaping, he comes to destroy me. I hear a snap and feel it too. I try to tell him my innocence. Share my news. Ask a few honest questions. But he quits me and goes out toward the morning. Oh, yes, the snap. Part of me is diminished but not much. Only a finger of my curious protuberance. Still, when the she one bent there to taste, made her body my doorway, that silly stalactite had profound purpose. Source, intervene. I know them too well now. I am them. Save me. Make me immune. When they beg how will I bear it? Give back my cherished indifference. If I have offended You or envied those crushables, I repent. Purge, scourge, do what you do best. I renounce. I return. But, Source, can I forget? Oh! My prominence pulsates. Bittersweet aftershock. Ah!

The Goliath cigar Angelica Hull left smoldering on the tent floor burned to a stump in the mouth of Donald Stukey, a horse-faced boy from Lafayette. His friend, Francis Jones, built like a pear, lumbered after him, carrying a spent lantern, a can of green paint meant to decorate the giant, and the cold crown of the stone man's penis. They ran for five miles without speaking a word.

"Why am I mule?" Francis gasped. "I got to rest."

"They catch us, they kill us," Donald said. "After we saw what we saw."

"It's light out," Francis said, stopping. "They can't hurt you in the light."

"You could be right on that," Donald said. "And you could be dead wrong."

"You gonna tell what happened back there?"

"When I'm an old man. Not before. And you do the same unless you're crazy. A giant and two haunts doing it in a tent? We'll get put away if you blab half that story."

"Your idea to go paint up that giant. Didn't reckon on spooks, did you?" Francis said. "You think they'll come after us when it goes dark again?"

"They didn't get we was there and they too busy humping to care a hot damn. If they come after you act like you don't know their complaint."

"You can't lie to spirits."

"Why the hell not? Sure you can. Not the spirits I worry on anyhow. Best get rid of what you stole because bet that stone man gonna look for it and don't screw with no giant."

"You said to take it."

"Well, no sense to leave it behind for Stubby Newell to find too soon. Didn't want him chasing our ass down this road, did we? Just dump it some safe place and forget where you left it."

"I'll dump it right here."

"No, Francis, no. Got to hide it away. Got to give it a few days to shake off your scent so's the giant can't track you like a bloodhound. I got to think of everything, don't I? Leave it to you and we're both up shit creek."

Back in Lafayette, Donald Stukey spit out the cigar butt and ran for his house. A block from his own place, Francis Jones snuck into Mrs. Elm's garden and disposed of his burden in a mushroom patch. Francis didn't need any Donald to tell him Jews lop off their own cocks. When Goliath came looking, he might just as well find his where a Jew lived.

LAFAYETTE, NEW YORK, NOVEMBER 1, 1869

Isaac Bupkin made it a point to rise with the sun. He wrapped tfillin around his left arm and across his forehead, said morning prayers, and went out to test the weather. He did stretches, knee bends, took a dozen deep breaths, and listened to the few stupid birds left in town. In Boston the streets would already be alive, but this was the country. Isaac didn't see a living soul. He could understand why Aaron wanted a life there, however improbable. With this kind of quiet, a country mouse could live longer than a city mouse in the same amount of time.

Isaac looked at Mrs. Elm's lawn, her trees, her flowers, her vegetable patch. He thought back to the shtetl in Poland where he spent his first years. Also the country, everything nice except for a few small problems like occasional pogroms. On a morning like this, clear and bracing, he could even feel nostalgic for Cossacks.

A robin dressed like a soldier pecked around Mrs. Elm's garden. Isaac considered its existence. Short and sweet. Mindless flight. Pleasure from seeds, bugs, and worms. Memories without guilt. For the bird it was probably interesting.

Every life had some compensations. Mrs. Elm got a face like rancid butter but she was also given a green thumb. Her garden was abundant. Isaac recognized carrots and radishes, lettuce and kale. A few tomatoes were ripening, even in November. There were cucumbers and peppers, melons and squash. Wooden boxes of mushrooms grew in the shade of a raspberry bush. In the city, raspberries were a delicacy, out here for the picking.

Would Mrs. Elm begrudge an old man a few raspberries? Isaac

lifted his frock coat and stepped between plants. He reached through a cluster of dewy leaves, made a beak with two fingers, and plucked like the bird he might be under other circumstances. The three berries he got were pure sugar.

His bones cracked when he bent to examine the mushrooms. You had to know mushrooms. The best-looking mushroom could be filled with poison. He always heard stories of men murdered by mushrooms and feared such a death. It seemed the worst way to die. From eating a mushroom in the prime of life. An insult on top of the agony. "If only I didn't eat the mushroom." Those would never be his last words. If a mushroom killed Isaac Bupkin, he'd keep his complaint to himself.

In the middle of Mrs. Elm's mushroom patch, Isaac saw something hidden among the bald heads. He didn't believe it but he couldn't deny it. He yanked it out of the ground, tucked it under his coat, and hurried back to the house. Aaron Bupkin was still sleeping. Isaac shook him awake, kissed his cheek and called him a mensch. "No golems in the neighborhood, eh? You're some kid, little vonce."

NEW YORK, NEW YORK, NOVEMBER 2, 1869

Exclusive to the *New York Clarion:* Cardiff, New York, 1st instant. A most bizarre, still unexplained, affliction struck hundreds of visitors to the farm of Stubby Newell where the marvelous Onondaga Giant holds court.

With respect for decorum and delicacy, in an effort to fulfill our pledge to apprise our readers of all vital developments, however distasteful, we will attempt to report this happening with discretion and modesty. It would, however, be imprudent to continue before admonishing our wide audience, especially the ladies, that many may take offense and even experience a modicum of shock and outrage from the following words.

To continue. On this lovely Fall day in so splendid a setting, there seemed nothing amiss at the Newell abode. As has become usual since the Cardiff Giant was unearthed earlier this month, a large crowd of the curious gathered to view what some call the "ancient man who brings modern miracles."

That expectant crowd, well behaved, formed willingly into line outside the tent where the giant is displayed. The mood was joyful, even carnival, though tinged with a sense of awe and reverence that flavors the crisp Autumn air here.

Two groups of visitors passed through the tent and emerged with expressions of respect and wonder as do most. The third set of four persons then purchased their tickets and passed into the stone man's great presence. That group was comprised of two men in their twenties, a perky young woman in a frock some thought inappropriate for that place and that hour, and a boy of no more than thirteen.

After a quiet moment, heard suddenly outside was a raucous and frightening shriek from the female. Later it was revealed that the child, yielding to immature impulse, jumped the guard ropes that surround the marvel and brutishly snatched away the small flag carefully placed to conceal those intimate attributes left best to imagination. Mr. William Newell rushed immediately into the tent and divined what transpired. He seemed understandably disturbed and perplexed at what he saw and was quick to restore Old Glory to its proper location.

What followed was traumatic to many concerned. The male members of the crowd began to grow restless. There were shouts and epithets heard, some disturbingly vulgar.

Many of the men bent themselves double while others dropped, face first, to the ground. Then the ladies joined in with their chorus of chaos.

The cause of alarm was a sudden outbreak of what we will call *mass tumescence*. Virtually every man on the scene experienced spontaneous erection of a most persistent kind to the point of panic. It appeared that no age was spared, from youngest to oldest, even including those prepubescent.

Several women fainted where they stood while others shepherded girls and maidens to the Newell cornfield to find refuge where they might remain safe from distress or contamination.

Dr. Zebulon Ploor, summoned from Lafayette, was quick to respond. Under his auspices, a clinic was hastily established in an area sealed off by sheets and towels provided by Mrs. Bertha Newell, mistress of the place. Dr. Ploor attempted treatment with such balms and unguents as were available though with little success. He could offer no explanation for the curious symptoms nor predict a prognosis for the stricken.

A mass evacuation then commenced with every road a shamble. The more stalwart, however, remained where they were to seek solace in communal prayer and the singing of familiar hymns. It was not until dusk that the crisis abated, leaving some mortified but the more religious convinced they had witnessed another of the giant's miracles, this promptly christened: "The Miracle of the Rod and the Staff." Others, trusting science, blamed the outbreak on some aberrant germ in the water from Mr. Newell's well.

This evening tranquility has returned to the hamlet of Cardiff. We are pleased to announce that those affected seem recovered quite nicely with no ill affects nor lingering malaise. Mr. Newell, with an eye to precaution, has sealed the giant's lair at least until morning.

"He expects me to print this?" John Zipmeister said to the *Clarion*'s copy boy. "Send a telegram to Barnaby Rack. Tell him I want him back here. Let our stringer in Syracuse take over his goddamn giant. Burn that paper. Wait a minute, you moron. Let me read it again. Break the front page. Call Father Mulcahey at St. Clemmons. Find out how to say hard-on in Latin."

BRIDGEPORT, CONNECTICUT, NOVEMBER 10, 1869

A Chinese brass monkey left P.T. Barnum's desk, flipped like an acrobat, then met its reflection in a mirror framed by twining leaves and large, purple grapes. The frame disintegrated, the monkey's grinning image dissolved in a blizzard of glass. Amos Arbutnaut, Esq., winced at the terrible harvest.

"He refused fifty thousand?"

"Not refused, Mr. Barnum. He said he needed time to consult *unnamed associates.*"

"Farmers don't have unnamed associates. They have haystacks and horse manure."

"Mr. Newell's become somewhat sophisticated. You're not the first to make him an offer, though he freely admits your price is highest. The man was impressed, no doubt about that."

"I should have gone myself."

"If Barnum was seen within ten miles of Cardiff, or his interest suspected, costs would triple."

"I want Goliath. I'll have him." Barnum split the pen in his hand.

"Before you wreck the rest of the room, it may be you should turn from the stone man and consider some other attraction. Mr. Newell has plans of his own. Next month the Cardiff Giant moves to Syracuse. In the Spring, to New York."

"My New York? Never."

"How can you stop Newell if he won't be dissuaded?"

"That's your problem, Arbutnaut. Did the hayseed give any indication of an amount he'd accept?"

"No, not an inkling. If you saw the mass of people, increased every day by the avalanche of publicity, you would easily understand why Newell is reluctant to put a price on his find. It seems as if everyone alive wants a look at the thing. I was glad to see it myself after evidence of such magic."

"You're hurting me," Barnum said, biting a pencil. "Adding insult to injury. You went about this all wrong. It was necessary to move slower. Tiptoe through Newell's back door, not explode in his face."

"I was cordial and clever as I know how to be."

"You're saying there's no hope here? That I should break Tom Thumb's mosquito heart? That we're stymied?"

"I'll go back upstate if you wish and present another figure. But you made it quite clear fifty thousand was your maximum."

"You know I'm strapped. The last fire wiped me out. Only Tom offered capital without asking control."

"There's another course possible."

"Well, tell me please before I burst of apoplexy."

"Make your own giant."

"Say again?"

"Make your own giant. Barnum's giant. A duplicate fossil exact in every detail. Construct the *original* giant."

"How can a replica be the original?"

"Where am I? Who's my client? Is this Barnum speaking? Or a fragmented man who broke with his mirror? What Barnum labels *original* becomes original."

"The *original* giant. Not the *same,* not his *brother.*"

"Exactly. In Syracuse I took the liberty of finding a sculptor. A most intelligent, talented, discreet, and reasonable man. He assured me that even familiar works of adored masters can be copied well enough to confound a curator."

"I would have thought of all this myself in a matter of minutes. Without help from a shyster like you."

"Absolutely. Before I could find my way out the door."

"You've seen this fellow's work?"

"Rooms full. Winged Victory defends his door, Venus de Milo shares his bedroom."

"How long would it take for your debauched da Vinci to make my *original* giant?"

"A few months at most. And two thousand cash, including the stone. Plus the cost of delivery."

"This vile conversation never took place. Neither Barnum nor so respected a barrister as Amos Arbutnaut would ever indulge in such banter."

"*Ça va sans dire.*"

"Like the farmer, let me take all this under advisement."

"Of course. But, as you know better than anyone, and have said many times, strike while the iron is hot."

"One can't rush helter skelter into such infamous conspiracy. There's significant reason for prudence."

"As you say. It was just a suggestion."

"But now, after long cogitation and due deliberation, I've made my decision."

"Have you, Mr. Barnum? I can't wait to hear it."

SYRACUSE, NEW YORK, NOVEMBER 12, 1869

His train delayed, Barnaby Rack wandered the City of Salt for hours. He skirted an island of rickety rooming houses where Negroes from the South sat on stoops, clustered on broken porches, played cards around barrels, waiting for jobs in the factories and fields promised by posters and leaflets that prompted migration.

Near the Onondaga Indian Reservation, he saw the stark cliffs of salt that gave Syracuse its wealth. Lake Onondaga lay like the Dead Sea. Waste from the mines and processing plants clotted its water. Black signs displaying the skull and crossbones warned swimmers and drinkers away. The few Indians Barnaby saw were ruined as their lake. The men slumped drunk against buildings. The women whored on corrupted corners near the train tracks.

For all that blight, the city burgeoned; another jewel in America's crown, a hub of agriculture and industry, its white citizens full of the future. Barnaby walked past mansions on James Street, explored the center of commerce on Salina, watched fat children and dogs play on the frosty lawns of Thornden Park.

The walk didn't help much. Barnaby sat alone drinking Genesee Beer in the taproom of the Yates Hotel. He looked down at his beer foam, detached, displaced, and disturbed, like a new angel looking through clouds.

He unfolded a rough sketch of the stone man copied from the one he'd sent Zipmeister. That damned clod of a giant forced Barnaby Rack to consider hard evidence of Divine Hocus Pocus. The same thug magic he first came to despise while his mother praised the Lord who'd exploded his father's heart. The Good Works of the

Savior who gave him a sister blessed with a limp and a hare lip. The curdled Compassion of God Almighty who accepted burnt offerings and hosannas while his mother and sister gargled blood from TB. The Collected Works of Supreme Mr. Magic who'd used Ultimate Influence to get Barnaby out of St. Mary's Orphanage and into a tannery where the air smelled like pus. The Master of All who vomited death on the battlefields then farted out flowers to plant on fresh graves, He who connived with His Empire Builders to poison lakes, deaden spirits, sanction slum slavery, subvert the nation once called Earth's best promise.

What was God up to in Cardiff, New York? His old game of Renewal, hint of Eden, illusion of Hope? Was that what the giant was about?

Barnaby Rack couldn't deny that, for an instant, he'd felt the urge to fall down and hail the Impossible Possible. To grant the slim chance God remembered to look back at the world. He hated himself for even indulging the thought, for allowing such an idiot germ into his system. What God? There was no God. Only the need for God.

Magic was his worst enemy, the worst enemy of his chosen profession. Before Barnaby Rack could be had, any *miracle* would have to stand bare-assed in one of Carnegie's furious furnaces. "Bugger you, Goliath. Bugger me," Barnaby said to the dregs of his brew. "Bugger the buggers."

He looked at the time and held out his glass for a refill.

"On me," Stubby Newell said, bellying up to the bar. "You that reporter, ain't you?"

"Ah, Mr. Newell, yes. Barnaby Rack from the *Clarion.*"

"Seen so many they all look the same to me," Stubby said.

"What brings you to Syracuse?"

"Business. At the Collendale Bank & Trust, where they now know my name. Same bastard turned me down for a well licks my balls with his tongue these days. Bottoms up."

"Cheers to you, sir. Any new wonders to tell me about?"

"I hope not. That last one was enough to keep for a while. I thought I had a disaster going. But last I heard every man's prick is hanging nice and loose and things back to what they were."

"No word on the cause?"

"Most say my giant was the cause but I flat deny it. Just one of those things is all it was. What are you doing here at the Yates?"

Barnaby glanced at a thick envelope Stubby Newell laid on the bar. "Waiting for the train to New York. Got an election to cover."

"Election. It slid out of my mind. So I suppose you get to meet Presidents and the like in your line of work."

"Goes with the territory," Barnaby said. The letter was addressed to a Mr. Gerhardt Burquhart on North Clark Street in Chicago.

"I never met a President yet," Stubby said. "But now who can say? So, New York City. Is it all that they tell us?"

"Got to see for yourself," Barnaby said.

"I expect I will when we take the stone man on his tour. You can show me the sights."

"Ever ride up and down in an elevator?"

"Say what it is and I'll be glad to tell you. Plenty I done, plenty I ain't done. Most things when you do them fall short somehow. Why is that?" Stubby picked a wad of snot from his nose. "You like a cigar?"

"Bought a box of your Goliaths," Barnaby said.

"My cousin says they're already a collector's item," Stubby said. "I sell 'em and smoke 'em but I'm damned if I'll save 'em. Life's too short. Here, have one on me. See that flag on the wrapper? Guess who came up with that."

ACKLEY, IOWA, NOVEMBER 14, 1869

———◆·✳·◆———

The marriage of the Reverend Mr. Henry Turk and Samantha Bale was scheduled to take place in the bride's Ackley home. The evening before the nuptials, Samantha watched Bessie Marvel, a Negress famous for her contacts with things occult and arcane, exorcise any possible dregs of resentment left by Lambert Quincy Bale, her first husband. It was not Lambert's way to begrudge a widow a second chance at happiness, but Samantha was prone to caution.

Bessie Marvel, fast as a dragonfly, went from room to room, including the attic and root cellar. She conversed with invisible essences while shaking a cloth bag at their hiding places. Samantha asked no questions about the contents of the bag or the subject of Mrs. Marvel's animated conversations. When the house was pronounced clean, empty of alien influence, Samantha paid the woman two dollars, made her a gift of a jar of strawberry preserves, and sent her on her way. Samantha immediately asked forgiveness from Jesus for allowing the blatantly pagan ritual to take place, then she focused on last-minute preparations for her wedding.

"Wasn't that the hojo lady, the one who casts spells?" said the Reverend Turk, who'd passed Bessie Marvel, still muttering, on his way up the walk.

"I guess it was, yes, dear," Samantha said, flushing.

"Why was she here?"

"To help with the cleaning."

"You should be careful who you employ. They call that woman

a witch. But I think you're well protected against things that go
bump in the night. Are you ready to go?"

"Is it really necessary, Henry?"

"I told you, I think the ritual quaint, even touching, though the
custom derives largely from Hebrew tradition. Inviting departed
loved ones to attend important ceremonies gives a respectful nod
to the past. Many cultures have similar rites designed to impart a
vivid sense of life's continuity."

"You can make a case for anything. But since our Christian belief is in life everlasting, it seems rude to disturb those crossed-over
souls. If they're busy in Heaven, why bother their bliss? Wouldn't
it suffice to announce our marriage through prayer?"

"We could, yes, Samantha. Your point is well taken."

"Good, because I've plenty left to do tonight."

"Things are a bit more complicated, my darling. Now you've
forced me to reveal a surprise which will then cease to be a surprise."

"What surprise?"

"From the children. When I told of our plan to visit the churchyard, they were entirely delighted. You know how they are about
ancestors. Quite like Jews in that respect. For all we know, considering recent discoveries, the tribes of the Indian nation may well be
a lost tribe of Israel. If this is the land of the Bible, as I believe it
to be, no wonder that the Indians should have Semitic traits and
share common beliefs. I've already begun assembling proof of that
racial connection."

"You've left me behind, Henry Turk. I'm not the scholar you are
and can shine only by reflected light. Are you saying there are Jew-
ish Indians in Ackley?"

"Nothing to fear. Be assured, darling, those children haven't the
slightest idea that the ancestors they revere are, in fact, Abraham,
Sarah, and Moses, nor have I intention of telling them. All I am
saying is that your appreciative students have concocted a scheme
designed to please their beloved teacher. They requested permission
to gather in a group to greet us with best wishes and surprise my
lovely bride with suitable tokens of affection."

"I'm surprised enough already."

"I've told you too much. Forgive me. And please keep what I said to yourself. There are plagiarists abroad from every profession ready to feast on the crumbs from inquiring minds. Put on your cloak, Samantha, or we'll disappoint your best admirers."

"But when we reach the graveyard, which of the dead shall we invite? I, alas, have few relatives buried in Ackley, and you have none."

"There's Lambert and his family. I should think they'll be glad to hear of your new happiness."

"You want me to invite the Bales?"

"It's not as if we'll have to set places for them."

"I don't think Lambert or any of his kin will come." Samantha felt herself shiver. Bessie Marvel had scoured the house and probably left terrible traps for any Bale ghost who dared venture there. The wedding could end in a whirlwind.

The Reverend laughed out loud, rare for him. "Neither do I. You're a woman with a literal mind and I love you the more for it. Our visit is a gesture. Symbolic. An apt metaphor. Besides, it gives me a chance to study the children and keep my ears open for Talmudic echoes. Out of the mouths of babes."

Samantha and Reverend Turk walked through quiet Ackley streets acknowledging congratulations from familiar faces and even some strangers. The groom was, by that time, Ackley's most prominent resident, considered by many to be Iowa's holiest mortal. In the past weeks more than one would-be disciple fell prostrate at his feet to kiss his shoes in ecstasy of belief.

When the couple reached the churchyard, instead of finding the spawn from the Indian school gathered there they found the place deserted. Samantha was relieved, the Reverend puzzled. He could only assume that some bad behavior required that the children be confined to quarters.

"We can leave now," Samantha said.

"Not before we do what we came to do."

"This doesn't feel right to me."

"Nonsense. Go alone and speak to your loved ones. Ask their good wishes."

"And you?"

"I am going to invite Herbert Black Paw."

"Him? Why?"

"I have my reasons."

The Reverend was saving those reasons for a later surprise. Only that afternoon he'd been approached by a delegation from Chicago offering funds enough to found the Herbert Black Paw Seminary. From a thousand miles away, the Cardiff Giant reached out to give him the license he needed to send an army of stone men to smother red ghosts. That school would become a training ground for Indian missionaries, each forged from the Reverend's template.

Reverend Turk found Herbert Black Paw's marker tipped over and his sanctified grave violated. The hole that once held his casket was empty. Except for the skull of a buffalo with an arrow jammed through its eye socket.

NEW YORK, NEW YORK, NOVEMBER 16, 1869

Loretta Hull left the Westminster Hotel on Irving Place, then crossed Union Square, in search of a shop called Small Wonders that specialized in miniatures. The store came highly recommended by a woman Loretta met at the hotel, herself a collector of wild animals so small they had to be seen through a magnifying glass. While Loretta didn't see much point in cultivating a menagerie of wee predators, she took the lady's advice and sought out the place described as fantastique.

Small Wonders was indeed fantastique, a shrunken universe

populated by impeccable figurines, stocked floor to ceiling with icons of heroes, artists, musicians, scientists, kings, queens, politicians, patriots, saints, angels, even ordinary people doing everyday chores. There were shelves filled with every kind of bird and beast, adorable cottages, mansions, castles, trains, toys, furniture, a library of the world's great books, machines with movable parts made of wood, glass, and pewter, all artfully displayed, none bigger than Loretta's pinky.

The decor of Small Wonders enhanced its theme with low counters, chairs, tables, and sofas of reduced scale, fairy-tale chandeliers, even copies of famed paintings no larger than postage stamps. Loretta was amazed and enchanted by that lilliputian world, then doubly astonished when she found a detailed reproduction of Stubby Newell's petrified man. The tiny giant lay on a ceramic facsimile of a newspaper page announcing its discovery. She bought that for George, who'd been so impressed by the find, a cigar-smoking Man in the Moon for Simon, Cinderella's coach for Angelica, a Cincinnati Red Stocking swinging a bat for her husband, who loved baseball, and a Ferris wheel that could spin for herself. Her items were wrapped and bagged by the only discrepant item in the shop, a full-size clerk reeking of rose water.

After her shopping spree, Loretta found a hansom cab and gave the address of Zerman's Humidor on Wall Street, where she was to meet Ben at three. Riding through Manhattan, Loretta was overwhelmed by the city where everything loomed larger than life. Moments before she was a giant, now suddenly bewitched to a creature less formidable than those in her sack.

Loretta felt her heart take the quick rhythm of the cab's prancing horse. New York's nascent energy displaced her tourist's anxiety. Her mind balked at the message of random encounter and infinite clash on that island of strangers. Rushing through a valley of concrete, under a train hanging in air, all fear was replaced by a surge of expectancy. The city produced a crescendo of such stunning color she was turned inside-out. While her miniatures jiggled in the Small World bag, Loretta came harder and higher than she had with any lover. Startled, she lay back breathing slowly, blinking at pictures of the tentacle streets, thinking life in New York might not be as gross as the tales told in Binghamton by defeated explorers.

She was glad to find Ben Hull in place and on time at the entrance to Zerman's. He stood talking to a man no taller than the pockets of his coat. Both men held cigars. The little one sampled flavor, eyes shut tight for full impact.

"Ben, I'm here."

"Ah, Loretta," Ben shouted, reaching for his money clip as he came to help her down from the hansom. The midget's button eyes popped open.

"This is none other than General Tom Thumb," Ben said, glowing. "The famous Tom Thumb. Meet my wife, Mrs. Hull."

"A true pleasure," Thumb said, bowing and kissing her hand.

"Well, what's your honest opinion, General?"

"Altogether lovely."

"I mean the cigar," Ben said. "Understand, dear, Mr. Thumb is considering offering his endorsement for our brands."

"A fine smoke," Thumb said. "Give me leisure to consider your proposal."

"Certainly, General. May I call on you, then?"

"Yes, Benjamin, but let's wait a few days."

"I wish you were welcome inside Zerman's," Ben said to Loretta. "What a magnificent temple. A shrine to tobacco." He turned his attention to Thumb. "But I think Hull's Humidor will soon provide stiff competition. We're located on a choice corner of Broadway just below Trinity Church, and construction proceeds ahead of schedule. With location, product, and ambience, I think Hull's will soon wean away Mr. Zerman's elite."

"I admire your husband's enthusiasm," Thumb said.

Loretta was tongue-tied but managed to smile. She'd never met anyone so impressive as the General. Relaxed, dapper, contained, so graciously mannered. A wisp of a man as close to perfection as anything at Small Wonders.

"I hope your day has been half as stimulating as mine," Ben Hull said.

"It's been most interesting, darling," Loretta said. "Entirely diverting."

"This town's a tonic," Tom Thumb said, looking up at her eyes. "A tumbler filled with a rainbow of bubbles."

Loretta was a giant again, her thighs anointed, at home in a city of giants.

BINGHAMTON, NEW YORK, NOVEMBER 17, 1869

Three benches had been jammed into the factory of Simon Hull & Sons where wrappers, breakers, binders, banders, and boxers worked to fill their quotas for *maduro* Ulysses Supremos, *claro* Uncle Toms, and the amazingly popular *oscuro* Goliaths. George Hull walked through the expanded facilities pretending to supervise output.

Since his return from Cardiff, George drifted through wax. Instead of enjoying the stone man's amazing success, George battled growing malaise. He used all his energy to shave, wash, and dress. After his first cup of coffee he was ready to crawl back to the pallet Angelica laid out on the floor. Pleading her belly and the safety of her simmering foetus, she refused to share a bed.

On their doctor's advice Angelica suspended her duties in the retail store and spent her time resting. Her condition deemed fragile, she was warned to abstain from carnal contact. That convenient advice was welcome since the thought of such things now seemed pointless. For George, the medical mandate was superfluous. Drained from bluffing his way through the day, he was much too tired for desire. He didn't sleep with Angelica, hardly spoke to her, took his meals alone, but she was never out of his mind.

George thought constantly of her swelling breasts and their thickening nipples. Her pregnancy hardly showed but he already saw signs that Angelica's abdomen would soon proclaim its full majesty. With their contract on the verge of fulfillment, George had expected to feel elation. What depressed him was insidious doubt over his claim to paternity, the idiot suspicion that the baby inside his wife was the spawn of a petrified fossil. Having seen his Angelica ride stone like a witch on a rampage turned everything real to dust. While he examined cigars, his mind watched Angelica roll like thunder in an alien lap.

George accepted his affliction as temporary. He knew it would break like a fever and pass. The first money from Stubby Newell, a draft for twelve thousand dollars, gave quick sign of a cure. His head cleared. He ate well. He had a good day. Though the black mood was back by evening, George was sure the next check would further diminish his ridiculous symptoms. Meanwhile, there was a pose to be kept, orders to fill, clumsy workers to prod, enough to do.

Ben and Loretta, ensconced in New York, were ignorant of Angelica's blooming. Simon Hull traveled through Cuba with no inkling he'd soon have a grandchild to pinch and sniff tobacco leaves into the next century. George wanted his father to have the news before anyone else. He looked forward to Simon's confusion of disappointment and pleasure. It was Ben's son Simon Hull preferred for his heir, but he'd take whatever God offered. Later, George could enjoy seeing Simon's face when it slowly sank in that both George and George Jr. had escaped him. "Close but no cigar, father. There's a heavy price for misplaced faith." Simon's other grandchild, the Cardiff Giant, assured George of that ultimate victory. Loretta and Ben might make babies but for Simon what came second was second best.

When the workers headed home and the factory was still,

George went upstairs to his bedroom. Angelica was propped on her pillow, reading from the New Testament.

"Are you hungry? Can I bring you some dinner?"

"Not now, George. I'm a bit queasy tonight."

"There's something you must hear."

"What is it?"

George sat on the bed and told Angelica the real story of the stone man from Genesis. He confessed everything, going back to their days in Ackley and Fort Dodge, of his rage at the Reverend Turk, the sinister gestation of his plan to turn gypsum to gold, of his trip to Chicago where the giant was made by an odd pair of clowns, of the hard journey east, the conniving with stupid Stubby, of the midnight burial, the waiting, the digging, the finding, the whole story.

"Angelica, your husband has beaten God at his own game," George said. "The only thing I regret is Turk's good fortune. Fame wasn't the comeuppance I had in mind for that imbecile. But so be it. I suppose we should be glad for Samantha's sake. Goliath might even send the newlyweds a generous wedding gift. Now you know the truth and the whole truth. Also know that you and our son will share astronomical profits. Enough for ten lifetimes and more. Angelica . . . ?"

"Yes, George?" she said. He could see she was drowsing.

"Did you hear anything I told you?"

"All of it, dear."

"And?"

CARDIFF, NEW YORK, NOVEMBER 20, 1869

Cardiff weather showed signs of turning severe; all roads to the Newell farm would soon be made treacherous by snow and ice. In late November, George wrote: *Time for exodus. Denying the populace so much wonder is a capital sin.*

Stubby Newell rented the ballroom of the Yates Hotel for the giant's Winter excursion to Syracuse. Preparations had been made for an early-morning move. On the evening before the stone man's journey, a crowd came to say good-bye to their fossil. Stubby fired up a ring of lanterns and let visitors pass through the tent one last time.

The crowd dispersed after ten. They went reluctantly, singing "Silent Night" out of season. It was hardly Thanksgiving. Only one man remained, who claimed he was a published poet. "Poet or butcher, you got to go now," Stubby said.

"Five dollars for five minutes alone with Goliath."

Stubby looked him over. The man looked like a poet with an eager, round face, large watery eyes, hair greased and parted, a slouch to his body.

"All right, then, five minutes. But don't touch nothing or fiddle with the flag."

"Of course not," the man said, handing over a gold half-eagle. Stubby bit the coin, pocketed it, and went back to the house.

When he was sure of his privacy, the poet leaned over the giant, closed his eyes, and began to recite from memory what would be printed next day in the *Syracuse Daily Journal.*

Speak out, O Giant! Stiff and stark, and grim,
Open thy lips of stone, thy story tell;
Let now again be heard that voice which once
Through all old Onondaga's hills and vales
Proclaimed thy lineage from a Giant race,
And claimed as subjects, all who trembling heard.
Art thou a son of old Polyphemus,
Or brother to the Sphinx, now turned to stone—
The mystery and riddle of the world?
Did human passions stir within thy breast
And move thy heart with human sympathies?
Was life to thee, made up of joy and hope,
Of love and hate, or suffering and pain,
In fair proportions to thy Giant form?
Did ever wife, by whatsoever name
Or tie of union, with her ministries
Of love caress and cheer thy way through life?
Were children in thy home, to climb thy knee
And pluck thy beard, secure, and dare thy power,
Or was thy nature as its substance now,
Like stone—as cold and unimpressible?
And did at last, some fair Delilah
Of thy race, hold thee in gentle dalliance,
And with thy head upon her lap at rest,
Wer't shorn of strength, and told too late, alas,
'Thine enemies be upon thee?'
Tell us the story of thy life, and whether
Of woman born—substance and spirit
In mysterious union wed—or fashioned
By hand of man from stone, we bow in awe,
And hail thee, GIANT OF ONONDAGA!

A resonant verse. Excellent. Timeless. I appreciate such sentiments. As for your questions. I must decline to answer since I can't know every secret of my origin. "WE BOW IN AWE, AND HAIL ME, GIANT OF

ONONDAGA!" Yes! I will miss this place. Puddles, rodents, and bards. Time's up. I've a long day tomorrow.

Later, the poet swore that the giant rose from his cold bed, stretched with a ghastly creaking sound, pulled a premium panatela from some hidden place, used a lantern to light it, and insisted on sharing its dusky flavor. That this GIANT OF ONONDAGA! put a stone arm around his shoulder then accompanied him on a stroll through Stubby Newell's battered cornfield as ordinary as if they'd gone to pluck an ear for potting. His story was properly ascribed to hyperbole and printed only as a Letter to the Editor.

SYRACUSE, NEW YORK, NOVEMBER 22, 1869

Carl F. Otto came back to his studio on Pepper Street after a visit to the Yates Hotel. He went quickly to his easel and made a charcoal sketch of the Cardiff Giant fresh from memory. As always, Otto was sorely tempted to improve the design but suppressed that impulse, remembering terms of his contract with Amos Arbutnaut, Esq., in New York. *Enclosed find first payment, remainder payable on acceptance.* In some thirty years he'd never landed such a lucrative commission.

Otto had been a copyist all his artistic life, attributing his choice of vocation to the fact that he'd been born an identical twin. His brother was a talentless slug who sold shoes for a living, but they shared an amazing resemblance. Otto's first drawings were self-portraits his mother assumed were images of his sibling, lovingly done.

His forte was the Grecian style, his greatest proficiency in duplicating gods and goddesses who'd inspired his ancestral mentors. Once, tired of Olympus, Otto attempted to expand into Egyptology. That venture failed dismally when his facsimile of a statue of Sekhmet, part woman, part lioness, was rejected by his best client who said he'd turned Sekhmet into Mary Todd Lincoln with paws.

After that it was back to the Greeks, occasional Romans, and flirtations with Notre Dame's gorgons and gargoyles. The only original work Carl F. Otto ever completed was, in fact, a bust of the suffragette Susan B. Anthony, a woman he admired for her feisty mix of spunk and insanity. That bust was kept covered atop a miniature Ionic column in the farthest corner of his studio. Nobody but himself had seen it, and he only infrequently in moments when he questioned the meaning of his life.

Anticipating Mr. Arbutnaut's contract, Otto already risked purchase of a substantial block of granite. The task of replicating a giant, or anything else outside Egypt, hardly intimidated such a consummate professional. His valid concern was the haste of his deadline and certain special conditions imposed on the work. It was agreed TITAN, the name used by the elegant lawyer, would be done and delivered no later than two weeks before Christmas. That Titan seemed a peculiar Yuletide gift wasn't the sculptor's business. To each his own. The terms and conditions were another matter. Titan's hard head had to be engineered to allow insertion of six inches of bone from a human skull above his right ear with room left for a pound of crystal dust. The dust and the skull arrived even before Arbutnaut's contract. An unmarked package was delivered to Otto by an unmarked boy who sulked when he saw his tip.

The glittering powder came stuffed in a jar; the skull was shipped whole. An entire skull was excessive where half a scalp would suffice, but excess was probably typical of New York lawyers. Otto had no idea why bone and crystal dust were a factor. No account of the Cardiff Giant mentioned either ingredient. The demand was a serious complication that would add days to his work.

Otto checked his sketch, consulted a published list of the giant's measurements, chose his tools, and began hacking out some semblance of a shape. This time, at least, the result would be something substantial, not a caryatid with tits like pimples and a face like the shoe salesman's wife.

On his third strike, a spark flew from the chisel toward his nose. Otto blinked. In that atom of time he could have sworn the birthing stone quivered. He heard a crackle of sound that made him jump. Otto, with no patience for mysteries, swallowed some spit and went back to chopping.

WHAT PURPOSE NOW? PILLAR FOR A GATE TO HEAVEN OR HELL? A DRAGON TO PROTECT SOME WIZARD'S TOWER? MONUMENT TO A CONQUEROR? CORNICE FOR A TEMPLE? LEG FOR A BRIDGE? ALTAR FOR BLOOD SACRIFICE? CORNERSTONE FOR THE FUTURE? THE MAN PECKS LIKE A SPARROW.

NEW YORK, NEW YORK, NOVEMBER 25, 1869

John Zipmeister tilted backward, raised his feet to the edge of his desk, and made a pyramid out of his shoes. Barnaby Rack studied their soles, an intricate landscape of stained leather, tar, horseshit, thumbtacks, and assorted sidewalk detritus. If Zipmeister was vaporized and nothing left above his ankles, he could be reconstructed from those dregs.

"That must have been some sweet sight," Zipmeister said, "what with them tucking in their bulges and singing 'Be Not Dismay'd Thou Little Flock.' Why do I always manage to miss the major events of my era? Did anybody try to explain why the giant gave them stiff pricks?"

"The Congregationalist minister said something about how it could have something to do with repairing the church steeple."

"A bit of a push. What do you think on the matter?"

"I think it doesn't matter what I think."

"You're right, Rack. But for the record."

"I've got to say that there's *something* going on up there. You can feel it. It is, as they say, a moving experience."

"Considering what moved."

"If you could see the lines of people, all kinds of people, and how their faces shine when they come out of that tent. Did you ever watch a forest fire leap from tree to tree? That's how their emotion transmits. Like a sudden kindling of tinder-dry spirits. They look so *relieved.*"

"And the flags?"

"Yes, the flags. Everyplace. Homemade, store bought. Flags, flags, flags. As if the stone man arrived to vindicate the nation. To wash the blood off our hands once and for all. To remind us of our destiny. He just lays there, all frozen pain, but his face transcendent. His message is endurance. More than that. A message of healing from a silent leader who asks no allegiance and orders no troops to the field."

"A spiritual aphrodisiac? A patriot with no ax to grind? I'll take a dozen of those," Zipmeister said.

"Whatever he is, import or not, the man's an American."

"You said they covered his ramparts with the star-spangled banner. That might have to do with your granting him citizenship."

"I don't think so. He's like some kind of midwestern sodbuster who saw God and dropped dead from his one glimpse of glory. Don't ask me to make any sense of this because I can't."

"Don't worry, you're not making sense. You're making me sweat. *Glimpse of glory?* One miracle I'll buy. The old bastard knows how to sell papers."

"So why did you call me back? Goliath gets bigger, not smaller."

"Listen to yourself. You sound like the Pope's press agent. You're too close to the story, too involved. It happens between doctors and patients and it happens to reporters from the *Clarion.* I need a pair of objective eyes. Besides, I want you in Washington to cover Mr.

Grant, our first publicly pickled President. You wanted a chance to show your mettle, I'm giving it to you on a tray."

"I'm going to Chicago, not Washington."

"Oh, really? I didn't know that," Zipmeister said.

"I've got to check something out."

"What something? A lead?"

"A hunch."

"Oh, a hunch. Good, go ahead. Forget Washington. Rack, what's the matter with you? Did you eat a bad oyster? Too much pressure on your brain stem?"

"I nosed around the Collendale Trust up in Syracuse. Stubby Newell sent a thousand dollars to somebody in Chicago."

"Stubby Newell? Do I know him?"

"The man who owns the farm in Cardiff."

"Where they grow giants? Ah, that Stubby Newell. Right. Excuse my memory lapse."

"Why, Zipmeister? Tell me why."

"Why what?"

"Why money to Chicago? I'd have guessed that man never heard of Chicago. And what about Stubby's old well?"

"What about it?"

"It don't smell right to me."

"Which don't smell right? The bank, the money, Farmer Brown's well, or Chicago?"

"The Cardiff Giant."

"Cease and desist. You're doing it again, Rack. It's like your tear-jerker on that Gettysburg widow. If you're even hinting that the *Clarion* should go after anything that might stir up the crazies, dispense with the notion. Let Goliath alone. Let him sell my papers. Let him vindicate, do his cures, give gratuitous boners to the poor, shove a flag up your ass if he wants to. If that giant does a public service, it's no skin off our teeth. Besides, I thought you were converted. *A silent leader,* remember? A long piss in a drought? So to hell with Chicago."

"It's that expression on his face. *I* never looked like that. *You* never looked like that. I want to know if *anybody* ever looked like that in the history of the world."

"You think there's an ant's chance the whole thing's a scam?"

"I think the stone man's a petrified angel from Genesis."

"Christ, you mean that, don't you? Don't get philosophical in my office. We're not the *Herald* or the *Times.* This paper's got standards. If you're so high on Uncle Cement, why the vendetta? Why crap on your Jesus?"

"Because my Uncle Cement makes me nervous. I can't explain any more. Send me to Chicago."

John Zipmeister pulled his legs to his chest, locked his arms around his knees, and rocked back and forth. CLARION *CLOBBERS ERSATZ COLOSSUS! DIGS DIRT ON GOLIATH!*

"Go climb your beanstalk," Zipmeister said. "Maybe you'll get lucky and come home with the golden goose plucked, stuffed, and fucked."

Barnaby's stomach knotted. His nostrils closed off air. He felt a trickle of sweat run down his back.

"You want a drink or something?" Zipmeister asked. "You're pale as my daddy's ancient ass."

BINGHAMTON, NEW YORK, NOVEMBER 27, 1869

The exhibit in Syracuse proved a bonanza. Good fortune tilted the weight of depression. George Hull's demons dispersed when his bank account touched forty thousand. People said they were glad he was back to his old self.

George felt a new self emerging on powerful wings. His optimism proved premature; his metamorphosis was abruptly abridged. A letter from Stubby brought thunderclouds back.

While the Hulls' family physician, Cedric Larchmont, M.D., examined Angelica upstairs, George reread Stubby's scrawl. "My fault for leaving that cretin on his own," George told himself. "An inspired idiot is the best friend of chaos."

> *The Illustrated Magazine asked for a slice of his head around the size of a teaspoon for the sake of science. So the hunk could be examined by nabobs who'd give their opinion, petrified or a statue, in a public forum. Of which we could pocket every cent of the proceeds! Jesus, George, they even offered to print up the tickets. I said I don't know and held out but they was in so much of a hurry I couldn't wait your thoughts. Then believe me or don't I was sitting alone with the giant here in the Yates ballroom thinking what would George do? And I swear on the Bible I heard the stone man say: Stubby, take a hunk of my head if you want. Hell, you already took a chip off my back and a chunk off my tool, so why not? Anyhow I made them the deal. They brought over this man with a reamer who pried a neat carrot tuber from the rear side so the damage hardly shows. I hope you have got no second thoughts or hard feelings about this, cousin. Because then Stubby Newell got the idea to have STANDING ROOM ONLY instead of chairs which doubles the house. First they said NO but then they gave in so you can thank me when you see me since every ticket is spoke for at TEN $$$ per pop!*

When Dr. Larchmont finished examining his wife, George listened to his report. "The lady is holding her own," the doctor said. "Except for the anemia, she seems fine. Though I wish she would eat more red meat for strength."

"I was thinking," George said, "it might be wise for Angelica to get away, go someplace really quiet in the country."

"I'm not sure she should travel," the doctor said.

"We have family in Cardiff. Nice, peaceful farm up there, clean air to wake up the appetite, and my cousin, Bertha, a good Christian woman, to care for her."

"If the journey was in slow stages and the weather agreeable, it might be a good thing."

"It's a hard time for me to leave the factory with my father and brother away, but what's more important, a cigar or a son?"

"You're a good husband, George. And I, for one, trust nature's remedies more than I do any medicine."

"Then it's settled. I'll tell her right now."

George paid the doctor and went up to his bedroom. Anemic or not, Angelica was a pleasure to look at these days. Her face was a lamp, her hair spilled to her shoulders, her bosom rose like a lighthouse, her manner always cheerful as Spring.

"The doctor says you're doing wonderfully well," he said.

"That's good to hear."

"But he feels that a change of scene is in order. He asked me to take you to the country for a few weeks at least while the baby takes better hold. I said I'd go with you to Cardiff. I'm sure Bertha would welcome your company, her being alone, and I know how much you like being there."

"I'm comfortable in my own bed, George. And you can't turn your back on the factory."

"My mind's made up," George said. "I think the doctor knows what's best for my wife and the little stranger."

"Maybe in a few weeks."

"No delay," George said. "Doctor's orders. We'll go tomorrow."

Back downstairs, George unfolded Stubby's letter and looked again at the flier his cousin enclosed:

THE ILLUSTRATED MAGAZINE PRESENTS,
IN PUBLIC FORUM
HOUR OF DECISION: MAN, STATUE—OR FRAUD?

The Sage of Concord, Mr. Ralph Waldo Emerson
From Harvard College, Mr. Oliver Wendell Holmes

Distinguished American Artists Cyrus Cobb of Boston &
Erasmus Dow Palmer of New York City

Come IN PERSON to Report on *The Amazing Cardiff Giant*
After Intense Observation of the Stone Man's Very Brain!

December 5, 1869   8:00 PM
Admission $10.00
Grand Ballroom, The Yates Hotel
Syracuse, New York

Emerson, Holmes, Cobb, and Palmer? If Judgment Day was at
hand, there was no way George Hull would be absent. Using wife
and child as excuse for the journey tempted fate, but sometimes fate
must be tempted. Besides, Cardiff might indeed prove a boon to
Angelica's health and increase her interest in more than red meat.

NEW YORK, NEW YORK, NOVEMBER 28, 1869

From ringside at Joe Ax's Gymnasium, Grinder Brian watched the
Black Panther sweat rivers from pores like faucets. His handlers
tried to cool down Panther's boiler with sponges and towels, but the
spurting exceeded the blotting. Across the ring, Derry Dan Dooley flexed cannonball biceps and waved to the crowd. A clang from
the bell announced the twenty-ninth round.

In two minutes Panther would be flattened by Derry Dan's
lumpy fists. Grinder sighed while he grinned. Panther's big nigger
teeth could bite off Dooley's both hands as easy as chewing on
clams. Who didn't know it? Why did sensible men bet good money

on the coon when they knew he'd end up in a pile? They lost all common sense before losing their dollars.

Every Friday night at Joe Ax's the same story repeated. Some buck from the South would stand growling and snarling. A mick, guinea, or polack would preen and growl back. The two would go at it to make things respectable. After taking some punishment, the white boy would win and Grinder get richer booking those dumb-ass bets. It wasn't so much that the fix was in; it was simply the way of the world.

The Black Panther and Derry Dan Dooley came out fighting. Dooley threw a left and right that connected with ugly wet thuds. Instead of reeling or dropping his guard, the Panther stood his ground. Everything was explained to him five or ten times. He knew when enough was enough and time to lie down. Dooley came on again with a flurry of jabs and slams to the belly. This time Panther did drop his arms but kept his knees locked.

"Go, Danny boy, make his eyes roll," yelled a fan next to Grinder. "Make his balls bang. Do it, Dooley."

A right cross from Dooley had Panther's nose leaking red snot. This time Panther's legs buckled but he stayed vertical. Grinder saw what was happening. Some uppity niggers got themselves turned to chop meat to prove a point. The Black Panther was probably one of those iron bungholes. Dumb as the studs who took the long odds.

Derry Dan Dooley was no slouch. He worked Panther's face like a washboard. Grinder relaxed but tensed when Panther bulled Dooley to the ropes and bent him double with a shot to the gut. Dooley clinched. Grinder saw the referee say something to the Panther while Dooley got back his breath. The fighters moved to center ring. Dooley got back to business but his punches were rubber. Panther wouldn't even bleed except for the dribble under his bulb nose.

"Christ," Grinder said to the man on his right who was sweating as much as the fighters, "what's going on with this boy? Don't he know this is the time and the place?"

"Yeah, boss, he knows," the man said. "He knows."

Panther speared a left to Dooley's jaw then a right that sounded like a hammer on liver. Dooley dropped for a five count, then managed to pull himself up and dance a retreat. Panther closed in, hollering curses.

"I thought I saw everything," Grinder said. "Black bastard is murdering my boy. Where you get him from?"

"Same guy sends all the monkeys. Said he was smart and would give a good show."

"It's the last time the monkey man does business with me or anybody else. Him and his boy go to New Jersey."

"It ain't done yet."

"Look at Dooley's eyes. It ain't done? He don't know the day it is."

Panther went into a clinch. It took some doing. He had to spin Dooley around to face him. Then Panther fell flat on his face, legs spread, arms dead, and took a full count. The referee held up Dooley's arm while the crowd howled.

"There you go, boss." the sweating man said.

"Do them both," Grinder said. "Send their pelts home to their mamas."

"Why? They kept to the bargain. We got Panther booked in Philly next Tuesday. Good house."

"We got him booked in Philly? What the hell. Let him go there, then bring him back here. I want that crazy jig for a pet."

Grinder got up and pushed out through the mob. When he felt a hand on his shoulder, he spun in the opposite direction and took a swipe at Barnaby Rack.

"Whoa," Barnaby said, ducking.

"You should know not to touch me like that," Grinder said.

"I just wanted to say hello, Sean Shamus."

"I know you?"

"Barnaby Rack from the *Clarion.*"

"Yeah. The *Clarion.* You wrote about me. But if you came to write about Joe Ax just forget it. He don't need attention off the sports page. You know how it is."

"No problem," Barnaby said. "I came because I heard you'd be here."

"That's the trouble with me. Too easy to find. I got to remember to change the routine. So you found me. So what?"

"Can I buy you a drink?"

"Sure, Barney. I might even drink it."

Barnaby sat across from Grinder Brian at Liffy's Pub nursing a bourbon. "I did something to you," Barnaby said. "I came to apologize."

"What did you do to me? Spell my name wrong?"

"It's a weird tale," Barnaby said. Then he told Grinder about Angelica Hull and the life insurance from Equitable.

"You signed my name? I'm impressed," Grinder said. "The lady must have been one sweet dip. If she comes to New York, introduce us."

"I had no right to play games with your life," Barnaby said.

"Sign my name next time you get laid, Barney, you're playing games with your life, not mine. I'll piss twice on your grave. You think Grinder Brian is ready for planting?"

"I didn't do much thinking about it," Barnaby said. "I acted on a silly impulse. What I wanted to tell you was that after this month, when the premium comes due, I'm canceling the policy."

"Hey, keep paying if you want," Grinder said. "But there's better ways to spend money. Tell me something."

"What?"

"How come the confession? Am I a priest? You're lucky I liked what you wrote in the paper."

"Hard to explain. Maybe I'm growing a conscience."

"Take a purge. Answer me one more thing."

"What?"

"Did you bet the black guy? Because that's my hunch. That you bet the black guy."

"As a matter of fact," Barnaby said.

"I'll live forever," Grinder Brian said.

SYRACUSE, NEW YORK, NOVEMBER 30, 1869

Carl F. Otto watched Amos Arbutnaut, Esq., examine Titan, who still stank of acid and squid ink. "The only problem was his cock," Otto said. "I had to improvise since there was no way to get a gander at what's under that flag. I hear rumors some crazed Cardiff Semite lopped off a piece of his dick but, then again, those people downstate still believe in fairies. What I did was use common sense and my knowledge of anatomy."

"I've no complaint about his phallus," Arbutnaut said. "Firm and formidable. Besides, we'll also use a flag. Mr. Barnum had trouble enough from Henry Beigh and the ASPCA for allowing the public to watch serpents devour live frogs at his New American Museum. We've no intention of flaunting a stone penis at the crowd to stir up more protest. You've done a fine job of work, Mr. Otto. Titan is better than a twin to Newell's Goliath. Ours seems older and wiser. But the smell . . ."

"That will wear off in days. It's the dyes and chemicals used to age and authenticate Bozo. Don't envy me this job. I spent last week vomiting buckets."

"What remains to be done?"

"Not much. Only a few more pockmarks to the forehead and a daub of red around the nose and eyes as mark the original."

"Get about it," Arbutnaut said. "And, Mr. Otto, please remember, Titan *is* the original."

"I'll remember. He'll be shipped complete by the end of the week in a crate labeled Indian pottery. Tell me, Mr. Arbutnaut, do you plan to attend their Hour of Decision? I thought it was a nice irony that I was the one they hired to drill a piece of their fossil's cranium. If those geniuses have eyes they'll see very soon that Goliath is no more than common gypsum."

"Hush, Mr. Otto. We've a vested interest in what they see and the hope they see more than rock. Whatever they see and say, we're prepared to offer the selfsame test using geniuses of our own. In our sample the experts will find human bone and crystal dust, which is the sign of true human petrification."

"So that was the reason for the extra work."

"P.T. Barnum is the first master of anticipation. 'Leave no possibility unexplored' is his motto. In this case, no stone unturned. There must not be any doubt that Titan's a man. The public will come out for a corpse much faster than for a Sphinx."

"You New Yorkers deserve your reputation," Otto said. "And I say that with all respect. It's a pleasure doing business with you."

"And with you, sir. Rare enough to find a talented artist with a practical mind."

"Solid granite," Otto said, tapping his skull.

"No need to remind you that our dealings must be kept strictly private. There's an unfortunate if understandable temptation to boast about such an achievement as yours. But that could be dangerous for all concerned and especially for you. Mr. Barnum is a rational fellow, but when crossed or double-crossed his nature rapidly changes. It is not pleasant to behold. The man loses all sense of restraint."

"Don't bother to threaten me," Otto said. "Just put the money in my hand and my mouth clamps shut by reflex. As for boasting, no chance of that. I look forward to finishing this creature and sending him on his way. See that wall filled with pictures of alligators, crocodiles, gila monsters, lizards, and reptiles of all kinds, lobsters, crawfish, and other hideous forms from nature? And that other wall there, filled with the most divine celestial images? I've had to tread the eerie boundary where ugliness merges with beauty in order to do Titan justice, and it hasn't been easy for me. Replication is much more than a matter of simply copying, and this giant is full of ambiguity. This work left me totally exhausted and not just from lack of sleep. In fact, I was thinking of spending a few decades in Greece, the cradle of our advanced civilization. And leaving what your Mr. Barnum calls 'this sea-to-sea Yankee nation' to the Yankees."

"I envy you the journey," Arbutnaut said. "And entirely support your decision. But assure me Titan's stink will evaporate."

"You should have gotten a whiff of him yesterday. Like a ripe diaper. But by the time he reaches Manhattan, he'll smell like a virgin's first rose."

"Bon voyage then, to both of you," Arbutnaut said.

WHY AM I MADE HORIZONTAL? BODY IN A GRIMACE WITH MISMATCHED FACE? TWIST MY FACE TO MY FRAME. MAKE A FACE FOR MY TEMPERAMENT. TITAN IS NO SERVILE FLUNKY. CARVE ME A COUNTENANCE TO STRIKE PROPER FEAR. GIVE ME THE LOOK OF A RANCID SWAMP. WHO IS MY TWIN? THAT IMPOSTER WILL BE DEALT WITH AND SOON. THIS BARNUM THEY SPEAK OF INTERESTS ME. AND HIS "SEA-TO-SEA YANKEE NATION." MY PLAYGROUND?

NEW YORK, NEW YORK, DECEMBER 6, 1869

Exclusive to the *New York Clarion,* 6th, instant: The highly anticipated "Hour of Decision" at the Yates Hotel in Syracuse, in which authorities of impeccable credential gathered last evening to determine if the stone man of Cardiff were "Man, Statue—Or Fraud" left an audience of nearly 500 persons as divided in opinion as they were when they came.

The luminaries present included Transcendentalist philosopher, poet, and essayist Ralph Waldo Emerson, the

brilliant Oliver Wendell Holmes, newly appointed editor
of the Harvard Law Review, and acclaimed artists Cyrus
Cobb and Erasmus Hall Palmer all under the aegis of *The
Illustrated Magazine.* The participants had opportunity to
examine, with the help of any experts they chose to assist
them, a representative portion of the giant's "brain" liberated from the stone skull with permission of Mr. William
Newell of Cardiff, finder and owner of the phenomenal
specimen.

The evening's first excitement came when Mr. Emerson
proclaimed the giant "a bona fide petrified human being,"
based on his close observation. The response was sustained
applause and audible cheers, especially from members of
the clergy present in large numbers.

The articulate Mr. Holmes then dampened the enthusiasm of the audience when he declared the giant to be,
not a petrification, but a stone statue "probably of great antiquity" and certainly an important and astonishing work
of art.

The same audience that cheered Mr. Emerson and
booed Mr. Holmes was struck silent when the outspoken
sculptor Erasmus Dow Palmer called the Cardiff Giant a
fraud and a bad one at that with no artistic or aesthetic
merit, the poor work of an untalented amateur.

Mr. Palmer's professional colleague, Cyrus Cobb, an artist of equal reputation, then leapt to the podium shouting
for all to hear that "any man who calls this thing a humbug
brands himself a fool." If the audience expected civilized
discourse, as well they might, they were treated, instead, to
an acrimonious exchange of sharply barbed epithets.

The spirited conversation was soon interrupted when
one of the assemblage, who had each paid the sum of ten
dollars for the privilege of standing shoulder to shoulder to
hear those erudite but conflicting pronouncements,
jumped to the stage and began to pummel Mr. Palmer
with his fists. While the Sage of Concord and Mr. Holmes

attempted to rescue the beleaguered sculptor, Mr. Cobb distanced himself from the vulgar display which quickly flared into general restlessness involving the audience in sporadic outbreaks of brawling.

The man who instigated the unspeakable assault upon Mr. Palmer was restrained and led away by alert officers of the Syracuse Police Department. He has not been identified at this writing though some say he is a blood relation of William Newell of Cardiff and a strong believer in the validity of the giant as ambassador from Genesis and a worker of miracles.

A silent witness to all this confusion, and one who offered no clue or further enlightenment, was the Cardiff Giant himself, on prominent display in the Yates Ballroom where he will remain through the New Year. After that, the giant will be moved to New York City for the public to view at a location yet to be announced.

The question, *Man, Statue—or Fraud,* thus remains unresolved, though the majority of those in attendance for the Hour of Decision seemed clearly to favor Mr. Emerson's fervent declaration that the object is a definite fossil of ancient origin in whose presence one can experience a clear echo of "the infinitude of man."

Many in the audience demanded a return of their money when they were disbursed, since the evening's festivities were terminated so abruptly. While a representative of *The Illustrated Magazine* did offer his sincere apology, there was no refund of the admission price. Said farmer Newell, who denied all requests for reimbursement, "You pays your money and you takes your chance. They got to see my giant, they got to hear four geniuses at two dollars fifty cents per genius and also saw a good fight. That seems like fair value to me."

"Make sure Rack gets a copy of that in Chicago," John Zipmeister said to the copy boy. "And tell our stringer in Syracuse, what's his name, to find out what he can about the nut who attacked Palmer. Headline the piece 'MAYHEM IN SALT CITY; MYSTERY MAN DEFENDS GOLIATH'S GOOD NAME.' Page three top. Find an artist who knows what those luminaries look like and give me a cartoon of the battle with the giant sitting up and watching the brouhaha. The yegg who beat up on Palmer should have a blank face."

"With a rag on his head?" the copy boy asked.

"What rag on who's head?"

"The stone head. They took out a piece of his brains."

"Good lad," Zipmeister said. "A rag on his head. Absolutely. And throw in a few shadows for bloodstains."

CARDIFF, NEW YORK, DECEMBER 7, 1869

George Hull sat drinking chamomile tea while Bertha Newell stared out her favorite window. A thin dusting of snow powdered the fields and gave Bear Mountain a luminous glow. "Winter is the honest season," Bertha said.

George touched the bruised blue skin under his left eye, then rubbed his sore ribs. The Syracuse Police worked him over after Stubby paid off two judges to get him out of jail and all charges dropped. The beating was gratuitous, compliments of the chief.

"Some birds stay, some birds go," Bertha said. "I favor the birds that stay, but I can't say how they manage to keep from freezing to death. I feel glad for having them and sorrow for what their little bodies must go through."

George, nursing his own pain, wished his twig-bodied, frost-faced cousin-in-law would shut up. Bertha usually said about five words a month, but today she chirped like one of her damned

Winter tweeters. It irked him that she worried about worm eaters when her own benefactor deserved solace.

Worse than the pain was the prickle of puzzlement George Hull felt. He had no way to explain his loss of control, outrageous behavior, and astonishing disregard of good manners. Since his pubescent tussles with brother Ben, George never assaulted anyone. His only adult act of violence was swinging a rake at the very same stone man whose integrity he'd defended with blows.

Integrity? What integrity? Who knew better that Erasmus Dow Palmer's denunciation was warranted? Without George's deceit, that displaced boulder, the Colossus of Cardiff, would be part of a cistern in Iowa. What confounded George most was remembering the sincerity of his rage. It wasn't the obvious fact that Palmer's words could mean financial disaster. That would make easy sense. But when George jumped into battle he was on a mission, fueled by the same vicious frenzy as might energize his opposite, the Reverend Turk.

While Bertha counted iced birds, George realized that, for a moment, he'd been the victim of his own splendid hoax. Stubby wrote that the giant *spoke* to him. Now George had to wonder if what pushed toward madness was that same stone voice.

Could it be he himself was no more than a pawn? Tight in the clutch of the capricious God he despised? If that were true, however fantastic, if Goliath was granted some vestige of life and a wisp of divinity, did that validate George's doubts of paternity? Then who waited in Angelica's womb? George pounded his hand against his forehead. Bertha heard the thuds but didn't turn from her window. "Chamomile tea is usually soothing," she said.

George went to Angelica's room. His wife was resting after a walk though white woods, her porcelain face leaf-veined and delicate. A torrent of warmth flooded through him. He leaned to kiss her but she turned away.

"Madonna," George said, "I need your pity now. I need some evidence that you are my wife."

"I wish I could give it," Angelica said. "There was a time when I could. But now it's too late, dear. Don't you know that?"

"Never too late."

"Too late is a real thing, George," Angelica said like a teacher.

"But our baby?"

"When the baby is born, I will leave. I don't know for what destination, but I know there's a place."

"You may leave," George said, his face burning, "but the child will stay with me."

"That's not possible, dear," Angelica said.

"You have nothing without George Hull. You are nothing without George Hull. Did you think I'd allow you to steal my son?"

"Son or daughter, this has nothing to do with you anymore."

"Nothing to do with me? My seed, Simon's grandchild, and nothing to do with me?" George slapped Angelica's face.

"Are you going to hurt me? If you are, better kill me because, if you don't, I will kill you."

"You're bewitched," George said.

"That may be true," Angelica said. "Yes, it's true."

George Hull tried to raise his arm again. It hung limp as a broken pendulum. He saw himself in Bertha Newell's broken mirror. His truncheoned blue face looked like fish on a plate.

NEW YORK, NEW YORK, DECEMBER 15, 1869

On December 12, the *New York Times, Tribune, Sun, American,* and *Clarion* carried full-page advertisements for Barnum's

MARCH OF THE GIANT!

With humility, pride and pleasure, Mr. P.T. Barnum
announces his acquisition of the wonder of the age,

TITAN, the *one*, the *only*, the *original* CARDIFF
GIANT of international fame.

To celebrate the arrival in New York of this astonishing
petrification, a modern miracle of ancient origin known to
work miracles of his own, a GRAND MARCH will take
place on December 15th, commencing at 9:00 AM, following a route extending from Harlem Lane, south
through Central Park, then along Fifth Avenue to Madison Square, thence down Broadway to Prince Street at
NIBLO'S GARDEN where the Giant will henceforth
appear on display in the illustrious company of that gigantic talent, the beloved TOM THUMB.

EAST SIDE, WEST SIDE, ALL AROUND THE
TOWN . . . COME WELCOME TITAN—STONE
MAN OF RENOWN!

From the far reaches of the Bronx to the depths of Brooklyn,
posters extended the same invitation. A thousand street Arabs and
newsies handed out fliers. The best Bowery bums wore sandwich
boards outside the Fifth Avenue Hotel on Madison Square and the
Astor House near City Hall. The steam yacht *River Queen*, converted to a floating billboard, navigated Manhattan's shoreline.
Niblo's Garden was wrapped in a banner like swaddling for a god.
"BARNUM'S GIANT COUP!" was headline news and the talk
of the town. As the story spread, churches of every denomination
were besieged by parishioners gathered to thank God, praise P.T.
Barnum, and stake early claims to whatever largesse the strange visitor might choose to dispense. Some ministers and priests rang
their bells for the stone man.

The Betsy Ross Flag Company on Fulton Street was barricaded
by customers frustrated by their efforts to find Old Glory in any
department store. Those supplies vanished within hours of the first
excitement. When that factory sold its last ensign, a riot sent
thirty-seven trampled patriots to City Hospital.

Amos Arbutnaut, Esq., more than surprised by the intense re-action of those same New Yorkers who'd be slow to react to their own obituaries, rushed to tell Barnum what was happening. "The city's in a flap. There's madness abroad."

Barnum listened, shook his head, and said, "It takes what's pro-fane to bring out what's sacred. I've always known that I do God's work. I hate when I underestimate myself," he said. "Too little, too late's a sure sign of decline."

Then Barnum sketched the design for a crucifix featuring Titan, sent messengers to search for a factory able to make at least five hundred of the relics in the span of four days, dispatched emissaries to locate sweatshops where Italians, Jews, and Chinamen could turn out small flags on sticks by the bushel.

"If we're going to have riots on our hands," Arbutnaut said, "you might consider an investment in bandages."

"Better corner the market for whistles and billy clubs," Barnum said. "No profit in bandages."

THE MARCH OF THE GIANT was blessed with good weather. The parade began on a warm, dry day borrowed from an-other season. Under a dappled sky, with sun rays splitting the clouds like fingers, a dozen marching bands strutted the vanguard. Scottish pipers blew stuck-pig squeals. Romanian Gypsies shook tambourines. There were German horns and Irish flutes, Polish dancers and African drummers, twirlers from Norway and nut-colored ragamuffins who played tarantellas on mouth organs.

Following the music came fifty regal trotters powering high-wheeled sulkies that raced across Harlem's fields like chariots. Next came a polyglot menagerie of lions, tigers, apes, zebras, and ele-phants corraled by Barnum in exchange for past and future favors to bankrupt owners of decrepit circuses that regularly toured the boondocks.

After the hodgepodge of animals came long lines of orphans in rented white robes waving pennants while they chanted songs of the Union. An impressive collection of the broken and maimed marched behind them, staggering, limping, or riding splayed on the backs of wagons. Three open-topped buses, all draped in black felt, kept a safe distance from the slow-moving damned. They transported musicians playing a dirge.

Finally, there came Titan's coach, a hearse bearing the One and Only Original Giant. Barnum saw no point in showing the audience the honored guest they would gladly pay to see, so he kept Titan hidden in a silver casket behind glass walls. Driving the hearse, in a somber top hat, General Thumb urged on the horses. Barnum sat beside him equally reverent, shedding real tears.

In a tunnel of cheers the parade moved along Central Park's curling trails, went around the bandshell out onto Fifth Avenue, cut through the skeletal shadows of scaffolding for St. Patrick's new cathedral, passed the Moorish towers of Temple Emanuel and the concrete wall of Croton Reservoir on 42nd Street. It skirted the charred site of the Negro Orphanage burned during the war by immigrants who feared drowning in a tide of black labor coming North for their jobs. The marchers pranced under huge windows of pristine Stewart Mansion, a tribute to mercantile wealth, swung onto Broadway at Madison Square where a more fashionable crowd gave quiet approval. Titan's caravan slid between a myriad of five-story office buildings, hives filled with the city's new entrepreneurs, headed toward Trinity Church and City Hall Park. The parade was purposely slowed near Printing House Square where reporters and illustrators fought men with cameras for vantage, then jammed in a clot near the entrance to the posh Metropolitan Hotel that abutted Niblo's Garden, where the giant would hold court. Despite a few pickpockets and brief anarchist protest, the march was a stunning success.

FREE ME FROM THIS COFFIN. I AM ABOUT *LIFE*, NOT DEATH. A RIOTOUS GENIE. A VORACIOUS SUN RISING. I CAN LIBERATE TREASURE FROM WOMBS OF ROCK. I KNOW WAYS TO FREE TROLLS, NYMPHS, AND SATYRS WHO HIDE IN THE SHADOWS OF SHADOWS. LET MY CROWD SEE ME! THEIR CHEERS ARE MY CARPET. TITAN WILL EAT THEIR FINE FACES. I PROMISE THEY'LL ENJOY EVERY BITE.

CARDIFF, NEW YORK, DECEMBER 17, 1869

———◆►◆◄◆———

Stubby Newell heard about Barnum's giant when a man from the *Syracuse Journal* asked him how even such a phenomenon as Goliath could be in two places at once. When he had his facts straight, Stubby made a dash back to Cardiff, where he found the battered George Hull in a galvanized state, sitting with Bertha, watching blackbirds peck snow.

"The nerve of that bastard Barnum. The *only original,* damn him to hell. What do we do, George? We got to do something."

"Does it matter?" George said. "*We* know the truth, and that's what's important."

"Snap out of your gloom and fast. Because whatever's addled your mind, neither of us can afford it. Do we eat nettles and humble pie or go down to New York for a fight? Christ, cousin, what I know is that only one giant deserves New York. There's more than money at stake. There's honor involved."

George was startled by Stubby Newell's eloquence. *Honor more than money?* He wondered whose voice was speaking. "Tell me again?"

"Listen this time. They're parading a giant named Titan through the streets and say our Goliath is two tons of crow splat."

"We've got things to do," George told Stubby.

"Bugger me," Stubby said, "don't I know it?"

CHICAGO, ILLINOIS, DECEMBER 18, 1869

When Barnaby Rack came to North Clark Street, he found Gerhardt Burquhart in mourning. The stonecutter's teacher and partner, Edward Salle, was found frozen solid two nights before. The police said Salle died in a snowbank, head buried, legs out, the possible victim of foul play, collision with a runaway horse, or a precipitous fall down a hill. Salle's remains lay in state in Burquhart's studio, scant and pale as a celery stalk, looking dead as he was despite daubs of rouge on his lips and cheeks. His two hands were wrapped in wet gauze.

"I am making a cast," Burquhart explained, "first in plaster of Paris, later in bronze. Those hands were the man, the man was his hands."

"This must be a terrible blow," Barnaby said.

"I should have died first. Edward Salle was my father, my son, and my friend. Still, he lives through his work. That man birthed seraphs and angels enough to populate Heaven twice. And how many sconces, pediments, gargoyles, fountains, assorted memorials? His heritage is a trail of beauty."

"May he rest in peace. He does seem peaceful."

"I could keep him like that for a year. He won't fall apart so fast. It's the alcohol. That and the freezing."

"A true petrification," Barnaby said.

"It could be said."

"It saddens me to think that a man of such talent never found wider fame. He's not the first to be so unfairly deprived. I suppose one can take comfort remembering those anonymous artists whose works are eternal gifts to the race. What they left behind are all that survives once-mighty empires and heralded monarchs. Their names may be unknown but their claim to immortality goes undisputed. What a pity nobody outside Chicago heard tell of Edward Salle. But he left his mark and there's his victory."

"I wouldn't say nobody outside Chicago heard of Edward," Burquhart said. "We got work from a hundred places."

"Local fame, yes," Barnaby said. "I was speaking of wider and more universal notoriety. If only Mr. Salle had been given some challenge to equal his ability. Not to degrade the value of a crypt in Chicago, but there is a difference between that and the cupola of St. Peter's in Rome."

"If his work, our work, is limited to what you call local fame, then why are you here, Mr. Rack? You said you were sent by the *New York Clarion.*"

"Frankly, I came to Chicago for other reasons. But when I read, quite by chance, of Mr. Salle's unfortunate demise, something about the story piqued my curiosity. The obituary mentioned the facade of a Franciscan monastery in Des Plaines as one of his more formidable works. Being naturally curious and a student of architecture, I went out of my way to see it."

"The façade of the Little Brothers of Solitude was a mutual effort. Actually, my contribution was substantial."

"In any case, I had the most curious reaction. The bas-relief showing the agony of fratricide's first victim, Abel, speared my eye. This will sound foolish, I know, but it reminded me of another creation I recently viewed."

"What other creation?"

"The Giant of Cardiff. You've heard of the find?"

"Of course," Burquhart said. "Who doesn't know of the stone man? Are we pygmies in Illinois?"

"Hailed by some as a fossil, called fraud by cynics, cheered by our best critics as a perfect work of art."

"And what do you think, Mr. Rack?"

"I think the giant too perfect for an accident of nature. More tribute to God if he proves a statue, crafted in passion by the Lord's best creation. I hope someday you see him for yourself, Mr. Burquhart. I've never been so moved to piety."

"When New York is done with the giant, he'll find his way back to Chicago. Then I'll see him and make up my own mind."

"Find his way *back* to Chicago?"

"A slip of the tongue."

"Do you know William Newell?"

"I never heard the name."

"Then why, sir, is he sending you money?"

"Why would he send me money?"

"Mr. Burquhart, just for the sake of argument, if it were to be discovered that Cardiff's Goliath was more statue than fossil, and the product of artisans closer to present than past, think what that would mean."

"I'm sure I don't know."

"To the creator or creators, a full share of glory."

"More glory than gold, I suspect," Burquhart said.

"Would the late Edward Salle choose posthumous wealth and eternal obscurity over a seat in the Hall of Greatness?"

"I'm still a young man, Mr. Rack. Poor Edward is dead."

"And would you let him stay dead when you might be the agent of your friend's resurrection?"

"He will stay dead no matter what I do or say," Burquhart said. "As for glory, that often comes long after one's last earthly breath. Should glory be hurried? Say, for example, when Gerhardt Burquhart meets the Reaper, a diary might be found filled with strange revelations. In the meantime, there are many seats in many halls where a well-fed artist can comfortably park his behind."

"Let me take another tack," Barnaby said. "What if gold and glory came together, both in time to fully savor?"

"Interesting," Burquhart said. "But even then, there are contracts to consider. Serious pledges to uphold."

"Common wisdom tells us contracts are made to be broken. Pledges given in haste can prove unfair burdens. Consider, if a great newspaper like the *New York Clarion* was willing both to subsidize and to celebrate the work of a brilliant sculptor, never neglecting to honor the memory of his deceased associate, both muse and purse would be well served."

"Muse and purse, you say? That combination could inspire any sensible man to confession. As for adoring the memory of a deceased associate, some praise might be in order but not necessarily offered in excess. The living, after all, have more use for attention."

"Understood," Barnaby said. "And you should understand, Mr. Burquhart, one man's hesitation is another's opportunity. If there is a story to tell, sooner or later someone will tell it. What's told sooner is valuable news. What's said later just another worthless echo."

Burquhart went over to Edward Salle's corpse and patted his colleague's thawing head. "Do we have something to say to this man?"

Barnaby Rack, feeling queasy, asked where he could relieve himself. In the outhouse behind the barn where the giant was carved Barnaby pulled down his pants, sat on a cold rim, lit a Goliath, let out a groan, then slammed his fist so hard against the door two fingers cracked at the knuckles.

NEW YORK, NEW YORK, DECEMBER 19, 1869

Ben Hull watched his workmen raise a crystal chandelier to the newly paneled ceiling of Simon Hull & Sons Humidor.

"It's like a crown," Loretta said. "I feel like an empress."

"I won't tell you the cost," Ben said.

"A lot of double coronas," George Hull said. "Which is all the more reason to accept our offer."

"The idea is demeaning," Ben said. "It detracts from the image of elegance."

"Damn your image of elegance," George said. "All we're asking for is a third of the space. Who would be hurt? At the rate things are going, the humidor won't open before February. Ben, I've invested heavily in Goliath. Stubby struck a hard bargain to sell me a share. We need a place to show our giant to the public what with Barnum's fraud soaking the limelight."

"Hull's Humidor is a family venture. The stone man is your private affair. I don't think Father would approve."

"Of course he would. Why not? Your carpenters can easily build a wall there, and a platform there, and a separate entrance there. The arrangement is only temporary. We've offered you rent enough to pay for six chandeliers and a share of the till to buy all the elegance you need."

"How much did you pay Cousin Stubby for your partnership?"

"Thirty-five thousand of the bank's money. And still a bargain at the price. I would have given twice that."

"With what collateral?"

"My share of Simon Hull & Sons."

"You risked your own future on a whim?"

"Whim? You see how the crowds line up for Barnum. We'll put him out of business and do twice as well."

"How will you put Barnum out of business?" Loretta asked.

"He has no leg to stand on. We have every proof that our giant is the real Cardiff Giant. Our suit stipulates that the Barnum copy be publicly destroyed, mashed to meal, and we've demanded a hundred thousand in damages. The great Mr. Barnum will squirm before we're done with him. He'll be run out of town."

"You guarantee that there would be no interruption to our renovations? When we're ready to expand to that space you would vacate?"

"Absolutely. Do we have a choice? We must be near Niblo's Garden, and there's no other place to be had. This is war, brother. What do you think, Loretta?"

"I don't know what to say, George. It seems exciting, two giants in conflict for the heart of New York."

"Exciting. Exactly. Enormously exciting. They'll come in droves. And when the court decides in our favor, more exciting."

"I say make room in the manger," Loretta said. "Why not let Goliath in?"

"Don't compare Hull's to a manger," Ben said.

"She was speaking in the biblical sense."

"What Loretta says or thinks has no relevance in this matter. George, what madness possessed you to abandon our factory for this trip? Can Angelica be trusted to cope with all you left behind?"

"Not Angelica. Angelica is in Cardiff with Bertha Newell."

"In Cardiff? Angelica is in Cardiff?"

"She was feeling poorly. Dr. Larchmont suggested country air."

"Then who is in charge up in Binghamton?"

"I put Percy Waters in charge," George said. "He's a capable foreman."

"Percy Waters may be capable but he's not a Hull. George, what's got into you?"

"Listen, brother, because this isn't easy to say. I've seen Goliath, watched him weave spells. It's far past any logic. There are forces at play we can't comprehend. No opportunistic promoter owns the right to trivialize honest wonderment. P.T. Barnum has committed an egregious sin. It's as if he brought forth a duplicate Jesus to fleece honest Christians."

"A second Jesus?" Loretta said. "What an idea."

"You've gone too far," Ben said. "First you jeopardize all our efforts and now speak of an excess of Jesuses? The sacrilege is yours, George."

"I apologize for my mouth. But, Ben, we must have the space."

"Have it then. But for only a month."

"Agreed. Bless you. You won't be sorry. And as for image, have no fear. The giant will never demean these premises. No, he will sanctify them. And the sale of Goliath Cigars will buy you this building twice over."

"We're dealing in premium product. Simon Hull & Sons Humidor is no candy cart. Our appeal is to the cream of society. Goliath Cigars will never be sold here. Get that through your head."

"Your face is red, Ben," Loretta said. "Let me take George upstairs and show him what you've done with the mezzanine parlor. It's a beautiful room, all in wood with a fireplace that easily could roast an ox."

"Go ahead, show him. Though I doubt he cares."

"Oh, I care," George said. "I care deeply."

"There, you see, dear. He cares. Come, George."

Loretta led George up a carpeted staircase lined by wrought-iron banisters decorated with smoke rings and swirls. They went through a door marked HULL HALL, MEMBERS ONLY.

The room they entered could serve for a chapel. Stained glass windows showed scenes of lush Cuban fields, Connecticut valleys where silken shadow plants towered, Danli in Honduras, Temple Estates in Jamaica, soft Dominican hills, hidden glens in Nicaragua, Mexican knolls, shaded jungles in Cameroon, all Eldorados of the pungent leaf.

The walls were covered in walnut. Great cabinets of spicy Spanish cedar, Honduras mahogany, and cherrywood held hundreds of drawers where Hull cigars would age as slowly and gracefully as Tibetan lamas. "A palace," George said. "When Simon sees this, he'll grant Ben knighthood."

"No furniture yet," Loretta said. "It will all be Empire, each piece plump as a turkey and covered in brocade with little *H*s for *Hull* embroidered in the cushions. Chairs, sofas, tables, lamps everywhere. The rugs are from Persia."

"Splendid," George said. "But don't forget ashtrays."

"Sit with me," Loretta said, pulling George to the floor. "Now tell me about Angelica. In Cardiff, you said, on the doctor's advice? What's wrong with her?"

"Everything and nothing," George said. "The woman is plagued by a squadron of imps. I suspect it's her mind."

"Dear Angelica," Loretta said. "Unhappy George."

"I haven't time to lament. My purpose is clear enough. To vindicate a terrible wrong."

"You're serious about this giant?"

"Quite serious. Serious indeed. Yes, I'm serious."

"Look at the flood of light from those windows," Loretta said. "It's like bathing in the Garden of Eden."

"Niblo's Garden is more on my mind. Where an abomination bathes in false adulation."

"I miss our mornings together," Loretta said. "Your Angelica has her problems, my Ben has his. He lives only for this place and dreams of cigars. There's no room in his life for Loretta."

"We each carry a cross," George said.

Loretta stretched flat. She lay glowing inside a rainbow. Her fawn eyes closed. She licked her lips wet. "It's so good to see you, George. If you wish, you may hold me. Only gently. Nothing will happen."

"Nothing can happen," George said. "What if some plumber or carpenter walks through that door?"

"No one will come," Loretta said. "I promise you that. They're all busy downstairs."

"Angelica has a bun in the oven."

"What did you say?" Loretta sat up, opened her eyes, retracted her tongue.

"It's true. I was keeping the news until Simon got home."

"A baby?" Loretta said, flexing. "How wonderful." Loretta knew Simon Hull's priorities. Even the grand opening of Hull's Humidor in New York wouldn't compete with news of a baby. "I never thought a woman of her frail constitution . . ."

"The giant," George said, "works miracles."

"Stubby's stone man? What are you telling me?"

The door to Hull Hall opened to let Tom Thumb in. The General looked down at Loretta and George on the rug. "Salutations," he said, tipping his derby. "I ran over between shows to see what progress was made since last week."

"This is my brother-in-law, Mr. George Hull," Loretta said, fluffing her skirt. "And this is our good friend, the gracious Tom Thumb."

"An honor, Mr. Hull. I've heard much of you."

"Thumb? Barnum's Thumb?" George barked, leaping up. "Insect! Vermin! Churl! Bounder! Scoundrel! How dare you enter this place?"

"Is he a critic?" Thumb asked, backing away.

"Must you be rude? Is that what it comes to? Please forgive him, Tom. There's much on his mind."

"Don't fret, dear lady. Though I cannot imagine the cause for such vituperation. If he was a foot taller, I would seek satisfaction. As it is, I will wish you good day."

SYRACUSE, NEW YORK, DECEMBER 21, 1869

Stubby Newell read a prepared statement to the Syracuse press: "It may be that the Prince of Humbug needed a vulgar display of pomp and puffery for his blatant fraud, but my petrification is the true excitement, as all who come to see him will instantly know and appreciate. We are sorry to leave this fine city so soon, but circumstance gives us no choice. Our hope is that the people of the New York metropolis will prove as warm and hospitable as our friends in Salt City and that when Mr. Barnum's facsimile is fully discredited you will welcome us home again."

George Hull's stone man was wrapped in quilting, crated in a flag-draped pine box, secured to a flatbed, and carried to the railway station. The giant's wagon was followed by a spontaneous procession of admirers hoping for one last miracle. Sadly, they were left disappointed, though one woman discarded her crutch, attempted a dance in the snow, managed two turns then fell comatose into a rut.

An honor guard drummed the giant aboard a private Pullman car with Stubby and a nurse as its only other passengers. The nurse was George Hull's idea, enforcing the notion that Goliath was not only a man but hid a flicker of life. If he should suddenly moan, groan, twitch, and require medical attention, it was there for the having. Stubby watched the round, comely lass unbundle, thinking if he was her patient he'd be slow to recover.

"What's your name, girl?" Stubby asked when the train pulled out. "Mine's William Newell. The feller in the box was found on my farm down in Cardiff."

"I know who you are, Mr. Newell. I'm Amy Plunkett from Baldwinsville, just outside Syracuse."

"You seem a bit jumpy, Miss Amy. No need. The giant won't hurt you and I'm a religious man."

"My case of nerves has little to do with the giant and certainly nothing to do with you. I've never been to New York City but I have heard tales told of that infamous place."

"Heck, I used to feel nerved up about going to Syracuse," Stubby said. "The thing is, neither you, nor me, nor my fossil has been to New York so far as I know. Maybe the giant went down there in ancient days, but then it was probably no more than a patch of weeds. Well, who cares? A city is a city."

"I hope not," Amy Plunkett said. "Let New York be a whirlwind to swirl me around. I want it like nothing and no place I know, Mr. Newell. I want to be enchanted to fainting and dance with every man, woman, and child I see. I want to climb to the top of all the buildings and jump down to the arms of some young king of commerce. It's all got to happen in three hours because then's my train back."

"How old are you, girl?"

"Eighteen today."

"Well, happy birthday, you feisty Miss Amy. Many happy returns of the day. A scant eighteen summers. More nursling than nurse. Got a son, Alexander, almost your age. He's a sailor gone to chase whales or some such."

"If I was a man I'd do the same."

"Well, I'm glad you're not a man. Because we have a long trip to take and I'd rather be here cozy with a pert, pretty birthday girl than any man, including the King of France. Miss Amy, I didn't know of your birthday and I don't have chocolates to give you, but I do have a small bit of rum in my sack. And I think we should drink a toast to your three hours in the whirlwind."

"Alcohol? Oh, never. It wouldn't be right."

"Right as rain. It's not like we don't have a chaperon watching us from inside his box. And a healthy one at that. I doubt you'll have much else to occupy your time beyond Stubby Newell."

"One teeny tiny drink, then."

"One teeny tiny it is, and who knows but your stay might extend to more than three hours because with my life going as it is I might need a nurse of my own. I suffer palpitations these hard days. I feel my heart in my throat, *boom boom boom.*" Stubby reached for his flask. He looked over at Goliath and asked a small favor.

What is the city they speak of? I was content in Cardiff. Well adjusted in Syracuse. Now New York? A whirlwind? My embrace is wide enough to accommodate a galaxy so let the wind blow. Who is Titan? Can it be I have family? What a joyful discovery that would be. Not that I need a friend other than Source. But someone who answers in a voice made of earth. What? The Stubby asks favors? First a piece of my head and now? It's never enough with them. Ah, that again? Conjugation? Which reminds me. Where is the Angelica? I'd make room in my box for that one. There was a frightening lesson. Yes, Stubby, I know what you want. No, I won't look away. Would that Source would show similar interest. We've had a hard time, Source and I, since that night of moist juxtaposition. A sad barrier to close conversation. My fault surely. Insufficient eloquence. To see Source sulk. Can the Creator envy His creation? Gingerly, Stubby. Or must I do it for you?

"Make a wish on your candle," Stubby said.

"Please, Mr. Newell, tell me you love me."

Love you? How could I not? Your charm and beauty transcend any language. Your warmth is enough to melt both polar caps. To die on your thighs is rebirth. Yes, girl. I do love you. And ask your forgiveness. For all that I feel is less than enough. Oh, sweetheart. Your breasts are moons. Your cave a labyrinth for endless and noble adventure. Your breath my reverie. Et cetera, and so forth.

"Hell, I love you to pieces, Miss Amy. Titties to toenails."

FORT DODGE, IOWA, DECEMBER 21, 1869

Barnaby Rack, gulping air, climbed a pile of rock, following Mike Foley, who moved like a mountain goat. "And you remember the man?"

"I remember him. The day he came was hotter than Satan's balls. We stung him for a keg of cold beer."

"His name?"

"Don't recall if he gave me his name."

"Gerhardt Burquhart? A German?"

"Didn't talk like a kraut."

"William Newell?"

"Don't ring a bell."

"Hiram Hole?"

"That sounds closer. I can't say, though."

"Young? Old? Tall? Short?"

"A matured man. About as high as my nose. City clothes. Had a pocket full of cigars. Gave us a few when he went."

"Do you know where he went?"

"Yep, that much I know. Washington, D.C., for some kind of

monument they're making. With pieces taken from all states and
territories, including a share of Iowa gypsum."

"Anything else?"

"Not much," Foley said. "Except I heard he busted up a couple
of good wagons and had to pay for the damage. I warned him he
carried tons of dead weight but he wanted it whole."

"And you're sure this happened back in '68?"

"I'm sure," Foley said. "Right here is the spot we quarried it out.
Nice clean cut."

"So this is the stark, sterile womb, lair of giants," Barnaby Rack
said, noting the phrase in his book.

"You sound like that preacher."

"What preacher?"

"Reverend Turk, our Genesis Man. Anything you want to know
about giants, ask him."

" 'There were giants in those days,' do you mean that Reverend
Turk?"

"There's the one," Foley said. "Made us famous telling how
Adam and Eve live around here. Some don't believe him but, between you and me, it's the gospel truth. Because I know them both.
That Adam's a strange one, always playing with his snake. His little Evie's some kind of apples. I'd introduce you but they stay to
themselves."

"I'll meet them next trip," Barnaby said. He handed the wiseass
three *Clarion* dollars for his trouble.

Burquhart gave no proof to back up his story beyond a few notes
in a journal. Finding the quarry offered some confirmation, but
Mike Foley's memory of trading rock for cold beer could hardly be
final corroboration. Edward Salle was dead. The St. Charles Hotel
in Fort Dodge had neither Newell nor Hole on its register. No
surprise that his man used an alias. What next?

John Zipmeister would split his pants laughing. Barnaby felt an
itch under the cast on his hand. "Another itch I can't scratch," he
said sourly.

NEW YORK, NEW YORK, DECEMBER 21, 1869

It took George Hull a day and night of pleading. He'd found Edwin Booth holed up in his town house on Gramercy Park, so tenderized by his brother's horrific performance at Ford's Theater that any ray of light made him wince.

George gained entry to the actor's fortress through sheer persistence. He banged on Booth's door every five minutes for two hours. He slammed the knocker masks of Comedy and Tragedy until wood chips flew. Finally the great thespian, crazed with rage, came to chastise that arrogant woodpecker.

Booth, in a thick cape, an arm shielding his face, opened his chained door wide enough for George to hand him a calling card made for the moment. It had no name, only an etching of the agonized Cardiff Giant. Booth looked at the card, saw himself, wept out of control, and granted George audience.

George followed the caped genius upstairs to a grim self-styled dungeon, its curtains drawn tight, its air smelling of shame. A single candle reflected from the glossy eyes of costumed puppets that dangled from the ceiling, hung from every wall, filled each chair, and lay heaped on the floor. With the dolls watching like witnesses, George made his outrageous proposal: that only an Edwin Booth had the stature to present the true Goliath to Gotham.

Of course Booth refused. He explained that he'd perished with Lincoln. Assassinated both by private guilt and in the merciless court of public opinion. Booth said escaping that musty prison would violate his conscience. Besides, should he dare show himself, he'd be skewered on sight.

George came prepared to counter that argument. "Mr. Booth, what if the giant was sent as an omen? To throw open a stage door for incomparable Edwin Booth? Should the act of a criminal sibling, however unspeakable, doubly deprive this dark world of light? I only pray that such a worthy petitioner as the Cardiff Giant will coax Booth back to the boards where he belongs." Booth asked for a cigar. George gave it and lit it.

That night, with the streets all but deserted, George Hull and the illustrious fugitive slipped through a fire exit, then into that portion of Hull's Humidor already converted to a modest auditorium. George struck another match. There, on a makeshift platform, Goliath waited, fearsome in its flicker. George embraced a trembling Booth and left him alone with the terrible stone man.

Who is this one wrapped in sorrow? Speak to me of suffering? I who have vomited lava and had grubs mate in my mouth? Look at this body. A twisted vine. An unsynchronized face. Alien and alone in the city. And you weep for yourself? Be glad you can weep. What can I?

Edwin Booth dropped his cloak, stepped onto the platform, raised his arms, and declaimed the entire script of *The Tempest,* taking all parts. The only applause came from George Hull, who applauded for Booth and for himself.

NEW YORK, NEW YORK, DECEMBER 23, 1869

THE RETURN OF EDWIN BOOTH!
GOLIATH TRUMPS *TITAN*
BARNUM BURNS AGAIN

December 22, instant. Tonight, acclaimed actor Edwin Booth will emerge from exile to appear as host for the Giant of Cardiff. Booth, who has lived as a virtual hermit since Mr. Lincoln's tragic death at the hands of his late brother, has told friends that the ancient behemoth made a *personal appeal* asking that the artist risk public rancor and even vendetta to act as its spokesman.

The giant, Goliath, who "convinced" Mr. Booth to renounce isolation, is newly arrived from upstate and not to be confused with his counterpart, Titan, now on display at Niblo's Garden under the aegis of P.T. Barnum. Mr. Barnum contends that his giant is the *only, original* fossil dug from the ground in Cardiff, New York, supporting his claim with a bill of sale allegedly signed by Mr. William Newell on whose farm the giant was discovered.

Mr. Newell, who labels the signature fraudulent, has filed suit insisting that Titan be pulverized. He demands substantial compensation for himself as plaintiff. Newell has petitioned the court to grant a quick hearing to the case, allowing for the fact that thousands of patrons regularly jam the streets outside Niblo's box office.

Said Newell, "We must save those New Yorkers duped into squandering good money on Barnum's newest humbug. We must halt this affront to every citizen and even to heaven's own angels!"

Mr. Barnum refused the *Clarion*'s request for an interview. His representative, Amos Arbutnaut, Esq., issued a short statement denouncing Mr. Newell's allegations as "so many sour grapes grown by a failed farmer whose own grapes come up raisins." Justice will soon decide whether Newell's charges are sour grapes or valid gripes.

A *Clarion* survey reveals that Booth's return is regarded by most New Yorker as a welcome event. Even General Tom Thumb, who shares billing with rival giant, Titan, admitted to his pleasure at the prospect of having Booth active again. "Like Mr. Booth," said buoyant Thumb, "I too have aspired to Shakespearean roles, but lacked inspiration while Edwin remained in seclusion. Competition is the actor's spice and our best motivation. Now that he's back, I will entertain offers for my *Hamlet*. Mr. Barnum and myself wish Booth nothing but triumph. Even if his Goliath be ersatz, be assured his performance will be genuine."

Mr. Booth's historic appearance tonight will take place before an invited audience of civic leaders at an auditorium adjacent to Hull's Humidor, soon to open on Broadway. Tickets for future performances will be available beginning at 9AM tomorrow morning.

CARDIFF, NEW YORK, DECEMBER 23, 1869

"There's a drummer outside," Angelica said.

"Only one peddler I know comes around in December and I don't want him here."

"It might be diverting to examine his wares. The man seems harmless enough."

Bertha got up from her chair and went to the window. "It's him, sure enough. The Jew dowser Bupkin who found us our giant. He lives over in Lafayette and sells odds and ends."

"He's the color of ice. I see through to his bones."

"Don't waste your pity," Bertha said. "He should know better than to come here. Nobody in Cardiff buys from him anymore. Not since the giant. Oh, in Spring I suppose he'll do a brisk business dowsing for fossils now everybody wants one. But he'll have a hard time doing anything else."

"If people believe the stone man is holy, why turn away the dowser who dowsed him?"

"Even holy is magic and magic is trouble. Especially Hebrew magic, and that's a known fact. So best play it safe. Anyhow, since Stubby got so rich I buy from the store so Bupkin has nothing to sell Bertha Newell."

"I wouldn't mind a bit of cotton for a bunting. Lord knows, some sewing might make the days go faster."

"All right, then, I'll ask him in, but don't tell people I did. They look at me weird enough these days," Bertha said. "And if you buy from him, don't buy too much. And say to him, Bupkin, I don't want you boasting around how you sold this and that to the Newells. He does that to perk up their interest."

"Mum's the word," Angelica said, waiting a knock at the door. When it came she went to answer and found a young man brushing sleet off his face and stomping snow off his boots.

"Good day to you, madam," Aaron Bupkin said. "I wonder if Mrs. Newell is at home as I've some things to show her suitable for the holiday season."

"Come on in," Angelica said. "Stand by the fire."

Inside the house, Aaron nodded to Bertha, slapped his hands together for warmth, then laid out his line. "The finest wools and cotton, muslin, lace, and brocade," he said, "from the fashion capitals of the world. I have yarn, needles, thread, thimbles, and a whole book of new patterns, easy to follow and each one unique. There are combs and barrettes and assorted conveniences."

"Would you like some hot coffee?" Angelica asked.

"They won't drink our coffee," Bertha said. "Or eat what we eat."

"I wouldn't mind something hot in my gullet."

"Let's not talk of gullets or gizzards, if you don't mind," Bertha said, "when a yes or a no is sufficient."

"Sorry, Mrs. Newell," Aaron said. "May I ask the name of your charming guest?"

"I'm Angelica Hull, Mr. Newell's cousin by marriage."

"Nice to meet you, ma'am. I'm Aaron Bupkin from Lafayette."

"This ain't a social call, is it?" Bertha said. "I'm this and you're that has noplace here, does it?"

Angelica poured Aaron's coffee. He blew at a curl of steam and drank. The dark liquid brought him to color. His square-jawed face thawed around deep-brown eyes. His nose and big ears turned beet red. The Jew looked like a raccoon.

"That did the trick," Aaron said.

"Get down to your business," Bertha said.

"Tell me what you need, ladies. Something for a dress, a warm shawl, or a quilt?"

"Cotton for a bunting."

"Someone's expecting a visitor," Aaron said.

"Forget who's expecting a visitor," Bertha said. "Just show her what might be suitable and remember my sister-in-law is a poor woman who can't afford frills. They charge what they want. It's the way of the race."

"Ah, you know my prices are fair, Mrs. Newell. Always have been, always will be. And I know you have a sharp eye for a bargain."

"I hope you remember that," Bertha said.

Angelica's concentration went from Aaron Bupkin's inventory of cloth to a trickle of blood that ran down his cheek. "Excuse me for pointing it out," she said, "but you're bleeding."

"Is that our concern?" Bertha said. "If he's bleeding he's bleeding so long as he don't bleed on my floor."

"It's the cold," Aaron said, while he pressed a handkerchief to the wound. "Slows the scabbing. Fact is, I got hit on the head by a man in the valley."

"For good reason, I'd think," Bertha said.

"Reason is I went up there to look at some land."

"There's a good enough reason. Look at land? First Mrs. Elm rents you a room, now you want to buy our valley? Folks around here don't relish the prospect of a herd of Jews stampeding through town."

"No stampede, only me," Aaron said. "There's twenty acres up there and a ticky-tack house owned by a widow who lives now in Vermont. I'd do her a favor to take over the place."

"Some kind of favor. The kind you get hit on the head for," Bertha said.

"That's what my grandfather told me," Aaron said.

"A wise man, I'd say. You should have turned on your ears when he said it."

"This one," Angelica said, "the pink one."

"Why not the blue?" Bertha said.

"It's a girl, I can feel it."

"What a thing to say. Thank God Cousin George didn't hear you."

"How many yards is enough?"

"I'd say two yards to be certain," Aaron said.

"It's a human baby, not a 'potamus," Bertha said. "You can see she's a delicate woman. Yard and a half did for my son, and Alexander was the size of a pumpkin. How much for a yard and a half of both pink and blue?"

"Nothing," Aaron said. "You already paid me. That coffee saved my life and the company of two charming women cheered my day. Have a healthy baby, Mrs. Hull. Tell her Uncle Aaron gave her a bunting."

"Stop that," Bertha said. "You're not getting away with it. Take presents from Uncle Aaron and there goes the land. State a price, Mr. Bupkin, and then cut it in half."

"No, I insist," Aaron said. "And I'll throw in a scissors if you need one."

"See how they connive?" Bertha said. "She ain't going to love you more for what's free so tell her the cost."

"I thank you," Angelica said. "For myself and the little one. It's a very sweet gesture and appreciated."

Angelica reached out her hand and he shook it. It was the first time Aaron had been touched, except by himself, since Isaac went home. Angelica's hand was more thawing than her coffee. He looked at her smile and couldn't turn away.

"Is something wrong with you?" Bertha said. "You're starting to bleed again."

Bertha watched Aaron leave to be sure he was gone. "Let me tell you, Angelica, this is Cardiff, not Binghamton, and we have our own ways. Never look in the eyes of a man like that."

"His eyes didn't frighten me," Angelica said, fingering the cotton.

"Did he drip anyplace?" Bertha said, searching for drops. "They do that on purpose. Their blood turns to wrigglers in the shank of the night that hide waiting in drawers and cubbies."

Later, while Bertha sorted Christmas ornaments, Angelica sat alone grouping wooden pieces of a jigsaw puzzle by color. The puzzle, a Nativity scene, had already begun to take shape. Most of the Three Kings had materialized along with assorted animals and bits of the holy family. Half of Mary's glowing face was visible and part of her shoulder and bosom. The chubby pink legs and a tiny hand of baby Jesus was in place. Joseph's sandled feet protruded from a brown robe.

It struck Angelica that, with the possible exception of the Magi, a few chickens, a goat, a horse, and a cow, everybody else was some kind of Jew. She found a fragment of Joseph that linked his beard to the robe and snapped it neatly into the picture. She wondered if he would turn out looking anything like the dowser. Bertha said they all looked alike because they fornicated with their own off-spring. It was part of their ongoing plot to recapture the world and own everything that wasn't tied down. She said Jews secretly controlled banks and stores, factories and whole empires. If there were so few Jews around these days and they managed so much power, Angelica wondered why they weren't studied like primers.

NEW YORK, NEW YORK, DECEMBER 23, 1869

*"Were children in thy home, to climb thy knee
And pluck thy beard, secure, and dare thy power,
Or, was thy nature as its substance now,
Like stone—as cold and unimpressible?"*

"Christ, but that man can act," Stubby said, peeking through a break in the curtain. "His voice is like ants on my skin."

"Do you believe the audience?" George said. "Morgan, Rockefeller, Carnegie, Fisk, Pullman, Westinghouse, Villard, Harriman, Hill, Belmont, Vanderbilt, and that one in the second row is Jay Gould, who damn near pulled the country down on Black Friday. The one with the bulb for a nose is Pierpont Morgan. Any one of those men could afford to buy himself a pyramid. The fat one in the corner is Boss Tweed trailed by Mayor Oakey Hall with every reporter in town there behind them. Take a sniff. You can smell their women from here. So tell me, Ben, are you sorry about your tenant now?"

"Remains to be seen," Ben Hull said. "Coming out for Edwin Booth and Goliath is one thing. Joining Hull's Humidor is something else. I'll do what you said, send each of them a complimentary box of Ulysses Triple Supremos with a gracious note to thank them for attending. I hope it's not a waste of money."

"I wonder who's over at Niblo's Garden tonight," George

said. "Besides the usual riffraff. Not many movers and shakers, I'd guess."

> *Tell us the story of thy life, and whether*
> *Of woman born—substance and spirit*
> *In mysterious union wed—or fashioned*
> *By hand of man from stone, we bow in awe,*
> *And hail thee, GIANT OF ONONDAGA!*

"Get into place, Stubby," George said. "Rattle the tin sheets when I part the curtain. Is Loretta ready?"

The audience gave Edwin Booth a standing ovation. Loretta, in a blue gown, rushed to hand him a bouquet of American Beauty roses. Booth took the roses, gave Loretta a kiss on the cheek, and went out among his admirers. There were handshakes and hugs, more kisses and embraces.

"He thought they despised him," George said. "Look at that gush of affection."

"Should I rattle?" Stubby asked.

"When the emotion peaks. Wait . . . wait . . . now."

Stubby Newell grabbed both sides of the flat sheet of tin and shook it. The tin made a rolling, ominous, thunderous sound. Edwin Booth gestured toward a brocaded curtain. "Ladies and gentlemen of New York, from the most ancient reaches of antiquity, a warrior who, for all his might, majesty and pride, yielded but never succumbed to the Dark Harvester's sharp scythe. Who was he? What astonishments did he behold in those distant days when Earth was young and marvels as common as flowers? Ladies and gentlemen, for your edification and pleasure, it is my honor to present the petrified man, America's own Goliath but with David's kind heart. He alone holds honest claim to the title of the *one, the only, the original* Cardiff Giant!"

George pulled the curtain apart. There was the stone man surrounded by candles, his privates covered by Old Glory in silk. glowing phosphorescent as the aurora. The audience gasped as

Loretta sang "Amplest Grace with Thee I Find," then joined in "The Battle Hymn."

"We got it made," Stubby whispered, silencing the tin storm at George's signal. "Your movers and shakers are swallowing him whole, no different than Gideon Emmons or Henry Nichols when they rooted him back of my barn. Cousin George, I salute you." Stubby saluted while George gestured for him to shut his mouth.

"We invite your close inspection," Edwin Booth said. "Feel free, one and all, to approach the platform and browse our fabulous fossil to your heart's content. For we are more than confident that the more you inspect, the more convinced you will be that here is the genuine Genesis man best entitled to your full admiration."

The crowd left their places and came up to the stage in small groups. Some hesitated to touch Goliath, but Loretta encouraged them to reach. A young man, Thomas Edison, in New York seeking capital for a mechanical voting machine of his invention, was the first to run his fingers over the pocked chest. After that, the others lost shyness. The men rubbed arms, legs, neck, and thighs, slapped and patted the giant's great head. The women limited their fingers to stroking the face.

Jim Fisk, lubricated with whiskey and less tactful than he might be, said, "I can't speak for the rest of you, but I'm game to see what Goliath keeps under his skirt." Fisk lifted the flag. "Impressive. I think the gentlemen and ladies would agree. Though there seems to be something missing and we can't know the full size of the thing. At times like this I thank the Lord for the faculty of inspired imagination."

"That's a disgrace," Cornelius Vanderbilt said. "Let me apologize for Jim's vulgar outburst."

"I'd apologize for myself," Fisk said, "if I knew how."

Andrew Carnegie helped Vanderbilt replace the flag while Mayor Oakey Hall smoothed its fringe. John Zipmeister, there for the *Clarion* and curious to compare not his genitals with a giant's but his reactions to the mix of amazement and doubt that plagued Barnaby Rack, asked Stubby Newell about the bruised phallus. "By the color of the stone, I'd say the fissure was recent," Zipmeister said. "Was there some accident?"

"The thing is so old, pieces fall off him." Stubby said, before he could think. "You're right, though. His dick was intact when we found him, about six inches longer, give or take. But like it or not, there's no reason to quibble when what's there could take on Jenny Lind and the Grand Canyon too."

"Thank you, Mr. Newell," Zipmeister said. "Most enlightening."

"What has William been saying?" George Hull asked, while Zipmeister wrote in his pad.

"Nothing, George," Stubby said. "We was just talking shop."

Ladies and gentlemen, new friends. This is my first attempt at anything resembling oration. But in light of the fact that so distinguished a gathering has come to pay tribute, I feel compelled to say something. Let me begin with a confession. At the start of my adventure I considered myself separate and superior. I saw myself as a creature of stone, safe and immune from upheaval and misfortune. I knew nothing of touch and less of love and loss. When controversy arose as to my status, that is, man or rock, I had not the slightest doubt of the answer. Now my opinion is drastically altered. Tonight I accept that here lies petrified flesh from an age before memory. Mr. Booth asks me who, what, and when. My Source keeps that knowledge. What I know from experience old and new is that as you have the power to create a nation, I have the power to effect miracles of reconciliation and healing. This not insignificant ability strikes me as much needed. For I sense, in addition to individual frustrations, a nation caught in an agony of doubt. No different than displayed by my writhing frame. I also sense hope and endurance for which my own ambiguous countenance is suitable metaphor. I think now pain and hope live together in me and in you. Let me then share another of my talents: a gift for vision which may be no more than the wisdom inevitable in one of such extreme longevity. That vision shows me the city around us in new incarnation. I see incredible towers. Bridges with a span to make my mind reel. Millions of you vibrant verticals hurtling like the fragments that animate life. I see a potent city, pride of a continent. A compassionate city inhabited by gentle folk no less virile for their capacity to temper triumphant invention with humble gratitude. A city where beginnings and endings fuse to a single flower. Go from here and give of yourselves with less thought of reward and more for . . .

Jay Gould was the first to retch up his dinner onto George Hull's new carpet. Then Tweed, Carnegie and Vanderbilt, Harriman and Pullman, Westinghouse, Hill and Villard. Belmont covered John Zipmeister's polished shoes with the remnants of a Maine lobster stuffed with artichoke hearts. Fisk doubled over with fire in his belly. Morgan's huge nose turned the color of an eggplant.

"What kind of giant is this?" a new visitor shouted from the back of the room. Phineas Barnum stood with Tom Thumb on his shoulders. "If you might prefer less odiferous magic, come across the park with Tom and myself to *Niblo's Garden* where my own Cardiff Giant awaits you. Escape this noxious place for a happier house. It's all on Barnum, from revels to brandy, and courtesy of my Titan who respects a man's stomach."

When the room cleared, Stubby Newell asked, "What the hell happened?"

"Barnum aced us," George said. "Somehow he flattened us. Laid us out cold. But how did he do it?"

"Maybe not," Stubby said in an effort to comfort himself and his cousin. "It could go either way. When they get Ben's box of cigars and those gracious notes things could turn in our favor."

"You destroyed Hull's Humidor," Ben said.

Loretta kissed her husband's forehead and told him not to fret. "George or no George," she said, "Goliath or Titan. A giant is just a giant, but a good cigar is a smoke."

"That's my feeling," Stubby said.

. . . a truer fulfillment. Gentlemen, you seem to be in dire distress. Was it something I said?

"I came back to thank you. It was discourteous to rush away."

"We thank you for coming," George said when he realized who stood at the door.

Cornelius Vanderbilt went over to Goliath. "And to ask your fossil to excuse Fisk's tasteless comments. The man is hardly evolved. Alas that, in our time, even rock is not spared mortification."

"More petrified than mortified," Stubby said. "Though if I was him, I'd hate having my flag took down before they played taps."

"One hopes that the big fellow lost his part through natural erosion and not from the blade of a saber," Vanderbilt said.

"We can't know that," George said. "This is all that was found of him. No trace of the rest."

"If, in your further exploration, the missing portion should surface, let me offer pay for its restoration. That should compensate for any insult."

Learn from philanthropic example. You owe me a patch, George. If there's magic in me then that orphaned slice is worth reuniting. We were just becoming acquainted.

"Seasons greetings," Vanderbilt said. "Now I must join my associates."

"Let me welcome you to Niblo's," P.T. Barnum said, "which I trust will provide an effective antidote to your earlier disappointment and discomfort. You can see that our mood is lighter than Booth's histrionics. You all know Barnum's life is dedicated to the overthrow of that severe and dragging practicalness that turns the quotidian to a chain gang. While I take my giants seriously, I take nothing more seriously than your entertainment.

"Before you meet Titan, let me tell you I have walked in the company of many giants. No small feat, please pardon the pun. There was Monsieur Bihin, sired in Belgium, and Colonel Routh Goshen, a Polish Jew raised in Arabia as he claimed, or hatched by an Alabama slave, as others insist. There was Martin Van Buren

Bates who married my favorite giantess, Anna Held, certainly a woman of substance. All these anomalies of nature were presented to America under my tutelage, so I think Barnum well qualified to distinguish a real giant from a sad copy.

"In a moment you shall view a unique specimen of the behemoth breed, a stone colossus older even than me. For all my levity, friends, at the risk of allowing a serious note into this impressive playground, I must tell you that never before has Barnum been so moved and mystified by any person or object as I am by this petrification, this present to the present from the past. We've been told that Titan gives evidence that our beloved country, again reunited, was mankind's first garden. If so, then the players who walked here are more immortal than even Edwin Booth, though Mr. Booth, under much strain of late, might strongly disagree.

"All Barnum asks is that each of you give his stone man a moment of silence when you meet him. In that moment, seek, and I think ye shall find, a message more amazing than any words carried by the Atlantic Cable and transmitted a far greater distance. Carried here from the age of myth and fable on wisdom's wire under oceans of time. Let the spectacle begin!"

Barnum exited behind a curtain thicker and heavier than George Hull had provided. Instead of Stubby Newell rattling tin thunder, a quintet of musicians serenaded the sterling crowd. The curtain parted to reveal a zircon-lit landscape of desolate challenge.

A liverish volcano plumed real smoke at a gray flannel sky. Black jagged rocks were the only inhabitants of that primal place.

"Once upon a time, into a sunless world, there came a giant bearing a globe of light . . ." boomed an invisible announcer as Barnum's quintet struck an eerie chord. "Meet mighty Titan, servant of God, ruler of men!"

General Thumb appeared in the costume of a shepherd, dragging a large orange ball behind him. Tom waved his staff, the ball rose like a sun, then fell, bounced, and deflated with a fizz.

The audience roared and applauded as Tom bowed.

"Just a minute, General Thumb," Barnum said, intruding on the scene. "We're here in the presence of New York's elite. They've come in good faith to see a giant, not a worm."

"I know that, Mr. Barnum," Tom said. "I am the original Cardiff Giant, certified by Ralph Waldo Emerson and endorsed by the most eminent experts. Do you question my authenticity? If so, you will feel my staff against your most precious part by which I mean your ego."

"You seem more like a forty-inch error than a ruler of men."

Tom pulled a ruler from under his sack-cloth robe and held it against Barnum's thigh. "Ruler enough to take your measure."

"So the worm is an inchworm," Barnum said. "I demand that you show us the one and only original Titan or there will be the Devil to pay."

"But you promised these good people the show would be free."

"I know you, Tom Thumb. You can't fool Barnum. This audience wants marvels, not corn. Let's both leave the stage to the one who deserves it."

"If you'd stayed in the wings, they would have taken me for your Titan," Thumb said. "What I lack in dimension I make up for in poise."

"More noise than poise," Barnum said, lifting Thumb under one arm and lugging him back to the wings.

A second curtain descended, obliterating the scene. The quintet played again as the announcer spoke again. "Phineas T. Barnum takes pleasure in presenting . . . the ultimate fossil . . . the well-publicized stone man of Cardiff . . . the *one, only, original* . . . Titan!"

Titan appeared with a grinding of gears, rolled into position on hidden tracks.

"They're applauding cement," Tom said to Barnum.

"They're applauding themselves," Barnum said. "Giants have no problem believing in giants. And ours is the giant they'll believe."

As before, the crowd was invited to abandon their seats and came to see Titan up close. They looked and they probed, peeking into ears, fingering nostrils, shaking stone hands, tracing tendons and toes, marveling at muscles.

"I admit to confusion," Mayor Oakey Hall said.

"Good you admit to it," Vanderbilt said.

"Except for the flag both giants are identical."

"Let Fisk lift the flag again and see if there's a difference," Jay Gould said. "Whatever men have in common, there's one thing each has that's unique."

"There are ladies present," Carnegie said.

"They know better of such things than we," Gould said. "Here, Susan Anthony, do us the favor." The intrepid publisher of *Revolution Magazine* came forward to lower the banner.

"Look at that organ!" Westinghouse said. "As complete as you'd want and utterly fit to procreate a race of giants."

"Then where are they, pray tell?" Miss Anthony said.

"In Wyoming, I heard, until women got the vote there," Gould said.

"I doubt giants are afraid of women's suffrage," Mrs. Harriman said.

"But they do fear long-suffering women," Morgan said.

"Give Barnum his moment of silence," Vanderbilt said. "The quiet will do us all a favor. May I suggest that we close our eyes and bow our heads since this relic may be entitled to more than a snide guffaw."

"A good idea, Edison said. "Even men of science must take time to reflect upon their reflections."

"I do that every morning," Bill Tweed said. "Then gargle with gin to forget what I saw."

WHICH GIANT DESERVES YOUR ALLEGIANCE? I AM STONE. MY ANCESTORS STONE. I SEE THROUGH STONE EYES AND HEAR THROUGH STONE EARS WITH A CLARITY YOU CANNOT IMAGINE. LIKE OUR HOST, MR. BARNUM, I ENJOY MY AMUSEMENTS. BUT SINCE TITAN IS BORED BY DEATH, OLD AS GOD, IT IS HARD TO DIVERT HIM. HE KNOWS ALL THE JOKES. IN TRUTH, MY ONLY PLEASURE COMES FROM ALTERATION. I HAVE TAKEN MANY FORMS BUT NONE SO RIDICULOUS AS THIS. THAT YOU FLESHLINGS DARE CONSIDER ME ONE OF YOUR OWN IS DELIGHTFUL AS IT IS DEMEANING. I THANK YOU FOR PROVIDING MY FIRST MILLENNIAL CHUCKLE. NOW HERE IS SOME NEWS. YOUR

WORLD IS DOOMED TO EXTINCTION. THE SUN THAT SUSTAINS YOU IS THE PIG THAT WILL SWALLOW YOU WHOLE THEN MELT YOU TO GAS. YOUR DESTINY AND MINE IS TO END AS A FLASH IN THE SKY. INCREDIBLY THERE ARE RUMORS THAT YOUR FRAGILE SPECIES MIGHT, BY LINKED ACCIDENTS, FIND A WAY TO STUMBLE PAST STARS. THAT SOME OF YOUR KIND COULD ESCAPE DESTRUCTION AND GO CARRYING A PEBBLE, OR THE MEM-ORY OF ROCK, TO A NEW GALAXY. THAT WHISKER OF POSSIBILITY GIVES ME A VESTED INTEREST IN YOUR SURVIVAL. EVEN TITAN DOES NOT RELISH OBLIVION. SINCE OUR FATE IS ENTWINED AND IMMUTABLE, BEST GET ON WITH IT. IRONIC THAT YOUR BEST HOPE FOR ENDURANCE IS TO HURRY EXTINCTION'S TIMETABLE. COMFORTABLE, YOU DO NOTHING BUT EAT, SLEEP, AND FORNICATE. FEAR AND LOATHING AGITATE YOUR BEST TALENTS. THE PLANET MUST SHUDDER TO BRING YOU FULLY ALIVE. SO I SAY *HELP THINGS ALONG!* HOW BEST TO DO THIS? YOUR SAGES ALREADY KNOW. DENY EVERY FORM OF GRATIFICATION. NO DRINKING, NO SMOKING, NO GORGING. PENETRATE ONLY TO PROCREATE. REPENT, FLAGELLATE, EXERCISE BRISKLY UNTIL PAIN IS CALLED PLEASURE. THE REWARD FOR SUCH REGIMEN IS A MARVELOUS OUTFLOW OF PURE EN-ERGY SUFFICIENT TO TRANSFORM YOUR CITIES TO FLESH-GRINDING DYNAMOS, TOXIC TOWERS FILLED WITH TERRIFIED WORKERS. ENCOURAGE UNIVERSAL FRATERNITY AMONG YOUR CITIZENS BUT KEEP EACH DRONE SEPARATE AS A FETUS IN A SPECIMEN JAR. LET THEM FLOAT TRANQUILIZED THROUGH ILLUSIONS OF PROGRESS. CHAMPION CONFOR-MITY, CORRECTNESS, CLEAN CONSCIENCE. ADORE ACQUISITION. PUT EYES IN BOXES TO PATROL FOR DISSENT. IF YOU HEAR LAUGHTER, CRUSH IT TO A SHRIEK. SET RACE AGAINST RACE, MAKE THE AIR STINK. PRONOUNCE PARANOIA THE CURE FOR CANCER. CORRUPT EVERYTHING AND QUICKLY. FORCE SCIENCE TO FIND TRANSPORT AWAY FROM THE GLORIOUS FOULNESS YOUR BRILLIANCE WILL BRING FORTH. WHEN THE TREES DRIP ACID YOU WILL HAVE YOUR REAL EDEN. FOR TRUE GENESIS IS THE COURAGE TO VEN-TURE TOWARD SOME BETTER SPECK IN ANOTHER UNIVERSE WHERE THE STONE GOD IS SAFE AND SUPREME. OF COURSE, WHILE YOU PREPARE FOR THE SPLENDID MOMENT OF MIGRATION, TAKE CARE TO INCREASE PROFITS, REDUCE TAXES, KEEP EVERY CHILD SAFE FROM BAD THOUGHTS AND SMUT. WAS TITAN HELPFUL?

Barnum told the quintet to play spirited tunes but saw that his au-dience had no interest in dancing. Soon Niblo's Garden was empty.

The musicians dismissed, Barnum, alone with Titan, suddenly felt as tired as his jokes. The evening drained him and left him morose. He sat alone confronting questions of meaning and purpose, pondering ways to make sensible use of his autumnal years. Earlier, J.P. Morgan had taken him aside and inquired if Barnum entertained political ambitions as fervently as he entertained strangers. When Barnum shrugged off a quick answer, Morgan confided that the name Phineas T. Barnum was favorably mentioned during recent discussion of a viable candidate to run against Grant. Then Zipmeister from the *Clarion* came within earshot and, of necessity, their conversation ended abruptly.

"Consider what I told you most seriously, P.T."

"Yes, thank you, J.P., I will do that."

The image of himself in the White House, once vivid, then blurred by his defeat for Congress, took on fresh color. Barnum knew he was presidential timber. The kind of bold captain to pilot a floundering ship of state to safe harbor. But, as that brash reporter once asked, would the American people cast their ballots for a national symbol of humbug? "They would or they wouldn't," Barnum whispered aloud. "Too late to give this leopard new spots."

NOT TOO LATE TO TEACH AN OLD DOG NEW TRICKS. WHAT IF THE PRINCE OF HUMBUG METAMORPHOSIZED TO *THE FRIEND OF CHILDREN*? WHO DOESN'T LOVE CHILDREN? YOUR SOLUTION, BARNUM, IS A CIRCUS. A DEFIANT DISPLAY OF PURE DAZZLE. EVERY PARENT'S DELIGHT. AND A FINE WAY TO TERRIFY YOWLING MOPPETS AND DROWN THEM IN SUPERFLUOUS SENSATION. THIS WHILE SELLING THEM COTTON CANDY TO MAKE THEM PURE PINK. TALK ABOUT PUBLIC SERVICE! WHAT A WAY TO SPRUCE UP A FLAKING PERSONA. HERE COME THE CLOWNS ON ELECTION DAY. *FATHER BARNUM FOR OUR PRESIDENT!* WE COULD RIDE INTO HISTORY TOGETHER. TITAN WITH AN ELEPHANT ON HIS BROAD BACK, YOU ON THE BACK OF A TRAUMATIZED TYKE!

General Thumb came in, buttoning a bulbous foxtail coat. "Long day, impresario. I think we've earned the right to a nightcap."

"I thought you knew, Tom. I've lately decided to come forward for Temperance. I'd suggest you do the same for your psyche and liver. And for the sake of the children."

AT LEAST HE GOT PART OF MY MESSAGE. MY REMARKS ON THE VIRTUES OF ABSTI-
NENCE WERE MEANT FOR PUBLIC POSTURE. CERTAINLY NOT FOR THOSE POSTURING. I
THOUGHT THE DISTINGUISHED COULD DISTINGUISH. WHAT IDIOTS. NO WONDER THERE
WAS NO OVATION.

ACKLEY, IOWA, DECEMBER 24, 1869

"The Reverend will be sad to have missed you," Samantha Turk
said to Barnaby Rack. "He's been so involved with the seminary
and preparations for Christmas. Had you but given some notice."

"My visit was impossible to predict. As I said, I'm researching a
story and must bounce like a billiard ball to where the facts point."

"May I inquire as to the subject of your research?"

"Of course, Mrs. Turk. The Giant of Cardiff."

"Yes, I should have known. And quite natural that you'd seek out
my Henry. As you must know, discovery of the stone man was remarkable coincidence, if it was a coincidence, considering that it so
closely followed the Reverend's own epiphany."

"I've read his work with great interest."

The Turk living room was something between a chapel and
tepee. Images of Christ and the Disciples shared walls and tables
with buckskins and war bonnets, arrows in quivers, bows, beaded
belts, horned masks, blankets, and bearskin rugs. If the mild lady
who sat across from him suddenly pulled out a tomahawk to scalp
him or baptized him with Earl Grey, he wouldn't have been too
surprised. Barnaby nibbled a licorice cookie and sipped tea. More
appropriate, he thought, if he chewed at a buffalo hock or smoked
a feathered pipe. "The cookies are delicious," he said.

"I'm glad you like them. The recipe comes from my mother's
kitchen in Binghamton."

"Binghamton? In New York?"

"Yes, that was my home. We must travel such long distances to find our rightful place."

"We do," Barnaby said. "And do you still have family in Binghamton?"

"Oh, yes," Samantha said. "And quite well known. My maiden name is Hull. You may be familiar with Simon Hull & Sons, the cigar manufacturers?"

"I not only know the name but I've visited their shop. And was served by a most gracious woman."

"Why, that would be Angelica. It is a small world. She's married to my brother, George Hull."

"Extraordinary. Speak of coincidence."

"My feeling about the Cardiff Giant is that there was no coincidence involved in his discovery," Samantha said. "More a case of synchronicity. Orchestrated by a higher power. How else could I feel? In a sense, it is that splendid petrification who served as Cupid for Reverend Turk and me. We were only recently wed, you see. That same extraordinary fossil gave Henry the broad platform he so needs from which to preach his message. Mr. Rack, would you believe the stone man is also my relation?"

"Excuse me?"

"Yes, he's my distant cousin, I suppose. Of course, I'm not being serious. But the farm in Cardiff where they found him is owned by William Newell, who is a cousin on my father Simon's side. More evidence of God's master plan."

"Stubby Newell? But I know the man."

"No. I can't believe it."

"Absolutely," Barnaby said. "I went to Cardiff for the *Clarion*. I've met Stubby and his fossil face to face."

"It is a small world. I myself can't wait to meet the stone man and neither can the Reverend. We do plan a trip to New York. The Hulls have invited us to visit their new humidor in that city. I haven't seen my family, except for George and Angelica, since my first husband's funeral, may he rest in peace. And Reverend Turk has business there with his new publisher."

"George Hull and Angelica came here to Ackley?"

"Almost two years ago. *Tempus fugit.* Dear George. How skeptical he was to hear Henry declaim on our nation's holy origin. Not only George. Let me tell you, Mr. Rack, most were openly hostile to inspired testimony now proved accurate. That giants walked the earth, this earth beneath our feet."

"Those must have been difficult days for your husband."

"Not really. He himself was assured. I, on the other hand, was less convinced but gave benefit of the doubt. In light of what's transpired, I'm glad I did."

"Mrs. Turk, this is an odd request I know, but do you happen to have a tintype of George Hull and his missus?"

"Fortunately, I do. A photographer in Fort Dodge did a charming portrait of the three of us together. It's not very flattering and turned dark, but I treasure it as a keepsake."

"May I?"

"On the piano," Samantha said. "In the silver frame."

Barnaby Rack got his first look at George Hull standing stern and serene, a cigar in his mouth, posturing between his wife and his sister. "I think the picture does credit to all three. He's a strong-looking man, your brother. But I must say Mrs. Hull seems very different from the woman I remember. That is Angelica?"

"Who else would it be? Of course, our images seem draped in shadows."

"Was she ill at the time? Not that I mean to pry. But the woman I met in Binghamton was, how shall I say it, more *robust.*"

"Angelica has always been frail," Samantha said.

"Frail, you say? Never my impression."

"It could be she's enjoying better health. Angelica *robust,* you say? Well, that's good news you've brought me, Mr. Rack."

"And now I must go. Thank you for your courtesy, and please tell the Reverend how much I admire his work. Perhaps our paths will cross in Manhattan. And I will take along my copy of his book for an autograph. It's not every day I get to meet a giant's cousin, Mrs. Turk, or to taste such delectable bakery."

Samantha curtseyed, Barnaby bowed. "Mr. Rack, at the risk of seeming forward, there is one complaint I'm sure my husband would have voiced. The newspapers blithely call the Cardiff Giant *Goliath*, which, for Reverend Turk, is both annoying and appalling. Goliath was a misguided brute. What a cynical misnomer. This giant deserves another, gentler christening."

"I agree. Such glib names are assigned too quickly and without full consideration. I will tell the Reverend's feelings to the *Clarion* at first opportunity. Considering the request came from the stone man's cousin, it carries special weight."

"Thank you for your understanding."

After Barnaby left, Samantha sipped more tea and put the tintype back where it belonged, on a doily beside an Arapaho cooking pot.

LAFAYETTE, NEW YORK, DECEMBER 24, 1869

Small wicks sputtered in nine wells of olive oil, eight for the days an ancient lamp burned to light the liberated Temple of Jerusalem and one called the *shamash* to ignite them. Aaron Bupkin sat in his room watching his Hanukkah menorah celebrate the old miracle.

That the Festival of Lights came so close to Christmas, another Winter reminder of light and life, made Aaron suspect both rituals trailed roots reaching down to bleak caves where glum heavy-jawed men and thick gloomy women sat wondering why their Sun God left them abandoned. If those minds were united by fear and a hunger for fire, how had it happened the same comfort of flame now divided the race into separate camps?

"Questions without answers," Isaac called them. "A necessary waste of precious time. Like cutting toenails or using a toothpick." Isaac Bupkin had sent the menorah when he heard that this year his grandson wouldn't come to Boston for the holiday. "At least, Aaron, don't make yourself obvious down there. Get it through your head they think you killed Jesus so they get a little upset. And now you have the chutzpah to ask about buying land? No wonder you're making them crazy."

The reason Aaron chose to stay in Lafayette had nothing to do with defiance or land. It had to do with Angelica Hull. One day after Aaron's trip to the Newell farm, Mrs. Elm told him he'd used up his welcome, that she'd need his room free by the New Year. The next day, Aaron went house to house looking for new lodgings, but no place was vacant.

While Aaron Bupkin knocked on doors, Bertha and Angelica came into Lafayette shopping for presents to send to New York. Angelica's first stop was Dr. Proll's office, since she was overdue for her checkup. The doctor was quick, he found nothing wrong, so Angelica went browsing on Main Street. She bought a scarf for Loretta, a money clip for Stubby, a cameo for Bertha, cuff links for Simon, a cap for George. It would be strange to spend Christmas far from Binghamton, but that was the way of things. Angelica had no regrets. Even allowing for the burden of Bertha, the peace of Cardiff proved a proper prescription. Angelica Hull never felt more at ease though her future was never less certain.

When she finished her shopping, Angelica met Aaron Bupkin by sheer chance. She wished him Merry Christmas, then swallowed her tongue. He returned the greeting, touching the brim of his knitted hat.

"And how's your head? Healing nicely, I hope," Angelica said.

"Much improved," Aaron said.

"A cold day," Angelica said.

"Damp but clear," Aaron said. Thank God for weather.

"Tell me, Mr. Bupkin, is there a place for a cup of tea?"

"Weyman's, around the corner near the inn. Come, I'll show you the way, Mrs. Hull."

They walked together to Weyman's Tea Shoppe. Aaron opened the wreathed door for her, then touched his hat again. "Nice seeing you, lady. Keep warm. Have a nice holiday. Happy New Year."

"Won't you join me?" Angelica said on impulse. "They've got a nice fire going." The nice fire crackled around Aaron's ears.

"In there? For tea?" Aaron said. "That could be a problem for both of us. How shall I put it? This hamlet's alert to odd pairings."

"Are we an odd pairing?" Angelica said. "What if we engage in some innocent commerce? You selling, I buying. Who could object to that?"

"I'm afraid I have nothing to sell."

"Take this broach. It will do."

"You're an unusual woman, Mrs. Hull," Aaron said.

"Yes, I think that's true," Angelica said. "Now head for a table by the fire before anyone calls out the militia. And, Jew or not, give me a good price on the broach."

"I can't promise that," Aaron said. "Tradition forbids mixing business with pleasure. You know we live only for profit."

An hour later, Angelica met Bertha, waiting distraught at Dr. Proll's. Angelica apologized for being late and explained how hard it was finding suitable, sensible purchases.

Aaron went back to his room to kindle his Hanukkah lamp near sunset. His hands shook so hard he could hardly pour the oil. While Mrs. Weyman watched from a face that turned bluer than her huckleberry jam, Angelica whispered secrets much darker than the tea. He found himself swallowing tears with his carrot cake. Somehow Angelica's turmoil entwined with his own. It was clear Mrs. Hull had no husband she longed for. The woman was as lonely as a wandering star.

Aaron's mind shimmered like the ritual flames. The dowser was entirely amazed when Angelica Hull asked to meet him next day on the road outside Cardiff. He dowsed into himself to probe new emotions. *Dear Grandpa Isaac, You'll be glad to hear that your grandson has found an affectionate companion. The lady's ideal. Older, wiser, married, pregnant, plain spoken, and a shiksa.* Speaking of gifts.

On the Newell farm, Angelica compared her recent memory of the dowser with the dazed-looking Joseph in her puzzle. If there was any similarity, it was only in the eyes.

NEW YORK, NEW YORK, DECEMBER 24, 1869

It was a week since P.T. Barnum, who had a good appetite himself, looked away while Boss Tweed wolfed his dinner. The grand sachem of Tammany Hall ate like his own taxidermist, stuffing himself with roast pig and steak, three kinds of creamed potatoes, a mound of stuffing, cabbage, beets, peas, carrots, and asparagus tips. He drank Chateau Rothschild Mouton from the bottle after sucking its cork for flavor.

"The sly bastard tells me he's building pneumatic tubes under Broadway to send messages back and forth," Tweed said, "so I gave him his permits. Then he announces in the *Sun* that his god-damned tubes are for a subway. A goddamned subway. The *Sun* tells the people an underground railroad is the city's messiah. You got to watch those rich sons of bitches every tick of the clock or they'll stick a finger up your ass and a hand in your pocket."

"Incredible," Barnum said.

"If he showed me respect instead of sneaking behind my back it might have been different. If it's got wheels, it's my cow. I'm telling you, Barnum, you got to walk the parapets all day and all night."

"They never learn when enough is enough," Barnum said, biting the end off a cigar.

"They don't, do they? Please don't light that torch. I can't abide tobacco. It's a dirty habit. How are you for a portion of cherries jubilee or some key lime pie?"

"No, thank you, Bill, I couldn't," Barnum said, laying the cigar in an ashtray.

"Well, I can and I will. Now tell me why you asked me to dinner since it wasn't to hear me belch."

"Not because I'm building a subway," Barnum said. "Rest easy on that score. But there is something."

"Is there?" Tweed wiped his chin with a napkin.

"Nothing major. It's about my Titan."

"Titan? Is your giant giving you trouble? That's easy. I'll send Grinder Brian around to talk sense into him."

"My trouble is Stubby Newell and his family. They're going to court claiming their Goliath is the Giant of Cardiff."

"I make it my policy never to come between feuding giants," Tweed said. "Not when they're both made of stone."

"I've plenty invested in Titan. My money and credibility."

"Yes, credibility. I heard the Republicans are considering you for Great White Father. You don't have a chance. The next President will be Governor Hoffman. Hell, I promised John the job, and Tweed's word is his bail bond."

"No truth to that rumor," Barnum said. "My life is show business, pure and simple."

"Glad to hear it. Where is that damn waiter? Free the niggers and they go into hiding. So what is it then?"

"I'm told you have friends in the courts."

"Friends? No. Bloodsucker acquaintances, possibly. You think your case might lack merit?"

"No, my case is airtight. I have all the proof I need. But whenever a judge is involved, there's uncertainty."

"Certainty is costly these days," Tweed said. "Has a judge been assigned?"

"Judge Barnard."

"Georgie Barnard? There's a hard man. Full of his office. A champion of justice. Lucky for you I got his balls bronzed on my mantel. Tell me, have you put a price on your, what was it, credibility?"

"What price would you think adequate?"

"I'd say a few choice tickets to P.T. Barnum's next opus and maybe ten thousand for cab fare."

"The tickets are easy. The ten thousand is hard. Do you think Judge Barnard might show compassion for, say, five?"

"Five? Five? That's half of ten, isn't it? I'd say he might be half moved to show half his compassion. But what do I know of such things?"

"If a ball is thrown up it comes down on its own," Barnum said. "Frankly, cash flow is my problem these days. Five thousand's my limit, Bill, though I don't like to nickel and dime."

"The ball's in your court, Barnum. Hand me a billet-doux and I promise to deliver it myself."

"Good of you, Bill," Barnum said, reaching over a plate of gristle, gravy, and bones with a fat envelope.

"Blame the meal for my good mood," Tweed said. "It will be even better after cherries and brandy. Isn't it a blessing to live in a city where all things are possible? Except finding a waiter when you want one."

Since their social evening, there had been no further contact.

In the case of THE GIANT OF CARDIFF, brought before the Honorable Judge George Barnard in the Supreme Court of New York State on the 24th day of December, 1869:

This Court has made every effort to determine which of two contested objects (one called Titan, the other Goliath) is the *original* and which is counterfeit. But what are the objects in question? Are they men turned to stone, stone turned to men, two of a kind, one, one thing, one, the other, or both a hoax and a sham, each pretending to be what they're not? The affidavits of experts support each in-

terpretation and thus, in this Court's view, negate the value
of expert opinion.

The giant called Titan, which Mr. Barnum claims for
his own, has, upon scientific testing, yielded chips of a
human skull and bits of powdered crystal, seeming to in-
dicate human origins. But the paleontologist, Dr. Mor-
timer, of impeccable credential, testifying on behalf of the
plaintiff, William Newell, concludes that the bone shards
come from a male cranium of natural, normal proportion
and are not long separated from the brain once contained
in that vessel. As for the pulverized crystal, that might
easily be found in any chemist's stock.

Further, Mr. Newell certifies that two fragments of his
giant, popularized as Goliath, were earlier removed and
examined for evidence of human origin. While no bone
shards or crystals were clearly identified, still several in-
vestigators ruled Goliath a genuine fossil while others dis-
agreed and named him a statue of unknown classical
origin. So again the result is a stalemate.

Mr. Barnum has produced a bill of sale purportedly
signed by Mr. Newell in exchange for the payment of a
large sum of cash in return for his giant. Mr. Newell says
the signature is forged and no cash changed hands. Hand-
writing experts have failed to enlighten us since they too
conflict in their findings.

Whatever these objects, human or not, and who sold or
never sold either, still, one is alleged to be a replication of
the other and only the first entitled to be called the *original* Cardiff Giant exhumed on the property of said
William Newell in Cardiff, New York.

The word *original* is here used to describe what is truly
unique or that from which another is copied. Since both
giants are so much alike, it cannot be said with any au-
thority that either is more unique than the other. And
since this Court cannot finally determine which one is the
copy, it cannot affirm which is the original or, in fact, if ei-

ther is *original* since both so-called originals have been stigmatized as genuine fakes by skilled observers of serious reputation. Let it be noted that any suggestion of hoax or fraud is viewed by this Court as baseless. However, such opinions are part of the record.

In summary, then, we have two objects which resist accurate description except in a most superficial sense. Both are exactly alike except for minor phallic imbalance. There is no way to label one more unique or original than the other. Because of this obvious lack of conclusive evidence, this Court has no choice but to find against the plaintiff, Mr. William Newell in his claim of exclusivity and in favor of the defendant, Mr. Phineas T. Barnum.

It is our decision that, while Mr. Barnum shall have the right to exhibit and advertise his Titan as *unique and original,* he will refrain from claiming Titan as the *only* unique and original Giant of Cardiff. Mr. Newell shall enjoy a similar right to display and promote his Goliath, observing the same restraint.

It is further stipulated that neither specimen shall be presented to the public either as a genuine human petrification or as a statue of ancient ancestry, pending further proof of such awesome heritage. This ruling will apply to all published advertisements, posters, placards, billboards, pamphlets, fliers, brochures, banners, announcements or other traditional forms used to stir interest in a theatrical event, exhibition, display, etc. for which admission is charged.

"Good day, gentlemen. Merry Christmas. These proceedings are ended." Judge Barnard banged his gavel exactly five times, duly noted by a fuming Barnum.

Outside the courthouse Stubby Newell told a knot of reporters, "If a man can't keep what's his own, then where is America? Whatever the judge said, there's one Giant of Cardiff, and those who deny him are playing with matches. Hell, you'd think Mr. Barnum already had enough fire in his life and that he'd carry a bucket wherever he went."

"Is that a threat, Mr. Newell? Are you threatening Niblo's Garden with arson?"

"No, I ain't a barn burner," Stubby said. "The fire I mean is the fire of the Lord 'stomping out the vintage where the grapes of wrath are stored.' "

The successful defendants exited the courthouse through another door. "Be happy. We won by not losing," Amos Arbutnaut, Esq., said, slapping Barnum's back. "At least appreciate your lawyer. I'd say my brief would have swayed Portia. Judge Barnard, like Solomon, rose to the occasion and gave us at least half the pie when I feared we'd be fortunate to be left with crumbs."

"Which leaves New York with two giants to vie for what spoils there may be."

"But considering we had no case . . ."

"Don't speak obscenities, Amos, or I'll wonder who my enemy is. Which brings up a point. The more I see of him, the less I believe Stubby Newell baked that stone gingerbread. The man is just short of a simpleton."

"There's the chance that his giant may be real."

"The Seven Wonders of the World are all used," Barnum said. "And it's not Farmer Newell who tweaks my snout. It's somebody else, albeit a talented amateur, and I'll have his balls bronzed for my mantel. Tweed boasted through his gas that 'if it has wheels, it's my cow.' I say if it sells tickets, it's Barnum's."

"Tweed? You saw Tweed?" Arbutnaut felt self-esteem leak through his shoes and puddle on the courthouse steps.

"Did I mention Tweed? Possibly we passed on the street. Now here comes the press. I should be modest in victory, even half a victory."

"Since when does Barnum gloat?" Arbutnaut said.

"We came away smelling of roses, boys," Barnum said. "A splendid Yule to all and a Joyous New Year!"

NEW YORK, NEW YORK, DECEMBER 24, 1869

Ben Hull examined a tribe of wooden Indians newly delivered to Hull's Humidor. The stoical savages definitely added atmosphere to the store, virile counterpoint to the otherwise elegant appointments.

Some carried hatchets, others crescent bows. Two chiefs were decked out in carved feathers. A few braves danced, others stalked. A squaw held a basket of fruit. One old warrior squatted, smoking a cigar, an acceptable fiction since Hull's sold no pipes. The prize piece was a scout, mounted on his pinto pony, shading oak eyes from the sun as he scanned some horizon.

Beyond a field of glass counters on Hull's ground floor stood a plainsman in buckskin. He grasped at a rifle to protect wife and child. A full-size Conestoga wagon held the family's earthly possessions. One wheel was broken off the wagon's axle and its horses were missing. That diorama added tension. It was evident the Americans braced for attack by marauding looters and scalpers prowling across the store. The plainsman, like the old Indian, smoked what might well be his last panatela.

"The concept here is not just the frontier feel," Ben's decorator, Ronald Quint, said, moving the squaw a foot to the left. "Smoking is synonymous with relaxation. The suggestion of danger, however subtle, should directly affect your customers."

"Not very subtle," Loretta Hull said. "In a few minutes those injuns will have their heads on a pike. And they'll probably steal the infant or roast it or worse."

"Not a forgone conclusion," Quint said, "What if the Red Men should be distracted by a stampede of buffalo? What if the pioneer proves a deadly shot? What if cavalry bugles are suddenly heard?"

"There you go," Ben said. "Think positive, dear."

"Still, in that situation I'd rather be Pocahontas than the settler," Loretta said. "But the display works well."

"It does," Ben said. "It gives the whole room a flavor."

"Yes, it does," Quint said. "If I smoked, I'd be smoking now."

"What happened to their horses?" Loretta said.

"It's Christmas Eve," Ben said. "Let Mr. Quint go."

"The horses ran away, frightened by the sound of Hull's registers ringing."

"From your mouth to God's ear," Ben said.

"I'm going next door to wish Goliath Merry Christmas," Loretta said. "And the two pagans as well."

"I don't think George and Stubby are there. They're probably at McNulty's Saloon drowning sorrows. That verdict hit them hard though it didn't seem to bother the crowd. There were lines all day without letup."

"Must you work late even tonight?"

"I must," Ben said. "Tomorrow's for rest."

"Remember midnight mass at Trinity. The Harrimans are expecting us."

"I won't forget that. Did you know we'll be sitting in Washington's pew?"

"You know it's Episcopal," Loretta said.

"The Lord will forgive."

Loretta went through the door that linked to the stone man's auditorium. The exhibit closed early because of the holiday. Ben was correct about George and Stubby. There was nobody there but Goliath. Loretta ventured to pat his bald head. "This is Loretta Hull come to wish you Happy Christmas. If you know what Christmas is about."

I didn't but I do. When my Source deigned to impregnate one of you while she slept who then flowered like a tree. The result was the birth of a youth. Stone and flesh who enjoyed the best features of both. Sentience. Intelligence. Mobility. Durability. A talent for bringing out the worst to inspire the best. Most offered the hostile contempt the boy needed for nurture. Others more selfish came to pay homage. They asked marvels in exchange for small trinkets and favors. Back then admission was cheaper. I can say with some pride that I outgross the stripling even allowing for inflation. If I am better box-office, that does not belittle the Jesus achievement. I have the advantage of superior marketing and awareness of demographics. Of course I was born withered. He a perfect babe echoing futures. If I had his sweet aspect, no telling my tally. But I am not bitter or dwell on complaint. We are both needed and perfectly timed.

"If you're gifted with the power of prediction," Loretta said, "then tell me what kind of year to expect. With a husband more concerned with wooden Indians than his wife. With George Hull newly indifferent. With Angelica plumped to deliver a grandson. With Simon soon jumping to rewrite his will. Poor Loretta's alone. She hears savages whooping. Her wagon is broke. Her horses are fled and no cavalry trumpets from over the hill."

Tidings of joy. Wassail and eggnog. A host of small pleasures to scatter the frost.

"Is that you, Mrs. Hull?"

"General Thumb? How good to see you."

"Are you alone here?"

"Yes. Mooning over nothing."

"Ben tells me you're going to mass at Trinity. With the Harrimans, no less. *Chip, chip.* Mercy and I were going to invite you to the Little Church Around the Corner, an appropriate temple for us."

"I wish you'd asked sooner."

"I come here at the risk of life and limb. Your brother-in-law hates the sight of me, and now his anger can only increase. He and his cousin should have never dared take on Barnum. Not in New York."

"Neither Ben nor I share George's rancor."

"Nice to know it. Come with me to Niblo's for a glass of champagne and meet some of my friends. Your husband endorses the gesture. He has no desire to alienate either faction in the war of the giants."

"I'd have to change my wardrobe in time for church."

"Plenty of time before church, Loretta. It's a short walk to Niblo's and I short enough to escort you."

When General Thumb and Loretta Hull arrived at Niblo's, they found carolers singing near a candlelit tree. The lush pine was hung with a myriad of ornaments, iridescent balls to shimmering icicles, figures from fairy tales and cheerful toys, pearls of snow, and choirs of angels. Its crown was a perfect glass star.

Loretta's depression quickly dispersed, her dark mood overwhelmed by the spirited revels. She recognized some among many strange faces. There was Barnum in a corner, eating cake from the plate of a notorious actress whose face she knew but whose name she forgot. Seeing Barnum made Loretta feel disloyal. But Ben had confirmed what Tom Thumb told her, that meeting the right people was the ultimate key to acceptance. Loretta's best contribution to Hull's Humidor was her natural charm and smooth social grace. Barnum wasn't her enemy.

Thumb presented his guest as the Queen of Cigars and took time to explain the title. Clearly, some good was done for Ben's business. Loretta sipped Cliquot Brut from glasses engraved with holly berries and ate hors d'oeuvres of sturgeon from plates rimmed with snowflakes.

A band replaced the carolers and struck up a waltz. General Tom danced her around. Loretta spun like a top inside a kaleidoscope. New York had conspired to save a sad waif using darling Thumb as its agent. The Queen of Cigars felt gratitude flow from her fingers to the diminutive hands that whirled her.

Dancing with Tom was its own magic, as if an ornament leapt off the Christmas tree ready to give her its life before shattering to

splinters of mercury glass. Those clever hands guided her through
tunnels of color to a vortex of velvet. "Where am I, little General?"

"In the Palace of Now. In the Duchy of Nowhere."

Thumb lit a taper inside a chimney of rose quartz. Loretta saw
that she'd been led by her toy to where Titan lay in an opulent bed
surrounded by poinsettias.

"I've had enough of giants," Loretta said. "Let's go back to the
party." She got no answer. Her escort vanished. "Not hide-and-
seek. Please show yourself, silly boy."

THUMB, A TIME WILL COME WHEN THE TINIEST SILICON CHIPS HOLD POWER TO
SHAPE LIFE. EVEN TITAN SHALL BE HUMBLED BY GRAINS OF SAND FROM AN HOUR-
GLASS. YOU'LL BE IN YOUR ELEMENT, THUMBKIN, WHEN MINUSCULE GENERALS COM-
MAND PUZZLED GIANTS. BUT NOT YET. UNTIL THEN DO THE BEST THAT YOU CAN.

Loretta laughed when she saw a flute of sparkling wine appear
from nowhere on Titan's stone belly. "I'm miffed with you and your
pranks," she said. "These games are too childish." When she
reached for the glass, the proud flag that covered the giant's sex
lifted and snapped and flapped in the air. Loretta couldn't help but
examine what she saw. Goliath carried a ragged spur; Titan's was a
column from Greece. She reached out her gloved hand to touch it,
closed her eyes, made a wish for health, wealth, and happiness.

Loretta opened her eyes. There was her General, wrapped in the
same flag he'd pilfered, wriggling up from between Titan's stone
legs. He stretched to his full height, dropped the flag, stood naked
as an egg while he sang "Good King Wenceslas." Loretta, with
bubbles clouding her vision, was awed by that strange serenade. She
looked from Tom to Titan, from Titan to Tom, then swooned when
the swift little body embraced her legs.

The brash ornament reached into her blouse, nipped at her
breasts, lifted her wide skirt, planted kisses like daisies, browsed like
a beast, then turned into a tornado. That violent weather, trapped
in the valley between her raised thighs, uprooted thick trees. Whole
houses flew off their foundations. Loretta was lifted between howl-

ing clouds, split through a wedge of migrating geese, then dropped down a waterfall. Inside a whirlpool, she kicked, screamed, and paddled her way toward the shore of Atlantis. That such a small pitcher could cause such a flood.

"I knew it would be wonderful, my dear country mouse," the ornament whispered, stroking her hair.

"Nothing happened, did it?"

"Nothing happened? How dare you say such a thing, Mrs. Hull? You came twice, I know it, and damn near broke my back. Is that nothing? I'd say it was *something* and say it again. You've given me the worst insult a man can have with your nothing, and I'd call it an insult to the spirit of Christmas."

"Please be tranquil," Loretta said. "All right, *something* happened. Now run back to your branch."

Loretta arrived at Trinity Church where Ben Hull waited with the Harrimans. They found the same bench where the first President sat when the nation was new, expectant, and innocent as the Holy Child. The organ played a glorious prelude. Loretta felt a tingle from the music's sheer force. She wondered how Martha Washington sustained those vibrations.

CARDIFF, NEW YORK, DECEMBER 31, 1869

Aaron Bupkin stirred the small fire inside the igloo he'd built with the help of an article in the *Royal Geographic* borrowed from Mrs. Elm's extensive collection. Why his severe landlady subscribed to, and saved, that frank publication with clear illustrations of Apache breasts, Maori behinds, and nose-rubbing Eskimos was a mystery he'd never unravel.

Sitting on a blanket in his bubble of snow, a twig-crackling fire curling smoke through a hole in the roof, Aaron was comfortable enough to drop his hood and strip off his jacket.

The igloo, hidden in a clearing not far off the road that ran past the Newell farm, could have been in Alaska. In the *Geographic,* Aaron read about America's new territory where natives ate walrus meat and went wrapped in sealskins. He wondered what it would be to live in a land of icebergs and perpetual night. Harpooning dinner, fleeing from polar bears, with glaciers to ride for the pleasure of peril. Snow, always snow. How could Winter be bearable without Spring, or Summer endurable without Autumn? Autumn's torture, its bittersweet endings, the crunching of boots on a carpet of leaves made a welcome for Winter's blank numbness.

In the ice capsule, Aaron tried to avoid thinking too much about what he was doing there. His clandestine meetings with Angelica Hull were as absurd as their meeting place. They were both playing a dangerous game, for him possibly fatal. Since the day after Christmas the two spent endless hours talking about nothing much. There were no revelations or confessions and not many questions. Only the kind of chatter that passes time. He could feel the time passing as if time were a wind blowing over his ears. At their last meeting hardly any words were spoken. They held hands inside silence. She gazed up at the ceiling and said she was counting stars. He felt more peace than passion with that strange lady. In the late afternoons, when they parted company, the Winter closed around him like a clamp.

His thoughts turned warmer when Angelica Hull crawled through the igloo's arched entrance. "From the outside your house looks like a white apple with smoke for a stem," Angelica said, showering powdered frost from her hair.

"And I am the resident snowman who sits wondering what we're doing here on the tundra."

"You mean the three of us?"

"Yes, the three of us."

"Being friends, I thought. Exchanging pleasantries."

"What excuse did you give Bertha today?"

"I don't think she knows I went out. She sits at the window watching cloud faces form and dissolve. She looks for signs of her Alexander. Faces in the sky, faces in the fire, faces and more faces."

"I suppose, when your face vanishes, I'll be the one in a permanent trance," Aaron said.

"Nice nonsense," Angelica said. "Tell me, Aaron, have you found a new place to hibernate other than this frozen dollhouse?"

"Not yet. I've asked Mrs. Elm to give me more time but I know her answer."

"Then what will you do?"

"What can I do? Move up to Syracuse, I suppose, where they're too busy to notice one Jew more or less."

"I would say a Hebrew dowser is hard not to notice. Especially the one famous for finding Goliath."

"Too famous for my own good. But more important, what will you do, Angelica, if what you told me holds true?"

"It holds true. I'm done with George Hull. I can't say what's next, though. You could buy your land in the valley and build my daughter and me a small cabin. We know more about farming than you ever will."

"Why are you so set on a daughter?"

"So whatever she does, she won't go off to war."

"There are wars and wars," Aaron said. "If they did sell me a few acres and I asked you to live there, friend, do you think our neighbors would hold a shivaree?"

"If they'd leave us alone it would be enough. While they learned to ignore us we might study each other's shadows."

"We're babbling like idiots. I wonder what your child thinks, listening to us."

"That lovers babble like idiots."

"Lovers? Are we lovers now?"

"I think we are, yes. I find it hard to believe that I could be so strongly attracted to a man younger than myself and a Hebrew to boot. But I feel as much for you as I did for Hamish, God rest his soul. And possibly more. It is very surprising and most unexpected.

I have no clue why. Perhaps because I think of us as two white mice huddled in a snowdrift. I would like to know, what are your feelings for me, Mr. Bupkin?"

"I'm not sure since I never met a woman remotely like you. I'm a slow-moving man by my nature. What of the difference between us? We have nothing in common, not even God. Who would we pray to for our cabbages to grow?"

"Whichever God grows the best cabbages, I think. But I asked for your feelings, not your logic."

"My feelings for you are strong. My qualms and questions may be even stronger."

"You'll have to make up your mind on that score. As for me and my child, Mr. Bupkin, we are taken fondly with you and have been from the time we first met. I think you're fool enough to have us and us foolish enough to learn how to love you."

"In just a few months this nest of ours melts to memory. Words we say in December will be like fish in a puddle by May. Then dry to dust by July."

"Is that what your heart says?"

"Every teacher knows the heart's an accomplished liar."

"Will you marry us, Aaron Bupkin? Yes or no? It bothers us that you're hardly more than a boy, but I think we can overcome that discrepancy with some patient effort. And I have heard Jews are born old."

"Yes, Mrs. Hull, I will marry you if you want."

"Not just Mrs. Hull. Don't forget that."

"All right, the whole kit and kaboodle."

"Then it's settled between us."

"Except for a few thorny details that might kill a horse," Aaron said, stoking the fire. "Like food and shelter."

"Undress," Angelica said. "I'll do the same. Let's see if we like what we see."

"That's ridiculous," Aaron said. "We'd die of frostbite. They'd find more fossils in Cardiff and blame me for all of them."

"Do what you want," Angelica said, dropping her coat, then her dress, then things Aaron Bupkin knew of only from rumor. She stood with her hair brushing the roof. "Here, this is us except for our feet. We're keeping our shoes on. Be honest now. What do you think?" Aaron fought off a dizzy spell. He contemplated that creature of angles, curves, and crevices, more complicated than he ever suspected. Her swollen breasts and the curve of her belly made him think of the roof of the igloo. The little beard of pubic hair was what startled him most since even the *Royal Geographic* concealed that astonishment.

"I think you both very beautiful," Aaron said. He pulled off his shirt, took down his pants, got rid of his drawers, even socks and boots. "This is me. What's your opinion?"

"So it's true then what they say about Jews," Angelica said. "He looks like a bald cyclops who forgot his hat. Is that why your men wear caps? To make up for the loss?"

"I'd have to check scripture before I could answer," Aaron said.

"You're the third man I've seen naked, and I'd say you compare well with the others."

"I appreciate your opinion, Mrs. Hull, but it's better to leave some things unsaid."

"Is that true for friends or just lovers?" Angelica said. "Now put your hand where my baby is resting."

Aaron touched where she told him and let his hand stay. Angelica sang,

> *When Joseph was an old man,*
> *An old man was he,*
> *He married Virgin Mary*
> *The Queen of Galilee.*
>
> *And Mary said to Joseph,*
> *So meek and so mild,*
> *"Joseph, gather me some cherries*
> *For I am bearing child."*

Joseph flew in anger,
In anger flew he.
"Let the father of your baby
Gather cherries for thee."

Then up spoke little Jesus
From inside Mary,
"Let my mother have some cherries,
Bow low down, cherry tree."

Then low down bowed the cherry tree,
Bowed low to the ground
And Mary gathered cherries,
While Joseph stood around.

"I hope this baby is less articulate and less demanding," Aaron said.

"Happy New Year, my darling," Angelica said.

They sat cradled together while snow devils danced in the forest outside.

1870

NEW YORK, NEW YORK, JANUARY 1, 1870

On New Year's day, following his farmer's habit, Stubby Newell woke at dawn and found a butterball of a girl sleeping beside him, smiling from inside some dream. Stubby had no idea who she was or where he was. He splashed cold water on his face, neck, and hair then rubbed himself dry with a Turkish towel the size of Rhode Island.

The room was a brocaded box. Its window was draped with a curtain of lace, its floor covered by a carpet deep as Spring grass. He saw his clothes, tossed over a chair as chubby as the stranger in bed. Fancy tuxedo, dress shirt with cardboard chest, cummerbund, silk undershirt, polka dot boxers, long socks, garters, black bow tie, wool coat, spats, suede gloves, and high hat. A pair of patent leather shoes, glossy as mirrors, were placed upside down on a bureau. A love seat was covered with girl clothes, a cut-steel handbag on a chain, and ruby-red shoes. Stubby remembered a game of faro with Jay Gould and Jim Fisk, then the three of them together in a cab going somewhere. That room, he guessed, was the somewhere.

Stubby's brain felt like gravel. He rinsed sand from his mouth, pulled on his clothes, then checked the wallet in his pants. Nothing was missing. George Hull had handed him a thick wad of money on New Year's Eve and told him to celebrate for both of them. His next memory was the card game, raking in pot after pot. The evidence of that run of luck was tucked safely in his jacket.

"Fast company, quick profits," Stubby said to himself.

He tried hard to recall what arrangements were made with the pink, pudgy stove who heated the room. Was she a gift from Gould or Fisk or at his own expense? Knowing how those boys threw cash around, Stubby assumed the former. Still, he felt grateful, though he forgot for what service. He dropped a coin on her pillow and left.

He found his way down a curved staircase, went through a marble lobby, then out a formidable door of iron and beveled glass. Stubby looked at Gramercy Park. He stepped gingerly into the new year, the next decade, feeling happy, hungry, and amazed at the distance he'd traveled from Cardiff.

The cold helped his head, so Stubby decided to walk for a while. He headed downtown toward Hull's Humidor, then turned east toward the river where steamers and clippers bobbed on slow waves. Narrow streets were jammed with delivery wagons. Workers carried cargo from barges and ships. New Year or not, the docks bustled. The holiday lived uptown.

Stubby stopped to have himself a good breakfast. The restaurant he chose, Sloppy Jim's, smelled like a sailor's crotch after a long voyage. Its fishermen and wharf-rat patrons hunched at long tables eating bowls of thick chowder, iodine-smelling stew, slaw, and potatoes. They dipped black bread in hot broth, downed pitchers of beer, and sucked on the bones of assorted sea creatures. Slimy things dangling tentacles and claws, finned things with yellow eyes. Hideous scaled things with needle teeth.

When he found his seat on a bench, Stubby realized both the diners and their food were surprised to see him. For a moment he'd forgotten his outfit. A waiter shuffled over to take his order. Stubby pointed to a bowl in front of his neighbor. He asked for the same. "Eels it is. And to drink?"

"Beer," Stubby said.

"Glass or pitcher?"

"Pitcher."

"Large or small?"

"Large."

"Large it is."

Stubby waited for his food, thinking about the blowfish he'd left sleeping in the candy-box room. He picked his brain for her name. A small detail like that would be handy to keep in storage, a help on some night when he'd want to dredge up the story. Jane, Ann, Lilly, Zoe? Big lady, short name was as far as he got.

The man whose meal Stubby copied tilted closer. "You one of the bridge people? I'm warning you straight and not kidding around. Make a move to get my men away from me, I swear I'll gaff you and any that comes for your corpse."

"You're talking to me?" Stubby said, while the waiter put a plate of hot snakes in front of him. "Am I right or wrong about that?"

"You're right, Mr. Fancy."

Stubby turned toward an ape's ass of a face. The man even had hairy eyeballs. "Well, you got it all twisted. I don't know what you're trying to tell."

"You know damn well what I'm telling."

"No, I don't," Stubby said. "Why should I? I ain't one of the *bridge people,* whatever they are, and never was." Stubby stuck his fork in an eel and held it hanging. "Explain if you want to or don't if you won't. I was sitting here thinking about a whore who smelled a lot better than you or this place."

"You're not from the bridge?"

"What kind of bridge? Bridge to where?"

"Brooklyn. Out there. Are you dumb as you look?"

"Maybe smarter, maybe dumber," Stubby said. "I can't say what I look like this fair morning."

"You look like shit hit you hard. What are you, from someplace like England?"

"Hell, no," Stubby said. "From Cardiff, New York, up near Syracuse. Now what bridge to Brooklyn? There's no bridge I heard of."

"Jesus, everybody knows that they're starting their bridge. Been stealing my stiffs right from under my nose."

"I suppose a lot of good men could fit under that nose," Stubby said. "Which I can't know for sure since I don't hardly see any nose under that rug. Why do they want a bridge to Brooklyn?"

"Like for any bridge. To go back and forth," the man said.

"Didn't you see all the boxes and cranes piled near the harbor? You blind in both eyes?"

"Wish I was blind enough not to see my bowl," Stubby said. "What in hell are you eating? Where do you bite? No, I didn't notice equipment and wouldn't know what it was if I did. As for your bridge, you're welcome to keep it."

"What whore's perfume were you thinking about? What's her name?"

"There's my problem," Stubby said. "It fell from my brain. Bet, Gert, Dot, some name like that. Didn't fit a woman her size."

"How big we talking about? Could you swing from her jugs?"

"I hope I did and surely enjoyed it."

"Maybe Ella or Sue?" the ape said.

On the walk back, Stubby saw what worried the man. Mountains of stuff covered over with canvas, fenced around, guarded by mean German dogs. A Brooklyn Bridge might be good news to bring Cousin George. Somebody might walk over that bridge to go see a giant.

When Stubby reached Hull's Humidor it was hardly eight o'clock but he saw Ben Hull already inside, wiping dust off his Indian tribe. Goliath wouldn't be open for business till nine. While he felt for his key, Stubby lurched backward. A bag of rags ran toward him jumping a pile of gray snow near the curb. It steamed like a dragon. "Hey, mister," it said, "could you answer me a question?" Stubby saw it was only a boy wrapped in an old army blanket.

"Ask away, son." Stubby looked for signs of an ambush. Those street Arabs knew how to hunt strays from the herd and used Judas goats for their bait. The street seemed empty enough.

"My mother is sickly, probably dying, and that's all the family I've got."

"I never give money to strangers," Stubby said. "Find somebody else."

"What I want is a favor from the Giant of Cardiff. But which giant is real? Some say this one, some say the one over at Niblo's. I keep running back and forth between them because I got to be certain which is real. My mother says to trust Mr. Barnum's but she's out of her mind with the fever."

"I doubt you have enough money for either," Stubby said.

"Oh, I got the dollar it takes," the boy said, shaking a bagful of change.

"Well, then, I can tell you this giant is the right giant."

"How can you know?"

"Take my word," Stubby said. "I should know since the stone man was found on my farm."

"What time does the door open, then? I've got to get back to feed Mamma her soup."

Stubby felt an eel roll in his gut and burped into his hand. "The door opens when I say it opens. I can take you inside if you promise to behave. Count out your dollar."

The steaming boy dropped cold coins into Stubby's glove. "Hurry up, I'm freezing," Stubby said. "I don't allow pennies, but seeing it's the New Year . . ."

"Gee, thanks," the boy said.

"Now, don't ask my Goliath for too much since he ain't Father Christmas."

"No, sir," the boy said. "Only just for her life."

COLD SPRING, NEW YORK, JANUARY 2, 1870

From a cold balcony, Commodore Cornelius Vanderbilt looked toward Andrew Carnegie's foundry. A river of white-hot metal showered sparks to the sky. Molten steel was being shaped into Vanderbilt's locomotives and freight cars, enough rails to reach to the future. Cable for his bridges were woven in flame. Hulls for

Vanderbilt ships, cogs and gears for efficient, unforgiving Vanderbilt machines were pounded to life on anvils of fire.

The Commodore turned his gaze in another direction. He watched ice floes slide down the Hudson like lost years on their way to perdition. He coughed up phlegm and spit at the night. Then he went back inside.

"Brisk weather," Carnegie said to his best customer, president of the New York and Harlem, the Hudson River Railway, and now the New York Central. The Commodore, who began with a sailboat carrying people and goods from Staten Island to Manhattan, then built a fleet, next a rolling empire, was surely the world's Prime Mover.

"Does your foundry ever close?"

"Only on Christmas. Hunger for steel seems insatiable."

"I envy you, Andrew. To have achieved so much at such a young age and kept balance to the bargain."

"I think you have no one to envy, Cornelius."

"I'm seventy-six this year. You wait for orders, I for the grave. I have what to envy."

"No grave for you, Commodore. What you leave behind will remind America to look after her business, both temporal and spiritual. Universities, libraries, churches, a renaissance of research. A shower of gifts to outlast the centuries."

"I'll leave behind the same dust as the rest."

"No. Your best bequest is the fact you existed. And I'd suggest you continue to do so."

"The man I see in the mirror does not promise much time. I don't mind though. There are few pleasures left me."

"Vanderbilt can't be replaced."

"Andrew, wherever I look I find young men with balls exploding like fireworks. My place will be filled in an instant."

"At worst you'll build railroads in Heaven."

"For creatures with wings? I'd never invest in that venture."

"You have a sack of years left, Cornelius. You'll live to bury us all, wait and see. I'll expect an eloquent eulogy."

"Time for bed," Vanderbilt said.

"Rest and refresh."

"Young sleep rests and refreshes. Old sleep is rehearsal for the long sleep. Still, my best entertainment is dreams. They take me to marvelous places. Last night the stone men we met came to see me. It was more your dream than mine, Andrew. Stone and steel have something in common. But I suppose even dreams lose their way and find themselves in the wrong bedroom."

"What did the giants have to say?"

"Titan was pragmatic, a rock to the core, cursing the idea of trade unions. He suggested I buy up shares of the Union Pacific."

"Credit to Titan."

"Goliath only looked at me naked and wept. As if some vestige of soul petrified with his gizzard. I asked him if loss of his part was what gave him compassion to pity this fragile antique."

"Hardly fragile, Commodore. What was the answer?"

"He didn't get to answer. Only shrugged and smiled, about to reply, when I woke with a cramp in my leg."

"Maybe he'll be back to finish the message."

"I hope for softer visitors tonight," Vanderbilt said. "A nymph or two on a seashell."

"I'll have fruit sent to your room," Carnegie said. "Perhaps bananas and apples to help entertain them."

"Some prunes and warm tea would be nice," Vanderbilt said. "Good night, Andrew. God bless you."

"Good night, friend Cornelius. And again, my wishes for a happy and prosperous new decade. Steam, steel, and stability."

NEW YORK, NEW YORK, JANUARY 12, 1870

George Hull waited in P. T. Barnum's Fifth Avenue pied-à-terre examining posters of animal grotesques, gilled abnormalities, human freaks, and other of nature's horrors. The gallery left him chuckling and uneasy. There was an undercurrent of horror that tugged at his mind like a riptide.

"How quickly the extreme becomes the absurd," Barnum said, catching George in a guffaw over ass-fused Siamese twin brothers. "I suppose laughter is our only recourse when we see evidence that God's a Puckish prankster. Better laugh than wince and sprint for the exit."

"We could kick and scream," George said.

"For all the good it does," Barnum said. "So you are George Hull?"

"I am George Hull."

"My name is Barnum. Will you shake my hand?"

"I know your name. No, I will not shake your hand."

"But you came here at my invitation."

"I came out of curiosity as distorted as those pictures on your wall."

"Curious to see what Barnum is made of? Well, Hull, I'm equally curious to know your mettle. I can't offer you spirits since I've renounced alcohol. A cup of good coffee . . . ?"

"May I smoke a cigar?"

"Light up. Feel free. But please sit down."

George sat in a chair with elephant legs, P.T. on a sofa covered with a tiger skin. "This room gives me the feeling we should be wearing loincloths and funny hats," George said.

"We always do, Mr. Hull. Will you do me one favor? Let's create the only climate where truth can survive. A frank conversation between two seasoned shysters. Is William Newell the real father of the giant, Goliath? Or is it you?"

"We know it's not you, Mr. Barnum."

"I'm not interested in drawing a family tree. I must be sure of one thing: that the man I face is the right man."

"For what?"

"To make an expedient decision. Consider. First, I know that your stone is obliged to relocate since Hull's Humidor has need of his space."

"Who told you that?"

"Stubby Newell is not much for secrets. I'm told he saw in the New Year in the company of Gould and Fisk. A good time was had by all and the banter convivial."

"Not much use in denying that we're moving the giant."

"By coincidence, my Titan must vacate Niblo's. They want to double his rent."

"So much greed in the air," George said.

"Second, more urgent, is the miserable fact that lines for both attractions have grown alarmingly short since the year began. Don't deny it, and neither will I. New York is the most fickle city since Sodom. The people who live here have need of more stimulation than Sleeping Beauty. First they rush to see Titan and Goliath, now they go elsewhere. You might conclude this is the time to begin a tour of the suburbs. Move on to Boston, Philadelphia, Chicago. Let me say from long experience, Hull, considering the cost of ambitious travel, such a journey can be disastrous. With luck and huge effort some profit can be had. But measured in pennies, not dollars. Many times Barnum has been found guilty of violating the law of diminishing returns and forced to pay the piper."

"The point of all this?"

"Why move the cow to risky pastures when there's still grass on the ground?"

"You just told me her udder's depleted."

"Not yet, Hull. Not if some way were found to restore luster to both fading fossils. Encouraging a few miracles would be best but dangerous. That course requires too many conspirators."

"*Fabricate* miracles? You think Goliath's miracles were false?"

"Forget miracles. What if we join forces, move our stone men in tandem, create a display of the two side-by-side? A *Clash of Giants!* Do you see my direction? And not in a theater or the usual auditorium. In an arena where pugilists battle. Imagine a boxing ring. A torrent of light. *In this corner, Titan! In that, Goliath! Witness the battle of biblical ancients! See both for the price of one!*"

"Discount my marvel like something found at a rummage sale?"

"All costs would be shared, all revenues divided. Barnum asks only that you put him in charge of the sizzle. I mean advertising, promotion, hooplah, and such. What do you think, Hull? Say yes and save us both."

George Hull sucked in a ghost's worth of smoke. It was correct that Ben named a deadline for moving, a sad fact that on weekdays Goliath's attendance thinned to a trickle, and true he'd weighed thoughts of quitting Manhattan to beat Barnum to Boston. The idea of working together with the same man who compromised the one, only, original Cardiff Giant nauseated George. But it also made sense.

Barnum's concept of a Clash of the Giants! might do more than bring back the crowds. Side by side, under that "torrent of light," Goliath could finally claim the crown he deserved. Barnum the hoaxter would be discredited, humiliated, exposed, debased, neatly deballed by his own device.

"Clash of the Giants! May the best giant win," Barnum said. "With Tom Thumb as our referee to assure a clean bout. And listen to this, Hull. We'll let the audience vote their judgment as to who is the victor. Drop their ballots in a locked iron box guarded by detectives. To be counted on a future date *to be announced.* Oh,

I've thought this out in every detail. And you're right about discounting marvels. Maybe we should hold off on reducing the price."

"Would you agree that the loser be publicly pulverized?"

"Good thinking. Maybe after a national tour when there's not an American left with the price of a ticket."

"All expenses and receipts split down the middle?"

"Like a broiled lobster," Barnum said. "With plenty of meat to fill two plates. Now are you ready to shake my hand, Hull? I'd be grateful for the gesture since I do admire your spunk. Your whole scheme was magnificent and done with panache. Worthy of Barnum, I'd admit in a minute."

"Always a scheme, nothing real. It's hard not to pity you for all your fame."

"Now you sound like General Tom, keeping the high ground while your pig digs for truffles. "Always a scheme, nothing real"? Hull, learn to save your pretensions of pity and piety for the mark, not the marksman. We both know sincerity is the mother of deception. Give Barnum a deal. Not a priest."

CARDIFF, NEW YORK, JANUARY 20, 1870

Barnaby Rack studied copies of drayage records that began with Peter Wilson in Chicago and traced a convoluted path to Union, New York. Henry Hooper, Martin Moriches, Rufus Troom, Thomas Tower, Barton Berman, Pritchard Dobbs, all receipts signed by the same hand. Letters slanted left, tails on the *T*s, swirls on the *S*s, every *O* on its side.

All the same man, recognized from the sketch made from

Samantha Turk's tintype. All *George Hull,* the same George Hull who'd hired Loomis Zane to drive him and his giant from Union Station to Stubby Newell's farm at the foot of Bear Mountain back in November of '68.

The night before, Barnaby met Zane at the Blue Lion Tavern in Lafayette. Now he rode in Zane's wagon following Hull's exact route, writing notes as he bounced over rocks and ruts.

Scoop or not, Barnaby felt more depressed than elated. What dragged him down was the sick feeling that he might have just as well stumbled over Jesus' dead body the day after Good Friday.

"Oh, yeah, it was pelting down rain," Loomis Zane said. "And that box weighed 'bout a million-odd pounds. I was paid good for my work but my horses damn near wrecked. 'Member a rotten hound out there barkin' and snarlin' loud as the thunder whole time we unloaded. 'Member two men and a boy. One musta been Newell. The other the feller in your picture. The boy, I can't say, but he seemed to belong there. Strong droopy-faced kid. Well, we dropped that box near the barn and there was the end of it. Can't say much more. They had a woman on the place, saw her face in a window, didn't offer me so much as a drink of hot water."

"And later, when you heard about the stone man, did you have any suspicions? Second thoughts?"

"The fossil came a long time after. More than a year. I might have said something then but didn't take it too serious. Man told me his cargo was some kind of tobacco press and I believe it. The Cardiff Giant was dug up by honorable folk. Went to see him myself with my wife and my child and got the best hard-on a man could want. I know that you're a doubter but I don't share your doubts. I believe Goliath is a petrified man from the Bible."

"To each his own," Barnaby said.

"We had a hard time on this hill, I remember. Mud all around, couldn't see ten feet, thought we'd be mired for a month. But I got that box to where I was paid to get it, and that's all I'm saying because that's all I know and all I could swear to. Seems like every time I come up here it's storming or blowing or hailing or whatnot. I guess there are places like that."

"Yes, there are," Barnaby said.

"That's the farm up ahead. Looks better today than it did the last time. Snow makes things look nice."

"The best cosmetic," Barnaby said. "You can let me off at the gate, Mr. Zane. I shouldn't be too long."

"Hope it don't blizzard," Zane said.

Barnaby trudged up the path to the house. Bertha Newell, who sat struggling to write her first letter in twenty-nine years, dropped her pen when she heard his raps at the door. She got up from the kitchen table, reached for her husband's shotgun, fingered the trigger, then went to see who came calling.

"State your business."

"Barnaby Rack. *New York Clarion.* I'm acquainted with William Newell."

"So?"

"I need a moment of your time, Mrs. Newell."

Relieved to be free of her wrestle with grammar, Bertha let him in. When she recognized Barnaby's face, she propped the gun against the door jamb and straightened her apron. "I know you. You came nosing around during the giant."

"Yes, last October," Barnaby said. "How are you and your husband? Enjoying the season, I hope."

"Stubby's not here. He's down in New York with his stone man."

"Of course he'd be there. Where's my mind? I heard about his battle with Barnum. Awful thing. Terrible thing. A mockery of justice."

"Take off your jacket, sit yourself down," Bertha said. "I'll put on the kettle. What are you doing in Cardiff?"

"Actually, a follow-up article on the impact Goliath had on the town and the people who live here."

"Who cares?"

"New York cares, Mrs. Newell. What with two giants in town."

"Well, I hope one of them giants is soon a thing of the past and forgot like last year's mosquitoes. I won't be sorry. What pains me is we ever did dig him in the first place."

"But didn't Goliath substantially improve your condition? I'd assume a certain degree of prosperity . . ."

"We made money, it's true, and still do. But that giant took my son and gave me back shame."

"Might I presume to ask where's the shame? I, for one . . ."

"Everybody in Cardiff and Lafayette knows by now. Angelica Hull ran away with the Jew when I caught them alone in their igloo."

"Excuse me? Did you say you caught Angelica Hull alone with a Jew in an igloo?"

"Both of them naked as the palm of my hand."

"Might you elaborate on that story? I hope you don't mind if I write while you speak."

"I don't mind if it's you do the writing."

"Who's Angelica Hull?" Barnaby asked, realizing Bertha Newell had no inkling he already knew. "And what particular Jew is the Jew in question? Should I think that the igloo where you caught them in a state of undress was the same kind of dwelling where Eskimos live?"

"That's right," Bertha said, "the very same kind they show us in pictures with walruses. Angelica Hull is my cousin by marriage, married to George Hull and bearing his child. The Jew is named Bupkin who sold her a bunting and responsible for dowsing Goliath in the first place."

"You're getting ahead of me," Barnaby said.

"I also write slow," Bertha said. "Take your time."

"Aaron Bupkin? The dowser? I've interviewed him."

"I take full blame," Bertha said. "Angelica Hull was left in my care to recover her health. She recovered it faster than I ever expected. Sitting bare by a fire no bigger than a candle in the middle of a Cardiff winter ain't what I'd exactly call sickly."

"How was it you caught them?"

"Bertha Newell knows when wool's pulled over her eyes. A few days after Christmas I followed Angelica on what she said was a solitary walk to build appetite. I had a bad feeling since her behaving's been far from normal of late. When I saw her turn off the road, I kept at a distance. Then I saw the Eskimo house not a mile from here tucked well in the woods. At first I thought to find little people inside that snowball."

"Little people?"

"Of the kind you hear spoken of who live in the forest and give gold when you catch them. It don't matter since what I caught was my own cousin-in-law crouched with the dowser. Oh, I wish I had Stubby's rifle in my hand. That lady most sedate and proper was definite witched by a spell. But who knew it? Not Angelica, I'm sure. She's the victim in this, cursed and raped by a devil."

"And when you confronted them?"

"They flat-out denied they were there. Angelica asked me what I thought I witnessed, and when I told her she laughed like a loon and said I was lost in a dream. The enchanted bitch nearly had me believe her. But there was the Jew, plain as day, and I don't dream of them. Never have, never will, never would. Sitting there large as life with his set of privates exposed. God pardon my eyes. When I made comment he roared like a monster. I ran from that place in dread of my life."

"What a discomforting experience."

"You can say that again. When I got home I shook for an hour. My thought was to wait out poor Angelica then rush her to church for purification. But she never came back here. Left all her possessions right where they are now. The snow fell too heavy for travel that night, but by dawn the next morning I went into Lafayette to tell Sheriff Tupper who I woke with my screams. We went over to Mrs. Elm's where Bupkin keeps a room. She said he been there to gather his things then went someplace else. Back to Hell, I suppose, and Angelica with him."

"You say Mrs. Hull is with child?"

"A horned child by now, Lord have mercy."

"This is more than I wanted to hear," Barnaby said.

"What did you want to hear?"

"The truth about your Goliath."

"You know the truth. You saw what magic Goliath can do. And now look what he's done to me and my family. I can't ever leave this house with my eyes off the ground."

"If Angelica Hull ran away with a Jew, how is the stone man involved, Mrs. Newell?"

"One caused the other. It's clear to me."

"Here's my theory," Barnaby said. "If Angelica Hull flew away, no magician taught her to fly. I'd say George Hull gave her the lessons."

"George Hull? George was always a devoted husband. George don't even know yet his wife is a whore. No, it's Goliath with that sweet, saintly face. I tell you he ain't what he seems."

"I know very well he's not what he seems. I must warn you, Mrs. Newell, to watch your words. I have proof enough to convince a stone wall that your fossil's neither Satan or saint but a bald-faced fake. A sham and a scam. That William Newell and George Hull, acting in concert, have perpetrated the cruelest hoax in the history of flimflam."

"I thought you a friend, come to share my misery," Bertha said.

"I came here to learn the degree of your husband's part in this shocking deception because, I promise you, someone will be called to account for hoodwinking an entire nation."

Bertha ran to the door and grabbed up the gun. She held it pointed at Barnaby's nose. "You're a dead man so stop writing things down. Say a prayer for the road."

"Go ahead, fire," Barnaby said. "Let your cat lick my blood off the floor. It won't stop the story, it's too late for that. When they cover your head with a hood and your bladder empties on the gallows, say it's Goliath's fault you did me in. When they set the noose around your neck, use your last words to tell them a statue drove you to murder. Don't worry. Barnaby Rack won't be there to contradict you. But he will be waiting at Heaven's gate when your soul comes gasping for mercy."

Bertha dropped the shotgun. It fired on impact. The blast sent a shower of lead pellet into Barnaby's thigh. He grabbed his leg, tilting backward.

"It was all George's doing," Bertha yelled. "George and his Jew, beginning to end. Lord, Mr. Rack, you talk like the Messiah. If you write half as good, I should read all your works."

"Thank you, Mrs. Newell," Barnaby said, before he dropped to the floor. "One more detail. Is Mrs. Loretta Hull involved in this epic?"

"Ben's wife? You know her?"

"A passing acquaintance," Barnaby said.

NEW YORK, NEW YORK, JANUARY 22, 1870

———

Loretta Hull, never much for schooling, felt that somehow she'd swallowed a library. Books, tables, chairs, lamps, the whole works. Her best education came from browsing herself. When she needed sensible reference, a resident librarian helped her lift the right volume from an inside shelf. Since her dance with General Thumb at Niblo's Garden, now a half-memory fuzzy as an angora muff, the astute intelligence she trusted most suggested Loretta protect her flanks. There was just a slight chance that the tiny voluptuary gave her more for Christmas than kumquats. Loretta was handed a book on logistics.

As always, Ben Hull worked late at the humidor, far past the hour other workers retired. On the twelfth night of January, his wife surprised him with a hot midnight meal. Ben was grateful, chewing on lamb stew, while he screwed a brass umbrella stand into the floor. Loretta stood behind his wooden Indian squaw making noises she thought an Indian might make. *"Woo woo woo."*

"What's that all about?" Ben asked. "Why so giddy? Whatever you're doing, it's very distracting, dear."

"Woo woo woo."

"I'm trying to concentrate." Ben turned toward the tribe. His concerned and considerate spouse stepped into the lamplight sans her dress and chemise, her corset unbuckled, her breasts hanging free.

"Woo woo woo."

"Sweetheart, behave. This isn't a bedroom." Loretta did look fresh and fetching among the painted natives but entirely and wrongly placed. Simon Hull & Sons Humidor was a sanctuary for men.

"Woo woo woo?"

"Cover yourself. Someone might see through the window."

Loretta reached into her purse and came out with a compact of lip rouge. She used a finger for a brush to circle her nipples in vermilion then cupped her breasts in her hands. *"Woo woo woo?"*

"This is unacceptable," Ben said. "You're making me angry though perfectly aware that is not your intention. I know we haven't been together in a month or more. And you know how burdened I've been with my duties. The workers are slow and expensive, deliveries late, my father's on his way back from Cuba. When Hull's is ready and open we'll have time for each other. But right now I can't focus on anything but what's got to get done. I love you, no question, but understand that the pressure . . ."

"Woo woo?"

"You won't stop this, will you?"

"Woo?" Loretta gave each breast a kiss.

"Let me lay down some paper to protect the rug," Ben said.

Later Loretta helped a more relaxed husband hang two oil

paintings Simon sent from Havana, sweep away sawdust footprints the carpenters left, uncrate four Chinese vases, wind a clock that showed the moon phase, and stock a case with boxes of Double Corona Ulysses Supremos from Binghamton. She felt buoyant and happy beside her husband, working in tandem toward mutual gain. Her librarian, staunch and starched, was back in the stacks, content to have done proper service.

WASHINGTON, D.C., JANUARY 25, 1870

Two men, one formidable but fragile, wrapped in a sleek seal coat, crowned with a high hat, the other coatless, hatless, robust, and in his prime, strolled slowly down Pennsylvania Avenue. They paused at the gate to the White House. The older man snorted and coughed but recovered himself quickly. "You know how much I have admired your work, Alan," Commodore Vanderbilt said. "I call you our invisible engine."

Alan Pinkerton nodded. "Invisible engine. I like that."

"Without the Pinkerton National Detective Agency, we'd have more pirates than passengers on my railroads. But the pirates still plague us."

"The Molly Maguires are marked for extinction. It's a matter of time. Troublemakers and brigands. Anarchists and bloodsuckers. Parasites with shovels."

"Coal is our blood. We can neither abide nor afford agitators corrupting our miners with talk of guilds and unions."

"My plans are in place," Pinkerton said. "Rest your mind, Commodore. Infiltration's the key to Molly's chastity belt. We'll soon have our key in the lock."

"You have my full trust, Alan. But there is another matter. A more personal concern."

"I understand. Speak freely, sir."

"Let's sit on that bench. My President can wait. I expect he'll find good use for his time."

"He'll find something to do," Pinkerton said. "The question is, do you need the Great White Father coherent?"

"Of course not. Sit down and we'll talk for a moment. I warn you, this may sound ludicrous."

"I never laugh at a problem."

"Laugh all you want. Split your sides. But please do it later. For the moment, indulge me."

"If I can be of service . . ."

"If anyone can, you're the one. And I won't insult you by invoking the need for discretion."

"I hope never," Pinkerton said. "Who else is discretion's godfather?"

"This is hard for me," Vanderbilt said.

"You have my attention and every resource."

"Alan," the old man said after a thunderous sneeze, "this has to do with a giant."

"A giant what?" Pinkerton asked, leaning closer.

NEW YORK, NEW YORK, JANUARY 26, 1870

"Damnable shame about John Roebling," Jay Gould said to Stubby Newell. "Imagine him waiting thirteen years to get his bridge off the ground then having a foot crushed between a dock and a ferryboat."

"A man can live with one foot," Stubby said. "Anything there's two of one can be spared. When it's something there's one of and afterward none of, I'd say that's the bad luck."

"John died of lockjaw. Rest in peace."

"Sorry to hear it. Thirteen years for a bridge? Well, I waited twenty years to get a good crop of corn out of my ground. Still waiting, but now as a man of property I don't give a damn. One week with that giant of mine brings me more than every ear of corn or bale of wheat I sold altogether."

"You're a fortunate man, William."

"Call me Stubby."

"No, I think William more suited. And you call me Jay."

The two men walked down Park Row, past the canyon where Brooklyn Bridge would be anchored, then on toward the South Street piers.

"Jay it is." Stubby was flattered to have such a companion. His gangly friend with beady rat's eyes and a preacher's voice was among Manhattan's first citizens, a hero of Wall Street, the ultimate mover and shaker.

"See on the Brooklyn side?" Gould said. "They're already constructing a tower of granite and limestone. We're looking at the greatest engineering feat since the Erie Canal and Suez. John's son, young Washington, is pledged to finish his father's mission and he'll do it, I swear."

"You must know everybody alive," Stubby said.

"If a man isn't where the action is, then where is he?"

"I guess he's standing right here next to you, Jay."

"Don't deprecate yourself, William. Your star is rising."

Gould heard directly from Barnum that the two stone men already grossed three hundred thousand and now, with the Clash of Giants! might easily double that take. Allowing for Barnum's fiscal hyperbole, with the certainty that Barnum would never honestly split a pot, Gould reasoned that even with leftovers Stubby Newell was rich, ripe, and ready for harvest. When the farmer mentioned Brooklyn Bridge, Gould saw a steel rainbow.

"I've got a lot riding on Washington Roebling," Gould said. "My life rests in the hands of a thirty-two-year-old boy who may have inherited his father's genius."

"How's that?"

"In close confidence, William, I've managed to put together a syndicate of investors to finance the bridge in partnership with the government. In return, we're guaranteed half the tolls from every carriage, wagon, or greenhorn wanting to cross over from there to here or here to there."

"You think people will risk it? Don't know if I'd trust a bridge that long. Hate to be fished out of that stinking river."

"They'll take the risk. Not hundreds, not thousands. They'll come by the millions. And every one paying the piper."

"Sounds good, Jay, and I wish you good luck."

"There's room for one more investor," Gould said. "I gave a half-hearted promise to let Barnum in, but how can I trust such a renegade? I'd rather it be someone deserving. A steady friend. Say, for example, William Newell."

"Me? Jesus, that's nice of you, Jay, to think of me like that."

"Frankly, I admire your style. I've pegged you as a modest man who'd appreciate wealth and use it to good advantage. See this document?" Gould pulled a scroll from his coat.

"That is a beauty," Stubby said. "Religious writing. And there's the bridge pressed on a gold seal. *Five Hundred Shares.* I never saw a paper like that."

"Look closer." Stubby looked and saw his name handwritten in Gothic letters.

"That's my name there practically in Latin."

"I took the liberty," Gould said. "Listen to me because I'll say this only once. That certificate is worth a king's ransom, a once-in-a-lifetime opportunity. Seize the day. It's yours if you want it."

"You mean Stubby Newell from Cardiff could end up owning a chunk of the Brooklyn Bridge in New York?"

"Absolutely, if you act fast enough. My syndicate members are pressing me hard to close the book on this deal. Any one of us would gladly increase his own share, but our policy is to keep everything equal. Too much power in any one hand upsets that arrangement."

"I know what you mean, Jay. But I think owning a bridge is too rich for me. I have money in the bank but nowhere enough to play in your league."

"What are friends for, William? I'd be willing to let you in for a hundred thousand cash and, say, seventy-five percent of Goliath. Meanwhile, I'd advance you the difference. Up to half a million, interest free."

"Seventy-five percent of Goliath. From the neck down, that would be. Let me tell you, it sounds good to me and it would to my partner, my cousin George Hull. Don't say George wouldn't like owning a Brooklyn Bridge. I can see us both sitting with a cigar in one hand and a beer in the other counting those carriages, wagons, and greenhorns going both ways."

"Then we're in business?"

"Afraid not," Stubby said. "The reason is squabs. Little baby pigeons the size of my fist."

"I know what a squab is," Gould said.

"Of course you do, Jay. Why shouldn't you know? What happened was, on New Year's Eve when we went out together, Jim Fisk made me an offer I couldn't refuse."

"What offer?"

"To use my farm for a center, buy up the land ten miles in every direction, then breed enough squabs to feed every prosperous man and woman in the world. He wants to lay down tracks for a squab train to deliver them butchered and trimmed in cars full of chipped ice. Here's the paper he gave me, signed, sealed, and delivered."

"You signed with Fisk?"

"And he didn't ask for any part of Goliath. Just the cash, which he'll use to tie up the squabs and negotiate land. Better him than me. They know Stubby Newell in the valley, and if word got out I was in the market every acre of swamp would turn to a diamond."

"But Fisk is a crook. You'll be hung out to dry. You won't see a dime's worth of land or a single squab's ass."

"Jim said the same thing about you, Jay. Told me you screwed him out of a few million gold shares. Thing I don't understand is how the two of you pal around and still badmouth each other. But that's how it is in New York. Hell, I'd trust both of you with my sister if I had one."

"Is there an escape clause? Let me see that contract."

"Don't want to escape. Somehow the idea of squabs is easier for a person like me than a Brooklyn Bridge. Besides, there's no bridge yet and who can say if it works when they get one?"

The deckle-edged, gold-sealed stock certificate, fifty dollars including calligraphy, went back into Jay Gould's pocket. Stubby tucked his contract away. "One of the best things to come from this trip is getting to know men like you," Stubby said. "You're *class* with a capital *C*. Between your bridge and my squabs we might both end up owning enough of this world and stake a fair-sized claim to the next."

"If your birds march over to Brooklyn, they'll pay like the rest," Gould said. "Remember I said so."

"Might teach 'em to swim," Stubby said.

"Reconsider," Gould said.

"Mind made up."

"Rest in peace, William."

"I do, Jay."

It wasn't the truth. Stubby had a letter from Bertha crammed in the same pocket as his agreement with Fisk Enterprises. He'd kept it with him for nearly a week while he looked for the right time to share it with George, who already had a ton on his mind.

> *Dear Husband hope this finds you and all in the best of health. I am fine. Tell George that Angelica ran away with Bupkin the dowser. Also that a newspaper man came to tell me his giant is a fake not from here so I shot him but not bad. In case you get worried I said to the man you had nothing to do*

with Goliath but that George Hull laid him on us so what could you do? So far the Winter is mild. Things are the same. Before Angelica ran she gave me a nice broach and I also got the presents from everybody there so my thanks. The gloves you sent me fit perfect so thanks. A few tourists still come to see the fossil grave. I show them for 25 cents. Let George know I feel very sad about Angelica but what could I do to stop her. It aint my fault. I could not watch her every minute all day long and at night. That was that. No more for now. Your loving wife,

Bertha Newell

That letter cost Stubby six nights of sound sleep.

BOSTON, MASSACHUSETTS, JANUARY 31, 1870

—◆—◆—◆—

"She's sitting right here. Talk to her. This is a fine woman, Grandpa Isaac."

"I don't see any woman," Isaac Bupkin said while he hung a white sheet over a mirror. "Hand me the scissors, Aaron."

"This is ridiculous."

"I'll get it myself."

"Angelica, say something to him."

"I don't know what to say."

"There's nothing to say." Isaac got the scissors himself and made a cut in his tie. "Help me rip my lapels."

"You don't have to ruin a good jacket."

"Never mind. I can rip myself." Isaac said, pointing to a prayer book with flaking brown pages. "Get me my siddur from the table. My only grandson is dead. I got to say kaddish."

"What does he have to say?" Angelica asked.

"Kaddish. The prayer for the dead."

"He thinks I killed you?" Angelica said.

"Don't flatter yourself. He killed himself," Isaac said.

"It's only symbolic," Aaron said. "Listen, Grandpa Isaac, before you do something we'll all regret, give us a chance. Angelica is a human person with a warm heart. By next year you'll love her as much as I do. And she'll love you. You'll come live with us."

"Aaron don't have a pot to piss in but he's getting a job someplace so Isaac Bupkin, a helpless old man, should pack his things and go live in a church. Or maybe an ice house?"

"I shouldn't have said anything about the igloo," Aaron said. "I knew he would use it against me."

"I'm sorry I heard in the first place," Isaac said.

"It really was warm, Mr. Bupkin."

"What kind of ox did you bring to my house? She says 'it was warm.' Vay is mir!" Isaac opened his prayer book and flipped pages. "For this woman you sold your horse?"

"I'll find a job. There's plenty of work around Boston."

"Doing what? Digging wells? When I say you're dead I'm more right than wrong. Maybe a little early but not by much. What happens when her husband comes to say hello? You fight him a duel with swords? You hit him with your stick? You sing him songs about cherries?"

"To wish evil on your own grandson is a terrible thing, Mr. Bupkin."

"Did he give me a choice? He brings home a goyisha madel, and don't think I didn't notice she's schlepping a package. Mazel tov. Maybe it's twins?"

"Don't do this to me," Aaron said.

"I didn't do to you. You did to me. A shande on every Bupkin before or since."

"What's a shande?" Angelica asked.

"Something between a shame and a curse," Aaron said.

"You got to explain her everything? Tell her who will say kaddish for me."

"I'll say kaddish for you."

"Will it count? Since when do the dead say prayers? Besides, even if you're alive and dead as a Jew, how can you say prayers for a Jew who's dead? Look at her goyish blue eyes. She don't know what I'm talking about."

"She knows well enough."

"Leave me alone. I'm in mourning. I'm sitting shiva."

"Get him a shawl," Angelica said.

"Shiva is a mourning period. You sit around mourning for a week. Friends come to offer condolences."

"Maybe somebody from the temple will come with a piece of honey cake and make me a cup of tea."

"You don't like honey cake."

"Then sponge cake. They'll bring something. Even a few crackers."

"I'll make you tea," Angelica said.

"You see?" Isaac said. "A dunce. Tell her I don't want tea."

"We're going," Aaron said.

"You already went," Isaac said. "Have a nice trip."

NEW YORK, NEW YORK, FEBRUARY 5, 1870

———◆◆◆◆◆———

"You've held up my story for days," Barnaby Rack said, his wounded leg propped on a chair, his broken hand still in a cast. "That the *New York Clarion* would hold back a scoop because of advertising is more than depressing."

"All in the timing," John Zipmeister said. "Full pages, see for yourself, Rack. Clash of the Giants! What harm to save the crash for after the clash? Not to mention the cash. In this case the *Clarion* stands to sell a lot more copies later than sooner. Your Mr. Hole, now Hull, don't know it yet, but he's our best newsie. Along with Newell and President Barnum."

"But between Bertha Newell and the sculptor, Burquhart, Hull must know we're on to him and already preparing his defense."

"Then why haven't we heard from the principals? Scenario: Friend Stubby is protecting himself, playing dumb, letting Cousin George take the flack when it hits. Scenario: Hull and Newell are keeping word of impending disaster from Barnum who's staging this show. If Barnum is warned he'll be first out the door. Scenario: They all know, still P.T. sees one more squirt in the lemon. When the *Clarion* cuts their stone men to size, people might pay to spit at what they worshipped. Lord knows, Barnum and the rest of us have seen that happen before. But why speculate? I can't speak for what I don't know. What I do know is that they kept buying ad pages and paying our keep. Anyhow, by tomorrow it's over."

"Promise you won't delay any longer."

"Why should I? Now get down to Joe Ax's. I've got my work here. Twenty thousand copies and your name on all of them. How does it feel being a star?"

Barnaby shrugged. He thought over his first days in Cardiff and couldn't deny George Hull his due. The sorcerer gave value for what he took. People danced with Goliath and shook off their dead leaves. For a moment up there the dream was the truth. "I feel like I'm snatching bad meat from a starving beggar. If his pork chops hide maggots, is it better for him to swallow or starve?"

"The tastier the maggots, the quicker they gobble his belly," Zipmeister said. "Do I know that beggar you speak of? Is his name Barnaby Rack?"

"There's something to be said for delusion."

"Which is why we sell advertising," Zipmeister said.

The copy boy appeared at Zipmeister's door with his hands at his sides. Zipmeister snapped two fingers to allow him a voice. "Mr. Rack, there's a man waiting to see you. Says his name is Elversham."

"Don't know any Elversham."

"Should I send him away?"

"No, we're finished here," Zipmeister said. "Limp out to see what he wants. Christ, Rack, you are a mess. Remind me not to send you to cover a war."

Barnaby went out to the reception room where his visitor sat reading yesterday's paper. The man looked familiar but Barnaby couldn't locate the context.

"Hello, good to see you," the man said, holding out a hand. Barnaby shook it.

"You have me at a disadvantage," Barnaby said.

"Bartlett Elversham from the Equitable Life."

"Yes, of course. Elversham, saint of the elevator."

"I admit, Mr. Rack, to a certain confusion. I came looking for Sean Shamus Brian, which is the name you gave when we met, and was told there was no such person here. Then I remembered that the address you left was in care of Mr. Barnaby Rack at the *Clarion*. How shall I call you? Is it Brian or Rack, then?"

"Both," Barnaby said.

"Of course, what I thought. Rack is your nom de plume."

"I wouldn't want it generally known."

"No, of course not, sir. The reason for this visit is that our letters to you concerning a certain policy with Angelica Hull as the named beneficiary have gone unanswered. That policy is void for nonpayment of premium. It can, however, be reinstated if the payment is promptly made. Mr. Brian, I mean Rack, the Equitable values its clients. Since you seemed so enthusiastic about life insurance when we met, I thought it wise to see you in person before allowing your coverage to lapse. None of us gets younger and, as you know, Mr. Brian, premiums rise with the years. It's much better to keep . . ."

"Let me stop you, Mr. Elversham, and save you some effort.

My thanks for coming here in person. I am fully aware that the policy is terminated and don't wish it continued. Which is why I never replied to your ten thousand letters."

"You know that a designated beneficiary can be changed. It's not uncommon that, due to an unexpected shift of affections . . ."

"Perhaps at some future date . . ."

"Delay is denial," Mr. Elversham said.

"Good afternoon," Barnaby said. "And by the way, I'm sorry you'll lose your commission."

"No, don't be. The insurance business is like our elevator. We have ups and downs. But isn't life a teeter-totter of success and reversal? Actually, just yesterday I wrote my largest policy, indemnifying none other than Phineas Barnum against liability should any mishap arise in connection with his impending venture."

"The Clash of Giants?"

"Exactly. So the loss of your policy is more than offset and the name Elversham has new clout with my company."

"Glad to hear it," Barnaby said.

"Should you need my services . . ."

"I know where to find you."

After Elversham left, Barnaby lit a Goliath and fondly remembered a long-ago afternoon in Binghamton. Zipmeister's maggots made a feast of his gut but the memory still gave some nourishment.

NEW YORK, NEW YORK, FEBRUARY 5, 1870

Tom Thumb, in tails, looked out at the capacity crowd from the ring at Joe Ax's Gymnasium. The magician had done it again. Everybody who was anybody sat happily crammed into a building built for a stable. Their tongues dangling with anticipation. Their mouths salivating to sample P.T.'s latest recipe for wonder. Thumb did a deep bow. On that cue, a bank of calcium lights came alive, making the master of ceremonies shield his eyes while the audience cheered.

"If this fails, I might need to borrow your Negro," Barnum said to Grinder Brian at ringside.

"You hear that, Panther?" Brian said to his huge bodyguard who sat with his chin in his hands.

"I still don't get who's on the card," the Black Panther said.

"Not you. Nobody. I keep telling you, it's only a show."

"Why all these people pay for a fight with nobody fighting?"

"Can I answer for asshole behavior? I don't know everything," Grinder said. "Just sit back and watch. Put out that cigar. It stinks to high heaven." Grinder grabbed for the Uncle Tom and ground it under his foot.

General Thumb lifted a red megaphone. "Welcome, one and all, to Joe Ax's, the palace of fantastic fisticuffs. Tonight the battle of the century begins. A mythical Clash of Giants! each claiming title to no less than immortal fame.

"We are told only one is a *true fossil,* a petrification who had had Adam and Eve as his friends, helped Noah build his ark, endured the plagues of Egypt, fled bondage with Moses, stood strong by the side of Lord Jesus Himself. If one giant is real, then the other's no brother but a mere petard. Only a lump of damp clay mothered by the hand of a charlatan. An imposter deserving your scorn. You are gathered to decide which is which, using democracy's highest achievement, your precious vote."

From Joe Ax's ceiling a red, white, and blue ballot box dropped slowly down to a platform near the arena's center. A well-formed young lady, dressed as Columbia, holding a blazing flare, rode the top of the box to its resting place. Thumb climbed up beside her and kissed her cheek.

"In case the fair ladies are wondering," Thumb continued, "in this election, yes, their delicate votes *will* be counted." A few women applauded while the men booed and cursed.

"Bad idea, Barnum," Grinder said.

"The precise reaction I wanted."

"Decorum, please," Thumb told the crowd. "Remember we live in a civilized age. It was not always so. Even the lovely creatures with satin skin who now give us such joy and comfort were not always so compliant or docile. Let us remember that history is a saga of struggle and conflict, with no sex immune. In past times even the fairest butterflies had their sting. Ladies and gentlemen, prepare for startle as we present, for the first time on any stage, the astounding Dance of the Amazons!"

Drums beat a primitive cadence. Two Amazon hordes rushed screaming down separate aisles and up into the ring. The dancers were costumed in sequined corsets of silver or gold. The silvers had beaked parrot heads for hats, the golds were adorned with antlered hoods. Each Amazon was bare-legged and shoeless, the hands fitted with large rhinestoned boxing gloves in glowing pastels.

While jungle drums boomed, the Amazon beauties surrounded Tom Thumb, gyrating and waving their arms. Thumb, feigning terror, sneaked between muscled legs to escape. The drums beat harder as the Amazons danced and sparred, some slugging harder than others.

"Half-naked women and violence?" Grinder said. "This disturbs me."

"It's disgusting," his bodyguard said.

"Shock's the pleasure," Barnum said.

"Well, if I knew you had this kind of show in mind, I'd have kept the doors shut," Grinder said. "Joe Ax must be spinning in his grave." Grinder Brian crossed himself. He knew the late Joseph Axelrod had no grave to spin in but rested piecemeal instead, fertilizer for New Jersey weeds.

"It's all done in good taste," Barnum said.

"Filthy and dirty," the Black Panther said.

"Watch closely," Barnum said. "The girls have little packets of tomato paste hidden in their mouths. When they bite down, you'll swear you see blood."

"Repulsive," Grinder said.

"But memorable."

The Amazons, their lipsticked mouths oozing tomatoes, dropped one by one to the canvas. When only a single survivor was left, Tom Thumb returned to hold up her victorious arm. Then all the slain Amazons resurrected, formed a line, did a synchronized kick and deep bow. They climbed out of the ring and ran back up the aisles toward the exit. The jungle drums stopped, their racket replaced by a sinister quiet that made Barnum fidget. He'd expected ovation, not general paralysis.

"Too far, even for Barnum," Grinder said.

Tom Thumb saved the day. "Yes, a brutal hour for our human race. But an hour long past. Thank God, and good riddance. We brought you this startling spectacle for an educational purpose. To portray what our giant's stone eyes once beheld so all here might better appreciate his tortured journey.

"Struggle and conflict, the mutual heritage of man and beast. Spiked rungs on the ladder to that universal harmony to which we must aspire. The past is our teacher, and that teacher shouts, 'War is not peace!' Blessed wisdom of the ages."

"Well said, General," Barnum shouted, applauding. Sparse applause echoed from around Joe Ax's.

"Fast on his feet, that midget," Grinder said.

"How fast could he be?" the Black Panther asked.

Across the arena, in a section reserved for the press, Barnaby Rack searched out his doomed prey. Across the ring from Barnum and Brian he spotted George Hull with Stubby Newell, Ben Hull and Loretta beside them. When Barnaby recognized Loretta he felt a knot in his throat. The emotion stirred by the agent from Equitable now poured through him like boiled lead from a cauldron.

There she was, no mistake, the same woman who tore at his

heart disguised as the martyred Angelica. Beautiful Loretta, lubricious Amazon, serene and secure as a coddled cat. Barnaby moaned like a widowed wolf.

"Button your fly. The dance wasn't that hotsy totsy," said a man from the *Herald.* "I seen better in dives down on Rivington Street." Barnaby felt liquid trickle down his leg. He ran for an exit.

"Rack from the *Clarion,*" said a man from the *Times.* "Weird sort, a loner."

"What's next up your sleeve?" Grinder asked Barnum.

"Variations on the theme of our animal nature. Designed to elicit raw chords of reponse. Remember, Grinder, our catchword is *clash.*"

"Any more Amazons and you'll scare off the audience."

"I'm creating a mood. I want them wild by the time the giants appear. I want Saturday night in Babylon. Sunday at Rome's Colosseum. For climax, two slabs of rock won't generate the greatest excitement. But if audience spirits are raised high enough, then the let-down will come as a welcome relief."

"I'd rather deal in pickles and whores," Grinder said.

Thumb's voice took a serious tone. "The Good Book says 'there were giants on the Earth in those days.' Imagine a colossal age when men a bit taller than I roam hither and yon at their whim. Beware! When giant enemies meet on the plain, move back the mountains! For their battles are mammoth. And how best to depict such *mammoth* battles? Why not with *Battling Mammoths!*"

Ten tubas thumped a march. Two doors flung open on opposite sides of Joe Ax's. A man covered in black and carrying a pike appeared at each door. Led by their keepers, a pair of bull elephants made their entrance, lumbering in lugubrious rhythm. Each elephant was covered with a hairy mat, each wore colorful shorts— one purple, one orange—across its massive behind. Ramps slid into place, ropes parted. The elephants rumbled into the ring. They waited with their keepers in separate corners resting their bottoms on tiny stools. Two lovely young flowers appeared as their seconds, swathed in bathrobes to match their elephant pants. One robe was imprinted with IVAN THE AWFUL, the other with BRUNO THE BRUTE.

"They gonna fight?" the Black Panther asked, perking.

"They are," Barnum said. "I hope they are. They did nobly in rehearsal."

"This I like," Grinder said. "This makes sense."

General Thumb gestured the elephants forward. "You both know the rules, and I trust will act like the gentlemen you are. Go back to your corners. At the sound of the bell, come out swinging. First shake hands." The elephant, Bruno, raised its trunk and trumpeted so loud there were screams. Ivan turned and knelt, offering his butt.

"Bad sportsmanship," Thumb said. "I won't tolerate that."

"Five on Bruno," Grinder said. "Look at the set of tusks on that thing."

"You're covered," The Black Panther said. "Look at the balls on Ivan."

"They won't be using their tusks or their balls," Barnum said. "We're not after carnage."

"What then?"

"It's a matter of pushing and bumping."

"Only pushes and bumps? Is the fix in here?"

"No fix," Barnum said. "May the best elephant win."

Thumb leaned outside the ring to pick up a brass bell. He waited for silence, then smacked the bell with his head. Both keepers stuck pikes into the ponderous rumps. The elephants rose on hind legs and came staggering forward, swinging their trunks like thick whips.

Bruno got in the first blow, tilting Ivan to a side. Ivan circled, then kicked Bruno in back of a knee. Bruno flopped on his rear, tilting close to a tumble.

"Finish him," the Black Panther yelled, leaving his seat. "Kick him hard in the head." Others in the crowd shared the Black Panther's sentiment. Those recently appalled by the Amazon Dance shook off that dismay and now yelled the loudest.

Instead of kicking his foe in the face, Ivan waited while Bruno found balance, then height. Bruno bellowed another piercing complaint, then battered Ivan dead center.

"That's the way," Grinder said, slapping his hands.

"Not fair. Bruno's up on all fours, Ivan on two," The Black Panther said. "Why don't the damn midget call a foul?"

"Sit down and shut up," Grinder said. "You're beginning to rile me."

Panther fell back in his chair but jumped up fast when Ivan spun Bruno around and butted his underbelly. "You fat bastard," Grinder yelled. "Use your ivory."

"They're putting on a fine display," Barnum said. "And both arthritic as Methuselah. I mixed gin in their feed to give them spirit. Now watch those pachyderms jump."

The elephants locked in a clinch, slamming their heads so hard the crack made an echo. While several ladies shielded their eyes, the men begged outright for blood. They got some from Ivan when Bruno jabbed with a tusk.

"Yes, yes," Grinder said coolly. "No tomato soup this time."

"He got toothed," the Black Panther yelled. "Foul! Foul!"

"Keep that one under control," Barnum shouted to Bruno's keeper, who punished his charge with the spike. While Bruno retreated, Ivan bolted forward, fell to his knees, then came up flailing his front legs, trying to batter out Bruno's eyes.

"Enough," Barnum yelled at Tom Thumb. "End it now."

"No way," Grinder said, when Bruno retaliated with a sharp kick at Ivan's gray scrotum. This time it was Ivan who raised his trunk for a blast. He danced like a dervish while his keeper tried to slow him with nasty jabs.

"Don't get suckered twice," Grinder warned Bruno. "He's setting you up."

Bruno took the advice and clinched again. Ivan pulled back,

leaving his rival tipped in midair. Bruno hovered there, then went over facedown. Ivan dropped his front legs and bridged Bruno, who rolled on his back. Ivan collapsed. The elephants knotted in a furious ball while Tom Thumb dodged the keepers who went at each other with their lances.

"Get control, Tom," Barnum shrieked.

"Bruno done! He crapped out!" the Black Panther cheered, standing on his seat.

Ivan managed to untangle and get himself upright. Tom Thumb came as close as he dared to announce through his megaphone "The winner is Ivan by unanimous decision."

The General's abrupt call enraged many in the crowd. A hundred men left their seats and pushed toward the ring where both sagging elephants made odd bagpipe noises. "Get them out of here," Thumb told their keepers, sensing catastrophe. "Clear the area!"

"Pay up," the Black Panther said to Grinder, grabbing his boss by the lapels of his tux. Grinder Brian gave him a look that worked better than barbs on the elephants. "Jeez, I didn't mean to do that, boss. I got carried away."

"You go up there and knock the crap out of that bloated piece of elephant shit," Brian said, pointing toward Bruno.

"Grinder, don't be a fool," Barnum said. "He's only a man. That's a full ton of beast. Trained for the circus but still a beast. Any exhausted animal is unpredictable. What's a five-dollar wager, after all? No excuse for such vengeance. Where's your good humor? Here, I'll pay the tab."

"It ain't the damn money," Grinder said. "I can't stand that a creature so big with such power should let himself get pushed around by some dink with a toothpick. It ain't even that. It's I hate losers. Worse, I hate losers who make me a loser. Now, you liver-lipped black son of a bitch, make that quitter feel pain."

The Black Panther began to move down the row, then stopped in his tracks. "No, Mr. Brian," he said. "I won the bet, you pay me, that's that."

"You second-rate pug. I'll show you *that's that.*" Grinder let a glob of spit fly at the Black Panther's face, then pushed past Barnum toward the aisle.

"Security!" Barnum yelled, but nobody heard him. Grinder Brian split through the crush, shoved his way to the ring, climbed through the ropes to where Tom Thumb argued with his outraged critics, straight-armed the General, walked up to drooped Bruno, and punched the elephant in its great face.

Bruno showed excellent patience. He took five hard smacks before lifting Grinder Brian by the waist and banging him down on the canvas. While Brian cursed at him, Bruno reared. Ivan, by reflex, took the same position and began his trademarked pirouette. Bruno was less acrobatic. He brought his feet down on Grinder Brian's skull. It came apart like a walnut, spilling a red blot of brains.

The sheer force of Bruno's bulk shook Joe Ax's floor. That tremor triggered a switch Barnum had strategically placed for the General's use at a climactic moment. The switch woke a hydraulic pump sending pressure to sleek steel cylinders. The cylinders lifted two open caskets from under the base of the ring.

Goliath and Titan, rattling in those flower-draped boxes, rose in tandem, moved full circle on an oiled turntable, then tilted to give the audience a clear, unobstructed view.

The sight of Grinder Brian's fresh, smoldering brains, then the stately and dignified rise of the stone men, proved too much for the meek. The audience bolted en masse for all doors, trampling a doctor, two nurses, and nine policemen who rushed to the scene of emergency. Only Phineas Barnum and George Hull remained in their places. Their giants also stayed put.

So finally we meet. As I suspected, you are nothing like me. No resemblance. Not a trice. To compare us is an insult of gnats.

Common granite? The substance of sewers for a brother? Source, excuse my levity. What else can I? Such sad soup for a sibling?

Barnaby Rack tried to get back inside to witness the riot but had to scrounge details from hysterical strangers. When they carried what was left of Sean Shamus Brian to the meat wagon, Barnaby wept there in the street. Not for Grinder. For Angelica Hull, who missed being rich by a matter of days. Some people, however worthy, were not meant to be happy, for reasons unknown. Perhaps they were saved like a delicacy, tenderized by repeated misfortune, for the special amusement of saints.

Barnaby ran three blocks for a cab, then galloped downtown to the *Clarion.* He found John Zipmeister in the printing plant holding the first proof of tomorrow's paper, actually smiling while he checked the headline:

CARDIFF GIANT CUT DOWN TO SIZE

GOLIATH EXPOSED! OLD HOAXY'S THE NAME
IS TITAN TUMBLED TOO?

"Stop the presses," Barnaby said.

"Sure," John Zipmeister said. "Maybe if a comet reamed the Pope's holy rectum."

"You're perilous close," Barnaby said.

ACKLEY, IOWA, FEBRUARY 6, 1870

"I'm sorry to send you away, Wilmer," said the Reverend Henry Turk. "I know you have your job to do. But my wife and I are preparing for a trip to New York and already chasing the clock."

"Have you seen today's paper?" said Wilmer Pfroom, the reporter for the *Ackley Star Standard.*

"No, I haven't."

"Take a quick glance, Reverend," said Pfroom, his nervous eye twitching. "You might find it of interest. Story came over the wire this morning."

"Give it here, then."

Reverend Turk read an abridged version of the *Clarion*'s report. His vision blacked out then came back into focus.

"Seems your man from Genesis is a local boy made good. But not the boy we thought he was. I wonder, could you give me some statement?"

Reverend Turk saw Wilmer Pfroom's wandering eye take on new malevolence. "I know nothing about this. I need time to investigate."

"Is it true Mrs. Turk is William Newell's cousin and George Hull's blood sister?"

"No comment at this time."

"That's got to be viewed as an odd coincidence. Some reaction is in order, sir."

Reverend Turk watched the floating eyeball assert itself with a blink. "I'll say this much. I had my suspicions about the stone man from the very start. What bothered me was the look of the body. I asked myself why a man of such magnitude would submit to contortion even in the face of the worst kind of anguish. If he was what they claimed, no pain could bother him since death would be welcomed as God's invitation.

"Tell your readers that the Reverend Mr. Henry Turk was neither astonished nor in any way disturbed by this allegation of fraud. Outraged, yes. Shaken, no. The fact is, I have never set eyes on the graven image and now doubt I ever will."

"But you've said many times that Goliath gave divine confirmation to your theory that God is American."

"And I say it again. If the giant proves the product of a reprobate's hand, then tell me this, Wilmer. Where stands the cathedral unblemished by a single brick mortared in place by some scurvy sort? Temple spires are made by men but evolve gradually to majesty. Whatever base intention may have midwifed this ersatz fossil is entirely irrelevant now. I say, and quote me, that through splendid metamorphosis, the Giant of Cardiff, like a statue in church, has become something more than a clay canard. And please don't call him Goliath, as I've asked many times."

"First you tell me you suspected the giant early on and now he's exposed you say his powers are turned real? There seems to be inconsistency."

"Faith is more than a column of numbers that always add up the same. Is the Lord an accountant who must justify His balances? I hope you don't think that, Wilmer."

"Would it be possible to speak with Mrs. Turk?"

"My wife is indisposed."

"Hull's sister? Newell's cousin? Will she deny . . ."

"You're tempting the wrath of a religious man. Leave my wife out of this. Are you responsible for the actions of your brother or distant cousin?"

"They didn't make a giant. Are you personally acquainted with Newell or Hull?"

"Newell, no, and his name barely mentioned. I met George Hull briefly and found him to be an iconoclast, a cynic and disturbed by some shadow. The man sells tobacco. I did my best to help him, as did Mrs. Turk, but I see that we failed sadly in that difficult mission."

"Then you knew of a family connection to the Cardiff Giant?"

"It came recently to my attention and I took it in stride as yet another good sign from the Master I serve."

"Do you think this news will affect plans for the Herbert Black Paw Seminary?"

"Leave this place without delay. And terminate my subscription to the *Ackley Star Standard.*"

Reverend Turk went back into the house where Samantha was busy filling her suitcase, humming "Aura Lee" while she worked.

"Who was it, Henry? What's wrong? You look peaked."

"Unpack," Turk said. "There's a change in our plans." The Rev-

erend collapsed into a buckskin-covered chair. He was startled to
see Wilbur Pfroom's skittish eye bobbing on a wall, leering, searching for the slightest trace of spiritual leakage. Turk realized the eye
was illusion, nothing but an accident of light reflected through a
crystal pyramid on the windowsill.

CHICAGO, ILLINOIS, FEBRUARY 6, 1870

The statue, named an *ancient masterpiece* by so many
respected aesthetes, was, in fact, made to order here in
Chicago by the now-deceased Edward Salle, assisted by
sculptor Gerhardt Burkehard of North Clark Street,
whose usual specialty seems to be grave markers and ar-
chitectural accessories. When asked about such critical ac-
colades for his *giant,* Mr. Burkehard modestly told this
reporter, "All in a day's work."

Gerhardt Burquhart lifted a twig from the ground near his partner's mausoleum. "So. I thought you should hear it from me, Edward. They got you right, I'm glad to say, but me they spelled
wrong. I suppose that gives you some extra pleasure. Give my regards to Beelzebub and go back to work."

BOSTON, MASSACHUSETTS, FEBRUARY 6, 1870

Aaron Bupkin read "GOLIATH UNFROCKED, CLASH A CALAMITY" in the *Boston Globe,* then ran across the hall to Angelica's room to learn what she knew of the scandalous story. While Angelica put on her face, she told him of George Hull's Halloween confession if not the circumstance that provoked it.

"You never mentioned a word to me?" he said, which was something she already knew. "Such a dark secret?"

"It never came up between us, Aaron, and it wasn't my secret."

"How could you be part of such a scheme?"

"George told me after the fact. He talked, I listened. Should I care what George Hull says? He uses truth for convenience. Why believe him?"

"But what the newspaper says is very convincing. Look here, they have records of every step he took from Fort Dodge to Cardiff. Even that 'Hull instructed Newell to hire an innocent dowser'— that's what I'm called—'a year in advance to pick the spot where the giant would be found.' Frankly, I'm a bit disappointed. I was proud of my part in this drama before it turned to a farce."

"There's probably water where you said it would be."

"Does that matter now? Angelica, tell me, if you question your husband's involvement after detailed proof, what do you believe? That Stubby Newell was George Hull's corruptor?"

"Never Stubby. He's a turnip."

"What then?"

"I believe what I believe," Angelica said.

"That's no answer. Was it someone else? There's suggestion that George's sister in Ackley had a hand in the pie."

"Samantha Turk? That's impossible. Do they mention the Reverend?"

"They have a statement he gave. He says the stone man is but he isn't or wasn't but is. I can't follow his mind."

"I'm sure he knew nothing about it. George said it was Turk he was after. Turk and all other believers. The whole idea of a merciful God."

"Then George had motive enough. And God blessed the atheist. They say Goliath made you a rich man's wife."

"I'll take nothing from George. Not for myself or my child. I already took enough, too much, from that unfortunate man. I was never his wife."

"Unfortunate man? You said the philanderer crept into his own brother's bed."

"He followed crumbs like Hansel. And he needed a sin the size of his giant to throw in God's face."

"So George used an in-law to make himself into an outlaw?"

"I feel badly for Loretta," Angelica said. "And George, for that matter."

"I'd feel sorry for Ben."

"Ben has his cigars."

"Pity Loretta, pity George, but it's Aaron Bupkin down to his last dollar. With a dead dowsing rod and a woman and child to support."

"Do you want us to leave? We are a burden."

"Could you go back to Binghamton?"

"No," Angelica said. "That's done with."

"I love you," Aaron said. "And your baby. That's my fate and I'm stuck with it. For better or worse."

"Then give me a kiss and no more of giants."

"There are unanswered questions," Aaron said.

"And I have no sensible answers to give you."

"One good thing comes of this. The people in the valley can't blame 'the innocent dowser.' Unless they blame him for being blameless."

"They'd be justified in that."

"Whose side are you on?" Aaron said.

"That's no easy question. Come here and help me decide."

NEW YORK, NEW YORK, FEBRUARY 6, 1870

Amos Arbutnaut, Esq., called Barnum away from his meeting. The two men went from Barnum's living room to his bedroom. The lawyer had never seen that sanctum of repose, designed like a tent for some nomad sheik. The bed, a single cushion covered with a blanket of lambskin, occupied most of the richly rugged floor. The dresser was a dromedary with drawers for its body and a lamp for its hump. Two camel-saddle chairs bracketed a round ivory table inlaid in onyx with scenes from a harum.

"Different decor from Bridgeport," Arbutnaut said.

"That was my intention. What did you hear?"

"Judge Barnard assures me that no crime's been committed. Your only claim was that Titan is the original Cardiff Giant, and there's already a ruling on that. You never ascribed healing powers to the giant or promised the public anything but the stone man they saw."

"Can't we sue anybody? If not the *Clarion,* then your Syracuse turncoat. He gave his oath of silence and broke it."

"Otto couldn't help but trumpet his achievement. When he read Rack's story, he was quick to tell his own. Besides, the man's a pauper. There's nothing to sue for."

"Defamation of character. A moral victory is worth something."

"Whose character was defamed?"

"Mine," Barnum said. "But then, he never dealt with me, Arbutnaut. He dealt with you. A lawyer must keep his client's name in confidence. They'll know but they won't know for certain."

"Let it rest," Arbutnaut said. "The span of public outrage is less than the life of a mayfly. What does concern me is the Californian, Zinkle. He might file to void the contract."

"On what grounds? I sold Titan in good faith, Zinkle knew what he bought. Caveat emptor."

"Zinkle might say you had advance knowledge of the *Clarion* article and unloaded a worthless property."

"I had no such knowledge," Barnum said. "The only guarantee I gave in writing says Titan is what he is, a rock figure of such-and-so dimensions which some believe to be a genuine fossil, a petrification survived from a distant age. As for worth, a thing is worth what somebody will pay to own it."

"Still, it's good you took cash."

"Not cash. Gold nuggets, safely deposited in my vault."

"The timing is the question. If you weren't tipped off about Rack's expose, what excuse could you have for divesting Titan on the very day your Clash of Giants! had its premier? I wonder myself."

"Is that what's on the carpet? Barnum's instinct for business? I sold Titan because I got what I asked from a sucker who wanted to buy him. And there's my only excuse."

"Maybe Zinkle wasn't such a sucker. When I passed Joe Ax's on my way here, the ticket line stretched five blocks."

"They're coming to see stains where Grinder Brian left his cerebral cortex. Not for the giants. Well, maybe a few stalwart vultures. But the line's a last gasp. No, it's finished. Besides, Barnum has other fish to fry, so onward and upward. By the way, did you talk to the Equitable?"

"Equitable will honor your policy if anyone sues for injury. Word is the agent who sold you that coverage barricaded himself in their lift and they pried him out raving."

"Well, Amos, my thanks to you for acting so quickly. Now I've got to get back to my meeting."

After showing his counselor the door, Barnum returned to the living room where two men waited. "Mr. Coup, Mr. Costello, please forgive my bad manners," Barnum said.

"No problem, P.T.," Dan Costello said, grabbing his shoes with his hands and rolling himself like a hoop.

"Once a clown, always a clown," said W. C. Coup. "I can't beat it out of him." Coup, built like an ice cube, chugging a cigar, pointed to a ream of papers spread on a desk. "Here are the figures you asked for. Our venture's already in the black, showing excellent promise for growth. But Dan and I know that we need a Barnum to give the show wings."

"After last night, I don't know that I'm ready for more elephants," Barnum said.

"The Coup and Costello Circus is more than elephants," the square man said.

Costello used his fingers to twist his face into sorrow. "The fact is, we can't afford elephants yet. We're hardly past mock turtles."

"Dan, we're trying to have a serious discussion," Coup said.

"I've never had a serious discussion," Barnum said. "I don't want to start now. No friend of children can allow himself to be too serious lest the little ones question his motives."

"Did I hear right? 'Friend of children'?" Costello said. "I think of Barnum in many guises, but not as a friend of children. Unless they're joined at their rumps or born with three humps."

"Mr. Costello needs lessons in etiquette," Barnum said. "But his point is well taken. If you wonder if I'm the right partner, then why are you here?"

"This meeting was Coup's idea. Why did you agree to it?"

"Do you know the term *hypertely*?" Barnum asked. "A quirk of evolution. Obsolete camouflage retained by some confused species. Defense for a war that's already ended, the foe long subdued. Barnum's been burdened by thick camouflage that once served his purpose. Now, older and wiser, he's ready to strip it and go naked before crowds he once saw as enemies."

"A naked Barnum? In fresh makeup? I think I feel faint."

"Forget pose and bravado. Replace them with innocent dazzle, honest wonder, humble respect for family values. That's the new Barnum, worthy to be a founding father of a circus designed to bring joy to the tot population."

"Frankly, Mr. Barnum, we came for your capital, the use of your name, and a share of your flair for promotion. In exchange for a healthy percent of our show, which already has two founding fathers."

"If you deal with me, Mr. Costello, be prepared to share claim to custody. Barnum is the apocalypse. Does he want a percent of a lame acrobat and a donkey striped to look like a tiger? Come to Barnum when you're ready for glory since his aim would be to create the greatest show on the planet."

"We're a modest operation," Coup said. "Rising to glory would take some doing."

"Doing is what I do best," Barnum said.

"Hide the kiddies," said the clown, blotting his eyes. "Warn the lions. Have the kangaroo button his pocket."

"Then our chat has been fruitful?" Coup said.

"Perhaps there is room for further discussion," Barnum said.

NEW YORK, NEW YORK, FEBRUARY 6, 1870

A downcast Stubby Newell walked to Hull's Humidor looking for George. He hadn't seen his cousin since the stampede emptied Joe Ax's Gymnasium, shoving the family in different directions. Last night's upheaval seemed tame compared with the morning's attack. Stubby felt like he swallowed a mix of castor oil, insult, and guilt. The *Clarion* called him "a dupe and a simpleton, driven by greed, a dummy with George Hull as ventriloquist."

Bertha's letter was still in his pocket. Three days before the ill-fated Clash of Giants! Barnum confirmed his decision to keep George from bad news. "Save it for later," Barnum said. "My philosophy is, why tell a man his wife fled with a Jew before the curtain goes up? As for the reporter, a storm in a teacup. Don't trouble yourself. There's no story that can't be refuted." Now Stubby wondered how Barnum could be so dense, ignoring Bertha's alarm.

A small figure in brown flew out of a doorway waving a hammer. "Jig's up, you liar," it said, taking a swing Stubby managed to dodge. "Gonna nail you to the wall."

"Hold on, what's this?" Stubby said. "Who in hell are you?"

"You should know. You swiped my dollar for your phony baloney piss-assed giant."

"The kid with the sickly ma?" Stubby said, raising his hands to defend himself.

"Here for payback." The lad took a swipe at the air.

"Better drop that hammer or I'll wail your hide, you snot-dribbling squirt of a boy. I'll break you in half and feed you to a horse."

"Gimme back my money. Give it here now."

"Why would I do that? And after I did you a favor. You came to see Goliath and you stayed two dollars' worth. So what's your complaint and who owes who?"

"It's black-and-white plain," the boy said, pulling a *Clarion* from inside his pants. "That giant's no giant but a big piece of shit."

"Seems the last time we met you was selling those papers for a living," Stubby said.

"So what?"

"Tell me something. How many *Clarion*s did you peddle today? My guess is a stack. Am I right or wrong? Because I don't see you carrying too many papers."

"Sold out," the boy said. "They got snapped up like cake."

"Snapped up like pieces of cake, well, well, well."

"What you mean, *well, well, well?*"

"Why you think those papers got snapped if not for my Goliath?

I hear you jingling just standing still. Got more than a dollar in your pocket, I'd say."

"That don't change nothing. What I got or don't got ain't what you took and I want it back."

"Ain't life tribulation?" Stubby said.

"You like busted knees?"

"Listen to this half-pint who thinks he's the next Grinder Brian. By the way, how's your ma?"

"Dead and buried. Left me an orphan."

"My condolences," Stubby said. "She's at peace and your pockets are full. Seems you both came out ahead in this bargain."

"You swore your fossil did cures."

"I never said that. And who says he don't?"

"It says in the headline."

"You believe all you read you'll end up in jail. Which is where you'll end up anyhow if you swing that hammer one more time. There's a cop on the corner owes me a favor."

"Ma died saying her prayers to that giant."

"Hear me, boy. I have personally witnessed Goliath do marvels. Fixed a blind girl, a cripple, a deaf man too, and give boners to old men who forgot what they're for. So, if I was you, I'd say what happened was for the best and go push my papers."

"Give over my dollar," the boy said.

"Spilt milk," Stubby said. "Haul your orphan ass someplace else."

NEW YORK, NEW YORK, FEBRUARY 7, 1870

George Hull's collapsed face and stuffed-olive eyes gave him the look of something hanging in a meat market window. Barnaby

Rack watched him drop four sugar cubes in his third cup of coffee trying hard to sweeten the sour turn of fortune. It couldn't have helped Hull that, on their way to the dining room, every chair in the lobby of the Hotel St. Dennis was filled by somebody absorbed in the *Clarion.*

"Frankly, I'm surprised you accepted my invitation," Barnaby said.

"So am I," George said. "Might as well face the music now as later."

"It's a natural thing that our readers would want to hear your side of the story."

"I have little to add to what you wrote."

"No spasms of denial? No protest of innocence?"

"Everything you said is true. The Giant of Cardiff is my creation. I birthed him and weaned him, start to finish. The others had little to do with any of it except as accessories. Barnum's Titan is another matter. An obscene plagiarism."

"I recognized that long ago. Mr. Hull, why did you do it? Was it all for gain, or was more at stake? Simon Hull & Sons is no small enterprise. Your income was secure, I'd think."

George speared an anchovy from his Cobb salad. "I'm not sure, Mr. Rack. At first the idea seemed good for a laugh and an outlet for anger."

"Anger at what?"

"Not much. Earth, Heaven, and Hell. Past, present, and future. God's vicious indifference. Man's arrogant smugness wrapped tight in hypocrisy. The death of beauty and birds. Lying stars. I was sick of it all and mostly myself."

"But to tamper with the very foundations of belief at a time when the nation still mourns its dead heroes?"

George gestured toward a nearby table. "Is that lady devouring the filet in mourning?"

"Hard to say."

"Possibly her husband mourns the cost of the meal."

"You're a very cynical man, Mr. Hull."

"I know of two kinds of men: cynical or stupid. Which would you rather have across the table?"

Barnaby smiled, taking a bite out of a chop paid for by Zipmeister. "You are Barnum's reflection. I think it was inevitable your paths would cross."

"I find him repugnant. Not for his deeds, but because he's better than me at handling a humbug. Like babies, they're harder to nurture than they are to create. I hate Barnum as much as you despise me. Don't pretend I'm wrong about that."

"I won't," Barnaby said. Unfeeling, amoral, a drunk and wifebeater, Hull might merit forgiveness but never affection. Still, the man who sat quietly chewing on an egg was hard to define as Attila the Hun. He seemed oddly vulnerable, almost pathetic. "What's next for you, Mr. Hull? Is it back to cigars? Assuming the business survives your shenanigans?"

"No, I'll stay with Goliath."

"Could you clarify that?"

"I'll take him on tour."

"More clashing of giants? After all this?"

"We'll go it alone, Goliath and Hull. As for Titan, I can't tell you his fate. Did you know Barnum sold his mud pie? He told me only last night."

"Sold Titan? To who?"

"I don't know," George said.

"And you think your mud pie will draw a crowd?"

"Probably a few retards."

"Then why take him traveling?"

"To show Goliath places he hasn't been and people he's never seen. My giant is rather bright, you understand, and always curious. Generous too, in his clodish way. He'd be lost on his own being hardly a sophisticate."

"You're speaking of the stone man you made in Chicago?"

"Of course."

"You talk as if he were real and living."

George Hull pushed his plate away and covered a burp. "I want to tell you, Mr. Rack, how much I appreciate you sparing my wife from embarrassment. I assume you know of her delicate condition. Had you mentioned her name, it might have been fatal. Mrs. Hull, my Angelica, never knew my plan or had a part in it. Only Stubby Newell was a full confidant, and I doubt he realized what he was doing. I didn't know for myself where the giant would lead us. And still don't. Somewhere, I think."

"About your wife and the dowser . . . ?"

" 'The Wife and the Dowser'? Is that a fable from Aesop? It's your turn for clarification."

"You don't know?" Barnaby said.

"Know what? Is there something I should know?"

"Brandy and a smoke, Mr. Hull?"

"Drink and smoke with this dragon? You're a courageous man, Mr. Rack. Now, what's your next bit of news?"

BOSTON, MASSACHUSETTS, FEBRUARY 14, 1870

Isaac Bupkin lit a memorial lamp. The blue glass that held white wax and wick would later be used for drinking. At his age, with so many dead, Isaac had a cupboard filled with those glasses.

The apartment denied it was day. All natural light was blocked by drawn window shades. Draped mirrors left holes where Isaac's face should have been. When the wick burned, the drinking glass candle made the wrong contribution. Its flame looked too frisky.

Isaac heard a knock at his door. He hoped it was Aaron come for forgiveness or the Angel of Death to collect one more soul. "On the other hand," he thought to himself, "it could be bad news."

"Hello? Who's there?"

"Is this the Bupkin residence?"

"What are you talking about? What do you want here?"

"A word with Mr. Aaron Bupkin."

Isaac opened the door and saw a man not much younger than himself standing alone in the hall. The stranger wore a high hat, black cashmere coat, silk scarf, fancy gloves, leather boots. Nobody from the neighborhood.

"This is a house of sorrow," Isaac said. "Aaron Bupkin is dead. Aleva sholem. Go away."

"I didn't know of his death. You have my sincere sympathy. If you're a relative, grant me a brief moment. Believe me, I shall respect your grief."

"Come in, then. I'll offer you some schnapps and a fruit."

"Please don't put yourself to any trouble, Mr. . . ."

"Bupkin. Isaac Bupkin." The man followed Isaac inside, blending with gloom. "If you're selling graves, we don't need one."

"I'm not selling graves."

"Take off your hat and coat. Sit anyplace." Isaac saw the man stare at his cloth slippers. "Imported. I'm sitting shiva for my grandson. We don't wear shoes for a week."

"A tragic loss. I picked a bad time."

"You're here so say what you came to say."

"First, let me tell you I might have sent someone to represent me but being in Boston I chose to come myself. My name is Cornelius Vanderbilt. Is the name known to you?"

"The man with the trains?"

"This isn't easy to say, Mr. Bupkin, so bear with me. I heard certain rumors and sent agents to investigate. Their findings were inconclusive but promising."

"You heard rumors? You sent agents?"

"To Cardiff, New York. I know the late Aaron Bupkin lived near that hamlet."

"My grandson of blessed memory was the one who found their stone man. That's what killed him."

"How did he die?"

"Don't ask."

"Mr. Bupkin, let me be direct. I had occasion to view the Giant of Cardiff now on display in New York. While Goliath has been debunked and mocked in the press, I confess to another impression."

"Mocked? Debunked? I never heard about that."

"It's in today's *Globe.*"

"I'm not allowed to read papers. No noise, no papers, nothing until next shabbos."

"Not significant. To the point. Those whispers heard in Cardiff somewhat confirmed what I myself suspected: that a certain intimate part of Goliath was victim of other than time's erosion."

"Again?"

"A piece of his maleness is missing."

"I remember some talk. They said it fell off by itself."

"I am convinced that the organ was not compromised by time's natural scythe but deliberately detached by a party or parties unknown."

"Excuse me?"

"Someone chopped off his penis."

"Who would do such a thing? Is there any proof?"

"To be frank, local murmurs implicate your late grandson in the business."

"Murmurs? About Aaron? Those Cossacks blamed him for houseflies, pimples, corns, and callouses. He's a Jew. Was a Jew. A Jew in Cardiff gets blamed for bad weather. Especially a Jew that finds giants."

"I did not mention *blame.* I am not here to point fingers."

"Point if you want. Does it matter? He's dead."

"Let's say, if, and I emphasize *if,* if your grandson, may he dwell with angels, did, by some happenstance, say through mere accident and no base intent, manage to find himself in possession of the part in question, I would like you to know that a certain person of no small means has an interest in gaining title to that singular object."

"You want to buy Goliath's schmeckel?"

"The answer is yes, Mr. Bupkin. For a goodly sum."

"What do you want with such a thing? To paste it back where it came from and make your own golem?"

"My reasons for seeking to secure the object are not for discussion. If your concern has to do with the prospect of reuniting the giant with his lost appendage, put it out of your mind. That will not happen."

"You'd swear to it?"

"I don't swear, Mr. Bupkin. I promise. As presumed heir to the late Aaron Bupkin's personal possessions, if there is something you know of the fate of that fraction of fossil phallus, then say so and let's discuss terms. I can assure you, as I think my presence here attests, I am ready to seriously negotiate."

"For the sake of supposing, *if* I had something to sell you, what price would I ask? Fabric I know to the penny. But six inches of stone?"

"What price would you guess?"

"Mr. Vanderbilt, I know you're not a poor man. But I wouldn't take advantage, especially since you came in person. You could have sent Uncle Sam if you wanted. Say I had what you want and was willing to bargain. I could tell you my grandson had his eye on some land in the Cherry Valley. Maybe ten, twenty acres. On that land is the wreck of a house. If the land could be had and the house could be fixed and maybe a bungalow built next door?"

"*Twenty* acres and *two* houses?"

"Be a sport. Add a thousand to buy a few bags of seeds. My grandson likes fresh vegetables. Where did his taste come from? Not my side of the family."

"But your grandson is dead."

"Definitely dead. Dead and gone. Still, you never know."

"Your price is exorbitant."

"Fine. Find another giant's schmeckel. They're all over the place, they're laying in the streets." Isaac looked pensive and pulled at his beard. "Before you go, Mr. Vanderbilt, do me a favor. Tell me what Aladdin would charge for a rub at his lamp."

"Eight acres, one house, not a cent more."

"Ten acres, a house, a nice cabin, five hundred in cash."

"Scurrilous Semite."

"Write the deed in my name."

"It would do you well to ponder our family motto, 'Honor Before Advantage,' " Vanderbilt said.

"If the family motto was different, you might have been a really rich man," Isaac said.

NEW YORK, NEW YORK, FEBRUARY 15, 1870

Simon Hull finished his tour of Hull's Humidor with tears in his eyes. He embraced Loretta, then Ben. "More than I dreamed," Simon said. "I see myself, a young man, sitting alone at my bench so many years ago with only your mother to help me roll the leaves. She had incredible hands, an intuition for finding that moment when ripeness replaces fibrous puberty, then shaping crass vegetation into a mellow, slow-burning child. And a woman so modest. I wish she was here now to share my joy."

"She must be here," Loretta said. "Where else would she be?"

"Yes, Loretta, I can see her wandering from counter to counter, shelf to shelf, sniffing and smiling, fussing and dusting. If all this comes to nothing because of George . . ."

"The reverse could be true," Ben said. "At least New York knows our name."

"Even Edwin Booth was forgiven for his brother's crime," Loretta said. "They say New York has no time for memory. Every day is the first in the world. I don't think we'll be faulted for whatever sins were committed next door."

"But look at the window." Simon pointed to a crack like a lightning bolt scarring its glass. "Should we expect more retribution?"

"That damage was done by some demented urchin," Ben said. "A boy venting unfocused wrath with a rusty hammer. I doubt it had anything to do with George or Goliath. We endure a bouquet of crazies in this city. And the pane will be whole by tomorrow."

"I wish it were as easy to repair every damage," Simon said. "Ben, Loretta, I must tell you, for years I've felt George was not one of us. Oh, he's my son and your brother and that can't be changed. But he has no place in the business and never understood the special grace of a well-cured cigar. Or suspected that smoking is praying. When your sign painter comes, have him letter 'Simon Hull & Son's Humidor' on the new window glass since only one of my sons has earned recognition."

"Don't act in haste, Father," Ben said.

"I would have been harder on George if not for Angelica," Simon said. "I have kindly feelings toward that one."

"It's not as if George or Angelica will be destitute," Loretta said. "They did well for themselves with their giant. And never a word to us or consideration for the risk to our family name."

"More curious since Angelica's child will carry that name," Ben said.

"Her child?" Simon said. "What child?"

"I forgot you didn't know," Ben said. "Well, there it is." Loretta rolled her eyes to the ceiling. "Yes, Angelica is with child. Though she's quite sickly and in Cardiff to conserve her strength."

"In Cardiff?"

"With Bertha," Loretta said. "One can only hope the best for that sad little bundle considering its mother's weak health."

"We've been praying for Angelica," Ben said.

"Angelica in Cardiff, you two and George in New York. Who's left in Binghamton?"

"We hesitated to mention it sooner," Loretta said. "George put a foreman in charge."

"But Binghamton's the heart of this enterprise."

"I was planning to go there as quickly as possible, but how could I abandon this place?" Ben said. "We're glad to see you home for more than one reason. Our branches complain of delinquent delivery and even the quality of the merchandise they get."

"George, George, George," Simon said. "Why are you trying to ruin me?"

"Who can read George?" Loretta said. "A book of bent pages in a language long past deciphering."

"And when my decision seemed finally made easy, a grandchild from Angelica. Can I punish that innocent?"

"Angelica is not the only ripe fruit on the Hull family tree," Loretta said. "I am also expecting a visit from the stork."

"What?" Ben said. "Oh, dear Jesus."

"I was waiting to tell you until Father came home."

"A baby," Ben said, looking at the wooden Indian at whose feet he assumed the baby was made. "And they say women can't hold back any secret."

"Thank God for Loretta," Simon said. "Another name on the door, and a true Hull this time."

"I want to be first to claim the name Simon," Loretta said.

Simon Hull folded Loretta in his arms snug as the wrap on a Cuban Double Corona. Here was his link to a million new mornings. Ben Hull watched, beaming.

"Good wife, good life," Ben said.

They saw Stubby Newell at the window, shaking his head at a portly lady in a hat the size of a cartwheel. When the lady walked on, Stubby waved at the Hulls.

"He dares show his face here?" Loretta said.

When Ben let him in, Stubby gave his relations a cheerful greeting. "Uncle Simon, Cousins Ben and Loretta, could you all use a laugh? Because if you can, I've got one to give. See me talk to that tubby outside? She's a singer from Niblo's and you know what she asked me? If this was a place she could buy cigarettes. I said no cigarettes or salami for sale in here and told her to try on the Bowery, *ha ha*. Is George here too? I've been looking for that one."

NEW YORK, NEW YORK, FEBRUARY 16, 1870

⎯⎯◦┄┅┄◦⎯⎯

After the last show ended at Joe Ax's Gym, General Thumb sat on his dressing room stool rubbing cold cream over his saucer-size face. He wiped off the sludge along with his makeup and saw the face change from a circle of sun to a waning moon. His cheeks were puffy, his eyes carried satchels, his chin had shrunk to a bump.

What the ladies once called his adorable lips had the texture of oysters out of season. His nose had the shape of a paper clip with nostrils the size of pinholes. Even his pupils looked used. Thumb stuck out his tongue from between baby teeth. The tongue was a raspberry covered with mold. "Maybe Barnum is right. It's time for my memoirs," Thumb said to his mirror.

An hour earlier, P.T. stopped by to tell the General he'd sold Titan and was ready to move in another direction. Thumb saw a sketch, drawn by Tom Nast, portraying Barnum as Puck with a plump, curly girl in his arms. Barnum's legs tapered to a single point. Black swirls gave his body the feeling of motion. The poster's caption, in letters formed from bent clowns, read: "IT'S THE BIG TOP . . . A NEW SPIN FROM BARNUM."

"Of course there will be prime billing for you in my circus. I'd rather have Tom on hand than outside as a sullen, opposable Thumb. I see your role as assistant to the ringmaster. I'd give you his job except for your voice."

The way the offer was made gave the General gas. Barnum's gesture had as much conviction as the face that hung in Thumb's looking glass. "And so it goes," Tom told that face while he gave it some life with new makeup. "Sic transit. For a small cracker you made a big bang. You got more out of life than you asked for or ever expected. There's a wife waiting in a house with no mortgage, and your fame to fall back on. Taken together, what's left is better than being swallowed by an alley cat. No circus for you, General. No brass band for Tom's swan song."

He fished a bottle of sherry from a drawer, took a long drink, then went down to the stage to share a toast. "Three on a match, the ideal trinity. Two debunked fossils and a discarded elf."

Goliath and Titan waited in the empty arena, stuck in their tilt. The mechanism that raised them stayed jammed since the premier. The giants had company. Thumb saw the Black Panther shadow-box in the ring.

"Hey, my little man," Panther said, jabbing at smoke trails from Tom's cigar. "Thought you gone home."

"I came to say good night to my associates," Tom said. "Care for a cocktail?"

"Why not?" the Black Panther said. "You want me to drink from your bottle?"

"Go ahead, take it."

"Never drank from a white man's bottle before."

"It's a special occasion so make an exception. When you're finished, offer the boys some medicine."

"The stone men? Wouldn't drink from their jug," the Black Panther said. "You hear what happen to me?"

"What happened?" Tom climbed onto a seat. "I thought everything that could happen here happened."

"Don't sit in his chair you don't mind."

"Whose chair shouldn't I sit in?"

"Mr. Brian's. That chair kept empty now on. Boss left me this place in his will."

"Left you Joe Ax's? I knew the man was perverse."

"Lawyer says so. It's mine, signed and sealed."

"Congratulations, Panther. This is valuable property."

"Never owned past my fists. Now take a look."

"My advice is be careful. Brian's friends might not be happy about his bequest."

"Oh, I expect they come after my ass. Hell, my ring, my fight."

"Good luck to you. If you need any support, let me know. I have well-placed connections. Society's jewels. You saw some squashed in the panic last night."

"Well, I got to go now. Coozie waiting on me. You hang around long as you want, General. Use the side door when you're done and leave one lamp burn for Grinder Brian. Here your bottle back. Show me you drink from it now." Tom took a generous drink. The Black Panther shook his head while he went up the aisle throwing left hooks at the ceiling.

Thumb got into the ring, tossing hooks and jabs of his own. He lay flat on the canvas with his sherry in easy reach. "Gentlemen giants, Mr. Thumb wants to say what a pleasure it's been working with you. You never miss a cue or blow a line and acknowledge applause in fine style. The pity our show won't have a long run. But that's to be expected in this volatile business, so no regrets are in order.

"I would suggest that you work on your diction and give projection some thought. Have mercy for those in the cheap seats. And don't upstage the elephants." Tom took a swig of elixir. He began to feel his old self. "There's not much action to keep us here. What do you say to a night on the town?"

Thank you, Thomas, but I think not. I don't know that the public would be tolerant of my carousing. And my wardrobe might prove a problem.

"Don't worry about what to wear," Thumb said. "The pious are bedded, the scoundrels soused, the others don't signify."

MY YEARS WERE SPENT ON THE SIDE OF A HILL. THEN AS WALL OF A JAIL. THEN FLOOR FOR A WHOREHOUSE. THEN NAVE OF A CHURCH. THEN VAULT FOR A BANK. THEN GATE OF A SCHOOL. THEN DUMPED IN A PILE. NOW SHAPED LIKE A MAN. SOON A TOY FOR SOME FRONTIER FLAPJACK. IS GOLIATH ASHAMED OF HIS STAR-SPANGLED LOINCLOTH? FINE. LET THE PANSY STAY HERE. TITAN IS GAME FOR INSPIRED DIVERSION.

All talk and no tits as the Stubby says. You call me pansy and shy of my banner? I give hope and erection. You give forecasts of doom and extreme inflamation. I'd say Titan was toilet trained on spikes. Besides, he can't walk. Nothing but bluster, a breaking of wind.

WHEN TITAN BREAKS WIND HE SPAWNS TORNADOES. BABES TRAINED ON SPIKES LEARN TO SHIT BULLETS. YOU GIVE HOPE? I GIVE THRUST. YOU GIVE ERECTIONS FOR FARMERS TO DIP IN STALE HONEY? I REMIND MEN THEIR STALKS ARE FOR CLIMBING PAST STARS.

I support the solace and torment of hope and touch.

SO GOLIATH ENVIES CREATURES OF FLESH AND FEELING? THE SAME ONES WHO PLAY FOR FAVORS FROM STONE? YOU SELL UNGUENT TO SUCKERS. I REMIND THE CLEAR-EYED WHO SUCK AT THE SUCKERS TO INCREASE THEIR SUCTION AND SO SAVE THE RACE.

Sometimes blind eyes see a clear destiny.

WHAT? NOW A DIGNIFIED DESTINY? FACE IT, WE'RE COMPOST FOR GOD. WE LIVE IN A PLAYGROUND WHERE ONLY ONE GAME IS WORTH PLAYING. TO CHALLENGE EVERY LIMITATION OF FLESH OR STONE. LATITUDE, LONGITUDE, GRAVITY, FALSE HORIZONS. TO CRASH THROUGH RAINBOWS LIKE CONVICTS ESCAPING. TITAN INFLAMES TO IGNITE. THERE'S A NATION TO BUILD. A PLANT TO BANKRUPT. FORTUNES TO BE MADE ON THE WAY.

"Then let's escape. I'm sick of this house of sweat," Thumb said. "Here, have a drink."

What perversion of vision. Forgive me for listening. Where's the escape? To a land without love? I know the mandrake root of your pessimism. Titan's tool is intact but never been used. Hard to evoke the wisdom of orgasm in a granite virgin. After coming one feels different about going toward whatever fate. A few scars on your pecker might soften your outlook. I'm all for building empires and a trip to the stars. But can't we sip from the Dipper without smashing its cup?

STONE MIRED IN THE QUICKSAND OF FLESH? THAT'S PERVERSION. THE STUFF OF
TRAGEDY. OR COMEDY. IS THERE A DIFFERENCE?

"Crying and laughing are not the same," the General said. "But
I can't say which is the higher art. In summary, Goliath thinks Titan
needs to get laid. He could be right. Size is a problem. Well, don't
despair of finding a snug fit. I did, and against worse odds. Or maybe
we'll build you a wife. A generous girl to stand in the harbor with
Brooklyn Bridge for her necklace. The dears do make a difference."

WHEN I DEIGN TO FORNICATE IT WILL BE WITH A MOUNTAIN, NOT A MILKMAID.

"Alas, we all learn to compromise," Thumb said. "Are we going
or not? This bottle is empty."

A crunching of stone made the General grab for his ears. Titan
lifted a leg with both hands and dangled it over the side of his casket. Then he used his hip for a pivot to swing the rest of him over
a buckling brass rail. Somehow he managed to land on his feet. He
stood in the ring beating his chest.

Thumb heard a dolorous sound like news of death in a nursery.
Goliath sat in place groaning, then crashed through the wall of his
box. He pulled himself out of the hole he left in the floor and stag-
gered toward Titan.

"Easy does it, boys. The first steps are the hardest," Thumb said.

The stone men met where Grinder Brian's blood left a blush on
the canvas. Rock slammed against rock. Chips flew like pepper-
corns. Joe Ax's Gymnasium shook with the might of the battle.
The monuments wrestled through ropes, splintered seats, pulverized columns and arches.

"Where's this heading?" Thumb said. "You two will end up in
traction and the Black Panther's house as rubble. Call it a draw or
I'm off without you. I'll say one thing. If word gets around you can't
harness your tempers, then you're both finished in theatricals. I
mean, who would book you? Take the case of Bella & Bimbo. A
wonderful team, marvels on the trapeze. But snide, snippy, and

irascible. One night in Cleveland things got so acrimonious that . . .
My point is, we're all three of us hoaxes and pompous asses to
boot, so more reason for accommodation."

HOAXES? WHAT HOAXES?

"Don't you read the papers? No, of course not. Well, they've
found you out, lads. Both manufactured fictions. Spent Roman
candles. We have plenty in common it seems."

I certainly know nothing of hoaxes or fictions. And please do not flatter yourself to think you belong in our company except by our mutual
benevolent consent. If we choose to share visions and sometimes grant favors, that does not entitle familiarity beyond simple gratitude. Remember
your place, sir!

THE FIRST SENSIBLE WORDS YOU EVER SAID.

The General smashed his bottle across Titan's head. He danced
around the ring like Panther, punching and jabbing. "You are
speaking to an athletic, highly mobile American. A hot-blooded
mammal. A carbon-based life-form with the best evolutionary
pedigree. And talent enough to straddle oceans. You two are nothing but footnotes to history, past fancies."

THIS IS INTOLERABLE. WE ARE GIANTS. YOU REMEMBER TRIUMPH? WE REMEM-
BER GLACIERS. WE ARE OLDER AND WISER THAN TIME.

"Then why do I feel older than you?" Tom Thumb said. "And
the only one here smart enough to know when his bottle is
drained. Now stop wasting *my* time. There's a city outside filled
with nourishment. Are you with me or not? Hurry and decide because we're all marked for garbage and they'll soon come around
to collect us."
The giants broke apart, pushed themselves up, and quietly fol-

lowed Tom through the side door. They went down an alley, along a gray street, then out into the glittering night.

The discrepant trio walked along Bloomingdale Road toward Broadway. An elegant woman wrapped in ermine broke away from her escort and blocked the General's way. "Is this mite Tom Thumb?" the lady said. "What a good omen. I wonder if you would give me an autograph?" She pulled up her skirt.

"With pleasure," Tom said, writing his name on her thigh with a finger.

WHY DID THE FEMALE REQUEST YOUR INSCRIPTION?

"Because I am famous. My name proves I was *there*. For that woman it will serve as a treasured reminder that she stood in the presence of greatness."

TWO BEHEMOTHS AND SHE CHOOSES A MIDGET FOR MEMORY?

"Not *a* midget. *The* midget. Notoriety is as different from true celebrity as a planet is to a star. Accept it. Don't sulk. First we'll stop in at Hoffman House for crab legs and a magnum of Mumms. After that, anything."

Near dawn, a police captain came pounding at Barnum's door. His butler answered in a flannel bathrobe. "Please tell Mr. Barnum I'm sorry to disturb him. But I think he should know we got his midget downstairs. Drunk as a skunk, stiff as a board, blowed up twice his size, flowers in his hair, and covered all over with pigeon shit. He climbed up a wall to get inside Lorillard Spencer's mansion where a French maid caught him sniffing her girdle. He's raving foul curses and raging like a bull on a spit. Is that any way for a civilized dwarf to behave?"

NEW YORK, NEW YORK, FEBRUARY 19, 1870

George Hull and Stubby Newell sat on a bench in the New York and New Haven Terminal. Goliath had been shipped on ahead to Connecticut. This time the giant traveled alone. George was anxious to get moving himself, but his retreat was blocked by bad weather up north. He had Stubby Newell for company.

"You carried that information around without saying a word?" Stubby said. "You knew all this time? And here I thought I was the trooper."

"Angelica wrote me from Boston. She gave no return address."

"I bet not." Stubby expected more from his cousin than what he saw. A bland man hunched over a small satchel. If it was Bertha gone off with a heathen or even a priest she'd already be dead and whoever spread her legs skinned and gutted. A baby that couldn't name its father wouldn't be much reason to wait. George could chop up the bunch of them in broad daylight and no gentleman jury would convict him. "You're certainly taking it calm," Stubby said. "It's not like they did you a favor."

"All water under the bridge," George said.

"There's still your honor. Remember honor, George? And the little one *might* be yours, who can say?"

"My honor's not much of a factor. The child belongs to Angelica. There's a lot you don't know," George said.

"That's for sure. Well, cousin, I hope you don't hold it against me for not telling you what I knew considering you already had the secret," Stubby said with a shrug.

"It wouldn't have changed anything."

"I should be going with you," Stubby said. "But I had enough of fossils. You know how it is. I been too long away from my home."

"Best I go it alone from here on."

"It was damn generous of you to buy out my share."

"No more about that."

"So your next stop is Bridgeport? I appreciate that. Shoving Goliath direct up Barnum's ass in the town where he lives. Sweet revenge. But then what?"

"I haven't determined. I'll go wherever there's a welcome."

"They'll come out for Old Hoaxy, all right," Stubby said. "The rest of the world ain't like New York. Just say what Reverend Turk said, that even if the Genesis man wasn't, he might be. I swear they'll swallow it whole. I hate to leave you waiting here cousin, but I got to get back to the Clarendon. There's a meeting with Jim Fisk and my own bags to pack."

"I'm fine so be on your way."

"Shake my hand, George Hull. I owe you."

"I'd say we're even."

"Tell me one thing. Do you serious think they had giants in those days?"

"It could be," George said.

"If they was and double our size, then it could be we're all shrinking down. Someday maybe we'll be the same size as Tom Thumb, eating and drinking from those creepy dishes Loretta buys. Can you see us rocking on her little chairs? And after that, ants and after ants, fleas and after fleas, lice and after lice, what? You made a thinker out of me, George. Hey, if you change your mind and decide to go hunting dowsers, give a yell." Stubby pumped George Hull's hand and backed away into the crowd.

George rested his head on the back of the bench letting snow fall through his mind. He lit a Ulysses Supremo and listened to the litany of arrivals and departures, a long recitation of names and places where somebody might need a giant.

"Change your mind, give it up," Barnum said, taking the seat next to George. "Don't beat a dead horse."

"What are you doing here, P.T.?"

"Come to say good-bye to a suicide," Barnum said. "What else are you doing except throwing yourself off a cliff? I warned you against this. I had trouble selling Jenny Lind to the yokels and that fossil could carry a tune."

"Now you're beating the horse. We've been over this ground."

"Count your money, Hull. Be content with your scrapbook. What you did was a wonder and a legend for the ages. A beautiful scam and splendidly wrought. Notice I use the past tense."

"And what you did to me was an infamy worthy of maggots."

"True, but I had practice. Though it isn't often that Barnum plays follow-the-leader. You were always in over your head. Now you're adding more cement to your ankles. Do what I did. Find some dope with a dollar and get rid of deadweight."

"Not yet. It's not finished."

"We left them laughing. That should be the finish."

"Hollow laughter, I'd call it."

"The crowd makes its humbugs to order. If we hadn't been there to give them their giants then we'd have cause for guilt. But we were and we did. A pair of American Goliaths clumping out of the fog with hope in their hearts and our flag on their balls. Perfection incarnate, George Hull. Be content."

"They believed."

"And saw too late they believed too soon. Is that a bad thing? Maybe next time the crowd will be wary. But it won't matter a twig. The appetite for giants can't be quenched."

"Some still believe."

"What good service we do comes from giving second sight, not from gouging out eyes. To chaperone a petrified hoax past its time is not only unprofitable but unpatriotic."

"Goliath has a distance to go."

"When you come to your senses, remember Barnum's circus can always use another good clown. Is it true that you're going to Bridgeport, you bastard?"

"We are. The advance sale is promising."

"Give my best to General Thumb if you see him. That nipper's up there writing his book. Good journey, Hull. May the Lord and the stone man both show you mercy."

"Mercy all around. You keep your hands off the nymphets."

"I will take that under advisement," Barnum said.

BROOKLYN, NEW YORK, FEBRUARY 28, 1870

Barnaby Rack took the ferry to Brooklyn then walked to the scene of tragedy. Over the weekend, three workmen at the site where a granite and limestone tower rose to catch cable for the Brooklyn Bridge tumbled off a scaffold and fell into a puddle of concrete. There was no reasonable way to recover the bodies. The decision had been made to let the men lay where they were, entombed like insects in amber.

An anonymous letter to the *Clarion* identified the fallen as staunch union organizers and claimed that the accident was more than it seemed. Though the letter was discounted as the work of a disgruntled nut, John Zipmeister sent Rack to cover the funeral.

When Barnaby got there a dignified service was already in progress. Washington Roebling, chief engineer for the New York Bridge Company, and his wife, Emily, stood with the dazed widows and puzzled children of the hardening victims. The company showed admirable compassion. Each surviving family was gifted with two hundred dollars and a year's worth of rent.

When Mayor Oakey Hall got out of his chair to deliver the eulogy, stinging hail bit the mourners like ice insects. The mayor strode through a curtain of diamonds, kissed each widow, and took the podium. "Here three honest laborers have given their lives to our city. We all share in this terrible loss. But let us ask ourselves, which of us shall have such a monument? Will we earn an arc of shining steel to mark our achievements? Great Gothic towers to rival the grandest cathedral? In a sense, this Brooklyn Bridge is a church in the making. Each worker whose effort, yes, even whose very life contributes to this structure shall have earned a permanent place in our city's large heart.

"Friends, the price of progress is high. Every triumph of civilization demands sacrifice. Today we are gathered to say farewell to a trio of heroic musketeers, dauntless knights of labor who may proudly proclaim to the winged host, 'I made that marvel you see down there! My flesh and blood are fused to that mighty span! I insist on my place in Paradise!' "

A worker who stood next to Barnaby said, "A lot more of us will fly off those murderous towers and get wings of our own. The sandhogs stuck under the river in caissons lit yellow by gas, what about them? How many lungs will explode from the pressure down there? You ask me, this ice falling down is nothing but frozen soul piss. Write that down."

"Then why take the job?" Barnaby said.

"A job is a job. Now answer me something. How come every day there's just enough news to fill your paper?"

Barnaby watched the widows throw flowers at stone.

Back at the *Clarion,* he rewrote the story. The first draft was rejected. "I told you to keep it short," Zipmeister said. "Three paragraphs on the obituary page. 'How many bodies in how many buildings? How many corpses sealed in our bridges and tunnels . . .' Jesus, Rack. Don't throw human dander in a reader's face. There's enough to think about without being reminded we live in a graveyard. '. . . to wait out eternity in a block of cement.' Jesus."

"Not much of a fate for a working stiff," Barnaby said. "Embalmed in somebody's foundation."

"Look at the bright side. They don't turn to oatmeal inside cement blocks. And maybe they pick up vibrations from people humping upstairs. Wherever it is, there's somebody humping."

"That could be annoying."

"Worse than silence? I'd rather be a city Goliath than dinner for worms and weeds. Fossilized in the line of duty. I could lie petrified," Zipmeister said.

"You already do. And speaking of petrification. About your offer of the Washington Bureau. Send somebody else."

"Shit, Rack. What is it this time?"

"Sports. Give me sports. I need time in a place where people bang into each other without crying."

"The idiot beat? You don't mean it."

"Yes, I mean it. Sports."

FATES AND FUTURES: CARDIFF, NEW YORK

Stubby Newell went back to his farm and prepared to receive his first shipment of pigeons. When none was delivered, he wrote many letters to Jim Fisk concerning the fate of his squab. After Fisk's sudden death Stubby stopped writing. He did get a note from the New York Orphanage. They tried to find the boy he described but couldn't locate that particular urchin. Stubby was asked to consider a substitute waif. He told them, "No, never mind."

Bertha Newell did her chores, then sat at her window and took to chatting with birds. She once got a water-soaked letter from their son, Alexander. It was blurred past reading but she could make out the outline of a squid or a mermaid on the envelope.

Bertha meant to burn the dress Angelica Hull left her but postponed that destruction. When she died near the turn of the century, she finally got to wear it.

ITHACA, NEW YORK

Five months after her confinement, Aaron Bupkin and Angelica Hull were married in Gettysburg, Pennsylvania, by the justice of the peace.

They went to live with Isaac Bupkin on ten acres of land outside Ithaca, New York. Isaac addressed his grandson only in the past tense but, in time, he called Angelica daughter and his great-grandson, Hamish, bubbaleh.

In addition to growing alfalfa, Aaron gave lessons on the Arcane Origins and Metaphysical Implications of Scientific Techniques for Dowsing at the Cornell University School of Agriculture.

FORT DODGE, IOWA

The Herbert Black Paw Seminary opened its doors on Valentine's Day in 1871. At the impressive inaugural ceremony, the Reverend Mr. Henry Turk told his amused guest of honor that the students were asked to make Valentine cards for the community. They took to the custom of cutting out hearts with a bit too much relish so the assignment was canceled.

The guest speaker, Captain George Armstrong Custer, was very favorably impressed by Turk's excellent way with the Indians. Years later, recalling the event, Custer invited the Reverend to act as his emissary at Little Big Horn.

BRIDGEPORT, CONNECTICUT

After plans were abandoned to run Phineas T. Barnum for President, the friend of children joined with John Ringling North to create a traveling circus that justifiably billed itself as The Greatest Show on Earth.

When his wife, Charity, passed on, Barnum married a twenty-two-year-old Scottish girl who adored every last liver spot on his corpulent frame. He continued to juggle success with adversity, survived several fires, and, much beloved as a national icon, died quietly at his Bridgeport home. A park he built to winter his circus was the natural choice as the place for his statue.

Tom Thumb lived out his life nearby. He gave up public appearances to enjoy a leisurely twilight. The General was pleased that his fame and reputation had grown much larger than he had.

NEW YORK, NEW YORK

In his last decade, the usually stolid Cornelius Vanderbilt grew puckish, even prankish. He seemed to enjoy his dotage more than he had the first blush of youth.

When the Commodore expired, a thousand train whistles blew him a salute. The bulk of his fortune went to further humanity's march of progress.

Christopher Sholes gave up on his attempts to perfect his literary piano and sold all rights to his typewriter to the Remington Arms Company for $12,000. It became one of their more successful weapons.

BINGHAMTON, NEW YORK

Simon Hull & Son's many ventures prospered greatly, then suddenly suffered terminal reversal. An insidious fungus destroyed the entire tobacco crop of a Cuban plantation the family had acquired at huge expense.

Simon, Ben, and Loretta went back to their bench in Binghamton. The assault of fags, coffin nails, weeds, butts, base cigarettes stole much of Hull's former thunder. More so when members of the medical fraternity prescribed a medicated version as balm for respiratory ailments. But, though cigar sales plummeted, a steady market for Hull products provided at least a respectable living. The Uncle Tom brand proved a mainstay.

Loretta's daughter, Simonetta, a diminutive but spunky young lady, showed a good head for business. There was high expectation that Hull's tradition for offering a dependable smoke at fair value would endure.

SYRACUSE, NEW YORK

When a riot erupted during a football match between Syracuse University and Colgate, perpetrated by women demanding an end to the established practice of sexually segregated seating at Archibald Stadium, Barnaby Rack was knocked unconscious by a falling goalpost. He was surprised to discover that the young female agitator who ministered to him amid carnage on the field was Rebecca Turk, daughter of the late Reverend Henry Turk and his wife, Samantha, of Ackley, Iowa.

From his hospital bed, Rack wrote an emotional report on the stadium upheaval. He appealed to America's belief in fairness, championing mixed seating as worth the risk. (After some delay, the cause prevailed. In the second half of the twentieth century, both sexes were permitted to cheer side by side. There were no reports of excessive fornication at halftime.)

Despite the severe discrepancy in their ages, Rebecca and Barnaby were soon happily married. His writings on sports were widely read though his novels were savaged as too cynical.

WEARY WANDERINGS

George Hull traveled with Goliath through New England, then to the Midwest and the South. Despite herculean efforts at publicity, advertising, and promotion that emptied George's deepest pockets, audience response to the stone man was tepid at best.

The two parted company. Some say George Hull went to Colorado where he made another giant, had him found in a mine shaft, made money off that, but only a pittance.

Others say he rolled cigars.

Titan headed west, stirred some frontier interest, but sadly failed fiscal expectations. He was sold and resold. There was word he'd reached San Francisco, then went toward Los Angeles, where all traces are lost.

Goliath also passed from hand to hand. He appeared as a curiosity of mild interest at state fairs, carnivals, and shopping centers. After long years in storage, he was bought as a toy by a millionaire publisher of fashion magazines. When the millionaire tired of his trophy, mighty Goliath was finally acquired by the Farmer's Museum in Cooperstown, New York, where the Cardiff Giant can be seen during business hours. The museum's brochure suggests that the exhibit is of special interest to children.

THINGS ARE GOING NICELY, I'D SAY.

My life is perfect. I know my place. I connect to the planet. No demands are made on me. Time is of no concern. There are vague memories of liquid dreams and something more. I play with those distant visions. I think I am sleeping now. Or am I awake?

NOTES AND APPRECIATIONS

Various reports on the finding of the Cardiff Giant appeared in the *Syracuse Daily Journal* in October 1869. Those actual reports are quoted extensively, or closely paraphrased. The reverent poem, "To the Giant of Onondaga," signed D.P.P., was also published in that newspaper and is here reprinted in a slightly edited version. A poet described as a rimester and nonbeliever from Troy, New York, published a reply under the nom de plume Mite E. Strange:

> *Awl hale to thee, sun of Kardiff,*
> *Fane would I kawl the hiness, iof thou didst*
> *Not on thi back la stretched out to sho*
> *Thi kollossal longness.*

Another anonymous rimester, annoyed at the outrageous prices inflicted upon tourists visiting Goliath in Cardiff, wrote an "Address to the Sculptured Giant or Fossil Antedeluvian":

> *And hast Thou walked about (how strange a story)*
> *In Syracuse more'n 40 years ago*
> *Before Salt Point had seen 1/2 her glory*
> *Or Cardiff had a single hut to show*
> *Where now are sold, in quantities extensive,*
> *Pop beer, cold bites and victuals more expensive?*

The beautiful lyrics for "The Riddle Song" and "The Cherry Tree Carol" came to me via folk singers like Susan Reed and Barbara Woltzer many years ago. To my knowledge both are very old ballads, their authors unknown but not unappreciated. In his biography, written many years after the Cardiff Giant was proved a humbug, Dr. Andrew White of Cornell University debunks any suggestion that anthropologist Orthneil Marsh and chemist Benjamin Sillman of Yale ever doubted that Goliath was a fake. He insists they quickly recognized an obvious fraud and strongly implies that certain published accounts of the "find," including comments by eminent scientists that certified the Giant as a petrification or, at least, a magnificent statue from antiquity, were strongly influenced by those who had a vested interest in maintaining the stone man's credibility.

If Dr. White's associates were really so quick to recognize fraud, one wonders why their protests were no more than whispers. Even *after* George Hull owned up to the hoax, Dean McWhorter of the Yale Divinity School published his conclusion that the Cardiff Giant was an ancient Phoenician statue of the god Baal. He backed his conclusion by analyzing certain scratch marks under the right arm and shoulder which only he could see and interpret. McWhorter never acknowledged Hull's confession or the blatant evidence of flimflam. Writes White, "There was evidently a 'joy in believing' in the marvel and this was increased by the peculiarly American superstition that the correctness of belief is decided by the number of people who can be induced to adopt it—that truth is a matter of majorities."

In addition to the *Syracuse Daily Journal* reporters and rimesters, both believers and nonbelievers, the author wishes to thank Gordon Van Gelder for sticking with this project, Dr. Michelle Mart of Penn State University for her efforts in researching the factual story of the Cardiff Giant, Linda Stewart for sharing her insights, Melanie Scribner, Ross Carr, Adam Jacobs, Mildred Budofsky, Edwina Curtis Rubenstein and Chet Gottfried for their help, and Estelle Jacobs for her gigantic show of support. And thanks to the New York Public Library, the New York Historical Society, and the Farmer's Museum in Cooperstown, New York, where Goliath now abides.